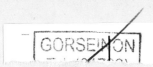

Praise for J. R. Ward's Black Dagger Brotherhood series

'Now here's a band of brothers who know how to show a girl a good time'
Lisa Gardner, *New York Times* bestselling author

'It's not easy to find a new twist on the vampire myth, but Ward succeeds
beautifully. This dark and compelling world is filled with enticing romance
as well as perilous adventure'
Romantic Times

'These vampires are *hot,* and the series only gets hotter . . .
so hot it gave me shivers'
Vampire Genre

'Ward wields a commanding voice perfect for the genre . . . Intriguing,
adrenaline-pumping . . . Fans of L. A. Banks,
Laurell K. Hamilton and Sherrilyn Kenyon will add Ward
to their must-read list'
Booklist

'These erotic paranormals are well worth it, and frighteningly addictive . . .
It all works to great, page-turning effect . . . [and has] earned Ward an Anne
Rice-style following, deservedly so'
Publishers Weekly

'[A] midnight whirlwind of dangerous characters and mesmerizing erotic
romance. The Black Dagger Brotherhood owns me now. Dark fantasy
lovers, you just got served'

J. R. Ward lives in the South with her incredibly supportive husband and her beloved golden retriever. After graduating from law school, she began working in health care in Boston and spent many years as chief of staff for one of the premier academic medical centres in the nation.

Visit J. R. Ward online:

www.jrward.com
www.facebook.com/JRWardBooks
@jrward1

By J. R. Ward

J.R. WARD
BLOOD FURY

piatkus

PIATKUS

First published in the United States in 2018 by Ballantine Books,
an imprint of Random House, a division of Penguin Random House LLC, New York
First published in Great Britain in 2018 by Piatkus
This paperback edition published in 2018 by Piatkus

1 3 5 7 9 10 8 6 4 2

A CIP catalogue record for this book
is available from the British Library.

ISBN 978-0-349-40935-1

Printed and bound by CPI Group (UK) Ltd, Croydon, CR0 4YY

Papers used by Piatkus are from well-managed forests
and other responsible sources.

MIX
Paper from
responsible sources
FSC® C104740

Piatkus
An imprint of
Little, Brown Book Group
Carmelite House
50 Victoria Embankment
London EC4Y 0DZ

An Hachette UK Company
www.hachette.co.uk

www.littlebrown.co.uk

Dedicated to:

Jillian and Benjamin Stein,

who are living a True Love story

GLOSSARY OF TERMS AND
PROPER NOUNS

ahstrux nohtrum (n.) Private guard with license to kill who is granted his or her position by the King.

ahvenge (v.) Act of mortal retribution, carried out typically by a male loved one.

Black Dagger Brotherhood (pr. n.) Highly trained vampire warriors who protect their species against the Lessening Society. As a result of selective breeding within the race, Brothers possess immense physical and mental strength, as well as rapid healing capabilities. They are not siblings for the most part, and are inducted into the Brotherhood upon nomination by the Brothers. Aggressive, self-reliant, and secretive by nature, they are the subjects of legend and objects of reverence within the vampire world. They may be killed only by the most serious of wounds, e.g., a gunshot or stab to the heart, etc.

blood slave (n.) Male or female vampire who has been subjugated to serve the blood needs of another. The practice of keeping blood slaves has been outlawed.

the Chosen (pr. n.) Female vampires who had been bred to serve the Scribe Virgin. In the past, they were spiritually rather than temporally focused, but that changed with the ascendance of the final Primale, who freed them from the Sanctuary. With the Scribe Virgin removing herself from her role, they are completely autonomous and learning to live on earth. They do continue to meet the blood needs of unmated members of the Brotherhood, as well as injured fighters or Brothers who cannot feed from their *shellans*.

chrih (n.) Symbol of honorable death in the Old Language.

cohntehst (n.) Conflict between two males competing for the right to be a female's mate.

Dhunhd (pr. n.) Hell.

doggen (n.) Member of the servant class within the vampire world. *Doggen* have old, conservative traditions about service to their superiors, following a formal code of dress and behavior. They are able to go out during the day, but they age relatively quickly. Life expectancy is approximately five hundred years.

ehros (n.) A Chosen trained in the matter of sexual arts.

exhile dhoble (n.) The evil or cursed twin, the one born second.

the Fade (pr. n.) Non-temporal realm where the dead reunite with their loved ones and pass eternity.

First Family (pr. n.) The King and Queen of the vampires, and any children they may have.

ghardian (n.) Custodian of an individual. There are varying degrees of *ghardians,* with the most powerful being that of a *sehcluded* female.

glymera (n.) The social core of the aristocracy, roughly equivalent to Regency England's *ton*.

hellren (n.) Male vampire who has been mated to a female. Males may take more than one female as mate.

hyslop (n. or v.) Term referring to a lapse in judgment, typically resulting in the compromise of the mechanical operations of a vehicle or otherwise motorized conveyance of some kind. For example, leaving one's keys in one's car as it is parked outside the family home overnight, whereupon said car is stolen.

leahdyre (n.) A person of power and influence.

leelan (adj. or n.) A term of endearment loosely translated as "dearest one."

Lessening Society (pr. n.) Order of slayers convened by the Omega for the purpose of eradicating the vampire species.

lesser (n.) De-souled human who targets vampires for extermination as a member of the Lessening Society. *Lessers* must be stabbed through the chest in order to be killed; otherwise they are ageless. They do not eat or drink and are impotent. Over time, their hair, skin, and irises lose pigmentation until they are blond, blushless, and pale eyed. They smell like baby powder. Inducted into the society by the Omega, they retain a ceramic jar thereafter into which their heart was placed after it was removed.

lewlhen (n.) Gift.

lheage (n.) A term of respect used by a sexual submissive to refer to their dominant.

Lhenihan (pr. n.) A mythic beast renowned for its sexual prowess. In modern slang, refers to a male of preternatural size and sexual stamina.

lys (n.) Torture tool used to remove the eyes.

mahmen (n.) Mother. Used both as an identifier and a term of affection.

mhis (n.) The masking of a given physical environment; the creation of a field of illusion.

nalla (n., f.) or *nallum* (n., m.) Beloved.

needing period (n.) Female vampire's time of fertility, generally lasting for two days and accompanied by intense sexual cravings. Occurs approximately five years after a female's transition and then once a decade thereafter. All males respond to some degree if they are around a female in her need. It can be a dangerous time, with conflicts and fights breaking out between competing males, particularly if the female is not mated.

newling (n.) A virgin.

the Omega (pr. n.) Malevolent, mystical figure who has targeted the vampires for extinction out of resentment directed toward the Scribe Virgin. Exists in a non-temporal realm and has extensive powers, though not the power of creation.

phearsom (adj.) Term referring to the potency of a male's sexual organs. Literal translation something close to "worthy of entering a female."

Princeps (pr. n.) Highest level of the vampire aristocracy, second only to members of the First Family or the Scribe Virgin's Chosen. Must be born to the title; it may not be conferred.

pyrocant (n.) Refers to a critical weakness in an individual. The weakness can be internal, such as an addiction, or external, such as a lover.

rahlman (n.) Savior.

rythe (n.) Ritual manner of asserting honor granted by one who has offended another. If accepted, the offended chooses a weapon and strikes the offender, who presents him- or herself without defenses.

the Scribe Virgin (pr. n.) Mystical force who previously was counselor to the King as well as the keeper of vampire archives and the dispenser of privileges. Existed in a non-temporal realm and had extensive powers, but has recently stepped down and given her station to another. Capable of a single act of creation, which she expended to bring the vampires into existence.

sehclusion (n.) Status conferred by the King upon a female of the aristocracy as a result of a petition by the female's family. Places the female under the sole direction of her *ghardian,* typically the eldest male in her household. Her *ghardian* then has the legal right to determine all manner of her life, restricting at will any and all interactions she has with the world.

shellan (n.) Female vampire who has been mated to a male. Females generally do not take more than one mate due to the highly territorial nature of bonded males.

symphath (n.) Subspecies within the vampire race characterized by the ability and desire to manipulate emotions in others (for the purposes of an energy exchange), among other traits. Historically, they have been discriminated against and, during certain eras, hunted by vampires. They are near extinction.

the Tomb (pr. n.) Sacred vault of the Black Dagger Brotherhood. Used as a ceremonial site as well as a storage facility for the jars of *lessers*. Ceremonies performed there include inductions, funerals, and disciplinary actions against Brothers. No one may enter except for members of the Brotherhood, the Scribe Virgin, or candidates for induction.

trahyner (n.) Word used between males of mutual respect and affection. Translated loosely as "beloved friend."

transition (n.) Critical moment in a vampire's life when he or she transforms into an adult. Thereafter, he or she must drink the blood of the opposite sex to survive and is unable to withstand sunlight. Occurs generally in the mid-twenties. Some vampires do not survive their transitions, males in particular. Prior to their transitions, vampires are physically weak, sexually unaware and unresponsive, and unable to dematerialize.

vampire (n.) Member of a species separate from that of Homo sapiens. Vampires must drink the blood of the opposite sex to survive. Human blood will keep them alive, though the strength does not last long. Following their transitions, which occur in their mid-twenties, they are unable to go out into sunlight and must feed from the vein regularly. Vampires cannot "convert" humans through a bite or transfer of blood, though they are in rare cases able to breed with the other species. Vampires can dematerialize at will, though they must be able to calm themselves and concentrate to do so and may not carry anything heavy with them. They are able to strip the memories of humans, provided such memories are short-term. Some vampires are able to read minds. Life expectancy is upward of a thousand years, or in some cases, even longer.

wahlker (n.) An individual who has died and returned to the living from the Fade. They are accorded great respect and are revered for their travails.

whard (n.) Equivalent of a godfather or godmother to an individual.

BLOOD
FURY

ONE

hen you had everything in the world, it never dawned on you that there were chances to miss. Opportunities that were only temporary. Dreams that could not be fulfilled.

As Peyton, son of Peythone, hid his eyes behind blue lenses, he stared across the training center's break room. Paradise, blooded daughter of the King's First Adviser, Abalone, was sitting one-eighty on a not-fancy chair, her legs dangling over one arm as her back rested against the other. Her blond head was down, her eyes reviewing notes on IEDs.

Improvised Explosive Devices.

Knowing what was on those pages—the promise of death, the reality of the war with the Lessening Society, the danger she had put herself in by joining the Black Dagger Brotherhood's training program for soldiers—made him want to take the notes away and rewind time. He wanted to return to their old lives, before she had come here to learn how to fight . . . and before he had learned she was so much more than an aristocratic female with a stellar bloodline and classic beauty.

Without the war, though, he doubted they would have ever grown close.

That terrible night when the Lessening Society had attacked the

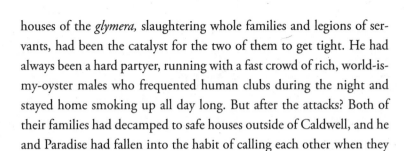

houses of the *glymera,* slaughtering whole families and legions of servants, had been the catalyst for the two of them to get tight. He had
always been a hard partyer, running with a fast crowd of rich, world-is-
my-oyster males who frequented human clubs during the night and
stayed home smoking up all day long. But after the attacks? Both of
their families had decamped to safe houses outside of Caldwell, and he
and Paradise had fallen into the habit of calling each other when they
couldn't sleep.

Which had been most of the time.

They had spent hours on the phone, talking about nothing and
everything, from the serious to the stoopid to the silly.

He had told her things that he had never shared with anybody:
He'd admitted to her he was scared and that he felt alone and worried
about the future. Had said out loud, for the first time, that he thought
he had a drug problem. Had worried about whether or not he could
cut it in the real world away from the club scene.

And she had been there for him.

She was the first female friend he had ever had. Yeah, sure, he had
fucked raft loads of the opposite sex, but with Paradise, it hadn't been
about getting laid.

Although he wanted her. Of course he did. She was incredibly—

"Admit it."

As Paradise spoke up, he snapped to attention. Then looked around.
The break room was empty except for the two of them, everybody else
either in the weight room, the locker rooms, or loitering out in the hall
as they waited to leave for the day.

So, yeah, she was talking to him. Looking at him, too.

"G'head." Her eyes were very direct. "Why don't you say it finally."

He didn't know how to respond to that. And when the silence
stretched out between them, he felt like he'd done a line of blow, his
heart turning his rib cage into a mosh pit, his palms getting sweaty, his
lids going venetian blind from the blinking.

Paradise straightened in the chair, shifting her long legs around and crossing them primly at the knee. It was a reflexive move, something that came from her lineage and her aristocratic upbringing: Every female of her station sat properly. It was just what one did, no matter where one was or what one was wearing.

Crate & Barrel or Louis XIV. Lycra or Lanvin. Standards, darling.

He imagined her in a gown, dripping in her dead *mahmen's* jewels, under a ballroom's crystal chandelier, her hair up high, her perfect face radiant, her body . . . moving against his own.

"Where's your man," he said in a rough voice—one that he hoped she blamed on his weed habit.

The smile that hit her face made him feel old and ugly-wasted, even though they were the same age and he was sober.

"He's just getting changed."

"Big plans for the night?"

"Nope."

Yeah, right. That blush told him exactly what they were going to do—and how much she was looking forward to it.

Popping his sunnies up, he rubbed his eyes. It was hard to believe he was never going to know what that was like . . . having her under him as he rode her, her naked body his to explore, her thighs spread wide so he could—

"And don't change the subject." She sat forward in that chair. "Come on. Say it. The truth will set you free, right?"

As the compressor behind the soda machine kicked on, he glanced over at the food service counter, where meals and snacks were offered when they were logging classroom and gym time. Even though the Brothers were letting the trainees out into the field for proper engagement with the enemy, there was still a lot of theory and hand-to-hand and weapons work that was done on a regular basis on-site.

At least two to three nights a week, he ate here—

Wow. Check it. He was trying to distract himself.

Peyton swung his stare back to her. God, she was so beautiful, so blond, with those big blue eyes . . . and those lips. Soft, naturally pink. Her body had gotten a little less curvy, a little more muscular, since she had started working out so much, and the power was a turn-on.

"You know," she murmured, "there was a time we didn't keep anything from each other."

Not really, he thought. He had always kept his attraction to her on the DL.

"People change." He stretched and cracked his back. "Relationships, too."

"Not ours."

"What's the point." He shook his head. "Nothing good can come from—"

"Come on, Peyton. I can feel you staring at me in class, out in the field. It's so damned obvious. And listen . . . I know where you're coming from. I'm not naive."

The tension in her was obvious, her shoulders tight, her mouth thinning out. And hey, what do you know, he hated the position he was putting them in, too. If he could stop it, he would, but feelings were like wild animals. They did what they wanted and to hell with what they trampled or bit or kicked in the process.

"As much as I try to ignore it"—she pushed her hair over her shoulder—"and as much as I'm sure you want to feel differently, it is what it is. I think we need to talk about it so we can clear the air, you know? Before it starts to affect us or the others out in the field."

"I don't think it's resolvable." *Not unless you want to go on a two-hundred-and-seventy-five-pound diet and lose your mate.* "And I don't think it matters."

"I disagree." She threw up her hands. "Oh, come on. We've been through so much together. There's nothing you and I can't handle. Remember those hours on the phone? Talk to me."

As Peyton wondered why in the hell he hadn't brought a bong with him, he got to his feet and played trailblazer with the dorm furniture that had been arranged with the care and precision of a game of marbles: The various seats, couches, and tables were willy-nilly'd all over the place, the result of different study groups and some questionable betting over push-ups, sit-ups, and arm wrestling having fucked the arrangement.

When he finally stopped, he turned around. And they both spoke at the same time.

"Fine, I'm in love with you—"

"I know you still don't approve of me—"

In another burst of synchronization, they shut up together.

"What did you say?" she breathed.

Gun. He needed a gun. So he could shoot himself in the foot in fact, as opposed to just in the hypothetical.

The door to the break room swung open and her male, Craeg, strode in like he owned the place. Big, heavily muscled, and one of the best fighters in the trainee class, he was the kind of guy who could use a rusty nail for a toothpick as he sutured up his own wounds in the middle of a burning warehouse with two *lessers* coming at him and a scared golden retriever puppy under his arm.

Craeg stopped and looked back and forth between them. "Am I interrupting something?"

Novo barely made it to the industrial-sized metal trash bin in time. As she bent in half and threw up, nothing but water made an appearance, and when the heaving passed, she rolled off the rim and let herself fall to the mats. Easing back against the cold concrete wall, she waited for the world to stop spinning around her.

Sweat fell like tears down her face, and her throat was on fire—although that was less about the vomiting than the sawing inhales she had been taking as she deadlifted. And don't get her started on her lungs. She felt as though she had been trying to find oxygen in the middle of billowing hot smoke.

Clank. Clank. Clank . . .

When she was able to, she lifted her head and focused. Across the weight room, a massive male was doing leg presses in a slow, controlled fashion, his forearms bulging from where he was gripping the pegs by his hips, his thigh muscles carved in stone, veins popping out everywhere.

He was staring at her. But not in a creepy way.

More like in an okay-is-it-time-to-call-a-doctor manner.

"I'm all right," she said, looking away from him. Although with his headphones on, it wasn't like he could hear her.

I'mallright. I'mallright. NoreallyI'mallright—

Leaning to the side, she snagged a fresh white towel from a stack on one of the benches and mopped up. The Black Dagger Brotherhood's training center was a case of state of the art, best of the best, professional grade all the way: From this iron dungeon of self-inflicted pain to the firing range, the classrooms, the Olympic pool, the gym, and then the medical clinic, PT facility, and surgery suites, no expense had been spared, and upkeep was just as meticulous and costly.

With a final clank, the male sat forward and did a pass of his own face. He had dark brown hair that had recently been cut, the sides so tight they were nearly shaved, the top left long and loose. His eyes were some kind of brown, and he had an all-American kind of look—well, except for the fangs, which were straight-up Bram Stoker, and the fact that he was not any more human or American than she was. The white muscle shirt he had on was stressed the fuck out trying to stretch over his enormous pecs, and his dark, hairless skin was just the same, taut nearly to the point of structural failure across his six-pack and lats.

He had no tattoos. No false airs. Unfancy clothes. And he rarely spoke—if he did open his mouth, it was always logistical, like, what machine was she going to use next, or was this her towel? He was unfailingly polite, distant as a horizon, and seemingly unaware she was a female.

In short, this stranger was her new best friend. Even though she didn't know his name.

And they did spend a lot of time together. At the end of every in-house night for the trainees, the two of them were here alone, the Brothers working out during the day, the other trainees already exhausted from whatever they had been doing in class.

Novo always had juice left in the tank, though.

Fuck 5-hour Energy or Xenadrine. Personal demons were waaaaay better for getting your ass in gear.

Oh, and then there was the other reason she preferred to vom into a Hefty bag rather than hang with the others while they waited for their bus to take them down the mountain.

"You're bleeding."

Novo jerked her head up. The male was standing over her, and when she frowned, he pointed to her hands.

"Bleeding."

Lifting one of her palms, she saw that, yup, she certainly was leaking. She had forgotten her gloves, and the bar that she had been holding the five hundred pounds with had cut into her.

"What's your name?" she asked as she pressed the towel into the raw spots.

Man, that stung.

When he didn't answer, she looked up again. And it was at that point that he placed his hand over his sternum and bowed.

"I am Ruhn."

"You don't have to do that." She folded the terrycloth in half and re-wiped her brow. "The bow thing. I'm not a member of the *glymera*."

"You are a female."

"So?" When he seemed honestly confused, she felt like a bitch. "Anyway, I'm Novo. And I'd shake your hand, but yeah."

As she flashed him what he had pointed out was injured, he cleared his throat. "It is nice to meet you."

His accent was like hers, without the haughty, long vowels of the aristocracy, and she instantly liked him even more. As her father had always said, rich people could afford to talk slow 'cuz they didn't have to work for a living.

Which made that group of entitled lightweights really hard to respect or take seriously.

"Are you joining the program?" she asked.

"For?"

"The training program?"

"No. I am just here to work out."

He offered her a smile—as if that encompassed his entire life story as well as all his plans for the future—and then he went over to the chin-up bar. The reps he did were unbelievable. Fast, but controlled, over and over again, until she lost count. And still he kept at it.

When he finally stopped, he was breathing deeply, but hardly taxed.

"So why don't you?"

"What?" he said with surprise. Like maybe he had forgotten she was still sitting there.

"The training program. Why don't you join us?"

He shook his head sharply. "I'm not a fighter."

"You should be. You're really strong."

"I am just used to manual labor. That is where it comes from." He paused. "You're in the program?"

"Yeah."

"You fight?"

"Oh, yeah. And I like it. I like to win and I like to inflict pain on others. Particularly slayers." As his eyes popped, she rolled her eyes. "Yes, females can be like that. We don't need permission to be aggressive or strong. Or to kill."

When he turned away, re-gripped the chin-up bar, and resumed his workout, she cursed at herself.

"Sorry," she muttered. "That wasn't directed at you."

"Is there someone else here?" he said between reps.

"No." She got to her feet and gave her head a shake. "Like I said, sorry."

"It's okay." Up. And down. "But . . ." Up. And down. ". . . why aren't you . . ." Up. And down. ". . . with them?"

"The other trainees?" She looked at the clock on the wall. "They're happy to chill before the bus comes. I hate loitering around. Time to go, actually. See ya."

She was just at the door when he spoke up. "You shouldn't do that."

Novo glanced over her shoulder. "Excuse me?"

Ruhn nodded to the trash bin. "You throw up a lot when you exercise. It's not healthy. You push too hard."

"You don't know me."

"I don't have to."

She opened her mouth to tell him to keep his God complex to himself, but he just turned away and resumed those chin-ups of his.

Oh, right, she thought. Fucking *fine*. Why don't I just go watch Tasty vids on BuzzFeed and take selfies in yoga poses.

#nothrowupzone

With her temper surging, she *so* wanted to pick a fight with him. Even though she was tired to the point of butt-hurt, and he might have a point about the barfies, fuck that. Live and let live, you know?

Or, live and let self-destruct.

Potato, potahto.

But whatever. No reason to argue with a stranger about something she had no intention of doing any differently.

Out in the corridor, the air was cooler—or maybe that was just a case of perception, the long concrete-walled chute to the parking area making it seem like there was a whole lot more air available for the taking. Forcing herself to walk forward, she headed to the locker room she and Paradise used as the only two females in the program. And the second she pushed her way in, she closed her eyes and considered going home sweaty and disgusting.

Sonofabitch.

That goddamn fragrance.

Paradise's shampoo was like spray paint on the walls, carpeting on the floor, ceiling fans whirling at a thousand miles an hour, strobe lights and a disco ball: In the cramped room, it took up every square inch of space.

What was worse? It wasn't like the female was hateful or incompetent or a Barbie doll that could be written off as Taylor Swift in a Nirvana world. Paradise had been the one who'd lasted the longest during that hellish orientation, and she was a crackerjack in the field, with shockingly fast reflexes and a dead-on shot that had to be seen to be believed.

But there was another thing she was good at.

And even though Novo had no right to care and no reason to notice and zero fucks to give, it was sublimely annoying to watch Peyton sneak those looks and linger in those doorways and pull those double takes whenever the female laughed.

The only thing that was even more irritating? That the shit was on Novo's radar at all.

Peyton, son of Peythone, was nothing she was interested in. After all, some things, like not volunteering for a major limb amputation, were self-evident.

Plus hello, personal history.

Not with him specifically. But still.

So the fact that she'd even noticed the guy's addiction to that other female was enough to make Novo want to beat her own ass.

As she turned to head for the shower stalls, she caught sight of herself in a full-length mirror—a fixture she was very sure wasn't in the males' locker room.

Which was really just so damned sexist—

Her thoughts dropped the mic on that familiar rant as her reflection registered. Her eyes had become hollow pits, and her stomach, left bare between her sports bra and her leggings, was concave, and her legs were swollen with muscle except for the tight bony knots of her knee-caps.

No hips, no tits, no female identifiers . . . even her long hair was bolted in a braid that hung as if in retreat down the powerful fans on either side of her spine.

Novo nodded at herself in approval.

She wouldn't want things any other way.

Paradise could keep the chick shit and all the sidelong stares in the world. Far better to be strong as opposed to sensual. The latter got you admired . . .

The former kept you safe.

TWO

"Nope," Peyton said. "Not interrupting anything at all."

As he smiled at Craeg, he thought, Yuuuuup, it's totally cool. I just told your girl I loved her while she thought I was still stuck on not wanting her to be in the training program. So yeah, conversationally speaking, we just faced off in a duel, where she had a gun and I had two paper clips and a rubber band. But it's fine.

Although, hey, while we're on the subject, maybe you want to slice my nut sac off and put my two veg in your back pocket? 'Cuz I won't be needing them anymore after this.

Beelining for the door, he didn't look at Paradise. In fact, there was a good possibility he was never looking at her again. But he was careful to guy-it-up with Craeg as he passed the male, giving him a clap on the shoulder.

"Can't wait for tomorrow out in the field." Unless he hung himself in the bathroom at home. In which case he was gonna be a no-show. "Good workout tonight. Fan-fucking-tastic."

Especially if you counted the body slam he just did to his own ego.

That little bitch wasn't getting up again. Probably needed reconstructive surgery and a prosthesis.

Out in the corridor, he stopped and cursed. He'd left his fucking duffel in the break room, but he was *not* going back in there. Nope. No reason to catch the drift of the Paradise/Craeg Reunion Kiss #45,896, which would be followed by the OMG-guess-what-Peyton-just-said's. The good news? Craeg was so into the program, and team leadership, and fighting the true enemy, that there was a strong possibility his bonded male wouldn't be reaching for a dagger right now.

Still, it was probably a good idea to head down to the parking area. If only to buy himself some lead time on the run-away.

Even he wasn't dumb enough to take on a bonded male. Especially one who was trained to kill things.

As Peyton checked his watch and started striding off to the reinforced steel door at the very far end, he pulled a thank-fuck. Fifteen minutes and the bulletproof bus would be ready in the parking area to take them back to the drop point. If Craeg went apeshit on the ride into town, surely someone would help a guy out. Boone was a straight shooter and would intercede, and maybe—

Instantly, Peyton's entire body went on high alert, his skin flushing with heat, the hair at the back of his neck triggering up, his blood pumping as hard as if he were on a sprint.

He stopped again and turned around slowly.

Novo was emerging from the female locker room, her hard body in leathers and a leather jacket, her Nike duffel over one shoulder, her black hair slicked back and braided down her spine.

"Hey," he murmured as she came up to him. "You looked good tonight."

She always did. And not just with her hand-to-hand form, either.

"What you mean"—she kept going past him—"is that I beat you."

"Not how I remember it."

"Huh. Guess my putting you flat on your back caused a little brain damage, then."

As an arousal punched at the fly of his slacks, Peyton discreetly rearranged himself and fell into her wake. Out in front of him, she moved like the boss she was, all attitude and competence, and yes, he totally looked at her ass—and wanted his hands all over it.

His mouth, too.

Something about her brought out the animal in him, ever since the first night he'd seen her. He didn't want to make love to her. He wasn't even interested in sex from her. He wanted straight-out fucking, the kind that left marks on skin, and ruined furniture, and broke lamps.

"I won in the end," he drawled.

Now she was the one pulling a halt-and-pivot, that long rope of hair swinging around and hitting her on the hip. "Because I slipped while I was submitting you. My foot *slipped*. That's how you got your advantage."

"I still pinned you in the end."

"I took you down."

"And I won."

As fire lit up her teal-blue eyes and her fangs descended, he focused on her mouth. In his mind, he shoved her back against the hard concrete wall and she fought him and they kissed like they were going to die after they were done banging. Raw. Furious. With orgasms that altered their brain chemistry for nights afterward.

"You didn't win," she gritted. "I *slipped*. And if the ball of my foot hadn't gone out from under me, you would still be on that mat like a carpet."

Peyton moved in closer and lowered his voice. "Excuses, excuses."

With the way she glared at him, it was clear she wanted to hit him. Break his legs. Stab him.

And he wanted all of that, too. It was punishment for his dropping that bomb back in the break room. It was self-harm done by someone else, a vital, painful distraction that took his mind off the fact that he gotten way too real with the wrong person, at the very wrong time.

Shit, had he really just told Paradise he loved her?

"So when are we going to fuck," he said in a guttural voice. "I'm ready to stop ignoring this."

Novo narrowed that stare even harder. "Never. How's *never* sound to you?"

"You want it."

"Not from you."

"Liar." He leaned in a little closer. "Coward. What are you afraid of—"

Her free hand whipped out and locked on his throat, her thumbnail pressing into his jugular and pinching off the blood supply. "Watch yourself, pretty boy. Or I might do some aesthetic damage they can't fix."

Peyton closed his eyes and swayed. "I want you to."

Covering her grip with his own, he forced her nail further into his skin until blood welled. And as her eyes flared, he removed her hold and looked at the red smudge on her thumb.

"You want a taste?" he drawled, bringing his blood to her mouth. "Open for me."

When her jaw flexed like she was clamping down on her molars, he rubbed her own thumb on her lower lip, banking on the temptation becoming too strong for her to resist—

Her pink tongue licked out and then she took over from there, sucking her finger in deep and making a show of rolling it around . . . until he nearly orgasmed in his pants.

But just as things were reaching taking off, she abruptly stepped back and looked away.

"Snowstorm, people."

At the sound of a male voice, Peyton did some f-bomb reps in his head. And then he glared at Axe, who was coming out of the office.

"What do you mean?" Peyton muttered.

Their fellow trainee sauntered over. Axe was neo-Goth'd, half-tat'd, and a good guy—once you got past the fact that he looked like a serial killer. He'd just settled down with an aristocrat, one of Peyton's cousins, so now he was in the family so to speak, and Peyton was glad. With everything the way it was going out in the world, at least he knew Elise was not just loved, but safe from the enemy.

"We're stuck here." Axe flexed his heavy arms like they were sore. "They can't get us out. Bus is canceled."

"What the hell?" Peyton pictured his weed stash in his bedroom like it was a long-lost relative. "I got plans."

"Take it up with management, my man. I can't help you."

The problem was that they couldn't just dematerialize off the mountain. The Brotherhood compound, which included this subterranean complex, was in a highly secured location: For one, the trainees were not privy to its whereabouts, and that was information you didn't want to have, anyway. Who needed to know where the First Family stayed? All that got you was on the short list of torture targets if there was an assassination attempt. But even more to the point, the property was covered in *mhis,* something that both blurred the landscape visually and also made it virtually impossible for anyone who didn't know the coordinates to dematerialize on or off the acreage.

So yeah, nobody in the class was going any-fucking-where.

Shit, he'd thought the ride back to Caldwell proper was going to be bad? This was a frickin' nightmare. Trapped here, with Paradise and Craeg, until at least five or six o'clock the following night when it was dark enough to bus out? Assuming the blizzard quit by then?

Peyton looked over at Novo. She and Axe were talking about the IED stuff Paradise had been studying, and as he watched her lips move . . . he thought about all the places she could put them on his body.

Well, now, he decided, at least the Brotherhood let people booze up if they were off duty. And with the right kind of persuasion? It was beyond time for him and Novo to find some privacy and put it to good use—and that would do double duty keeping him away from the flying fists of one half of the Happiest Couple on the Fucking Planet.

This was an opportunity. Not a crisis.

Goddamn it. He tasted amazing.

As Novo kept a convo going with Axe, it was just a surface-level tennis match of words and terms they'd learned in class. Underneath all those conventional syllables, she was back in the moment when she had taken a part of Peyton into her . . . and liked it.

He was still staring at her, his body poised as if it were ready to take hers down to the floor, all kinds of heat and erotic intent rolling off of him like strokes she could actually feel on her bare skin.

The aggression and the hunger were a surprise considering his refined bloodline, but not a shock given who he was. For a rich boy, he had proven to be a cunning and tenacious fighter, strong and strangely fearless. Now . . . the question appeared to be whether she wanted to see what kind of lover he was—

"—Paradise's birthday," Axe was saying to him. "Elise told me you guys were going to meet to make sure shit was tight."

Novo refocused as Peyton nodded. "I'll call her tonight. I think we're all set."

"When is this?" Novo heard herself ask.

As date/time/location were shared and there was more gum-flapping around the whole celebration, she retreated into her head again.

Yeah, not her scene. Two or three hundred members of the *glymera* under the age of a century, doing a Stella McCartney/Tom Ford mix-and-mingle fueled by top-shelf liquor, finger foods on silver trays, and aristocratic privilege?

Just shoot me now, she thought.

And that was before you added Peyton staring at the birthday girl like she had stolen his soul and put it in her Chanel bag.

"—coming, right?"

When there was a pause, she glanced at Axe. "What?"

"You have to come," the guy muttered. "I need someone I can stand to talk to."

"Why don't we skip it and go to The Keys?"

"Those days are over for me."

"Oh, that's right. You got your happily ever after, so you're too good for us sluts."

And no, she didn't give a shit that she sounded bitter . . .

Okay, maybe she was sorry she was being a bitch. But the guy had been a legend down at Caldwell's infamous sex club. Why anybody would give that up for just one person, she couldn't fathom. It was a buffet exchanged for a cupboard full of the same can of soup, decade in and decade out. Plus that whole eggs-in-one-basket thing? Not for her.

She'd only had to learn that lesson once.

"You go there on the regular?" Peyton asked her with a remote expression.

As he narrowed his stare on her, it was tempting to point out to Mr. Anachronism that females were *shocker* allowed to drive cars, own real property, wear pants. And civilization hadn't crashed and burned into the mountain of Everything Was Better Before.

"I'm a member." She crossed her arms over her chest. "You got a problem with that."

"So when are you taking me?"

She hid her surprise. "You couldn't handle it."

"How do you know?"

Novo looked him up and down. "I don't, but you're not interesting enough to me to find out."

Axe whistled under his breath. "Ouch."

Peyton ignored the guy, a cold light entering his eyes. "Challenge accepted. What night?"

Novo shook her head. "That wasn't a challenge."

"I think it was. And although you didn't spare me any courtesy, I will rise above and refrain from pointing out that you're lying. Just like you did a minute and a half ago when you told me you didn't want to fuck me." He put his hand over his mouth. "Oh. Whoops. Did that just come out?"

"Will you two cut the shit and get a room already," Axe drawled. "No offense, but rom coms make me sick."

"This is not a romantic comedy," Novo ground out. "It's a murder mystery with an obvious ending."

"I have to agree with her on that one." Peyton reached forward and ran his fingertips along Novo's collarbone. "A good orgasm is known as the little death. And I'm more than willing to die for you. A little."

Before she could slap his hand away—or break out the bodily harm—he sauntered off with a smile.

"Where's some booze," he said over his shoulder. "I need a drink if I'm going to make it through today stuck in here with all of your denial."

Novo crossed her arms over her chest. "He is *such* an asshole."

"Everyone needs a hobby." Axe shrugged. "And he clearly likes pissing you off."

"If you tell me to stop encouraging him, I'm going to punch you in the junk."

Axe put his palms up. "Not it on that one. Besides, your presence alone is enough encouragement. What are you going to do, take your own skin off?"

"Yeah, right. Paradise is the one he wants, and don't read any bitch into that. She is more than welcome to hold that exalted position. And likewise, if he wants to continue hitting that wall until he blacks out, have fun with that."

Axe regarded her for a long moment. Then he offered his palm. "A hundy says that you're the one for him."

"I don't bet."

"Coward."

She jerked her hand forward and grabbed him hard. "Fuck you. And it's on."

"You can't do anything to dissuade him."

"That's my S.O.P. with the bastard. I'm not stopping now."

"Not what I meant." Axe shook his head. "This is out of your control. And his."

"Like you're an expert."

"I am." The male shrugged his powerful shoulders. "Just been through it myself. That's how I know how this is going to turn out."

As the fighter walked away, he had all the calmness of someone who could see the future, and Novo hoped he enjoyed that superiority—while it lasted.

She was going to enjoy spending his Benji.

That much she was clear on.

THREE

As Saxton stood at a long window framed by green velvet drapes with golden tassels and embroidered sashes, he stared out into a blizzard and braced himself to go ice-bath. He had his brief-case in one hand, his Gucci scarf in the other—and his intense distaste of cold weather all around him.

The Black Dagger Brotherhood's mansion was on top of a mountain, and the wind gusts at this higher altitude were like an invading army bearing down against its great stone walls. The blasts came in waves and from different directions, and as he watched the snowflakes blow at their mercy, he was reminded of what schools of fish looked like, going this way and then that way, in delineated chaos.

I don't want to do this anymore, he thought.

As the conviction struck, he told himself the ennui concerned merely the month of January—which, in upstate New York, was a miserable season unto itself, cold, dark, and dangerous if you got stuck outdoors for long. He feared, however, there was more than the dead zone between December and February in play.

"You going to try for home?"

He glanced through the archway of the billiards room. Wrath, son of Wrath, the great Blind King, had arrived in the foyer, and the male was just so huge, harsh, and aristocratic, a straight-up killer in black leather—with a beautiful, kind-faced golden retriever by his side.

Saxton cleared his throat. "I'm not sure, my Lord."

"You got a bedroom here."

"You are most gracious." Saxton lifted up his briefcase even though the King could not see it. "But I have work to do."

"When was the last night or day you took time off?"

"I have no need to."

"Bullshit. And I know the answer and don't like it."

In truth, it had been forever. The King's nightly audiences with members of the race required much follow-up and paperwork—and on top of all that valid work, there might also be a little self-medicating, distraction-seeking going on.

As if on cue, a pair of voices echoed throughout the grand open space and Saxton took a deep breath. Blay and Qhuinn were coming down the gracious staircase, each of them carrying an infant, the bonded couple laughing. When they got to the bottom step, Qhuinn put his hand on the small of Blay's back and Blay looked over at the Brother, his eyes lingering as if he could have stared at that handsome face forever.

The shaft of pain that went through Saxton's sternum was as familiar as the sinking feeling in his gut, the one–two punch of Blay's no-it's-him-I-want-not-you choice making the idea of battling the Nor'easter very appealing. After all, the other option was to take advantage of his unused room there and try to sleep under the same roof as the happy pair and their two beautiful young.

Sometimes, nothing made you feel older and more worn out than the happiness of others. And yes, that was uncharitable—but that was why it was good that inner thoughts were things one shared only with oneself.

"My Lord, do enjoy Last Meal." Saxton pinned a smile to his face even though, again, the Blind King would not know it. "I believe I will—"

"Join us for Last Meal? Fucking awesome. Come on, we'll go in together."

Saxton cleared his throat and began to construct a false engagement, an imperative that could not be denied, an overriding principle—

"I'm waiting," Wrath muttered. "And you know how much I love that shit."

With a sag, Saxton recognized this was an argument lost before it began. And he also was more than aware that the King's patience was as short as his temper.

After that little warning shot across the bow, Wrath's next move could well be a draw-and-quarter out back in the snow.

"But of course, my Lord." Saxton bowed and started to remove his favorite Marc Jacobs coat. "It will be my pleasure."

Falling in line with his King, he walked across the foyer and entered the vast dining room, depositing his briefcase, scarf, and all that fine cashmere on a chair next to one of the sideboards. With any luck, one of the *doggen* wouldn't "help" by putting his things away. In a mansion this size? They could end up a mile off in some closet.

And storm or no storm, as soon as this meal was over, he was leaving.

Using his peripheral vision, he located the delightful family of four and strategically picked a vacant Queen Anne chair on the same side of the enormous table but down at the other end. The result was a good fifteen people between them—or there would be, when everyone was settled into seats. In the meantime, he made a show of micromanaging his already perfectly arranged silverware—and then taking an ungodly amount of time explaining to a patient *doggen* exactly how much cranberry and how much seltzer he wanted for his libation.

No alcohol. Alcohol made him, for want of a better word, horny—

and that was just going to leave him sexually frustrated. No one at home waiting for him. Nobody he really wanted to call in. Nothing to be done about that—

I don't want to do this anymore.

As the thought struck again, he decided maybe his King was right. Maybe he should take a night off, if only so he could find a release or two with some stranger. It would never be more than that. His heart was somewhere else, never to return, and sometimes, an anonymous body used as gym equipment was all that destiny offered—

Directly across the table, a large male figure pulled out a chair and sat down. And Saxton found himself sitting up a bit straighter.

It was Ruhn. Blooded uncle to Rhage and Mary's adopted daughter, Bitty. New member of the household. All around very decent, very . . . spectacular . . . male.

Strange, how someone that big could move in such a controlled, compact way. It was as if he commanded not just his arms and legs, but every cell, down to the molecule, on a series of separate, but coordinated, calls to action.

Amazing.

And yes, his simple clothes suited him. No tailored tweed suits with handmade shirts, a cravat, and ostrich shoes going on—which was Saxton's typical work dress. No, Ruhn was wearing a Hanes T-shirt under a navy blue knit sweater on top of Levi's. The male had pulled the sleeves of that knitted top up on both sides, and the tendons and veins of his forearms were a testament to both his strength and how lean he was. His callused hands were clean, with unbuffed, clipped-to-the-quick nails, and his chest was so broad that the poor sweater was—

"Hello, Uncle!"

As Bitty came skipping around the table to the male, Saxton shook himself out of his assessment. And yet his eyes quickly returned to where they had been.

"Hello, Bitty." Ruhn's voice was very nice, low and resonant, and the accent was that of a civilian of Southern extraction. "How are you?"

Nothing loud. And as the girl gave him a hug, those big hands were gentle and slow, the embrace careful as if he were afraid he might crush her.

And with the way he was built? He absolutely could.

"I'm good! Your hair is wet."

Indeed it was, the deep brown waves were combed back and already curling up thanks to the dry, furnace-warmed winter air.

"Did you just work out?" the girl asked.

"Yes."

"You're getting as big as my dad."

"Oh, not nearly."

Saxton smiled a little. The male most certainly was putting on weight, the however-many hours he spent pumping iron in the training center adding pounds to his pecs, shoulders . . . those arms. But he clearly was as self-effacing as he was careful with how he threw his body around.

As the girl sat down and continued to make conversation, Ruhn nodded and smiled a little more and answered in few words a veritable barrage of inquiry. Unfortunately, the forty-foot table was soon filled to capacity, and Saxton could hear no more.

That did not mean he stopped looking. While Marissa sat on one side of him, and Tohrment the other, and food was served on silver platters and in deep porcelain bowls, Saxton kept up a pleasant conversation while allowing his eyes to scan from time to time the opposite flank of the table.

Ruhn ate with his brows down tight, as if he were concentrating on every slice of his knife and each piercing tine of his fork. Whether this was because he was starving and determined not to scarf his food or because he was scared of dropping something, it was hard to say, but Saxton could extrapolate it was the latter.

Ever since Ruhn had come into the household, he had been nothing short of polite and quiet, and one had to feel for him. It was as if he were worried he would be asked to leave at the slightest infraction, but that was far from the truth. He was family now, because Bitty was family now—and, indeed, the way that male had behaved with respect to the welfare of his niece was truly extraordinary. With the passing of Bitty's mother, and Ruhn as the girl's next of kin, he'd had every right in the world to swoop in and take her away from Rhage and Mary.

Who had been fostering the young and desperate to adopt her.

But instead of being territorial, Ruhn had been selfless—and recognized the deep abiding love that the little family had found together. The male had insisted that the adoption go through and had signed away all his legal rights without any expectations for himself.

If that wasn't love, Saxton didn't know what was.

And in return for that compassionate act, Ruhn had been embraced by the whole household—not that the adjustment to Caldwell and the mansion still wasn't a struggle for the male. But he had nothing to worry about when it came to his future under the Brotherhood's roof; for as long as he wanted it, he had a home here.

Saxton had first met him during the process of adoption. But after he had helped with Bitty's formal adoption papers, he had made sure to stay far away.

Although the male's physical assets were legion, he had not given any indication that he was sexually open to or even aware of males—or anyone else, for that matter. And knowing the way the universe ran? Ruhn was utterly heterosexual, and God knew Saxton was beyond over wanting things he couldn't have—

Eyes the color of fine bourbon looked across the table without warning, and the shock of meeting Ruhn's calm, rather innocent stare made Saxton fumble his napkin off his lap. Which turned out to be a blessing as it gave him an excuse to bend down and get out of view.

Nope. He was definitely not staying the day.

He didn't care if he ended up stuck headfirst in a snowbank because he had guessed wrong dematerializing, there was no way in hell he was going to get trapped under this roof with unrequited love on the one hand, and unrequited sexual attraction on the other.

It was simply *not* going to happen.

He should have eaten in his room.

As Ruhn looked back down at his place setting, he tried to swallow the anxiety that rose every time one of these meals happened. So many forks and spoons on the sides of plates that had gold all over them. So many people who were as comfortable in this grand dining room as he was not. So many courses and servants and candles and—

"Uncle?"

At Bitty's soft inquiry, he took a deep breath. "Yes?"

"More rolls?"

"No, thank you."

He turned the silver basket down not because he wasn't hungry. Fates, he was starving even after having cleaned his plate. But he hated the way his hands shook and he was worried he would drop the basket and break all the glassware in front of him.

Please send it in the other direct—oh, thank God. Rhage was taking the thing back and putting it down between the sterling silver salt and pepper shakers and the golden candelabra.

Ruhn didn't understand how they could all just lounge back after they were finished with the entrée and chat casually, wineglasses held with confidence while plates were cleared around them, dessert coming in on more platters—

When he looked up and caught the King's solicitor staring across at him, he cringed and wanted to bark out, *Yes, I know I have terrible manners, but I'm doing the best I can and your cataloging every slipped pea and drip of gravy is making me worse.*

Instead, he dropped his eyes and wondered exactly how long he had to stay here before a bolt for the exit would be even marginally permissible.

Saxton, son of no doubt a Very Well-Bred Aristocrat of Noble Bloodline, looked at him a lot. Whenever Ruhn walked by or sat anywhere around the gentlemale, which fortunately was not often, those eyes followed him in disapproval and judgment. Then again, the attorney was always perfectly dressed in suits that fit his lean body like they had been stitched on it, and the male always was perfectly groomed, his blond hair off to one side with nothing out of place, his shave so close that even at the end of a long night, he appeared to be just out of the shower.

To a male like that? Of course someone who had come to the house with only two pairs of jeans, a better, a medium, and a bad T-shirt, and a single set of work boots, would be an insult. Add on to that the fact that Ruhn was illiterate and hadn't even been able to sign his name to Bitty's adoption papers? Come on. The distaste was as justifiable as it was obvious.

Maybe there was more to it, though. Maybe Saxton knew the truth about his past.

Ruhn shuddered to think about that. He'd been truthful about where he'd been and what he'd done, and he had to imagine that nothing was kept from the King's attorney. But who knew. And at least everyone else seemed to accept him—and when he really got up in his head about Saxton, he tried reminding himself of that fact. It still hurt and worried him, though.

In the meantime, all Ruhn wanted was to find a way to contribute to the household and earn his keep. The problem? There were *doggen* everywhere, and as much as he had tried to take over some basic repair duties around the estate or work in the kitchen, he kept getting shut down by all of them.

So he lifted weights and tried to pretend he was okay while he screamed inside his head and told himself that connecting with his dead sister's daughter made it all worth it.

Every night and every day were getting harder, however.

And as much as he hated to admit it, he was coming to the conclusion that he had to leave. He just couldn't stand being a fish out of water any longer.

Things were not working out.

"I love you, Uncle," Bitty said. Like she could read his mind.

Closing his eyes, he reached out and took her tiny, soft hand. Leaving her would be like putting his heart in cold storage. But he had done that once before.

He could do it again.

FOUR

$\mathcal{T}$he training center's gym was big enough so that it could be sectioned in half by an air wall and still have room for two full-sized basketball courts. The ceiling was fifty feet high and had caged lights, and rafters of bench seats rose like wings down both of the long sides. There were two scoreboards that could be lowered for games, as well as multiple hoops and backboard arms that were like-wise retractable. Finally, the floor was the color of honey, the heavily varnished and basketball-marked pine boards the kind of thing that squeaked your sneakers.

Peyton was chilling on a metal folding chair just inside one set of entrance doors, a bottle of Vishous's Grey Goose in one hand, an open bag of Combos in the other. The former he was halfway done with, the latter he was scraping the bottom of, the pretzel and cheddar cheese nuggets of processed goodness his Last Meal.

He really missed his bong, but the Brothers were not into the drugs—and besides, the vodka was doing the job well enough, a floaty disassociation making his head feel like a balloon on a barely-there tether to his spine.

He was also now horny as fuck.

Boone, Craeg, John Matthew, and Novo were playing a game of two-on-two, the echoing dribbles like a marching band that couldn't quite settle on a beat. Paradise—along with some others—was over on the bleachers, still with those notes, and that was why he was here on a single, right next to the exit: There was no way she could sidle up for a heart-to-heart without being obvious about it—and she wanted to talk to him. She kept looking over at him, trying to catch his eye.

Nope.

In the words of old-school Dana Carvey, *Not gonna dew iiiiiiit.*

Fortunately, she had Zsadist right next to her—and Paradise's studious nature couldn't help but get her to ask the Brother questions and point out things she had written down for elaboration.

You had to respect that about her. And given that Peyton wanted to avoid her for the rest of his natural life, the proclivity so worked for him—

A shout got his attention.

Novo had the ball and was driving to the basket, dodging Boone and then dribbling between Craeg's legs. Her dunk was Michael Jordan from the mid-nineties, all air, nothing-but-net, and the bucket won the game. As John Matthew came in for high fives, she smiled.

Truly smiled.

For a brief moment, she looked her age, her eyes sparkling, her face softening, her aura glowing.

"Suck it, douchebags," she said as she pointed fingers at Boone and Craeg. "Suck it good."

John Matthew and she fell into Hammertime, all precise coordination of athletic bodies with her rocking the #suckit chorus while the vanquished losers threw up their arms and bemoaned their pitiable fate.

Abruptly, Peyton forgot about everything else. Funny . . . how you could notice something new about somebody you'd known for a while. And the revelation about Novo?

She was desperately unhappy. Otherwise, this brief show of normal wouldn't offer such a frickin' contrast.

Sure enough, she happened to glance over at him, and instantly, she dropped the victory song and dance, her mask of cold, hard competence slamming down over her features. Turning her back on him, she went over to where Paradise was sitting and fished through a duffel, grabbing a water bottle.

But she didn't drink. She took out her phone and frowned at the screen.

When John Matthew came over and tapped her on the shoulder, she jumped and fumbled with the cell.

The Brotherhood had recently improved reception in the underground facility, so texts and calls now went through with greater reliability. And that was a blessing and a curse. Sometimes it was good to just be in the zone.

With a shake of the head to John Matthew, she disengaged and headed for the equipment room/PT suite, disappearing behind closed doors.

As the next game was organized and got started, Peyton watched Xhex and Payne go up against Butch and V. But not for long. After about five minutes of play, he got to his feet and started down the opposite flank of the gym . . . following in Novo's wake.

Saxton barely made it through dessert, and as soon as the parfaits and fruit started to be cleared, he folded his napkin and placed it next to his untouched sweet. After saying good day to those on either side of him, he pushed his chair back and retreated from the table along with a couple of stragglers who were likewise peeling off early: The Brotherhood usually lingered after the final meal of the night, relaxing and talking over coffee, wine, or aperitifs.

Which would feel like two lifetimes and a second-degree burn all over his body at this point—

"Are you really going home in this storm?"

Saxton looked over his shoulder and tried to hide his true reaction. Blay had come up behind him, napkin still in hand, as if the male had hurried from his seat.

Well . . . damn. It was so hard not to notice how beautiful he was, how kind, how smart and loving, how considerate.

"I shall be fine," Sax said roughly.

It was hard to put any faith in that, though, especially standing so close to the source of his pain. What he wanted to say? *I miss you. I want to hold you. I want to feel that wholeness again, that sense of purpose and—*

"The weather is really bad out there."

Saxton took a deep breath. "It's the work of a moment to get back downtown."

Blay frowned. "Downtown? Why would you—sorry, that's none of my business."

"I moved about three months ago."

"Wait, I thought you were at your Frank Lloyd Wright?"

"No. I sold it and bought Rehv's penthouse at the Commodore."

Red eyebrows rose high. "And what happened to your Victorian?"

"I sold it, too."

"You loved that house."

"And I love my new place."

"Wow." Blay smiled after a moment. "Well, you're moving up in the world."

"To a higher elevation, certainly." There was a pause. And then Saxton felt compelled to say, "Your young are doing well."

Blay glanced back at Qhuinn and the two bouncy chairs that had been brought in from the kitchen. "They're so much fun. It's also a lot of work, but between the four of us, we cover it." The male crossed his arms over his chest, but it was in a relaxed way. "God, I feel like I haven't talked to you in forever."

"We're both busy." And you're in love with someone else. "I'm happy for you. Everything seems to be working out for the best."

If you were Qhuinn, that was.

"For you, too. You and the King are doing an incredible job together. Which brings me to my point. Do you mind if I talk to you about something? It involves my parents' neighbor? I'd really like your take on what's happening."

Oh, so this wasn't about my going home in the blizzard. It was about work.

"Yes, of course," Saxton said in what he hoped was a level, calm tone.

As Blay started to lay out the facts, Saxton felt himself pull back from reality, the inner part of him retreating until he was tucked deep inside of his mind and his body, miles and miles away from this pleasant, largely uncomplicated discussion concerning real property.

Cruelty came in so many different fashions, did it not. And Blay was not being purposely mean. In all his un-complication and warmth and casual conversation, he would no doubt have been shocked to find that he was tearing a hole in the soul of the sad, hollow male he was speaking with.

"Forgive me," Saxton interrupted. "I don't mean to cut you off, but perhaps you could summarize this in an email and I could respond a bit later? If I'm going to leave, I should probably do it now."

"Oh, God, yeah of course. I'm so sorry. And your safety comes first, I shouldn't have even brought it up here." Blay put a hand on Saxton's shoulder. "Be careful out in the blizzard."

"Thank you." Although it is so much more intolerable under this roof, Saxton added to himself.

With a reflexive bow, he took leave of his former lover—and as he turned away, he was relieved to find that his coat and briefcase were still where he'd left them by the sideboard. Drawing his coat on, he crossed the foyer and let himself out into the vestibule.

At which point, he stopped and dropped his head.

His heart was pounding and he felt sweaty, even in the chill.

This really wasn't going to work. This whole thing in Caldwell. He loved what he did for the King, but the grind of being around what he had lost and was never going to have again was wearing him out.

Blay, and everything they'd shared for that brief time, was why he'd had to switch to living in a penthouse in the sky. The Frank Lloyd Wright house didn't name the requisite technology upgrades, and the pair of them had been together too much in that beloved Victorian of his—it had been their love nest when they'd sneaked out of the Brotherhood mansion in search of privacy: They had made love in the master bedroom. Lain side by side in front of the fire. Talked of private things and taken meals. Read books and newspapers. Sung in the shower and laughed in the claw-footed bath.

He'd had dreams of them settling there forever, raising a family of some description, enjoying the ups and enduring the declines of life.

So, of course he'd had to move somewhere else. He didn't want to catch glimpses of the male all night, and worry about the fighter when he was out in the field with the Brothers, and remember what it was like to have sex with him . . . and then have to go home and be stuck indoors where the last one on that list of mournful memories had happened on every flat surface and most of the bumpy ones.

It was hell—

Some kind of rhythmic noise got his attention and he frowned.

Leaning an ear to the outer door of the vestibule, he couldn't identify the sound, but he was fairly sure that whatever it was, it was directly outside.

If it were *lessers,* they would be banging the panels down, and it certainly wasn't that loud or urgent.

Setting the briefcase on the floor, he looped the scarf around his neck, tucked the ends across his chest, and anchored them by buttoning up the coat's front.

And then he opened the door—

The wind hit him square in the face and brought with it a slurry of flakes, his vision diminishing in the midst of the stinging onslaught. But the barrage didn't last. In the next breath, the gust shifted to another direction, and like a rock star drawing a crowd, the flurries followed the leader, leaving a vacuum that gave him plenty of sight.

Schhhht. Heave. *Schhht.* Heave. *Schht.* Heave . . .

Ruhn was shoveling huge loads of snow over his shoulder, the movements powerful and showing no sign of tiring, the path he was creating from the front entrance three to four feet deep in the drifts— and one had to wonder why he bothered. Nobody was going to try to come in that way before dawn, and certainly not afterward, even with the heavy cloud cover—

What a powerful body that was.

As Saxton traced the movements, the jabbing forward, the hauling back, the over and over again, something stirred inside of him . . . and it was a surprise. Ever since Blay had passed through his life, leaving behind a frigid, ruined landscape, Saxton had noticed no one, really. Sure there had been sex, but he'd quickly discovered that was no solution to his pain, and nobody had resonated with any depth. Yet here he was in a snowstorm, measuring the width of a set of broad shoulders, and the swing and twist of a torso, and a pair of legs planted with such strength.

As if Ruhn sensed the presence behind him, the male wrenched around. "Oh, excuse me. I'm in your way."

"Not at all."

A gust blew in between them, ushering a swirl of flakes through the distance that separated their bodies. Then Ruhn abruptly stepped back into the fresh snow and rested the business end of the shovel at his feet.

Dropping his head, he folded his hands on the handle and assumed the role of a servant male, prepared to wait through even the deadly rising sun if it was necessary for his social superior to move along.

"Why are you out here?" Saxton asked.

Ruhn's eyes rose in surprise. "I . . . there needs to be a path cleared."

"Fritz has a snowblower."

"He is busy inside." Those eyes refocused on the ground. "And I would like to help."

"Does he know you are doing this?"

Except that was a silly question. Regardless of Ruhn's station prior to moving in, the male was now a guest in the First Family's house, and as such, the idea he was doing manual labor out here in a storm? The butler would have an apoplectic fit.

"I won't tell anyone." Saxton shook his head even though the male wasn't looking at him. "I promise."

Those toffee-colored eyes lifted again. "I don't . . . I don't wish to cause any difficulty. But the truth is . . ."

Another volley of wind barreled into them, and Saxton had to shift his weight to keep from being pushed over. When things re-quieted, he waited for Ruhn to finish.

"You can talk to me," he said as the male stayed silent. "I'm an attorney. I'm used to keeping things to myself."

Eventually, Ruhn shook his head. "It just doesn't sit well with me."

"What doesn't?"

"Being here and not . . . doing anything." The male's eyes traced over the mansion's great gray profile. "It's not right."

"You're an honored guest."

"No, I'm not. Or I should not be. And I do not wish . . ."

As the male stalled out again, Saxton prompted, "What do you not wish?"

"I do not wish to be purposeless." The male frowned. "Are you truly going out in this weather?"

"Do I look so fragile?"

Ruhn bowed low. "Forgive me. I meant no offense—"

"No, no." Saxton stepped forward with his hand out, thinking he might reassure the male. But he stopped himself. "I'm just kidding. And I'll be fine. Thank you for your concern, however."

There was an awkward pause. And indeed, it was impossible not to notice that flakes had landed in that dark hair, and dusted those shoulders . . . and there was a scent in the air, a heady, sexy scent of a male in good health exerting himself . . . and God, in the midst of the blizzard, that rugged profile was the kind of thing that made one wish to loosen one's scarf.

"I best be off," Saxton said gruffly. "But do stay out here as long as you like. We all must let it out somehow."

On that note, he dematerialized himself off into the waning night.

In the midst of his scatter of molecules, he had a fleeting thought that when he came back the following evening, the entire mountaintop might well be free of snow.

Ruhn certainly seemed to have the strength for it.

FIVE

own in the training center's physical therapy suite, Novo was in a debate with herself as she held her cell phone to her ear and caught a barrage of blather.

"—good to talk to you! Oh, my God, it's been sooooo long. I mean, after you moved out and . . ."

As her sister's high-pitched voice played piccolo over the connection, Novo closed her eyes and hopped up on one of the massage tables. The pro for returning the call was that it was a rip-the-Band-Aid-off solution to a problem that wasn't going to go away: no pit in her stomach for nights while she put off what was inevitable.

When Sophy wanted something, she could be tenacious as a fresh coat of paint.

The con? Well, that was obvious. The female never called unless she had an agenda that benefited her, and the saccharine warm-up to the ask was bad soap opera acting draped over a hard-stack of narcissism. Oh, and if you pointed out that the female might as well skip that shit and get to the point? Then you enjoyed an hour-long crying jag that was as moving and authentic as a sock-puppet account on the Internet.

So yeah, as painful as it was, it was much more efficient to let Sophy waltz through the preamble. And it made Novo think of those Tums ads where the person eats something that fights back and slaps the crap out of them? Except in this case, it was her new Samsung going straight-up ninja on the side of her head.

"—Mommy and Daddy are so excited for Oskar and me. Anyway, I want you to be my maid of honor."

Wait . . . say *whaaaaaaaat*?

A cold flush shot through Novo's body—which was what happened when your prettier-than-you-are sister called to tell you she was mating your ex—and she distracted herself by getting annoyed with Sophy's insistence on referring to their parents by those human titles. Like, really. Do you have to pretend you're human just 'cuz you think it's cool?

And maid of honor? What the fuck? Were they doing a human ceremony and not a proper vampire one?

"Novo? Hello? Did you hear me?"

She cleared her throat. "Yes, I did—"

"I know this must be a shock to you." That voice lowered from Minnie Mouse all the way down to Michelle Tanner. "Novo, I realize this must be awkward. But you're my sister. It wouldn't be my big night without you."

Translation: It wouldn't be even half as much fun if I get the trophy without you being at the award ceremony.

"Novo?"

For a moment, she closed her eyes and imagined speaking from the heart: *I already know you won. You got him and you can have him. How about I just stipulate that here and now and we move along?*

Oh, and this was not a shock. It wasn't even awkward. In fact, this "happy" announcement was the culmination of exactly what Sophy had set in motion two and a half years ago. The only moderate surprise was that it had taken this long for her to get to the mating.

"Please, Novo. You have to be there."

No, she really didn't. The healthy thing to do was to politely decline the kind frickin' invitation, wish the female well, and pretend that she wasn't actually going to be legally related to the male who'd left her for her sister.

Unfortunately, that felt like a cop-out. A cowardly retreat. The larger part of Novo's makeup, the part that never said die, that refused to be beat, that would take physical amputation over losing face or pride, mandated that she go.

Just to prove to herself she was strong. Unbroken. Whole.

In spite of the tragedy that had happened after Oskar had pulled out of their relationship.

"Novo?"

"Yeah. Sure. I'll do it."

Cue the happy tears. The gratitude. The *Cosmo* magazine, Insta-gratuitous, Fakebook emotion: all for show.

As her sister started rattling off maid-of-honor duties and bridal-shower details—again, what was with the human bullshit? She was getting mated, not married—Novo shook her head.

"I gotta go."

"Wait, what? You can't. You have a job to do and we need to discuss this. You need to organize my shower and my bachelorette party, and we need to pick out dresses—"

"Bachelorette party? Shower? Sophy, what the fuck is all that?"

There was a pause. "Please watch your language."

Like you're the fucking Queen of England, Novo thought.

"And I never imagined you as prejudicial." Sophy went on the huff. "Humans have traditions that can be adapted around our ceremonies. Why not? They'll make my night more special."

Riiight. Because it's not really about the male you're mating. It's what you can post online for people to see.

"I'll do what I can. But I'm working."

"And you have a responsibility to me as your sister."

"I'm fighting in the war, Soph. Do you even know what that is? It's

44 J. R. WARD

the pesky thing that's been killing people like you and me for the last couple of centuries. And you want me to get all thought up about a party? Come on."

There was another pause. And the longer it continued, the more Novo wanted to kick her own ass.

If you were smart, you didn't provide a stage for theatrics. But she had rolled the red carpet out with that one.

"I have to go," Sophy said through what sounded like sniffles. "I just . . . this is my time for joy, Novo. I can't take your negativity. I'll try again with you when I'm ready."

As Sophy cut the connection, Novo dropped the cell phone from her ear. "Why . . . why couldn't I have been an only child."

Dealing with her sister was like a bad carnival ride: You knew exactly where the turns and the loop-de-loops were, the free falls and the too-tall-for-comfort heights, because you could see them up ahead. And meanwhile, your corn dog and your cherry-flavored slushy were clawing back up your throat.

If she'd only held her tongue for another minute and a half, she could have avoided what was going to roll out next. So close. She had been *so* close. The trouble was that her sister knew nothing of real pain, true sacrifice, actual loss. And that coupled with the narcissism and the histrionics? It was enough to make a sane person want to plate-glass-window their own face.

Looking around the neat, orderly room, Novo found that the past replaced the soaking tubs, padded benches, and shelves full of wraps, braces, and gel bottles.

Oskar had been a blond, too. Just like Peyton. Not as rich as him, however.

And when Novo had first met the male, she had had no idea how bad things were going to get. If she'd had even an inkling? She would have trampled whole neighborhoods to get away—

The door to the PT suite swung open, and Peyton appeared between the jambs with a bottle of liquor in his hand, an arousal in his pants, and the wild look in his eye of someone over the brink. In this current incarnation, the male was something right out of the Bad Idea Catalog.

And what do you know . . . a blond male with an able body was exactly what she wanted in her virtual shopping cart.

As Peyton stood in the doorway to the PT suite, he noticed nothing about the tiled clinical space . . . and everything about the female sitting on one of the padded tables.

Novo's powerful body was strung tight as a wire, sure as if she were about to jump off or maybe attack something, her hands gripping the edge of the cushioned work surface, her legs dangling free, the muscles of her arms carved around the bones that supported them thanks to all that pressure she was funneling down into her hands.

"Everything okay?" he asked in a guttural voice.

"Gimme."

As she extended her hand, he entertained a fantasy that she was reaching across the room for his hard cock. But no, she was after the Goose. And who was he to deny her?

Especially with that hooded look she was giving him.

"Say please," he drawled.

"No."

A bolt of lust funneled down into his sex and he smiled. "Careful, you'll make me beg."

"I'm waiting."

As he crossed the room, he did absolutely nothing to hide what was going on with his erection, and fuck yeah she noticed, her eyes dropping to his hips and staying there.

"Far be it from me to deny a female," he murmured as he held the bottle out to her.

She drank from the open neck like a boss, swallowing the vodka as if it were Sprite. And when she lowered the bottle, she nodded down at his hard-on.

"Who's that for?"

"You. If you want it."

She took another draw, and he waited for her to tell him, with no small amount of superiority, that she didn't. When all he got was silence, his blood rushed even faster.

"Is that a 'yes'?" he said as he focused on her lips.

"It's not a 'no.'"

"I'll take what I can get."

"Oh, that's right." Novo smiled with her fangs. "You can't have the one you really want and you're stuck here overday with me."

"Fishing for compliments? That's not like you."

"Just stating reality." She took another haul of the vodka. "You're my only option, too. So we're in this together."

"You make me blush with the compliments," he muttered. "No, stop. Really."

"You don't like being used? Hmm, maybe this is a life lesson for all those women and females you fuck at the clubs."

"It's not using someone if there's pleasure involved. Mutual, that is."

Novo laughed in a hard burst. "Is this the part where you tell me you've never had any complaints about your performance? Because that statistic would be a little more impressive if they had any way of reaching you afterward."

"Now, Novo, if you don't play nice, I'm going to take my vodka and my dick elsewhere."

"You're right. If we keep talking, this is not going to happen."

With that, she reached out with her free hand, grabbed the front of his shirt, and yanked him to her mouth, holding him in place as their lips met.

Crashed, was more like it.

There was nothing romantic or tentative or get-to-know-you about the contact. Potent sexual power burst between them, their tongues dueling, sensation overwhelming, instinct shutting down thought. Her taste was wildness and Grey Goose, her scent was heady as weed, and shit, he got to touch her—something he had wanted to do for so long. Bringing his hands to her smoothed-back hair, her neck, her shoulders, his heart pounded and he was ready to get inside of his her right then and there—

Had he shut the door tightly?

Breaking the contact, he panted as he looked over his shoulder and willed the panel shut tight and locked—and when he turned back around, she'd put the Goose on the floor and was pulling down her loose nylon workout shorts—

No panties.

Fuuuuuuuck, this was moving fast.

On that note, her hands went to the fly of his slacks, and in the work of a moment, his fine, loose pants fell to his ankles. He was also commando. 'Cuz this was exactly the situation he had hoped to be in. And what do you know, it was cup-runneth-over time: The next thing he knew, her thighs were wide, and she gripped his hips, her nails digging in. With a jerk, she pulled him forward, and he masterminded himself between them, taking his cock and angling—

"Oh . . . *fuck*," he groaned as they were joined.

She was so tight and hot, and he felt the sensation all over his body, arching above her as she lay back on the massage table. With his feet on the ground, he couldn't kiss her, but he could start pumping, that was for damn sure. Putting his hands on her hips, he rolled into her again and again, the momentum doubling and redoubling with ever-greater force—

It was hard to say when he first noticed she was just lying there.

For one, his body was all in for the sex, his blood thundering, the sight of his slick shaft penetrating her again and again scrambling what little was left of his blown mind. And as a corollary to all that, he was also having to concentrate on not coming—which was like trying to extinguish a house fire with nothing but your own thoughts. Yet, even in his frenzy, and in spite of the alcohol in his system, he noticed that her lids were closed in the frozen mask of her face, and her breathing was nothing-special as her head moved up and down while he fucked her.

Peyton slowed. Then stopped.

When he just stood there, his lungs screaming for air, the sweat dampening his silk shirt, she opened her eyes. "What's wrong?" When he didn't say anything, her brows lifted. "You finished already?"

Peyton blinked.

And withdrew.

With a curse, he bent down and pulled his slacks back up. "Yeah," he muttered as he redid the fly. "I'm done."

"I didn't think you were a quitter."

He looked away. Looked back at her. "Do you even care who you're with?"

Novo sat up quick. "Are you trying to slut-shame me? For real? 'Cuz if that is not a double standard, I don't know what is."

He picked up the bottle from the floor and managed to take a swig as he straightened. "Nah, I just want the female I'm fucking to do more than lie back and make a grocery list in her head."

"Ohhhh, riiiiight, I didn't perform enough for you." She put a hand over her heart and feigned like she was dying of regret. "I wasn't enough for Peyton, son of Peythone." Abruptly, she dropped the act and focused on him hard. "I thought you were going to take what you could get."

"Guess I don't want it anymore."

"Liar." Novo hopped off the table and he turned away as she pulled her shorts up. "You're such a fucking liar."

"Nope. Not on this one."

"You're not going to cry on me, are you?" she taunted. "Look at you, all lowered head over there."

"I was trying to give you privacy."

"After you were inside of me?"

Peyton headed for the door, taking his Grey Goose with him.

"Coward," Novo muttered.

He didn't reply as he came up to the exit. And as he stepped out, he hated to admit the truth about how he felt.

Weak. So fucking weak.

But for some reason, his feelings were hurt. Which was insane. The plan had been for the two of them to use each other. Fair trade. No emotions, just fucking.

It was his standard currency. So what the hell was his problem?

Left to her own devices in the PT suite, Novo felt like picking up the padded massage tables and workbenches and throwing them around the room until there wasn't one piece of equipment or medical supply that hadn't been destroyed at the molecular level. There were problems with that strategy, however. For one, anything with four legs was bolted to the floor. For another, as fucked in the head as she was, she didn't want to deliberately destroy someone else's property.

"Shit," she said as she stared across at the closed door.

Between her legs, a warm hum persisted, and goddamn it, her body still wanted to be where it had been—under Peyton, his sex buried in her own, that powerful penetration of his eclipsing the screaming in her skull. Except he'd been a revelation. In a bad way.

The purpose had been to wipe Oskar out of her head. Replace him with a different model. Make a male who didn't want her—and wouldn't even know the sex was happening—jealous because she was with someone else.

God, that sounded insane. And in any event, it hadn't worked, because she had found herself wanting what she was getting too much: Underneath that composure she'd locked herself down with, she'd been on the verge of an orgasm.

Their bodies had been made to fit together like that.

"Whatever."

Prowling around, she gave herself time to lose the scent of her arousal, and then finally reemerged into the gym proper with what she hoped was a suitable amount of nothing-special-going-on-here. Turned out, she didn't need to worry about a peanut gallery. The place was empty.

As she surveyed the vacant bleachers, the still nets, the empty court, her cell phone started to vibrate in her ass pocket—and when she took the thing out, she already knew who it was. Yup. Her mother. Ready to complain that she had been mean to Sophy, ruining what was supposed to be a joyous time for everyone.

Off in the distance, an eerie scream vibrated through the silence like a premonition of death.

It was that patient, Assail. The one who was locked in that room. She didn't know the details, but could guess by the sound he always made that he had gone insane.

Maybe she was next on that list.

Left to contrast that very real possibility with everything her sister was looking forward to, she considered going to the weight room for a second workout—when the calendar date popped into her mind for no good reason.

Closing her eyes, she felt herself sag.

She had gotten pregnant three years ago on this very night.

When Oskar, the male her sister was going to mate, had serviced her in her needing.

After which, he had promptly left her for different shores, as it were. Naturally, she had never told him that she was with young, and so he had no idea what had happened eleven months later.

As her stomach clenched and she considered throwing up, she thought, God, all of those events, from the pregnancy to the . . . nightmare . . . that became of it seemed to have happened to someone else—and a stranger, at that. She was different now than she had been. Stronger. Tougher. More resilient. Getting into the Brotherhood's training program had been proof of how far she had come, and fighting on the streets of Caldwell was a nightly reminder that she wasn't backsliding.

She was going to go to that mating ceremony. And she was going to be the maid of whatever the hell.

This was her final test. If she could manage to survive the ritual that united the pair of them for the rest of their lives? Then the fool she had once been was truly well and buried—and the loss that had nearly killed her was finally and forever locked away.

No weakness. No quarter given or taken. Nothing left of what she was . . . and no more fear that she could be hurt like that again.

Novo looked at the scoreboard that still had the last game's results on it. Home and Away. Home team had won by ten.

She was going to be fine, she resolved as she headed for the exit.

Oh, and she was absolutely going to forget she knew what Peyton felt like. Abso-fucking-lutely.

SIX

*T*he following evening, Saxton materialized over to the Audience House early, taking his form in the back by the Federal mansion's detached two-story garage. *Doggen* had come during the afternoon and plowed the blizzard's snowfall away, but he was careful as he walked over to the kitchen's entrance. Hot Gucci loafer soles were slicker than greased lightning on anything smooth and icy—and given how perfectly Fritz insisted things had to be done? The driveway and the parking area were like a sheet cake iced by Ina Garten.

As he entered a code and opened the door, he knew he was the first to come into work, but that didn't mean there hadn't been plenty of people in and out during daylight hours. Indeed, as he shut himself in, there were fresh pastries on silver trays, all carefully plastic-wrapped for freshness, a restaurant-sized coffeepot ready to be plugged in for brewing, and baskets of apples and bananas set to be arranged in the waiting room.

The first audiences wouldn't convene until eight p.m., but Saxton liked to make sure all the paperwork for each private meeting with the King was in order and that everything would run seamlessly, both for

Wrath's sake and for the subjects'. With as many as twenty different issues a night, there was a lot to keep track of. Certain audiences, like those seeking a blessing for a mating or the birth of a young, were straightforward and went relatively fast. Others, like those concerning the disposition of assets following a death, bloodline disputes, or incidences involving bodily harm, could be quite involved and require much follow-up and monitoring.

Proceeding into the staff corridor, he opened the first door on the right and flipped on the lights. His office was utterly devoid of accoutrement, no paintings or drawings on the walls, no *objets d'art* on the built-in partner's desk, nothing but law books on the plain shelves. There wasn't even a rug. Just two rolling office chairs on either side of the work space, a monitor he could plug his laptop into so he didn't get eye strain, and a series of locked cabinets containing files that were live.

All of his in-session notation was done by hand as the sound of tapping keys, no matter how soft, drove Wrath absolutely insane. So Saxton took notes with a Montblanc and then transposed them afterward, and there was a measurable benefit to the double-work. For one, he had a hard copy of everything in the event of a computer failure—not that V would allow that with his precious anti-Apple network and equipment—but more importantly, as Saxton typed up his cursive handwriting, he reinforced everything in his own head.

Sitting down, he took his laptop out of his briefcase and hooked it up to the keyboard that had been mounted on a slide under the desk as well as that screen that didn't give him a headache.

And then he stalled out.

"Come now," he muttered to himself.

Turning on the Lenovo, he got into his Outlook and was greeted by twenty or so work emails, a flyer from the Met, an ad for 1stdibs, and notices from Sotheby's paintings department and Christie's online watches sale.

He ignored all of that.

The bolded line that grabbed his eye and refused to let go was from *Blay Lock,* and the subject read *Follow-up.*

It had come in about an hour after Saxton had left the mansion the night before, but he hadn't been able to open the thing at home. Just the sight of the name made his loneliness condense into an ice-cold spear that nailed him square in the chest—and indeed, he would have much preferred to move the thing into junk mail and pretend he'd never received it. Avoiding his duty unto the law, however, was not an option, not even with his emotions tangled and twisted into this heartache he was so used to—and Blay was clearly seeking a legal opinion on whatever it was.

Calling the message up, it took him a minute to focus on the words that had been typed, and then the first thing he noticed was that there were no spelling mistakes, no grammatical issues, and perfect punctuation within the sentences. But that was Blay. He was a measured and methodical kind of male, who liked to do things properly and to their completion. And sure enough, the way he presented the facts and made the request was logical, respectful . . .

Saxton frowned as he read the five short paragraphs again.

And then once more.

Evidently, Blay's parents had moved a number of months ago into a house in a human development out on the very edge of suburbia. Saxton had never been there, of course, as that had been after his time, but he had overheard Blay tell folks that it was beautiful, with a pond out in the back, and a porch, and lots of room. His *mahmen* was not totally in love with the place, because it was too new, but she was adjusting.

The problem concerned a neighbor of his parents', an older female who resided on the large tract of land next to the neighborhood. Human developers who were acquiring acreage in the area were pressuring the female to sell her property to them so they could continue to expand and build a golf course and country club complex. But she didn't want to leave. She was living in the farmhouse that she and her mate had constructed back in the late 1800s and it was all she had left of him and their lives together. According to Blay, she didn't have too many years left, maybe only a decade or so, and her only wish was to stay where she was. Her granddaughter was worried about her safety, though.

The humans were banging on the door in the daylight hours, harassing her on the phone and through the mail, and sending her packages with threatening papers in them. It had been going on for a good six months and seemed to be escalating, in spite of the fact that the female had made it clear she wasn't going to move. Blay's father, Rocke, had even gone over to try to intercede one evening, chasing off a car, but nothing seemed to get through to the humans.

Saxton shook his head. It wasn't like the female or her family could go to the human police: *Hi, I don't exist in your world technically, but I am bound by your property laws and am having some trouble with trespassers. Can you help me out?*

Oh, and don't mind my fangs.

He could only imagine how worried the family was. Older female, alone, human agitators tormenting her while all she was trying to do was spend the last remaining years she had in peace.

And there was no telling where this would stop.

Humans were a lesser species, for certain. But they could be deadly.

As Saxton began to form a plan in his head, he tried to ignore the fact that his sense of purpose was contaminated by an irrational desire to be indispensable to Blay; to solve this problem, not just because it was his job, but because it might impress his former lover.

Which, naturally, in this fantasy hypothetical, led to Blay breaking off his bonded relationship with Qhuinn, leaving those two beautiful young behind, and volunteering to run away from Caldwell with Saxton.

Yes, all of that would come from one, perfectly modulated return email.

Well, that and successfully running off those thugs from the male's parents' neighbor.

As he rolled his eyes at himself, he started typing.

Romantic delusions aside, he was going to take this to Wrath and see what could be done. At the very least, he could do right by that defenseless older female, and there was consolation in that.

After he hit *send,* he swiveled around and pulled the venetian blinds up high enough so that he could see out to the snowy landscape. Everything had a thick layer of powder on it, the day having been cold, according to the human online weather reports. In the glow from the other stately homes, the landscape fluoresced blue.

Loneliness was just like winter, he decided. Cold and pervasive, trapping you inside your own head because what was outside was so inhospitable.

Was he never going to be warm again?

About three blocks over, in another mansion of similar size and distinction, though of Tudor, not Federal, style, Peyton stepped out of his shower and reached for a monogrammed towel. As he dried himself off, the air in his bathroom was so thick with steam, it was like being in a fogbank, the mirrors veiled with moisture, every breath as much water as it was oxygen, his skin tingling from the heat.

He'd just gotten home from the training center, the bus having dropped the lot of them off at a strip mall a couple of miles away, and he had an hour before he was supposed to be downtown in the field with the Brotherhood. He was hungry, hungover, and tired to the point of exhaustion—and that shower hadn't done shit to fix any of that.

And then there was his other little issue.

"God*damn* it."

With a series of nasty jerks, he wadded up the damp towel and threw it as hard as he could across the marble expanse. And then he just stood there, buck-ass naked, his feet planted on the heated floor, his hands locked on his hips so he didn't start trashing the place.

That . . . whatever it had been . . . in the PT room with Novo refused to go away. Every time he blinked, he saw her lying back on that table, her eyes closed, her face as composed as a fucking corpse's. And the visuals weren't the worst of it. That cynical, hard voice of hers kept banging around his head, mocking him, calling him out, making him feel like a fool.

After he'd left her, he'd gone to the break room, polished off the last of the vodka, and then headed three doors down to crash in a vacant inpatient bed. Throughout the day, the muffled screams of that psychotic male patient had warred with nightmares that involved Peyton being unclothed and in the midst of stinging wasps. Both had kept waking him up, and it was a toss-up as to which was worse.

When it had finally become dark enough for the bus to depart, he had sat right in front, in the first row of seats—because Novo was always toward the rear. And during the entire trip back toward town, he had been aware of her presence, sure as if her body were a beacon. But he hadn't heard her say one word.

The good news? He'd been so preoccupied that he'd barely given the mess with Paradise a second thought.

And now he was here, trying to get his head to calm the hell down so he didn't get himself killed when he went out to engage with the enemy—

The knock on his outer bedroom door was discreet, which told him who it was. Fucking *great*. "Yes," he snapped.

The *doggen* on the other side spoke in a haughty, well-modulated tone. "My Lord, forgive me. But your father wishes for an audience prior to your departure."

Okay, so one, the butler wasn't asking for forgiveness, at all. And two, this was a direct order. There was no fucking "wish" involved.

Peyton put his hands on the sink counter and braced his weight on his arms. "Did he say why?" he gritted. "I don't have a lot of time."

This was both true and not the point. The only thing guaranteed to make his head fuck worse than it already was? A royal summons from Daddy-o, the agenda of which was either Peyton's drinking or his drug use. These command performances had been a fairly regular occurrence over the past few years, and they always went sooooooooo well.

And come on. He had been a lot better since he had joined the training program. Well, at least until his cousin Allishon's murder. He'd fallen off the wagon since then, but who could blame him? He was the one who'd gone to her apartment and seen all of the blood-stains. And yeah, sure, fine, the fact that he was sweating out last night's vodka at the moment didn't bode well if he was hoping for a pass on the addiction front—or an at least partially credible counter-argument.

"My Lord?" his father's butler prompted.

He cursed. "Tell him I have to get dressed first."

"As you wish."

Oh, he didn't wish. Not fucking at all.

A good half hour later, Peyton meandered down to the first floor, and he took his sweet frickin' time making it over to the closed doors of his father's study. At any moment, he expected the butler to jump out from the pantry with a stopwatch and—

"He has been expecting you."

Bingo.

Peyton looked over his shoulder at the hall monitor. The *doggen* was looming as only an old-school servant of a Founding Family dressed in a uniform could, his average height pumped up to LeBron standards thanks to that holier-than-thou attitude.

"Yeah," Peyton drawled, "you mentioned that before. That's why I came down."

Man, if that *doggen*'s disapproval was any thicker, it would qualify as a coat of asphalt.

"I shall let him know you've arrived," the butler murmured as he stepped forward and knocked. "My Lord?"

"Send him in," came the muffled response.

The butler swung open the carved panels, revealing a grand expanse of mahogany, Oriental rugs, leather-bound books, and brass chandeliers. Long and tall, the room had an upper story of shelves accessible by a curved set of brass steps and serviced by a walkway with an ornate rail that went all the way around the second level.

As Peyton looked up at that gold-leafed balustrade, he was reminded of when he'd been young and convinced that a giant king's crown had been imported from somewhere and installed in the family's house.

Because he and his bloodline were just that special.

"Peyton. Sit down."

He shifted his eyes to his father. The male was sitting behind a desk that was as big as a king-sized bed, his back straight, his hands linked on the blood-red blotter. Peythone was dressed in a dark suit and had a tie knotted precisely at his throat, the button-down and the pocket square white. A discreet Cartier watch peeked out from the French cuffs, and the cuff links were gold with Burmese rubies.

When his father indicated the vacant chair across from the desk, Peyton realized he hadn't moved.

"How are you, Father," he said as he walked forward.

"I am well. How kind of you to ask."

"What is this all about?"

"Sit."

"Actually, I'm good right here." As he stood to the side of that chair, he crossed his arms over his chest. "What can I do for you?"

"You may sit down." His father nodded at the silk-covered seat. "And then we can talk."

Peyton looked around and got absolutely no support from the portraits that hung in front of the books, the softly crackling fireplace, the seating arrangements of armchairs and side tables.

Grinding his molars, he moved around and slowly lowered himself into the chair. The way he saw it, he might as well face the music, whatever it was—

"Must you wear those clothes in the house."

Peyton glanced down at himself. The leather jacket, heavy combat pants and steel-toed boots were standard issue in the training program.

If you could only see all the weapons underneath, he thought.

"What do you want from me, Father."

Peythone cleared his throat. "I think it's time to discuss your future."

And what future is that exactly? he wondered. As a feature on *Intervention*?

When his father went no further, Peyton shrugged. "I'm in the training program. I'm a fighter—"

"We both know that's a diversion—"

"The hell it is—and you wanted me to go into the program."

"Because I had hoped it would turn you into—"

"Someone like you? Yeah, 'cuz you're such a hard-ass."

"Watch your tone," his father bit out. "And permit me to remind you that your life is not your own. It belongs to this bloodline you are a part of, and as such, it is incumbent upon me to steer you in the proper direction."

Peyton leaned forward in the chair. "I am—"

His father talked right over him. "And accordingly, I have someone I would like you to meet. She is from a suitable family, and before you worry, she is widely considered a great beauty. I am confident that that part of all this will be to your liking. If you are smart, you will consider her fairly, without regard to any rebellion you might feel compelled to pursue as a result of my bringing this forth. I have your best interests at heart here, and I implore you to see that."

Implore? My ass you're imploring any of this, Peyton thought.

"Of course, if you fail to conduct yourself in a proper fashion"—his father smiled coldly—"I shall be forced to reduce your allowance."

"I have a job."

"Being a soldier does not pay for this." His father motioned around the study in such an expansive fashion, it was clear he was referring to the entire estate. And maybe half of Caldwell itself. "And somehow, I don't believe you would fare well without this standard of living. You are not that hardy."

Peyton looked off to the side, to a portrait of a male in nineteenth-century court dress. It was his father, of course. All of the portraits were of his father, each stage of Peythone's life displayed as if he were challenging anyone to argue with his station.

"Why do you think so little of me," Peyton murmured.

"Why? Because I have lived through feast and famine. Wars both human and vampire. I moved across the great ocean and established our base here before any of the other families did. I am the head of this great bloodline and have conducted myself with honor throughout the centuries, remaining faithful to your *mahmen,* and giving her you as a gift of my loins. I hold three doctorates from human schools and am a certified expert in the Old Laws. I am also a virtuoso violinist and speak twelve languages. Tell me, what have you done? Have I in some way missed your vast accomplishments, having noted only your ability to consume vast quantities of alcohol and whatever else you do in that room I provide you with under my roof? Hmm?"

Peyton let all that stand and considered getting up and walking out. Instead, he said softly, "May I ask you something?"

His father offered his palms to the lofty, vaulted ceiling. "But of course. I welcome any inquiries."

"Why did you want me to participate in the training center program."

"It was about time you brought some honor to this family. As opposed to burden."

"No . . ." Peyton shook his head. "I don't think that's it."

"Do they teach you to read minds there, then?"

Peyton got to his feet. "I think you made me go because you thought I was going to fail—and you were looking forward to adding that to the list of things you could lord over me."

His father did an excellent impression of offense. But the light in his eyes . . . oh, there was a nasty little light in there, and that was the truth, wasn't it.

"Of course not. Don't be dramatic."

"Yeah, that's what I thought," Peyton said as he turned away.

With every step he took toward the door, he felt worse: In his mind, he saw Paradise's expression as he had told her he loved her. Then he enjoyed that close-up of Novo lying there like she was enduring him. And the capper was that face of his sire's, the deep-seated dislike he had never understood simmering just below the fine patrician bone structure, which looked exactly like Peyton's own.

When he got to the door, he said over his shoulder, "I'll meet the female. Just tell me where and when, and I'll be there."

His father positively recoiled in surprise, but Peythone recovered soon enough. "Very well, then. I shall have it all arranged. And I trust you shall comport yourself with appropriate dignity—by my standards, not yours."

"Sure. Fine." He let himself out. "Whatever."

As he re-shut the doors behind himself, he was surprised at what he had agreed to. But then he figured . . . why not try his father's way. He didn't like the guy, didn't respect him, but shit was not going so well with Peyton in the Captain Kirk chair. All he'd managed to accomplish in the past five years was liver damage, THC cravings, and unrequited love.

Maybe another way would work better.

Things certainly couldn't get worse.

"My Lord," the butler started with condescension.

"Shut up." He glared over at the *doggen* as he strode for the door. "I'm armed and I now know how to shoot—and you cannot outrun a bullet, I promise you."

As his father's servant started to sputter like an old car engine, Peyton let himself out and kept right on going.

Please let me find a fight tonight, he thought. *If only so I don't come back at dawn still wanting to kill someone.*

SEVEN

As Novo materialized on the rooftop of a walk-up on Sixteenth and Trade, she had a gun on her right hip, one at the small of her back, two daggers on the front of her chest, and a length of chain inside her leather jacket. Her feet were locked in a set of shit-kickers, and her leathers were tight across her thighs and calves. A set of tinted goggles were strapped on her face and their purpose was two-fold: keep the cold wind out of her eyes to prevent tearing, and also dim the headlights and streetlights, which could blind as they flashed across white snow or jumped into your line of sight as you engaged.

As a gust came prowling across the urban landscape of walk-up apartment buildings and grungy little shops, her legs registered the chill, but that wouldn't last. Soon as she got moving, she wasn't going to feel a thing—and on that note, where the fuck was everyone else? Allowing her instincts to roam, she prayed for movement, the scent of baby powder . . . hell, even a human with a dumb idea—although all that was premature. She wasn't permitted to engage with anything until the Brothers and the other trainees arrived.

When a hand tapped her on the shoulder, she wheeled around—and outed one of her knives—

"John Matthew." She lowered the weapon. "Jesus. I didn't hear you."

The male moved his hands in the positions of American Sign Language, and she frowned as she deciphered the words. Good thing he was cutting a rookie some slack and going slowly, letter by letter.

"I know. I need to check my six. You're right."

She bowed to him, something she rarely did. But John Matthew was not just an expert in all kinds of fighting; he was also one of the few males she had ever trusted right from the onset. There was just a quality about him, a quiet calmness where he looked you right in the eye and yet didn't threaten you. To her, this equated to safety, something she was not used to.

He started to sign again, and she nodded. "Yes, I'd like to be paired with you tonight—wait . . . can you do that again? Oh . . . yeah, right, got it. Yes, I have extra clips, four of them." She patted the front of the jacket. "Here and here." She nodded again. "And a chain. What? Well, I think of it as the only kind of bracelet a female like me will ever wear."

John Matthew smiled, flashing his fangs. And as he put out his fist, she pounded it.

One by one, the others materialized at the position, Axe, Boone, Paradise, and Craeg showing up first, followed by Phury and Zsadist, and then Vishous, Rhage, and Payne.

"Where's the golden boy?" the Brother Vishous demanded as he lit a hand-rolled cigarette. "Peyton not gracing us with his damn presence tonight?"

To make it look like she didn't care one way or the other, Novo re-ran the same check of weapons and supplies she had just done for John Matthew—

The blast of heat that went through her body told her down to the split second when Peyton appeared from out of thin air.

But it was just awkwardness, she told herself. Just garden-variety awkwardness, based on hostility and resentment with maybe the smallest dash of embarrassed thrown in—because, hello, she had allowed herself to be vulnerable last night.

Even if Peyton didn't know it, she sure as shit did.

In retrospect, she shouldn't have used him like that. Not because it had hurt him. Hell, he didn't really give a shit; she knew that from the way he behaved with those bimbos at the clubs. No, it had been bad for her, ultimately.

Yeah, even twenty-four hours later, her body still wanted what it had been denied.

But whatever. No reason to think about it anymore—and what do you know, going out in the field and trying not to get killed while she attacked the enemy? Exactly the kind of imperative she needed to wipe everything else out of her mind.

Even Sophy and Oskar, too.

There was a brief review of positions and a reminder of engagement protocol and then an opportunity for questions, which none of the trainees took—everybody was clear on what was expected because it had been drilled into their heads in the classroom.

Hopefully, tonight they would take down a few *lessers*.

There were not many slayers left now, and she could tell the Brotherhood was getting focused on finally ending the war: There was a twitchiness to the warriors, a prickly awareness that seemed to be growing ever more intense—and that, coupled with some overheard conversations about the Omega, led her to believe that things were coming to a head.

What would the world be like without the Lessening Society? It was almost inconceivable . . . and it did make her wonder about what the trainees' role would be if there was no more fighting. Sure, you had to worry about humans, but that was a coexistence issue, not a head-to-head battle for survival.

Assuming those rats without tails never learned about the race.

If they did? That was game-on in a bad way for sure.

"Let's do this," the Brother Phury announced.

In pairs, they dematerialized to their quadrants, and as soon as she and John Matthew resumed corporeal form, they started off at a steady march in the road. Thanks to the storm, the sidewalks were impassable, nothing but deep footprints frozen into the snowpack like fossils in old stone.

Even though she and John Matthew had been assigned a grid ten or fifteen blocks to the west, the neighborhood was the same, all older walk-ups, the four- and five-story buildings narrow and housing some eight to ten rent-frozen units under their roofs. Cars were parallel parked with barely inches to spare, and as a result of the massive snowfall from the storm, the bumper-to-bumper line of vehicles was like one contiguous snowbank, only the brief flashes of the door handles and hints of body paint showing on the sides. Plowing had utterly impacted them all; it would be days of sunshine or hours of shoveling before the owners could move them.

As Novo swept her eyes around, she took note of the streetlamps. Most of them were dark, sometimes because a bulb was out . . . others because the glass headers had been knocked or shot off. What light there was came from the occasional glow from a window, either because the drapes were flimsy enough to let illumination pass or because the shade that had been pulled down had so many holes, it was basically an indoor shutter.

No humans were out, anywhere.

And as she measured the trampled trail that led into one of the walk-ups' front entrances, she tried to imagine what it was like for the people to be moving around in the daylight. Strange, that Caldwell had this other half, this alter ego of activity that none of them ever saw firsthand. Reflections of it filtered through in the form of news, and these tracks in the snow, and these buried cars, and the vague evidence of holed-up, closed-up, currently-going-nowhere apartment dwellers. But during their nightly sweeps they didn't get a true flavor of it, because the law abiders tended to head for cover and stay there after ten p.m.—

She and John Matthew both stopped at the same time.

Up ahead three blocks, a pair of figures rounded the corner. One was a little ahead of the second, and they were big enough so that they had to be males. Whoever it was, they were likewise walking in the road—and they also stopped as soon as they saw they were not alone.

Novo reached to her hip and palmed her gun, but she left her arm down with the nine at her thigh. In her peripheral vision, she noted that John Matthew did the same.

The wind was coming from behind them, and that was a disadvantage: If those were *lessers,* they would recognize the scents, but she and JM had no idea whether they were facing off with human thugs or slayers.

Either way, the rush of adrenaline and surge of inner power that went through her made her feel blissfully alive, her mind swept sparkly clean, her emotions flatlining like schoolchildren admonished by a teacher.

Her fighting instincts took over, her body becoming a tuning fork for information that could improve her attack.

Goddamn it, she wished the wind would change direction—

The pair of humans or slayers or whatever they were turned and walked back in the direction they had come from, re-rounding the corner.

As John Matthew elbowed her, she nodded at him.

And the hunt was on.

As Saxton concluded his presentation to the King, he fell silent and waited with patience for the response.

The Audience Room, which had been the mansion's formal dining room, was empty but for the two of them, the setup of armchairs by the fire vacant, and so, too, the lineup of extra seats that could be brought into a circle as needed. Off to the side, the desk that Saxton used was ready for the night, his orderly row of folders, a legal pad, and several of his pens everything he needed.

Wrath paced around the empty space, the footfalls of his shitkickers muffled by an Oriental rug that was big enough to carpet a Target parking lot. George, his seeing-eye dog, was off halter, but still on the clock, the golden retriever following at his master's heels, his big, boxy head and ruffled, triangle ears cocked and at an angle as if he were wondering if he needed to intervene in the event the course changed.

"Can't we just kill the developers who are harassing that old female," Wrath muttered as he stopped under a crystal chandelier that could have doubled as a galaxy. "I mean, it would be so much more fucking efficient."

Yes, Saxton thought. He'd assumed this would be the first response, and in fact, the King was completely capable of calling a Brother and sending them over with a loaded gun rightthisminute even though it was murder. Then again, Wrath didn't particularly care for humans even though his Queen had their blood in her. And actually, the first couple of times this kind of expedient solution to a Homo sapiens problem had been suggested by the King, Saxton had waffled on whether it was a joke. Then he'd been dumbfounded to have to talk the male out of it.

Now, this was old hat.

"There is merit to that, certainly." Saxton bowed in spite of the fact that Wrath couldn't see him. "But perhaps my Lord would consider, at least initially, a more measured approach. Something with more diplomacy, and fewer bullets."

"You are *such* a buzzkill." But Wrath smiled. "My *mahmen* and father would have approved of you. They were peacekeepers, too."

"In this instance, it is not for peace, but rather a lack of complication from human law enforcement that would be the goal."

"Fine. What do you want to do?"

"I thought perhaps I would go out and talk to the female to make sure her documents are in order with regard to ownership in the human world. And then thereafter, I would intercede on her behalf with the humans and try to get them to desist with the harassment. With it being wintertime, I can do both prior to the audiences starting here as there is plenty of darkness."

"I don't want you out there alone."

"We have no indication these humans are truly dangerous. And besides, I have lived quite readily without—"

"I'm sorry, what? Are you talking? I'm hearing this noise in the background." When Saxton fell quiet, Wrath nodded. "Yeah, I didn't think you were going to argue with me. You and Abalone are the only outsiders I trust with what I'm doing here. So no, I'm not rolling the dice with your life. Aside from the fact that I can actually stand to be around you ten hours a night, every night—which is a fucking miracle—there is the pesky detail that you know what the fuck you're doing."

Saxton bowed again. "You are most complimentary. I respectfully disagree with you about the hazard I may face, however, and—"

"You're going to do as I say." Wrath clapped his hands. "Great. I love it when we agree like this."

Saxton blinked. And then cleared his throat. "Yes, my Lord. Of course." He paused to choose his words with care. "I would just like to note, however, that the Brotherhood and the trainees are best used for guarding you here and being out in the field downtown. And if they're not on rotation, they are taking a much needed break for recovery. In terms of resource allocation, guarding me is of very low priority."

There was a brief silence. "I know who will do it. And we're finished with this, you and I."

As the King stared down from that great height of his, those black brows low behind the wraparounds, his incredible size dwarfing even the grand room, Saxton knew that, indeed, the discourse ended here. For all the collaborative work they did with the civilians, it was best never to forget that the male was a cold-blooded killer, well-versed first in the art and horror of war before he ever sat upon the throne.

"As you wish, my Lord."

EIGHT

As Ruhn walked up the Audience House's cleared front pathway, he burrowed into his old wool peacoat. He hadn't bothered with gloves when he'd left the Brotherhood's mansion, and inside the pockets, his hands were sweaty in the clenched fists he made.

Stopping at the top of the steps that led to the entrance, he couldn't help but remember the first time he had arrived at the gracious antique house.

He had come in search of his niece, Bitty, after he'd heard about a Facebook posting about his sister, who had passed. Back then, he had stood before these great doors with little hope, but much desperation, his long quest for news concerning his blooded relations presenting him with a new turn in what had otherwise been a barren, sad journey.

To what ultimate end, he had not known. In fact, however, it had proved to be one blessing after another, the sum total nothing short of a miraculous run of good fortune, fellowship, and generosity.

But perhaps that was all over now, and he had been expecting such a reversal. Sooner or later, the natural order of balance had to be brought to bear, and that meant that all of this must inevitably shift back, somehow.

An official summons to the Audience House by the King? What else could it be other than bad news?

And actually, he suspected he knew what this was about—

The door opened wide and the Brother Qhuinn stood to one side. "Wassup. You need something?"

Ruhn bowed low. "Forgive me. I have been summoned. Is this about the shoveling?"

"What?"

"The snow?"

As the two of them stared at each other—like both were hoping a translator would step in and clear up the confusion—Saxton, the King's lawyer, emerged from the Audience Hall along with a civilian male and female. The attorney was speaking in his usual calm and aristocratic manner.

"—you will receive an email from me detailing the remedies, and explaining the ramifications as to your cause of action—"

Saxton stopped short the second he saw Ruhn. And then his eyes did a quick up-and-down, as one would if they were sizing up an undesirable.

The male cleared his throat. "Greetings. Would you be so kind as to go in now? His Lordship is waiting for you, and I'll join you both in a moment?"

Ruhn looked at the couple. The Brother Qhuinn. And then took a quick glance behind himself at all the Absolutely No One Else behind him.

All right. Clearly, he was the one being addressed here.

He bowed to the solicitor. "But of course. Thank you."

Stepping through the tremendous crowd of people in the foyer—okay, fine, there were only four plus himself, in a space that was big enough to park eight cars in, but holy hell, he felt as though there was no room to breathe—Ruhn entered the great Audience Hall on quiet feet.

The King sensed his presence immediately, the great ruler straightening from a water bowl he was putting down by the fire for his dog.

As George gave a wag and then started in for his drink, the King looked directly at Ruhn even though Wrath was sightless.

"Hey." The ruler of all vampires indicated one of the armchairs by the fire without turning his head that way. "Sit."

"Yes, my Lord."

Ruhn bowed low and then hustled across the great patterned carpet. As he lowered himself into the armchair, he tried not to put all of his weight down too fast. He was well aware of his size, and the last thing he wanted to do was break the thing.

"So how you been?"

Ruhn fidgeted as the King came over. "I beg your pardon?"

Wrath sat down as the dog's rhythmic lapping continued in the background. "Pretty clear question, isn't it?"

"Ah . . . I am quite well, my Lord. Thank you."

"Good. That's real good."

George lifted his head and tongued his jowls back into order over the bowl, as if he didn't want to leave a trail of drips. Then he headed for his master, curling into a sit so Wrath could stroke his ear.

Unable to stand the silence anymore, Ruhn cleared his throat. "My Lord, if I may . . ."

"Yeah?" Wrath rolled his shoulder so it let out a crack that was so loud, Ruhn had to wince. "G'head."

"Do you wish me to vacate your premises?"

Those dark slashing brows dropped behind black wraparounds. "I asked you here. Why would I want you to leave?"

"The mansion, my Lord."

"What?"

"I can remove my things, if you wish, although I would like to stay in Caldwell to keep up with Bitty—"

"What the fuck are you talking about."

Not a question. More like a gun pointed to his head.

In the silence that followed, Ruhn glanced at the golden retriever—who promptly lay down as if he didn't want to be rude to the guest, but he had to vote with his master and therefore had to stay out of things.

"I assume this is about the shoveling last night?" Ruhn said.

As the King opened his mouth, his incredulous expression suggested there was more misunderstanding ahead, instead of less. "Lemme try this again. What the fuck are you talking about?"

Saxton entered and closed the double doors behind himself. "In a way," the male said, "it is a bit about the shoveling."

Ruhn cleared his throat and felt stupid. He should never have taken the aristocrat at his word. "I was only trying to help. I was careful so as not to score the stone steps and—"

"Okay, I don't know what you're going on about and I don't care." Wrath shoved his hair back with a slashing hand. "You're here because Saxton tells me you're looking for a way to earn room and board. So I've got a job for you."

Ruhn looked back and forth between them. "I don't have to leave?"

"Fuck no. What the hell gave you that idea?"

Ruhn didn't bother keeping the exhale to himself. "Oh, my Lord, thank you. Whatever you require of me, be assured that I shall do it to the best of my abilities. I cannot abide living off of your generosity."

"Great. I want you to take him out to visit a civilian of mine who is having problems with some humans."

Ruhn had to frown. "Forgive me, my Lord, but I cannot read or write. How could I ever help the Royal Solicitor with his work?"

Saxton stepped forward, and as he did, his scent reached Ruhn's nose—which seemed a strange thing to notice. Then again, none of this visit seemed normal at all.

"Our King," the male said, "would like me to be accompanied for the purpose of protection on my visit to the civilian. The Brothers, soldiers, and trainees are otherwise occupied in the field, guarding this house, or resting, and assigning one of them to this task would be a misappropriation of sorts."

Wrath put his palm up. "Look. I just want you to be there in case any of these humans comes down with a terminal case of the stupids. This is not a wartime situation, but I also don't like the idea of Saxton out there without anyone watching his back. And word has it . . . you know how to fight—very fucking well, indeed."

As Ruhn looked away, he could feel Saxton staring at him—and there was a temptation to deny or . . . at least diminish the past. Of course, he couldn't do that without contradicting his King—and outright lying. Besides, surely the solicitor had been told about him.

"Again, I don't anticipate either of you being in danger," Wrath pronounced, "but I can't promise that you won't find a little conflict. It is nothing you can't handle, though—not with what you've already faced."

As an old, familiar exhaustion settled with the weight of a mountain on his shoulders, Ruhn let his head drop and grew silent.

"You don't have to," Wrath said in an even tone. "This is not a condition for you to remain in the house."

After a moment, Ruhn looked up at his ruler. The great Blind King was staring across at him with such fixation, you could have sworn he had sight. And then his nostrils flared as if he were scenting something.

Abruptly, Wrath turned his head in the direction of his solicitor. "It's okay, I'll get you someone else—"

"I'll do it," Ruhn said roughly. And then he switched into the Old Language. *"I owe you a great debt already for allowing me unto your blessed home and permitting me to reside therein. To do this service unto you is an honor."*

Ruhn forced his body out of the chair and he walked forward to kneel at his King's boots.

But Wrath did not put the great black diamond out for the vow. "You sure about this. I'm not into forcing people to do shit—well, not people I don't want to kill for survival or sport."

"I am certain."

Those nostrils flared again. And then the King nodded. "So be it."

As the ring was proffered, Ruhn kissed the massive stone. *"In this and all things, I shall not fail you, my Lord."*

When he got back up to his feet, he glanced at Saxton. The solicitor was still staring at him, an inscrutable expression on those features that were so perfectly handsome, they were intimidating—and that was before you added in all those intelligent words he was always speaking or his perfect mannerisms or his fine and fancy clothes.

"If you will permit us, my Lord," the male said, "I should like to walk him out? And now would be a good time for you to take a break for some sustenance. We have three more hours ahead of us."

Ruhn was vaguely aware of Wrath saying a few things and Saxton answering back.

All he could focus on was the fact that he had gotten pulled in again.

The last thing he wanted to do was fight with anyone or anything, whether it was offensively or defensively.

He had left all that behind.

But he couldn't deny his King. Or the fact that yes, he could see why anyone would want to keep that solicitor safe. The gentlemale was so smart, and so integral to everything the King did here. Ruhn had heard the stories around the dinner table at the mansion. Saxton was indispensable.

With any luck, he told himself, he wouldn't have to kill anybody this time. He truly hated that part.

Even though he was very, very good at it.

Just humans.

As Novo and John Matthew rematerialized in the shadows downwind from the pair of winter night-wanderers, it was amply clear that they were not the enemy. Which didn't mean the two men weren't a potential threat and, therefore, killable. But proper provocation by them was required, and as much as she might have been able to engineer the shit, that was a pussy move—as well as against the rules.

Live and let live, unless forced into engagement.

"Damn it," she muttered.

John Matthew nodded. Then pointed back to where they had been. "Yeah, we better stay on track."

Twenty minutes later, they had covered the first leg of their sector and it was time to double-back. And it was so funny—while they cut over one block, she remembered the first couple of nights she'd been in the field. One of the big challenges to this kind of work was in not becoming frustrated that you weren't in a bare-knuckler every single minute you were out here.

Somehow, she'd assumed she'd be fighting all the time.

Yeah, not by half. The discipline to it all—and something she was still working on—was in staying sharp without becoming worn out as minutes turned into quarter hours and then half hours. You needed to be as fresh at the last second of the night as you were at the first, because you never knew when you—

As her new earpiece went off, she brought up her gloved hand and pushed it farther into place. *"Shit."*

Be careful what you wish for, she thought as she got her gun back out again.

John Matthew tapped her shoulder and she nodded. "Yeah, I'll flank left."

Seconds later, they dematerialized into a dogfight. Paradise and Phury were holding their own against a slayer, pushing the *lesser* back in the alley. But two more had showed up at the far end.

Novo made a quick calculation and lunged forward, going on the attack. There was too great a chance of collateral damage if she used her gun, so as she ran, she re-holstered that weapon and unsheathed one of her daggers.

With her fangs bared and a great rage in her heart, she hit the *lesser* on the left like a train, plowing it down before it knew what the fuck was happening. She stabbed it in the throat at the Adam's apple, and then, with her free hand, grabbed the front of its leather jacket and began to drive the back of its skull into the iced-over snowpack, again and again and again.

Black blood splattered up into her face, getting in her eyes and her mouth, the sickly sweet taste mixing with the frigid inhales that burned a path to her gut.

In the dim recesses of her mind, she knew she needed to move on to the other one. She needed to drive her dagger blade into the center of this goddamn thing's chest so it could go back to the Omega—and then she had to continue to help in the fight.

Her arm was like a piston, though, and the black stain in the snow under the impact spot grew ever wider. The fucking fantastic part? The slayer was aware of everything that was happening, the pain she was causing registering in its shocked expression and gagging breaths.

There was only one way to "kill" a *lesser*.

You had to stab them through the non-existent heart. So she could keep this up for a year and the piece of shit, this immortal murderer of her kind, would feel fresh agony with each and every strike—

A bullet sizzled by her left ear and she looked up. About fifteen feet away, another slayer had come into the alley, ready to play, and he had a poodle shooter in his palm.

Which would have been a joke, except he was aiming the gun right at her—any closer, it would have been point-blank.

Novo went into a roll, pulling the incapacitated slayer on top of her as a shield. In the process, she lost her dagger, but she had other options—digging for her hip, she took out her gun, shoved it through the various body parts flopping around her face, and started popping off rounds.

She caught the newest arriving slayer in the shoulder, the impact pitching him back on that side, but the wounding didn't slow the bastard down much—so she kept on shooting until her clip ran out. Good news? She blew the slayer right off his feet. The bad? In the next heartbeat, the undead was back and popping—bringing out a second gun.

Mother*fucker*—Novo scrambled through the floppy-limbed, stinking, oozing half-corpse on top of her for her own fresh clip.

Too late. Too uncoordinated.

She was going to be dead—

From the corner of her eye, she saw a flash of movement, and it didn't take more than a second to ID it: Paradise was bolting out of the shadows in a crouch, clearly ready to tackle the shooter.

Thank God. But Novo was taking nothing for granted. She managed to slap her backup clip into the butt of her gun and raise the muzzle, except she held her trigger, as she didn't want to hit Paradise—

Somebody passed right in front of Novo's gun—and directly into the bullets the slayer was discharging. The flash came from the left and moved so fast, she couldn't track whether it was friend or foe.

Except then she recognized exactly who it was.

Peyton didn't give Paradise a chance to do her job. He barreled into her and knocked her out of range and into a snowbank, eliminating the defensive strategy that had been engineered to save Novo.

The slayer with the gun got off two more rounds, which through nothing but blind luck missed, and then it took advantage of the opportunity to escape, pulling a turnaround and run-like-fuck—

He didn't get far. Zsadist was on him, a *pop!* and a flash of light announcing a quick dispatch.

And with that, thanks to all the other back-ups that had come on scene, the action was over as suddenly as it had presented itself.

"What the fuck is wrong with you!" the Brother Phury barked.

As he and John Matthew came pounding over in the snow, it was very clear that the silent fighter was every bit as Absolutely Batshit Rip Ass as the Brother was.

Novo shoved her *lesser*-blanket off to the side some and lifted her head so she could see the ass kicking roll out. Also started checking for bullet wounds on herself.

Meanwhile, Phury peeled Peyton off Paradise like he was cling wrap, and the Brother all but tossed that fighter across the city. As Peyton landed with disappointing agility, shit was on.

Phury marched across the snowpack. "You want to explain what the *hell* that was all about?" The Brother jabbed a finger at Paradise, who was back up on her shitkickers and brushing snow off her leathers. "You compromised our team, endangered two people's lives, and cost us a slayer."

Peyton crossed his arms over his chest and stared at a point over Phury's left shoulder. Then he paced around until he happened to stand beside Novo. "Paradise was in trouble."

"Excuse me?" the female said. "What was that?"

Peyton refused to look at her. "He had a gun. He could have swung it around and shot her in the face."

"Except that by the time he'd have seen me," she countered, "I would have had control of the weapon. He was fully diverted."

"You don't know that." Peyton shook his head. "You totally don't."

"Yeah. I do." Paradise stomped her way across the alley, meeting the male head-on. "I had made the assessment, and I was executing. If I didn't take out that gun, he might have killed Novo."

"And again, I'll say that you don't know that."

Novo rolled her eyes. *Thanks for your concern, asshole.*

And, p.s., why are you two having this argument right over me?

For fuck's sake, there was no getting up now, not unless she wanted to play full-contact ref.

Paradise threw up her hands. "But I didn't get a chance to find out, did I. Because you decided to be a goddamn hero when I didn't need one."

Preach, sister, Novo thought as she shoved the barely moving slayer farther off herself and sat up.

"This is unacceptable." Phury got his phone. "You're out of the field until further notice."

"What!" Done with that off-the-shoulder eye thing, Peyton glared directly at the Brother. "What for!"

"Not following protocol." Phury put his palm out. "Shut your mouth. I can assure you, nothing you say is going to help—"

The dagger came in a fat circle from out of nowhere, the stabbing motion on a trajectory directly for the center of Novo's chest.

A shout exploded out of her as she put her arms up to catch the forearm: The heavily wounded slayer had somehow found her discarded blade . . . and was doing its level best to return it to her. And the undead was hellaciously strong, even with all its leaks.

Especially as her grip slipped free because of all that black blood she had drawn—

The dagger plunged into her heart, penetrating through her bullet-proof vest.

There was no pain, which was probably not good, and as she fell back down on the snowpack, she was able to lift her head and look at the inexplicable sight of the weapon's handle, still in the grip of that slayer's fist, sticking right out of her sternum.

Oddly, she noted the way her breath exploded out of her in a white cloud, the exhale dissipating in the night as if it had been eaten. Or maybe that was her soul leaving her body?

Her last image was of the *lesser* smiling down at her, its crazy eyes rapt with triumph, its lolling mouth leaking black blood as it started to laugh.

And then its head exploded, bullets riddling it from some direction or another, bone getting pulverized, a fine mist of brain matter atomizing into the bitterly cold night air.

That was it for her.

She lost consciousness, a great black void swooping in, the Grim Reaper's robe curtaining down on her, its fabric so thick and heavy, she could neither fight nor deny it.

Her final thought was that this was the precise, inevitable outcome she had predicted from the moment she had filled out the training center's application. The only surprise? That it had come so fucking soon.

She'd been sure she would last at least a year or two.

NINE

As soon as Peyton saw that slayer sit up, he knew there was trouble. And then there was the flash of the dagger blade over the undead's shoulder, that grotesque, gape-mouthed face stretching into a crazy grin of hatred.

It was forever and an instant at the same time.

He did not need precise arc measurements to extrapolate where that razor-sharp point was going to end up, and there was no stopping the inevitable. The weapon did its duty, impaling Novo in the chest, going right through her bulletproof vest, finding home in a horrible way—

The sound of a gun going off at point-blank range rang loudly in his ears and he jumped back. But it wasn't the enemy. It was Paradise, standing strong and sure, doing her job: Her precisely put bullet blew apart the back of the slayer's head, bits and pieces of it falling like confetti, the black blood becoming a fine rain that landed like soot on the white snow.

Except the fucking *lesser* fell forward, instead of back, going limp on top of Novo—and the dagger.

As the blade penetrated even deeper, she jerked, her hands flopping, her legs kicking. And then nothing about her moved at all.

"Call Manny!" Phury said as he lunged forward and pulled the *lesser* off. "Call the fucking—"

"I have him now!" Craeg cut in.

Peyton weaved on his boots as he saw the hilt of the dagger down tight to Novo's leather jacket. The blade was in so deep, none of the steel showed. She was going to die—if she wasn't dead already.

And this was all his fault. Thanks to him, Paradise had disabled that enemy way too late.

As his legs went out from under him, he was only aware of the structural failure of his lower body because his vantage point changed from high to ground level. Nothing in him registered—no physical sensations, that was. Emotionally . . . he was in a firestorm.

Meanwhile, Zsadist jumped over and stabbed the remains of the *lesser* back to the Omega, and as the *pop!* and flash of light faded, everyone else got in close to Novo, crouching down, settling on one knee or both in the bloodstained snow. Peyton couldn't see much of her now, with Paradise and Craeg each taking one of her hands while Phury checked for a pulse and Boone settled in at her boots.

Oh, God, that dagger. Sticking right out of her chest.

Peyton swallowed through a dry throat. "Novo? Is she alive?"

Stupid fucking thing to say. Then again, anything from him was a waste—

Thundering footfalls. Coming up behind him.

Wrenching around, he looked to the source of the fresh attack. Except, no, there was no one there; it was his heart beating in his chest, the panicked rhythm rebounding in his ears with pressure.

Peyton raked his hand across his mouth and jerked open his leather jacket in the vain hope it would ease the suffocation in his lungs. Where was the fucking surgical unit?

Standing up, he leaned in to see over the heads of the other fighters . . . and nearly wished he hadn't. Novo was as white as the snow, her eyes open and fixed on something in the middle distance above her. Was she seeing the Fade?

Come back to us, he wanted to scream. *Look away from the other side . . . stay here!*

And goddamn it, he hated the slayer blood on her face. He wanted to wipe it off her too-pale skin, cleaning her of the war, of his mistake, of these consequences.

With a curse, he paced around, gripping his hair, pulling, pulling, pulling at it. His brain told him that if he could just think clearly enough, and picture himself exactly where he'd been standing when he'd made the bad call, he could somehow implant himself earlier in time—and undo this outcome by not trying to protect Paradise.

And then they could all be still fighting—or maybe, with the skirmish having been won, they could be standing around in a flush of buzzy, trippy victory, preparing to find the next battle.

"Is she alive," he said roughly. "Is she . . ."

Novo started to cough, and the red blood that came out made him so dizzy, he went down to the snowy ground again. Lowering his head, he braced both hands in front of himself and got ready to vomit. But nauseous as he was, he didn't throw up.

The rumble of the mobile surgical unit coming around the corner was like a choir of angels singing, and to make way, Peyton pushed himself across the snowpack until his back hit the wall of the nearest building. As the RV punched to a stop, Manny Manello burst out from behind the wheel, a duffel bag in his hand, a stethoscope around his neck.

"Don't move her," the human barked.

Instantly, everyone went hands-off, as if they didn't want to be the person who fucked shit up. And then they moved back to give the doctor room.

Peyton stayed where he was, his hands locking on either side of his head so he could hold the deadweight of his skull up. When he blinked from time to time, it was the only way he changed position.

He wasn't even breathing.

A minute later, Ehlena materialized in the alley with a backpack of supplies. And then Doc Jane arrived. And more Brothers.

From time to time, he could feel eyes passing over him, and there were whispers that he knew were all about what he had done. He didn't care about any of that. He just wanted to know Novo was going to live.

A pair of shitkickers marched across and stopped in front of him.

As Peyton looked up, the Brother Rhage said, "You didn't mean it, I know."

"Is she still alive?" Holy shit, that didn't even sound like his voice. "Please . . . tell me."

"I don't know. But we need to get you out of here."

"I swear I didn't mean for this to happen." He closed his eyes and pressed the heels of his palms into them, hard. "I don't want this."

"I know, son. We gotta go back now, you and I."

"What about her?" He dropped his hands. "What's going to happen to her?"

"Manny, Ehlena, and Jane are doing what they can. But we want all trainees back to home base. The bus is here."

Shit, he hadn't even noticed it.

As he struggled to get up, Rhage's big hand was there to help—and when he was on the level, the Brother started to pat him down.

"What are you doing?" he asked his teacher.

"Removing your weapons."

"Am I under arrest?"

Rhage shook his head. "No, you're looking really fucking suicidal."

Peyton had no idea how long it took to get back to the training center. Time had ceased to be something that could be measured in any kind of unit—it was more like the vastness of space, never ending, incalculable, larger than himself and anyone else. He also wasn't exactly sure how he came to be underground and in the Brotherhood's facility. He had no memory of the bus ride in, or of entering the facility, and he didn't recall how he'd ended up in the break room, sitting in a chair.

There must have been some ambulation involved. He sure as shit hadn't dematerialized down the corridor or been carried here. His brain was flatlined—

Oh, God, he didn't want to use that word.

Lifting his arms, he discovered that there was a bottle of booze in one of his hands—gin, this time, Beefeater. And the cap was off. And someone had had a quarter of what was in there.

With the resignation of a prisoner with a life sentence, he looked around the break room. He was alone, and the clock over there read that a couple of hours had passed.

How much longer would Novo be in surgery? he thought. Rhage had at one point come in and told him that she had been stabilized out in the alley, but that she needed more time in the OR here at the clinic.

Was she alive—

The door to the break room swung open, and when he saw who it was, he focused on the gin bottle. Ordering his arm to bring that open neck back to his mouth, he got frustrated when his limb refused to obey.

Interesting. It appeared that he had become paralyzed.

"How are . . . you doing?" Paradise asked from just inside the room.

As things could hardly get worse, he figured, what the fuck, and looked up at her. Her eyes were bloodshot and swollen from crying, her cheeks bright red from her having brushed away tears in the cold, and her hands were shaking as she zipped and unzipped and re-zipped her black fleece.

"Fine, and you?" he muttered.

"Peyton, come on."

"What do you want me to say? They stripped me of my weapons

because they thought I was going to off myself—and you know, I think that logic was very sound. Does that answer your question?"

When she just stared at him, he cursed. "Sorry."

Lowering his eyes, he turned the bottle around in his hands until he could inspect the little English guard on the label. Man, if there was only a way to change places with a two-dimensional drawing—he'd rather like to be nothing more than an image.

"Any word about her?" he asked roughly.

"Not yet. We're just out there pacing. Ehlena said it was still going to be a while."

"Is that why you came in here? To tell me that."

"I thought you had a right to know."

"I appreciate that." He took a shuddering inhale. "You know, I really should have just let you do your damn job."

"Peyton . . ."

Dimly, he wondered if she was going to say his name like that for the rest of their lives. Like it was a sob with syllables.

She came forward and sat down in the chair opposite him. "It was a mistake. Some kind of knee-jerk reaction."

"If she dies, I'm a murderer."

"You are not."

Peyton just shook his head. Then he looked at her and made his eyes stay put.

The wisps of blond hair that had escaped her low ponytail glowed in the recessed lights of the ceiling, giving her a halo—and that seemed apt. She was a saint, a female with a heart of gold.

And then he thought of that crackerjack shot that had blown that *lesser*'s head apart.

Okay, fine, she had a heart of gold and the marksmanship of a sniper.

With abrupt clarity, he remembered her back during orientation, helping him to keep going after he'd eaten those poisoned *hors d'oeuvres* and gotten sick, pulling him through until he had finally collapsed from exhaustion on the final leg of the brutal endurance test—after which she had kept going. He also had so many images of her in class, always paying attention, working so hard to prepare for tests, asking good questions. She brought the same focus and dedication to every part of the physical training, too, whether it was hand-to-hand combat, pumping iron in the weight room, or running obstacle courses.

She was utterly qualified to do the job she was in.

And what was more? He was willing to bet she never would have made the call he had back in that alley. She would never have stepped in where she wasn't needed.

"Knee-jerk," she had called his reaction.

No, it wasn't that. He'd been protecting her as if she were his female. Putting himself in danger to save her—when in fact, she hadn't required saving and wasn't his to worry about. If it had been anyone else tackling that *lesser*? He would not have interfered.

With a frown, he noticed that she was fiddling with something at her throat. A little charm on a chain. She'd never worn anything like that before, and God knew, her mother's jewelry was all statement pieces from major houses, not something so dainty and simple.

It had to be from Craeg.

White gold, probably, he thought. Not even platinum. And yet she no doubt thought it was priceless.

As he watched her slender fingers worry whatever the charm was on its delicate necklace, he had the very clear conviction that he needed to let go of his fantasy.

"Listen, Peyton, about what you said last night—"

"I said nothing. It was a joke. A bad-timed, stupid-ass joke."

The silence that followed suggested she had done the math on his Gronk/linebacker move on her in that alley and knew he was lying. But at that moment, sure as if the conversation was being broadcast over loudspeakers, the door opened—and yeah, of course, it was Craeg.

"They're closing her up now," the male announced in a hard voice.

Wow, Peyton thought as the male glared at him. That stare could do as much damage as a hollow-point bullet—and he should know, 'cuz he'd been shot in the head in the field.

"Is she going to be okay?" Paradise said as she got up and went to her mate. "Is she?"

"I don't know." The embrace the two shared was all about the mutual support—and didn't it make Peyton feel like an outsider. Appropriately. "She's in critical condition. But they're looking for volunteers she can feed from, which has to mean she's got a chance. Listen, are you okay if I give her my vein—"

"Oh, my God, yes. Of course."

Peyton spoke up. "She won't want it from me."

Those hostile eyes swung back his way. "No one is asking you."

Oh, so it's gonna be like that, Peyton thought. But it wasn't hard to understand the guy's position.

Fuck.

Before Craeg could throw down, Paradise put herself between them and pushed her boy back, palms to pecs. "Relax, okay? We do not need any more injuries on the team."

She lowered her voice at that point and there was a private exchange between the two of them, all quick words at a shhh'd volume. And then Craeg punched the door back open and left.

Paradise took a deep breath. "Look . . . I think we need to talk."

"No. We don't and we aren't."

"Peyton. What happened tonight—"

"Will never happen again. Mostly likely because they are going to throw me out of the program, but even if they don't, I'm not making this mistake again. You're on your own."

"Wait a minute. Excuse me? I don't need you looking after me. I can take care of myself."

"I know, I know." He rubbed his face. Took another swig from the bottle. Wanted to scream. "It's over, Paradise. Okay? It's done—and stop looking at me like that."

"Like what."

"I don't know."

There was a long quiet. "Peyton, I'm sorry."

"I was the one who made a mistake, not you." To cover up the double meaning, he shook his head. "I'll apologize to Craeg, too. You don't have to tell me."

The door swung open again, but this time, the Brother Rhage put his head in. "Okay, Novo's out of surgery, and at least she's alive. So you and I need to do an incident debriefing and then we'll make an appointment for you to get psych eval'd."

When Peyton didn't respond, the Brother nodded at the corridor behind him. "Come on, son, you gotta follow me to the office."

As Peyton got to his feet, he thought it was a sad commentary on your life when an interruption requiring you to justify an unjustifiable action was a step up from your other option—which happened to be a lively discussion about unrequited love with the object of your unreciprocated affections.

Ah, yes, choices, choices.

On his way to the exit, he put the Beefeater down on a side table, and as he came up to Paradise, he paused.

Reaching out, he put his hand on her arm and gave her what he hoped was a reassuring squeeze. "I'm sorry. For everything. It's all on me, all my fault."

Before she could respond, he released his hold and walked out.

In the concrete hall, the rest of the trainees, along with a number of Brothers, were milling around the clinical area, and everyone went statue as they saw him, shuffling boots halting, whispering words silenced.

He had no idea what to say to any of them.

So he just ducked his head and kept on going.

TEN

"You're going to want to take a right up here at that fork in the road."

As Saxton spoke, he pointed through the windshield even though the truck's headlights were already showing the way. Next to him, Ruhn was behind the wheel, one of the male's big hands resting comfortably at the twelve spot, the other palm on his thigh.

Bitty's uncle was a consummate driver. Smooth, steady, in total control of the enormous Ford-whatever-the-heck-it-was even though there was enough iced-over snowpack on the road to rival Alaska.

It was good to feel safe.

And then there was the fact the male smelled amazing. A clean, powerful scent, which was soap and shampoo and shaving cream, but none of the fancy kind. Then again, on Ruhn? Palmolive was a cologne.

"Next time we can dematerialize," the male said. "I'm sorry that I don't know the ins and outs of Caldwell yet."

Well, we could just have had you take my vein, and you could have followed me—

Saxton shut that thought process right down. "The drive hasn't been bad at all. In fact, it's been a while since I've ridden in a motorized vehicle. It's quite pleasant, isn't it."

He'd forgotten how hypnotic automotives could be, the quiet hum of the engine, the steady stream of warm air at the feet, the softly blurred landscape—which in this case was all about gentle rolling farm fields covered in pristine snow.

"May I ask you something?" he heard himself say.

"Are you too warm?" Ruhn glanced over. "I can turn down the heat?"

As the male reached for the dials, Saxton shook his head. "The temperature is perfect. Thank you."

After a moment, Ruhn looked across the interior again. "Am I going too fast?"

"No, you're a terrific driver."

Was that a blush hitting those cheeks? Saxton wondered.

"Anyway, I was just curious . . ." He cleared his throat and couldn't pinpoint why this felt awkward. "I was unaware that you had a background that involved fighting. I'm assuming it was in the war—did you engage with the enemy down in South Carolina?"

When there was no response, he glanced over. Ruhn's hand was no longer at ease on the wheel, his knuckles showing white—and those brows were now down tight.

"I'm sorry," Saxton murmured. "I have offended you. My apologies."

"No, it's not that."

The male did not continue, however, and their next turnoff arrived before any reply came.

"Up here, take another right," Saxton murmured.

Ruhn slowed them down, put a blinker on, and executed a directional change. Then, about two hundred yards farther, a discreetly lit sign reading Blueberry Farm Estates appeared at the side of the road.

Saxton spoke into the thick silence. "That's where his parents live—I mean, Rocke and Lyric. Blaylock's sire and *mahmen*. They were the ones who came to him with the issue, so the older female must be up here a little farther."

"Is this it?" Ruhn asked as they came upon a single mailbox with a hand-painted number on it.

"That's the address, yes."

The driveway into the property was unplowed, but there was at least one set of tracks marring the snow cover. Perhaps the humans who were harassing the female had paid her another visit?

"This will be bumpy," Ruhn said. "Hold on."

Saxton threw a hand out to catch the door as they lurched and lumbered off the plowed county road and onto a lane that could accommodate one car at the very most. Barren trees and brush choked the shoulders, as if Mother Nature disapproved of the ingress and was seeking to rectify the intrusion the only way she knew how.

Leaning forward, he glanced up and imagined in the warm months that a tunnel of leaves would form overhead.

And there was the farmhouse.

The manse was bigger than he thought it would be. He'd pictured in his head something the size of a hobbit cottage with maybe cock-eyed shutters and a chimney that looked unreliable. Instead, the structure was a proper brick house, with four twelve-paned windows on the bottom, a wide front door, and eight six-paned windows on top. The slate roof was solid and clearly capable of surviving the apocalypse, and yes, there were shutters, but they were all perfectly hung and painted black.

Smoke curled from both of the chimneys. Which were straight as arrows.

There was also a tree.

Or more . . . a Tree.

In the center of the ring in front of the house, a gracious, thick-trunked maple tree grew out of the ground as if it were reaching for the heavens, great limbs stretching out and upward, the shape so perfectly balanced, surely it proved the hand of Providence existed and that the Creator was indeed an artist.

And yet all was not bucolic and at peaceful rest.

The second-floor window on the left corner was missing a pane of glass. Or at least, he assumed that was the case as there seemed to be a piece of plywood fitted into one of the six squares.

For some reason, that chilled him in a way the cold weather did not.

Ruhn brought the truck to a stop in front of the shallow steps that led to that glossy front door. "We are expected, yes?" the male said.

"Indeed. Or rather, I called the granddaughter. I don't have a contact number for the female."

Saxton opened his door, the winter chill rushing in like it was hellbent on conquering the warmth they had artificially created, and as he put his Merrells into the snow, the squeaky, crunching sound was a testament that the ambient temperature was below zero. Taking a deep breath, the scent of wood smoke tingled in his sinuses and made him think of ads for Vermont.

There were lights on in the first floor, and through the parted curtains, he saw homemade furniture, the lines of which spoke to earlier ages, as well as walls covered in paper the flowered patterns of which had gone out of style in the Roaring Twenties.

This was not a life in decline, he thought, so much as the Old Ways preserved.

The front door opened just as Ruhn came around the bed of the truck, and the female in the doorway was in fact as Saxton expected: slightly stooped, with white hair cut into a bob, and a pleasant face that was deeply lined. But her eyes were alert and the smile was wide and the homemade dress was pressed and had a fine lace collar.

Given the way vampires aged, which was essentially in no manner at all until the very end of their lives, she had a decade, maybe more. But not much longer than that.

"You must be Saxton," she said. "The King's solicitor. I am Minnie. That's short for Miniahna, but please do call me Minnie."

As Saxton proceeded forward through the snow, he noted there had been footsteps coming and going off the front porch. "Yes, madam. And this is Ruhn, my . . . assistant."

From behind him, Ruhn mumbled something and bowed low.

"Please, won't you both come in."

As she stepped aside, Saxton went up the steps and Ruhn was right in line, following him into the warm, golden interior. The scents of cinnamon and something sweet permeated the air, making him realize he had forgotten to have anything for First Meal—and oh, was that beeswax?

Stomping the snow from his shoe treads on the mat, he glanced around. Directly ahead, there was a staircase with a carved wooden banister that had clearly been polished on a regular basis—and that had to be where he was picking up that undertone of lemon.

"I have made us tea." She indicated the front parlor. "If you'll sit down?"

"Of course, madam. I believe we shall remove our shoes."

"That's not necessary."

"It is but a moment." And what do you know, Ruhn was already working on the laces on his boots. "I hate to track in."

"I appreciate that," Minnie said. And as Saxton bowed again, the female smiled some more. "You have such beautiful manners. You remind me of my Rhysland, may he be blessed in the Fade."

"May he be blessed, yes."

"Do sit down in here while I bring in refreshments."

Minnie left and Saxton chose a seat on the sofa by the fire. Dutch tiles in blue and white had been set around the hearth, and there was a woven blue and white rug lain before the old brass fender. The rest of the room was done in Victorian red and navy.

Glancing over his shoulder, he looked out the window upon the snowy landscape. What a perfect place to read a book, he thought—and then he realized that he was alone in making himself comfortable. Ruhn was still standing over by the door, the male's hands crossed before him, his head tilted down, his body at rest as if he were prepared to be thus for however long they were in the house.

"Ruhn? Come and sit with me."

Ruhn shook his head and didn't look up. "I would prefer to wait here by the door."

"I believe it would be more awkward if you did not sit with us."

"Oh. Okay."

The male seemed to burrow into his peacoat even though the cold was well vanquished by the fire's heat, and Saxton had the sense Ruhn was trying to seem smaller. And sure enough, he sat down at the other end of the sofa slowly as if he didn't want his full weight on the furniture.

For no good reason, and probably a bad one, it was hard not to notice how close they were. The cozy couch was sizable for two—provided one of them wasn't as big as Ruhn . . . and their thighs were nearly brushing.

You're here to do your job, he informed his libido. *Not ogle your guard.*

Minnie came in with a tray, and before she got far, Ruhn was up off the sofa and taking the weight from her.

"Where may I put this?" he asked.

"Oh, right here. Please."

Ruhn delivered the tea to the coffee table, and as he bent down, the firelight caught in the longer hair on the top of his head and made it flash with highlights like new copper in moonbeams.

What would touching it be like—

"Saxton?" Minnie said.

As he snapped to, he saw that the female was staring at him in inquiry and he took a gamble. "I would love some tea. Thank you."

"It's Earl Grey."

"My favorite." He forced himself to focus and happened to look in the direction of the hearth. "I must commend you on those Delft tiles around the fireplace. They are extraordinary."

Minnie smiled as if he had just told her her young was the most brilliant thing on the planet. "My Rhysland, he brought them over from our home in the Old Country. He purchased them from a master human over there, and they had been around our hearth since 1705. When he decided that we must go across the great sea to find a better life here, he knew I was heartbroken to leave, and he removed them without my knowledge, packing them with care. It took us fifty years to be able to afford this land, and then another ten before we could build this house, but my Rhysland . . ." As her eyes watered, she took a handkerchief out of a pocket in her dress. "He did not tell me what he was about, and he installed them here as a surprise. He told me they were a bridge to our future, a tie that brought our past with us."

While Minnie sought to compose herself, Saxton leaned in to examine the tiles to give her some privacy—and then he was just plain captivated. Each of the white tiles had a little whimsical scene in the center done in blue, the depictions of windmills and landscapes, fishing boats and people at their work, executed in a breezy, painterly style and set off with decorative swirls in the corners. The overall effect was delightful—and they were worth a fortune. These were from the period of the masters.

"Do you take sugar, kind solicitor?"

Saxton nodded. "Yes, thank you, madam. Just one."

A porcelain cup was passed over to him, and he stirred the cube in the bottom away with a tiny silver spoon. Ruhn declined the tea, but took a big piece of cinnamon coffee cake.

"That looks delicious." Saxton nodded as a slice was offered to him. "I skipped First Meal."

"One has to eat." Minnie smiled. "I always tell my grandchildren that. Even though they are well past their transitions and living their own lives, I took them in when my daughter tragically passed upon the birthing bed. One never ceases to be a parent—are either of you mated with young?"

Saxton coughed a little. "I am not. No."

"And you?" Minnie asked Ruhn.

"No, madam."

"Well," she announced as she sat down in a rocking chair with her own tea. "We should rectify that, shouldn't we. You know, my granddaughter is unmated and quite lovely."

As Minnie indicated an oil painting behind her, Saxton dutifully looked over. The female was indeed quite lovely, with long, dark hair and even features. The eyes were objectively arresting, a keen intelligence radiating out from them, and the smile suggested she was kindhearted but no fool.

"She hated that old-fashioned gown I made her put on." Minnie smiled. "My granddaughter is of the modern era, and that dress is one that I wore long ago when I was her age. I made it for when I first met Rhysland and kept it safe. I suppose I hoped that it would help her see the value in settling down with a good mate and living the life I have. She has other plans, though—which is not to say she is not virtuous."

Saxton glanced at Ruhn. The male was likewise examining the portrait, and for some reason, whatever opinion he was forming seemed terribly important. Did he find her attractive? Did he want to meet her? As an unattached male, with an invitation from the head of the household, it would not be inappropriate for him to engage in a supervised meeting. He was not an aristocrat, and neither were Minnie and her clan, but there were still rules of conduct to be considered.

"You mention that you have other grandchildren?" Saxton asked. "I was aware only that you had a granddaughter."

Minnie grew pensive. "Rhysland and I also have a grandson. But we have not been as close to him."

"What do you mean? And forgive me if I am prying, but I am curious as it relates to your issues with this house."

There was a long pause. "It is not that I do not love my grandson. There is, however, a side to him that I struggle to understand and accept. He seems to rather prefer the easy road, and this was something that brought him into much conflict with his grandfather."

"I am sorry. Relationships can be complicated."

"Yes, I fear my grandson is about to discover exactly how true that is." Minnie put her tea aside and rose to her feet. "But that is his journey, not mine, to take."

The older female walked across the room, tilted a lampshade off-center and righted it . . . then moved an amethyst geode up and back on a side table . . . after which she straightened a throw pillow.

"Please tell us what is happening with your house, Minnie," Saxton said softly. "We're here to help you."

"That is what my granddaughter told me. But I believe this is much ado about naught."

"Both your granddaughter and your neighbors don't seem to think so."

"Are you referring to Rocke and Lyric?"

"Yes."

"Oh, they are such fine people."

Saxton looked at those blue and white tiles around the fireplace. And then refocused on the female. "Minnie, we will not let your property be taken from you unlawfully, whether it is by humans or vampires."

"You serve the King, though."

"And do you think Wrath, son of Wrath, is not powerful enough to reach into the human world? I assure you, he is."

"My *hellren* always said that humans were best left to their own devices."

"Forgive me, madam"—Ruhn put his coffee cake down, half eaten—"but that is only true if they are abiding by their own rules."

She smiled and went back to the rocking chair. "That's exactly what Rhysland would have said."

"Tell us," Saxton prompted gently.

It was a while before the female spoke. And when she did, it was as if she were relating the facts to herself—trying them on as if to determine whether the reality others were seeing was in fact what was happening.

"My beloved *hellren* went unto the Fade two years ago. My granddaughter, who lives closer to the city, told me to sell the house and come live with her. That would be such an intrusion, though, and moreover, this is my home. How could I leave him—I mean, it. The—subdivision, I guess is what the humans call it—next door was built right around then. I remember when I couldn't sleep during the days, listening to the hammering and all the trucks going in and out on the road. I was first approached about selling this property maybe six months thereafter. The humans liked what they were building and the houses sold well so they wanted to expand."

"Who came unto you?" Saxton asked.

"A man named Mr. Romanski. Or, no . . . wait, it was a lawyer or someone representing him? I can't remember. They sent me a letter first. Then they called—I'm not sure how they got the number. And when I replied to neither, they called again. More letters. Then people started knocking on the door during the day when I was downstairs. Rhysland had installed a little camera at the front entrance just before he passed unto the Fade and so I could see the human men. First it was only one. Then they came in pairs. It was once every other week. And then more frequently."

Saxton shook his head. "When did it escalate further?"

Minnie brought her hand to the base of her throat. "They started leaving these phone messages that I was in default on my mortgage? We don't have one. As I said, my *hellren* built this house two centuries ago. Then they said there was something toxic on the land—and it was at that point that human officials started calling from something called the EPA? They wanted to get on the property. I let them and they found nothing. Then it was a problem with human taxes that didn't exist. The water table. It's been . . . very stressful."

The older female glanced toward the windows. "Naturally, I cannot go out in the daylight, so I can't go down to meet with any of these human agencies—and this caused them to become suspicious. I had to ask a friend's *doggen* to pretend to be me and this made me feel even worse because I was imposing. And then . . ."

"What happened next?" Saxton murmured.

"Somebody shot out one of my windows two nights ago. I was downstairs at the time and I heard the popping sound and then the glass shattering all over the floor. It was in what would have been the master bedroom if I didn't sleep underground—"

At first, Saxton had no idea where the soft growl was coming from. And then he looked across the sofa. Ruhn had bared his fangs—which had descended all the way, their points like those of knives—and his already big body seemed to have swelled with aggression, becoming something huge and very deadly.

As Saxton noted the transformation, his brain bifurcated, half of it remaining engaged with Minnie and the story . . . and the other part?

All he could think of was what it would be like to have sex with that.

Abruptly, Ruhn closed his lips and appeared to catch himself.

Flushing, he said, "Forgive me. But I care not for you being treated as such in your own home. It is not right."

Minnie, who had become slightly alarmed herself, smiled once again. "You are a lovely young male, aren't you."

"No, I am not," Ruhn whispered as he lowered his eyes. "But I would keep you safe herein, if I could."

Saxton had to force himself back to the topic at hand. Otherwise, he was liable to stare at that face for the next night and a half.

Clearing his throat, he said, "How long ago was this again?"

"The night before last. I didn't tell my granddaughter, of course. I can't have her even more worried. But I did call Rocke and he came over to patch the glass with a piece of plywood. I ended up telling them everything—and now you came tonight."

Saxton thought of what he'd noticed on the approach to the house, that something-is-not-like-the-others up in that window on the second floor.

This was much more serious than he'd thought.

After Mistress Miniahna completed her story, Ruhn took the tray with all the tea fixings back to the kitchen. He was trying to be polite, and also make himself useful, but what he really wanted to do was inspect the farmhouse's lower level. There were shutters for the daytime that had been pulled into place along the rear of the house, and that gave him some reassurance—except he couldn't understand why the front ones remained open. She should have everything shut up tight.

As he went through the simple, spacious rooms, he noted the dining room along the back. The library off to the side. The small bathroom under the stairs. A pantry and a number of closets.

In the recesses of his mind, he couldn't help but note the woodworking on the moldings, the furniture, and especially the paneling and shelving in the library. Her *hellren* must have been a master carver

of the old-school variety, and for some reason, that made Ruhn feel
even more protective of Mistress Miniahna. Then again, these were his
kind of people, civilians who worked for a living and earned their way
honestly. Which was not to say that he did not respect the Brothers. As
soldiers, they worked just as hard, and in dangerous, even deadly, situations. No, he was thinking of the *glymera* . . . of Saxton's people . . .
although he meant no disrespect to that male specifically—certainly
the solicitor had risen above the shiftless nature of so much of his class,
for Ruhn knew well how much work he did.

But yes, the high-bred dilettantes.

In fact, maybe that was why Ruhn felt so disconnected in the mansion. Being surrounded by all the trappings of great wealth, he found
it difficult to reconcile who the people were with the assets of the highest social order of vampires. This house was his style, though. Grander
than he would ever live in on his own, but so lovingly built and enjoyed.

Those fucking humans.

Indeed, although he had made a vow not to return to his old ways,
he was going to happily sort this little difficulty out. By force, if necessary.

Backtracking into the country kitchen, he then returned to the parlor. Saxton was leaning forward on his cushion on the sofa, his hands
motioning in emphasis.

"—think we need to reach out to them on your behalf."

"Oh, I wouldn't want to be a bother," the mistress was saying. "You
all work for the King. You have more serious matters than this to address."

"It would be our pleasure to be of service unto you."

"No, I must insist you do naught. All will be well—surely they will
become bored of this soon?"

As Saxton brushed an impatient hand through his thick blond hair,

Ruhn happened to notice the way the waves resettled into place, riding a cowlick that was off to one side.

It seemed odd to note such a thing, and Ruhn was careful to redirect his attention to the mistress.

"Please," he heard himself say. "I would not feel right about leaving you here to fight them alone."

"Must it be a fight, though?" Old hands twisted in her lap. "Again, perhaps they will just tire of me."

Saxton spoke up. "They used a gun to threaten you. Do you think they are tiring—"

"Forgive me," Ruhn interrupted. "But I noticed when I was in your kitchen that the shutters along the back of the house are shut—and yet those in front are not? Why are they open?"

Miniahna flushed. "The windows are painted shut after all these years, and the only way to close the shutters is to do it manually from the outside. I had opened them before the storm so I could enjoy the moonlight—and to prove that I wasn't scared. But then the blizzard came . . . and I have been afraid to go out there alone. I promise you that I've been sticking to the rooms in the rear of the house except for tonight. With you coming, I figured . . . well, if I'm being watched, it is good for them to see that I'm having people in, that I'm not alone. Or was I wrong? Oh, dear, have I put you in danger—"

Ruhn put up his palm. "Do not think more of it. You did the right thing. But may I go and shut them for you?"

"Would you?" Miniahna began to blink quickly. "That would be such a help."

"Work of a moment."

Ruhn gave Saxton a nod and went to the front door to put his boots back on. As he let himself out of the house, the cold air made his eyes and the inside of his nose sting, but he ignored that as he stepped off the stoop and slid in between the hedges and the house. Closing the shutters one by one, he locked each set of them in place with hook latches.

A quick check on the sides of the house and around the back satisfied him that everything else was in order, and then he returned to around front.

He did not go back inside right away. Searching the big tree, he thought of those tracks in the lane.

On an impulse, he trekked through the deep snow to the truck and got out a flashlight. Triggering the beam, he trained the light up into the barren branches above him.

He found the remote camera off to one side, a subtle wink of glass flashing as the illumination hit the lens's reflective surface. But before he did anything about it, he continued his investigation, doing a one-eighty on the property. He located a second one around the back.

Killing the flashlight, he went to the front entrance, stomped the snow off his boots on the mat, and let himself in.

After he'd reclosed the door, he leaned into the parlor. "Mistress? You said you had a security camera—do you have more than one?"

"No, why?"

"No reason. Where is your camera located again?"

"On the corner of the house under the eaves, over there." She pointed to her right. "It's so I can see anyone who is at the door. Is there something wrong?"

He shook his head. "Not at all. I'll be right back. Just checking all the shutters."

Outside again, he located her monitoring device and then did another pass around the property just to make sure he hadn't missed anything. After that, he stepped out of view and dematerialized up into the big maple. Removing that camera, he ghosted around to the rear and took the other one off its mounting as well. Both had activation switches that were easy to operate and he turned them off—

and the units were small, so the pair fit into the deep pockets of his peacoat.

As he walked back inside once again, Mistress Miniahna looked up. "Is everything okay?"

"Yes, madam. All is in order."

"Did you see anyone?"

"No, I did not." He glanced at Saxton. "Perhaps she should have our contact information?"

"Yes, indeed." Saxton put an elegant hand into his jacket. "Here is my card—Ruhn, we don't have one for you, do we."

"I can tell you my number?" he said to the mistress.

"Here is a pen." She opened a little drawer in the side table next to her. "Will you write it down for me on his card?"

Ruhn froze.

But fortunately, Saxton smoothed the awkwardness over by taking what she offered. "Ruhn? What is your number?"

Swallowing hard, he recited the digits and tried not to feel as though he were stupid.

"Here you are." Saxton stood up and gave the older female the card. "Call either one of us. Day or night. I will do my own independent title search on the property, although I do not expect to find anything of note out of place. And then I will reach out to Mr. Romanski as your solicitor and see what we can do about your difficulties."

Mistress Miniahna stood and clasped the card to her heart. "I am very grateful. In truth, I hate to be an imposition, but I am not . . . my granddaughter is probably right. I should not handle this alone."

"You said your granddaughter is not far?"

"About twenty miles away."

Saxton nodded. "There is a good chance that things will get a little more messy before they get better. I cannot tell you to vacate your property, but I would advise it."

"I really would prefer to stay."

"We understand. Please consider the option, however."

After they both bowed low, and the mistress bid them best of night, Saxton put his shoes back on and they left and got in the truck.

"So I found something," he said as he drove them out the lane to the county road.

"Tell me."

"Here." He took the cameras from his pocket. "I only saw two. Maybe there are more, though."

Saxton held both in his palms. "Where did you find these?"

"The trees. They're watching her."

As Saxton said something vile under his breath, Ruhn turned out of the driveway and hit the gas.

"I could not agree more," he muttered.

For the next twenty minutes or so, the King's solicitor made some phone calls, one of which was to Vishous, and then there were a number of others where the person on the other end wasn't immediately apparent.

After that, they were just riding along, heading back to the Brotherhood's compound.

"I'm going with you when you go to talk to the humans," Ruhn announced.

"Yes, I should be ready tomorrow night or the next. I have research to do."

"And I'm going to make routine trips out there to the property." He felt Saxton look over at him. "You might let her know—or choose not to tell her. Whatever you deem best. But I can dematerialize there now that I know where it is, and I'll be discreet. I don't want her there all by herself, however."

"We need to talk about what happens if you meet up with any of them. Particularly if it's before I finish my investigation into the property records."

"I won't hurt them. But I shall not be gentle when I remove their presence from the mistress's property."

Abruptly, a strange scent reached Ruhn's nose . . . a dark spice. And it was strange. Whatever it was got into his nose and somehow into his entire body. He'd never smelled anything so good, actually. It was—

Ruhn frowned as something in his body shifted, a rushing instinct thickening his blood . . . thickening somewhere else on him, too.

When he realized he was aroused, he recoiled in the driver's seat, his hands gripping the wheel hard, sweat blooming on his chest and running up into his face.

This was sexual attraction, he realized with shock.

Toward . . . a male.

"Ruhn?"

He jumped in his seat. "I'm sorry, what?"

"Are you all right? You just made a strange noise."

Aware that his heart had begun to beat with panic, he swallowed through a tight throat. "I am well. Very well."

"All right. Anyway, Vishous wants to look at the cameras, and I will bring them to him. And then I will . . ."

As the King's solicitor continued talking, Ruhn tried to follow the conversation, filling in the breaks of silence with what he hoped were appropriately supportive and affirming nods and mm-hmm's.

Behind his eyes, all in his skull, however, he was screaming.

The one defining thing in his life, back as far as he could remember, was that he did not belong. Not even with his loving parents as he had grown up, not with what happened during the bad years, not when he was searching for his lost sister . . . and not even as he joined the Brotherhood and lived in their beautiful mansion and accepted material things that he had not earned.

He was someone who had been ever apart, and for the longest time, he had assumed—or perhaps prayed—that all of that isolation would be relieved by him finding, finally, the place in the world where he belonged.

This shocking attraction? To a male? It seemed just one more unwelcome reminder that he was never going to fit in. After all, that kind of thing might be accepted in the *glymera,* but never in the civilian class.

"Ruhn?"

Closing his eyes briefly, he said, "Yes?"

"You don't look well."

"I am fine. Worry not, I am well enough to do my duty."

And he would complete it, regardless of this momentary . . . whatever it was—after which he was going to take his leave of the household. He would find a station somewhere in one of the big estates here in Caldwell so he could still see Bitty, and he would resume his handymale ways, fixing and doing manual upkeep.

Until he was claimed by the Fade.

An unspectacular life, perhaps. But not all were granted grand destinies, and who was he to think he was special enough to warrant that, anyway. What he was certain of? He had enough secrets he needed to keep.

A strange, misplaced attraction to Saxton was not going to be added to that list.

ELEVEN

*P*eyton ended up not leaving the training center for the day, but then no one did. All of the trainees stayed—and he was careful to keep away from them. After his debriefing with Rhage, he left the office and considered joining the others for the food that he could smell in the break room. A non-specific rolling nausea and highly specific frontal-lobe headache cured him of that bad idea. And besides, the last thing anyone needed was Craeg snapping and going on the attack.

Although with the way Peyton was feeling, he was liable to leave himself undefended, accepting an old-school *rythe* of sorts.

At least Novo was still hanging on. Craeg had fed her and so had Boone, from what Peyton had been told. He had been surprised the Brothers hadn't been used, but then it seemed as though the clinical staff recognized that the trainees wanted to be the ones who helped their fallen soldier, even though the Brotherhood certainly had stronger blood.

God . . . he wished he could have given her a vein. And she had to be at least in and out of consciousness; otherwise she couldn't be feeding.

But again, no one asked him and he knew better than to volunteer.

Left to his own devices, he made his way down to where the classrooms were, and what was on the far side of door number three worked well enough: He took up res in the empty company of the tables and chairs and blackboard where Tohr had taught them about bomb making and detonation, and V had done a course on torture techniques.

Fuck algebra. They were actually going to use that stuff.

Well, the others were going to use it. Although Rhage had said nothing yet about kicking him out, he had to believe that was coming.

And therapy? With Mary?

Who were they even kidding? The last thing he wanted was to have to talk to Rhage's *shellan* about how he was *feeling* about what had happened. Hell, getting through the facts had been hard enough—and besides, it wasn't a great fucking mystery. Guilt, regret, shame.

Come on. Like, duh.

After he paced around for a while, he lay flat on the desk and stared up at the ceiling, his lower back pointing out that there was no mattress underneath him, his arm aching because he angled it up and used the thing as a pillow. As the day wore on, he would get up and pace again from time to time, trailing his fingertips on the slick tops of the tables they had all sat at while they had been in class.

He wanted to go back to the student part of things, when the learning had been theoretical. It had been a grand adventure back then.

He wanted to go back to before his cousin had died. Because that had seemed like the first of the bad dominoes to fall.

He wanted to go back to that alley. But he had recriminated enough over what he wished he had done differently there.

When the door opened, he was lying down again and he didn't bother to look over from his desk-bed. He knew by the scent who it was.

"Hey, Rhage." Peyton rubbed his face. "You got good news for me?

No? Well, at least I'm used to that—oh, wait, this is the part where you kick me out, right?"

"She's asking for you."

Peyton jumped to his feet before he was aware of moving. "What did you say?"

"You heard me." The Brother nodded out into the hall. "She's waiting."

Okay, this was a shocker. Unless Novo wanted to yell at him—and hey, if that was what motivated her to stay alive, he was good with being her punching bag.

Out in the corridor, he headed for the clinic area, and as he went along, he pulled up his combat pants and re-tucked his black muscle shirt.

But like she was going to give a shit how he was dressed?

At the door of her hospital room, he knocked—and when he heard a muffled response, he pushed his way inside.

Oh . . . shit.

Novo was lying prone in that bed with the high rails, her motionless body hooked up to beeping machines by miles of wires. Her skin was sallow, the yellow tint making him think about her liver—no, wait, was that the kidneys? He couldn't think. And her lids were down low, her mouth parted as if she were trying to breathe with the minimum amount of effort. Next to her, Ehlena was checking one of the monitors . . . and then the nurse put something in the IV line, using a syringe.

"Come closer," Novo croaked. "Not going to bite."

The nurse glanced over her shoulder and smiled. "I'm glad they found you. I'll leave you two to it—but Dr. Manello will be coming in very soon."

As the female left, Peyton went over to the side of the bed. Opening his mouth, he meant to say something appropriate. Nothing occurred to him.

Feeling like a fool, he went with: "Hey."

Yup, real original, profound stuff right there—God, why couldn't he have been the one to get stabbed?

Novo lifted her arm, or at least tried to—only her hand got up off the sheets. "Don't leave."

"Not until you tell me I have to."

"No . . . the program. Don't leave. I know that's . . . what you're thinking. I know . . . you're going to try to . . . leave."

For a moment, he considered pretending that hadn't been on his mind, oh, like, two minutes ago. But she looked so tired and worn out that he didn't want to waste her energy—even though he couldn't understand why she cared.

"We need . . . fighters," she said hoarsely. "You . . . good one."

"How can you even say that?" He pulled a chair over, sat down, and put his head in his hands. "How can you even . . ."

His voice drifted off as tears came into his eyes. He was so goddamn exhausted with being the fuckup, the asshole, the partyer, the rake . . . he was a poor excuse for a male of worth, and his father knew it just as everyone who had ever crossed his path did.

And now this incontrovertible evidence of his perennially poor judgment.

This. Here. Lying on this hospital bed. Just out of the operating room, where they had had to repair her heart.

Off in the distance, he heard that patient, the one who was losing his mind, scream like the male was also trapped in some kind of nightmare.

"Don't . . . leave . . ." she said. "Look . . . at me."

Scrubbing his face with his palm, he focused on her eyes . . . her beautiful, direct, intelligent eyes. And somehow, it was not a surprise that as weak as her body was, her stare was, as ever, alert and burning with purpose.

"I am so sorry," he whispered. "For what I did."

"It's . . . okay . . ."

"No, I was wrong." As his voice cut out, he forced strength into it. "I wanted to save Paradise, and she didn't need saving. She doesn't need it. She's as strong a fighter as any one of us. I don't know what I was thinking."

"You . . . love her." Novo's face tightened. "Not your fault. Emotions are . . . what they are. Trust me, I know this."

"I didn't want to hurt you."

"I know . . ."

As her eyes closed, Peyton panicked like she was dying in front of him, and he turned to those monitors with their graphs and their numbers and their blinking lights. None of them were showing any alarms. Were they working right?

But Novo didn't seem in any kind of distress. Her breathing stayed shallow, granted, but it was even, and her face didn't show any kind of pain.

She really was beautiful, he thought. So strong and unwavering, even in her weakened state.

"You can't leave the program," she mumbled. "Everything will fall apart. Brothers . . . will cancel us all—"

"I'm not in love with her," he blurted. "I'm not. I just didn't realize it until tonight."

Novo's eyes flipped back open. And then she shook her head a little on the thin pillow. "Doesn't . . . matter."

"You're right. It doesn't."

"Promise . . . me. No leaving . . ."

"We'll see—"

"My fault, too." As he frowned, she said, "I should have . . . stabbed *lesser*. Should have . . . finished job. I got distracted, too. Part . . . my fault."

"You're wrong about that—"

She put her hand out, like she wanted to stop the argument and

116 J. R. WARD

lacked the energy to talk over him. "I made mistakes . . . too. First rule is finish the job. I failed. I got . . . hurt because . . . of me, too."

Peyton had to blink a couple of times before he could be sure he wouldn't leak. "Let me take the responsibility. The Brothers can do what they want with me."

"We will fight again . . . together in field . . ." She took a deep breath and winced. "Soon as I'm . . . out of bed . . ."

You are such a female of worth, he thought.

And the more he dwelled on that conviction, the more everything in the room receded, the monitors, the antiseptic smell, the too-bright lights, and the too-hard chair. And then the airbrushed effect extended out even further, wiping clean the existence of the training center, the mountain they were on . . . Caldwell, the Northeast . . . the fucking planet itself.

Novo became all he knew, from the specks in her teal-blue eyes to the way her braid curled around and lay on her shoulder to how she put her hand out as if she wanted him to take it.

Extending his own palm, he clasped what she offered him and felt her squeeze with surprising strength.

"We will fight together again," she vowed.

Novo fought the ten-thousand-pound drag of pain and drugs in her body and tried to force what will she had into Peyton. The training program had to continue. Without it, she had no purpose and no outlet for all the shit she refused to feel and deal with: If she didn't accept her part in what had happened in that alley, and if she didn't forgive Peyton, the class was going to be divided, the Brotherhood was going to lose confidence and patience with them, and then she was going to be stuck going to her sister's fucking half-human mating ceremony with no battle armor against everything she had lost.

Without this work, these fights, her nightly routine, there was nothing to ground her. Pull her through. Keep her going.

And her salvation from oblivion all started with Peyton.

Forgiveness by her, here and now toward him, was the kind of thing that would spread to everyone else and re-bind the group. The other trainees would have to follow her lead—and p.s., she hadn't made up the shit about her being part of the problem. She should never have let the enemy just lie there on her like it had. Those slayer bastards were like rattlesnakes, capable of biting you even after you cut them in half. Peyton had definitely set the bad result in motion, but she had provided the slope.

It was a mistake neither one of them was going to make again.

Assuming they got the chance.

With what was left of her strength, she tried to keep her eyes focused on Peyton's face, but she could only get halfway to goal. Everything was fuzzy, as if there were panes of dusty glass between them.

What was clear? The scent of his tears.

And that was a shocker. Sure, she had needed open-heart surgery, but he was the perpetual joker, the playful resister who bobbed on top of everything. Not even a brush with death could make him get real . . . or at least, she wouldn't have thought it could—

I'm not in love with her.

That was totally not relevant, she told herself.

The door to the room swung open and Dr. Manello came in, his hospital scrubs traded for workout gear, a water bottle under his arm and a set of earbuds dangling from his hand.

"And we're awake." The human smiled. "Better than I thought you'd be."

"Fighter," she said in a voice that was more sandpaper than syllable.

God, she fucking hated to sound weak.

Dr. Manello came over and pounded knuckles with Peyton. Then

he leaned against the base of the bed. "Yeah, as a soldier, you are absolutely in the right line of badass work. You flatlined twice on our table,
which, to be honest, pissed me off. But you had your reasons. And
there was one point when I was convinced I was going to lose you for
good—you came back, though. Guess you decided you weren't done
with your work here on earth—well, and that six-chambered heart of
yours just kept working with us. Somehow, it hung on so I could do
what I needed to to fix that hole."

"Maybe it was more because my surgeon"—she took a deep
breath—"is talent? I mean, talented."

"Nah, I'm just a mechanic in scrubs instead of overalls."

He was lying, of course. Just as she had been coming out of anes-
thesia, she had heard Vishous say that there were only two surgeons
that he knew of who could have saved her—Doc Jane and Dr. Manello.
Especially because they hadn't had a bypass machine in the surgical
unit.

Whatever the hell that meant.

"So here's the plan." Dr. Manello did that thing medical people do,
scanning the monitors that were all around the bed like he was updating her chart in his head. "You're going to stay here for the next forty-
eight hours. And don't frickin' bitch to me about how long that is or
how amazing your species' regenerative powers are and how you can go
home at nightfall." He put his palm up as she opened her mouth.
"Nope, there will be no discussion. In another twelve hours, I want
you walking yourself up and down the corridor. All the way to the exit
and back every two or three hours—"

"Hoping . . . back to . . . work forty-eight hours."

Dr. Manello shot her an are-you-fucking-serious. "After you had
open-heart surgery. Yeah, right."

"Feeding? But I could . . . feed more."

"That'll help, sure. But you know what else is ammmmaaaazing?"

He lifted his head to the ceiling and got rapturous. "Staying the fuck in bed."

"I heal faster . . . if I feed."

"What's the rush? None of you are going back out in the field any-time soon." Abruptly, the surgeon shut his mouth, as if that were infor-mation he was not authorized to share. "Anyway, take a load off, eat chocolate pudding to soothe that throat I intubated, and we'll see how you go."

"Feeding, too."

"Fine, yeah, sure, take as many fucking veins as you want. But whether you turn yourself into Frank Langella or not, I'm only clearing you when I'm good and goddamn ready."

"Do you always curse . . . at your patients?"

"Only the ones I like."

"Lucky . . . me." But she smiled. "Do I . . . say thank . . . you . . . now?"

"Are you going to cry like a sissy if you do? 'Cuz, no offense, I'm a sympathetic weeper and I'd just as soon not have to go into the weight room looking like someone Mayweather'd me in the face."

"I never cry."

"Well, you've got a big heart, I'll tell you that much. I've seen it up close and personal." Dr. Manello put a hand on her foot and gave her a little squeeze. "You hit that call button if you need anything. Ehlena is right next door. I'm working out for the next hour or so, and then I'll be sleeping across the hall just in case you spring another leak. Not that I'm expecting that."

"Thank . . . you."

"You are so welcome," the surgeon said. "I love a good result. And let's keep it that way during recovery, okay?"

"Yes, Doctor."

"Good girl." He smiled. "I mean, good badass boss lady."

As her surgeon headed for the door, Novo admitted to herself that he was right. It was way too ambitious on her part to think she'd be able to fight in two days. The pain in her chest was incredible, the kind of thing she felt up in her molars and down to her toenails, even with all the drugs she was on. There was no way that was backing off by next nightfall.

She looked at Peyton. He was sitting in that chair like he was on the verge of bursting to his feet, his torso leaning forward, his hands planted on his thighs as if he were going to push himself up.

"What?" she asked him. "You look . . . as if you want . . . to be called on in class."

"Chocolate pudding."

Novo tried to take a deep breath and just ended up wheezing. "What . . . ?"

"He said you're supposed to eat it for your throat. I'll get you some."

"No." In fact, the more she thought about it, the more she wanted to gag. "Oh, no. Stomach . . . no."

"I just want to help somehow."

She stared at him for a while. In all the ways that mattered, Peyton was the very thing she detested in a male, all that *glymera* bullshit wrapped up in a package that, as much as she tried to deny it, even she recognized as attractive.

He was her sister's type, as a matter of fact.

Good thing Sophy was never going to meet him. Or Oskar would learn firsthand how it feels when someone you think loves you treats you like you're an iPhone 5 in an X world.

Actually, wasn't that a tempting fantasy . . .

What was the question? God, her brain was fuzzy. Oh, right . . . Peyton was everything she hated about wealthy high-society types who were too good for everyone else around them—but there was one part to all that which did work for her.

His blood was liable to be hella pure, to the point of being medicinal.

"What can I do?" he asked. "And if it's leave you in peace, I can do that for you, too."

In the back of her mind, a warning went off, the little *ring-a-ding-ding* pointing out that maybe, just maybe, it might be better for her to never know what he tasted like.

Although, come on, she'd already learned her lesson with males, and it had cost her a piece of herself. Literally.

She was not that stupid—and she really fucking wanted out of this bed.

"Let me . . . take your vein."

As she said the words, Peyton's eyes flared like that was the last thing he had ever expected her to say.

"Please," he said roughly as he extended his wrist to her.

Except he immediately retracted his arm and brought his own flesh to his lips. His brows tightened only a fraction as he bit into himself, and then he extended the punctures over to her.

Her jaw cracked as she tried to open her mouth, and things seemed hinged in a bad way by her ears, maybe part of the whole emergency intubation. But she forgot about all that as a drop of his blood landed on her lower lip.

The scent alone was like food in a stomach when you were weak from hunger, everything waking up with vitality—no, fuck that. It was like a hit of cocaine. And then she was extending her dry tongue and licking—

Dimly, she was aware of groaning as her eyes rolled back in her head . . . and not because she was dying. Oh, no, she was suddenly very alive. His taste. His taste was like a crash cart hooking up to her sliced-and-diced heart, the jolt that went through her chest, cranking her entire circulatory system into a gear with so much more power.

"Take from me," he said from a great distance. "Take it all . . ."

As he lowered his arm down, she formed a seal around his vein. Her first couple of draws were sloppy and uncoordinated—she cured that quick, though. Before long, she was taking the kind of long pulls you might if it had been years since you had been properly nourished.

Holy . . . shit . . . she had never had this kind of sustenance before. Craeg and Boone had volunteered earlier, back when she had been in and out of consciousness. And prior to that? It had been other civilians, just like herself. But Peyton was high-test to all that discount gas, to the point where the singeing path burning its way into her gut made her break out in a sweat—and sure enough, alarms began to go off, her heart thundering behind that recently sawed-open sternum of hers.

She really didn't care if she stroked out. Or if her cardiac muscle exploded all over everything. Or if her head popped off her spine, her feet grew fifteen sizes bigger, or she went blind, deaf, and mute.

Instinct, bred into her species, took over, the hunger owning every part of her.

And then her eyes locked with Peyton's.

She told herself this was about getting well, triumphing over her injury, making herself stronger. But the more she drank of him, the more she took of him into herself, it was clear there was another drive at work.

He was a meal she feared she was going to want again. Even when her survival was not at stake.

And she wasn't going to need only blood.

TWELVE

Down the corridor, in the weight room, Ruhn lay with his upper body on a padded bench, his legs bent, his feet planted on the floor mats. The bar he gripped with his hands weighed fifty pounds or more and was made of iron. The disks racked on either end totaled some seven hundred pounds.

As he popped the load off the supports, he held it up above his chest and breathed deep as he steadied all that weight. Then he brought the bar down to his pecs, controlling the descent, a triumph of strength over gravity. With first the right hand and then the left, he realigned his grips a little . . . and then he pushed up, taking the bar high as he exhaled with a *schhhhhhhht*. And then down. And then up. And then down . . .

He kept going until those pectorals began to seize and his biceps and triceps trembled and his elbows burned . . . and still he continued, to the point where he need to arch his spine to get the bar to its apex.

Sweat dotted his brow and then ran down into his hair and his ears. His thighs ached. His lungs ceased to work. His heart didn't so much pound as blow up with every beat.

And still he did not stop.

The idea that he had been attracted to someone of the same sex was something he had never confronted before. Sure, he was aware that those liaisons occurred, but he'd always assumed it was just something the aristocracy indulged. Where he came from? As a lowly civilian from a traditional background?

No, his parents would never have approved of this, his father especially. That male had been very adamant about what the proper roles were for both sexes, and they had not included masculine coupling. He had also been clear about the expectations for each person in the family, *mahmen,* father, daughter, son.

And you wanted your elders to approve of you, especially after a youth where you were bigger than everybody else and shy as a fawn in social situations.

In fact, Ruhn had nearly killed himself to live up to what his father had needed from him, what his family had required. The idea of letting them down—

Wait, why was he thinking like this? As if he had already had sex with someone of the same . . . well, sex, as it were?

Because you want to kiss him. Admit it.

As the thought went through his head, he threw his no-I-don't into the bar, shoving the weights up with the same kind of power he'd had when he'd first started. He absolutely did *not* want anything from that male. At all. Because if he did? Well, he'd already been through the nightmare of discovering a new, unacknowledged part of him, and that had been a horrible experience, to say the least.

He was not going through that again.

Nope—

All at once, his arms gave out on him, the muscles failing, the weight going in a free fall that resulted in the bar landing directly on his chest. The pain was instant and paralyzing, those seven hundred and fifty pounds compressing his lungs as sure as if a building had fallen on him.

Instantly, a face appeared overhead. "Help me get this off you—come on, push! Goddamn it, PUSH!"

It was the surgeon, Dr. Manello.

As Ruhn began to black out, he was dimly aware of a piercing alarm in the weight room—no, it was a whistle. The human was whistling through his front teeth as he tried to relieve some of the pressure by straddling the bench and pulling up on the bar with both hands.

It did help. Ruhn could breathe some and his vision cleared a little.

Two more people came running in and then the crushing load was gone off of him. He still couldn't inhale right, though. Had he broken his entire upper torso?

Dr. Manello's face came back, real close. "I am not opening another chest cavity up tonight, do you hear me?"

And then there was a mask over his nose and mouth, a forceful stream of oxygen making his cheeks blow out and his throat go dry. The air tasted weird, like there were pencil shavings in it or flecks of tin—and that, coupled with the plastic form-fitting piece over his mouth and nose, made him feel like he was suffocating worse than he had been when he'd been left alone.

When he tried to push the mask away, strong hands prevented him.

But he was even stronger. A surge of pure panic shot him upright in spite of the people around him, and he tore the oxygen feed free.

To settle any arguments to the contrary, he opened his mouth and dragged all the air in the weight room down deep. Immediately, there was a horrid cracking sound, like an oak branch snapping in half, and a lightning bolt of agony accompanied the noise—still, his light-headedness fled like an intruder chased away, his heart hammering in an even rhythm.

"Well, there's that approach to it, too," Dr. Manello muttered. "Is it all right if I take a look at you?"

As Ruhn was still having to concentrate to get the inhale/exhale thing right, he simply nodded.

"Can you lie down for me?" the doctor asked.

Ruhn shook his head. Nope, no way. The panic would come back and take over—and with a shiver of claustrophobia, he looked at the door. Thank Fates that it had a window out into the corridor, and he reminded himself that there was a place to escape out of—

Someone came at him with something.

With a quick mortal reflex, he slapped a grip onto the wrist and bent the arm in its joint socket so hard and fast that whatever person was attached to it went down on the mats.

"Whoa, easy . . ." The Brother Rhage broke the hold and put his body in the way. "Hey, look at me. Come on, son, you focus on me now."

Ruhn blinked. Blinked again. Tried to follow the command, but it was impossible. Rhage was jumping around like water on a griddle— oh, wait. Ruhn was shaking. Yup, those huge feet of the Brother's were not moving; Ruhn was the one with the over-motorization.

"Where are you in there?" the Brother murmured. "'Cuz I need you to come back so you don't hurt the doctor, 'kay?"

Something was wrong with his hearing. The volume was going up and down on the world, words fading in and out of mute with a randomness that required him to fill in the blanks.

Ruhn breathed in and out some more, and then he looked down, to where Dr. Manello was examining his own forearm like he was wondering if it was broken.

"I'm so sorry," Ruhn choked out. "Oh, dearest Virgin, I didn't mean . . ."

The doctor smiled up at him. "Nah, it's okay. Boundaries are good. Just next time, tell me to back off first before you strong-arm me, and then if I don't listen, go MMA on my ass. So are you ready for me to listen to your heart? This is not going to hurt you."

The human held up a little metal disk, which appeared to be attached to a cord that . . . went into the doctor's ears.

"Have you never been examined before?" Dr. Manello said softly.

Ruhn shook his head.

"Okay, this is a stethoscope. I put it here," the male pointed to his own chest, a little off of center, "and I listen to the beat. It's non-invasive—which means it doesn't hurt or cut into you. I promise."

Ruhn shuddered and then nodded—not because he wanted anything anywhere near him, but rather because he'd been unforgivably rude in hurting the man and wanted to make up for that somehow.

And it looked like submitting to whatever that was was his only chance.

"Can you sit up straighter for me?"

As he complied, pushing his spine higher, Rhage seemed to be encouraging the others who had come in to leave—and for that, Ruhn was grateful. What he needed right now was less sensory input, not more, and as someone who suffered from shyness, all those pairs of eyes staring at him, even if it was with compassion, were too much to handle.

"See? Nothing to worry about."

Ruhn looked down. The disk end of the instrument was on his pecs and the doctor was staring off to the side, as if he were concentrating on whatever was being transmitted to his ears.

"Does it hurt to take a breath?" the doctor asked. "Yes? Can I take off your shirt so I can see what's going on?"

Ruhn nodded before he could think better of it, and Dr. Manello and Rhage each took the bottom of his muscle shirt and peeled it slowly upward.

Like a young, Ruhn held his arms up for them—before he remembered why his shirt had to stay on.

Both of them gasped and froze.

And immediately, Ruhn wanted to curse. He'd forgotten about the markings on his back.

Damn it.

•   •   •

After Novo was finished feeding and had fallen into the restless sleep of the injured and healing, Peyton stumbled back to the classroom on numb feet, shaky legs, and a vertigo-scrambled inner ear. As he closed himself in, he wondered why the tables and the chairs, the desk and the blackboard, all looked completely unfamiliar, like he'd never been in the room before.

Made no sense. He'd been gone a half an hour, tops, and his short-term memory informed him that everything was exactly as he'd left it.

Then again, he was what had changed.

Turning the lights off and rolling onto the desk, he felt like he was nothing but bones in a loose sack, everything hard-edged and not well connected. Jesus Christ, what had just happened back there? Whatever, sure, on the surface, Novo had taken his vein, and that hadn't been the first time a female had done that to him. And hello, she was in a hospital bed, hooked up to machines.

The experience, though? The feel of her lips on the skin of his wrist, the subtle pulls, the lick of her tongue when she was finished?

Fuck his drug addiction. Give him a lifetime of that and he was never going to need another line of coke again.

Closing his eyes, he relived every part of it, from when he had scored himself to that first drop that had landed on her lip. Sensations rippled through him, heating his blood, making him even harder.

He fought the arousal.

He lost.

When he had been at her bedside, he had managed to keep things under control, rearranging his cock discreetly and staying tight. Here by himself in the dark? He felt like a fucking man-whore, but he was never going to sleep again unless he took care of things.

With a rough shove, he pushed his palm down the front of his combats and the instant contact was made, an orgasm exploded out of him, memories of Novo from class, sparring, out in the field, flashing through his mind, keeping things going. He even went back to when he'd been inside her, her bare sex accepting his penetrations like she had been made for him and him alone.

Okay, that was not such a great image, given that she'd only lain there.

Staying away from that one, he stuck to the others as he gave himself more access, ripping open his fly with two brutal hands, shoving the waistband down over his ass. With a grunt, he twisted to the side, his torso torquing as he gripped his shaft and worked himself even harder, the desk cool under his hot cheek, his free hand curling around the edge and squeezing so hard, his forearm nearly snapped in half.

And still he kept coming.

When he was finally drained, he closed his eyes and just breathed for a while—until he realized he'd made a goddamn mess all over himself and the front of his pants and the goddamn desk.

Thank God it was the middle of the day. With any luck, he could sneak down to the locker room, grab some towels and a set of scrubs, and get back here without anyone seeing him.

So yup . . . it was time to get up.

Uh-huh.

Right now.

Instead, he stayed where he was and wondered what would it be like to feed from her and actually remember it . . . her blood down the back of his throat, her body underneath his as he rolled her over and went for her throat.

He needed to go there. And not because he was shot in the head and in a medical emergency.

Yet even as the conviction went through his mind and started to re-wire things with all sorts of purpose-driven, results-oriented, get-naked-soon goals, he knew none of it was ever going to happen. She had made it clear all along that he wasn't her type—hell, even if she said she wanted to fight with him again, she didn't even like him. More to the point, their paths were going to stop crossing when he left the program.

Their time was totally coming to an end: she was going to continue to train and do the right thing by the species, and he had his career as a professional club douche to resume.

Busy, busy, on both their parts.

As his phone went off with a call, he ignored it and tried to get motivated for his walk of shame.

It was a good half hour before he made it down the hall and back. And after he had cleaned himself and everything else up, he laid himself flat on the desk again and passed out.

In his fitful rest, he was haunted by a lover with long dark hair, eyes of fire . . . and a will of steel.

THIRTEEN

As night fell the following evening, Saxton rolled over and looked at the other side of his bed. There had been a male in those twisted sheets. A body that he had used and which had used his own in return.

At the other end of the penthouse, a door shut quietly.

Saxton sat up and pushed his hair out of his eyes. Recollections of how he had spent the day made him feel hollow, and wasn't that a hangover he could have done without—and then there was the added fun of a dingy headache that came from too much champagne and not enough sleep.

When he was finally able to focus properly, he looked around at the sleek mirror-fronted bureaus and side tables, the black chairs, the soft gray rug, the pattern of evenly spaced hanging light fixtures that were like stars in the ceiling.

For no good reason, he thought of how he'd misled Blay.

He hadn't sold his Victorian house across town. Now, did he ever go there? Absolutely not. But the fact that he couldn't be in it anymore, yet nor could he let it go, had seemed like a weakness best kept to himself: It was a sad reality that he was paying property taxes on a shrine to a love that had gone nowhere.

Well, not exactly nowhere. He had been in pain for quite some time now, and that certainly felt like a destination.

Not a good one, granted.

With a subtle hiss, the automatic shutters on all the glass panels started to rise, revealing the twinkling lights of the city by inches, curtains pulled away by an invisible hand. And it was strange . . . as he considered once more how he had spent the day, he realized that for once, Blay had not been the reason for his little dalliance. Usually the male was. Yet in fact all those pneumatics had been caused by . . .

He frowned and rubbed his gritty eyes. But no. Surely he must have imagined that moment, when he and Ruhn had been in that truck, and Ruhn had looked over at him? It could have been anything.

Just because he found the male attractive did not mean that regard was mutual.

Still, there had been an undeniable trickle-down effect, a gnawing, restless energy that had ultimately taken him into his contacts list and through the entries of males and human men that he had availed himself of from time to time. Most of them were acquaintances, individuals he met at clubs or parties, and he never asked about their couple status. All he cared about, as did they, was that they could fuck well.

Not to put it too bluntly.

And the fact that he had chosen one with dark hair and a big, strong body? He supposed he could look at it as a sign of improvement. At least it hadn't been a redhead. Somehow, though, it was hard to be encouraged by the fact that he had traded one male he couldn't have for another.

"Enough," he said aloud.

Shifting his legs out from the satin sheets, he sent himself toward the bath, the subtle aches and click to his hip the kind of things he was used to after a day like the one he'd had—and he tried not to think of Blay and the past. Back when he had been with that male, the aftermath of the sex had been more about the warmth in the center of his chest and the side smile that had come unto him whenever he had thought about his love.

What he was experiencing now was nothing more than the mechanical residual of unaccustomed exercise.

As he entered the marble enclave, he kept the lights over the sinks off for a number of reasons, the main one being that the glow from the urban landscape provided him with more than enough illumination. And he also didn't want to look at himself in all the mirrors.

He took four Motrin as he waited for the hot water to get running in the shower.

Stepping into the multiple heads, he washed himself thoroughly and shaved using the anti-fogging mirror he'd had mounted in one corner. When he was finished, he was no more refreshed than he had been satisfied by the way he had spent the day—and for the first time he could remember, the idea of going in to work and losing himself in his nightly tasks held no prospect of enthusiasm or satisfaction.

And then as he toweled himself off, the sound of flapping terry-cloth made the emptiness of the penthouse seem like a black hole in space.

In the back of his mind, the idea of leaving Caldwell tantalized him yet again. Certainly, everywhere he went, there he was . . . but he had to believe that a fresh perspective would come if he lived in a different place and pursued a different kind of life. Perhaps as a teacher? There were people who still wanted to know about the Old Laws, and he was so well-versed in them now that he could easily design a curriculum—

When his phone went off out in the bedroom, he let whoever it was go into voicemail. But when the thing immediately began to ring again, he wrapped the towel around his hips and proceeded over to it—because, yes, he was that kind of male who thought answering a phone while naked was inappropriate, even if FaceTime was not involved.

Especially as it was likely Wrath or one of the Brothers—

No, not this time. As he checked the phone's face, it was not someone who was in his contacts, although the No Caller ID suggested it was from a member of the Brotherhood's household.

Vishous was into the untraceable.

"Hello?" he said.

"Saxton?" Ruhn's voice was instantly recognizable, and a surprise. Also carried with it an erotic charge, but again, that was just on his side.

"Yes? Hello? Ruhn?" There was some interference over the connection, some wind blowing or something. "I'm sorry, I can't hear you?"

"I'm out at Miniahna's." Fuzz. Rustle. "I just ran two men off her property." Wind blowing. "Where are you?"

"I'm at home. Downtown."

"Can I come see you?"

"Yes, yes, of course—let me tell you how to get here." After he provided directions, he cut in, "Wait, before you hang up. Did you kill the trespassers? Do I need to call for a body removal?"

Blustering sounds. "Not yet, you don't. But that is not going to last."

As soon as the call ended, Saxton rushed into his walk-in closet and pulled a pair of slacks on along with a white button-down shirt—and had to resolutely ignore the fact that he had quite a bounce in his step all of a sudden.

This is just business, he told himself. For godsakes, keep it professional.

Across town, in the wealthy zip code where mansions sat like crowns in the midst of manicured, snow-covered grounds, Peyton arrived on the grand doorstep of his father's house along with a marching band of exhaustion, his dull-thumping temples the bass section, the sharp shooters in his lower back the cymbals, and the grumbling cramps in his gut a tuba manned by a very low-skilled, but highly enthusiastic, player with a great set of lungs.

He couldn't decide whether he was hungry or nauseous.

And his first clue that the night was about to go from bad to worse—once again—came as he opened the front door: There was a sweet smell in the air that was utterly foreign. Perfume? he thought. Yes, that was it. But who could be wearing any—

His father's butler shot out from under the stairs as if the male were on roller skates.

"You're late." Eyes the color of old newspapers swept up and down him. "And you are not dressed."

Last time I checked, I sure as shit was, Peyton thought. These scrubs cover the naughty bits.

He kept that to himself. "What are you talking about?"

"First Meal starts in fifteen minutes." The *doggen* pulled up his cuff and flashed a watch like it was a gun aimed at a mugger. "You have missed libations."

Peyton rubbed the front of his skull with the heel of his hand. It was either that or take that timepiece and feed it to the guy—through his ass.

"Look, I don't know what you're going on about, but I haven't slept well since the day before yesterday, and there was a terrible accident last night in the field—"

"There. You. Are."

Closing his eyes, he thought, of course, his father. And that tone? It made the butler seem like a BFF.

Pivoting around, he caught a glare like a frying pan to the side of the face. Which was saying something considering his sire was wearing a custom-made tuxedo and was hardly the type to throw pans, much less punches.

But that stare was a stinger for sure.

"Hello, Father." Peyton clapped his palms together. "Well, good talk, and now I'm going up to bed—"

As he turned away, his father stepped in front of him, blocking the way to the stairs. "Yes. You are going to the second floor right now, but it is to change—because you agreed to meet Romina this evening. At this hour—actually, last hour, and where *have* you been."

"I don't know anything about this."

"I called you last night. Twice! So go up and put your tuxedo on so you don't embarrass me or that poor female any further." The male leaned in. "Her *parents* are here, for godsakes. What is *wrong* with you. Can you not, for one night only, be the son I need you to be?"

Well, jeez, Dad, when you put it like that, how about I solve the issue for the both of us and go hang myself in the bathroom?

#problemsolved

Peyton glanced over his sire's shoulder at the staircase and tried the suicide plan on for size. He had plenty of belts, for sure—and a nice sturdy light fixture in his bedroom.

Except then the image of Novo feeding from him came back, sharp as a knife-edge.

Yeah, no way he was offing himself. Not yet, at any rate.

Shifting his stare into the parlor, he started to form a fuck-off, fuck-you, and fuck-this combo that somehow encapsulated how little he cared about social bullshit after having spent the last twenty-four hours dealing with the reality that he had nearly gotten someone killed.

But all that came to a crashing halt.

Through the ornate archway, he could see into the elegant room, the silk sofas and chairs arranged with the marble fireplace as a focal point. Seated on the cushions, with her back to him, was a female with brunette hair pulled back in a chignon and a formal, pale blue dress that had some sort of tie or sleeving that draped like an angel's wing over the arm. Her head was down, and her shoulders were tight, as if she were holding herself together.

But just barely.

She didn't want this any more than he did, he thought. Either that, or she was feeling rejected by him because he hadn't showed up.

"Will you *please* get moving," his father demanded.

Peyton looked at the poor female a little longer and wondered where she would rather be tonight.

"Give me ten minutes," he said gruffly. "I'll be right down."

As he stepped around his father and took the stairs two at a time, he despised his family and its traditions and the *glymera*'s stupid fucking rules. But what he was not going to do? Leave some other schmuck like him out to dry, thinking she was lesser because of stuff that had nothing to with her.

He didn't know the female, but the way he looked at it, they were in the social cesspool together.

At least for this one meal.

FOURTEEN

As Ruhn materialized on a skyscraper terrace that was larger than the estate cottage he had lived in, he took a moment to internalize where he was. Saxton's home. Where the male lived.

He should have waited an hour and met with the attorney at the Audience House.

What had he been thinking—

You wanted to see him, a small voice said in his head. Alone.

"No, I don't."

The words he spoke out loud were lost in the cold wind that rushed at his back, the blustery, chilly gusts seeming to urge him inside. For a moment or two, he fought against the draft, leaning against the invisible hands pushing at him . . . but it was too late to turn back now. Not without making a mess of things.

Besides, this was not personal. They were working on something together.

"And I do not want to be alone with him."

With that resolved, he tried to figure out where he was supposed to knock, or ring a bell. The entire penthouse seemed to be made of glass, great panels lining up one to another down the front. Inside, there were few lights on, everything dim, the shadows of the furniture a landscape yet to be revealed by an artificial dawn.

So luxurious and fancy, he thought. It seemed all very sophisticated, just like the male who lived there.

Then again, someone's personal space tended to reflect who they were. Take him, for example. He was a squatter with no prospects, homeless but for the kindness of others. It made sense if you had no future and little of the present that you would also have no roof and four walls of your own.

Walking over and inspecting one of what he hoped were sliders, he wondered who lived here with the solicitor? He had never seen the male with a *shellan,* nor had there been any mention of one. But then a certain professional distance had always seemed to surround Saxton, even as it was clear that he was respected by all.

Surely there had to be a female somewhere in the picture. And didn't that fact make all of this even more uncomfortable—

He froze as Saxton came into the great open room, the male's stride sure, his blond hair gleaming under the dimmed ceiling lights, his impeccable slacks and super-white button-down looking tuxedo ready. Or, like, whatever you wore on top of all that.

The solicitor headed into the kitchen area, throwing out a casual hand to turn on lights that provided brighter pools of illumination from above. He started doing something at the counter, by the sink—he was preparing coffee and getting out mugs and a tray. But Ruhn noticed little of that. The things that registered? Saxton's skin was golden. His face was beautiful. His body was lithe.

What is this, Ruhn thought . . . especially as sexual arousal curled around his hips, sure as if hands were touching him—

Saxton looked over without warning and stopped as he saw that he was in the regard of another.

Moments turned into a full minute.

And then they both snapped back into action at the same time, Ruhn trying to pretend that he was just searching for a handle or an opening or something as Saxton came across and solved the problem for him.

"Good evening," the male said as he slid one of the panels back. "You invited me." As Ruhn heard the words leave his mouth, he closed his eyes. "I mean, I'm here. I mean . . ."

"Yes, you are expected."

When Ruhn didn't respond, Saxton stepped aside. "Come in."

Two words. Two syllables. A simple invitation. The kind of thing that was offered and accepted or rejected by humans and vampires all over the world.

The trouble was, Ruhn couldn't shake the awareness that it was so much more for him—and he couldn't handle it. He could handle . . . none of this.

"I should go," he mumbled. "Actually. Yeah, I'm sorry—"

"Why?" Saxton frowned. "What's wrong?"

I think I want you, that's what's wrong.

Oh, dearest Virgin Scribe, had that just gone through his mind?

"Ruhn, come in. It's cold."

Turn away, he told himself. *Just turn and leave, and tell him that you'll meet him at the Audience House in a little bit.*

"I shouldn't have disturbed you at home." He shook his head and prayed that the heavy beating of his heart was not something Saxton could hear or sense. "I apologize."

Across town, Peyton returned downstairs in exactly ten minutes, his hair wet and slicked back thanks to the fastest shower in the east, his tuxedo on and poppin'—and also a little tight across the shoulders, in the arms, and at the thighs, thanks to all the exercise he'd been getting.

As he entered the parlor, he did a quick check that the bar was stocked and open for business. Yup: Over there in the corner, an array of mimosas in slender flutes and Bloody Marys in squat glasses had been arranged on an antique brass cart.

My friends, I cannot wait for us to become reacquainted, he thought. But first things first.

"Ah, yes, my firstborn son," Peythone said in the Old Language from the armchair closest to the fire—and hey, points for the smile, old man; it looked almost sincere. *"Salone and Idina, may I present Peyton, son of Peythone."*

The couple were seated on the silk sofa across from their sacrificial lamb—sorry, daughter—and Peyton walked forward to them and bowed low, first to the male, who was your bog-standard *glymera* type, and then the female, who was wearing a dress the exact same blue color as her young. Which was creepy. He also didn't immediately recognize them, which was unusual. The aristocracy was small, and nearly everyone was their own uncle's first cousin. They must be from out of town, he thought. Maybe down South?

"It is my pleasure to meet you," he said. *"Please excuse my tardiness. I have been unforgivably rude."*

Blah, blah, blah.

"You are even more handsome than I have heard," the *mahmen* said, her eyes going wide. *"So handsome. Is he not handsome? Such a handsome male, fresh from his transition."*

You are no MILF, he thought. *So stop looking at me like I'm fresh meat.*

God, he hated this.

"Enough with that, Idina," Salone grumbled before he switched things to English. "Now, Peyton, your sire indicated you are in the Black Dagger Brotherhood's training program—something that we have only just learned this night. I suppose we may give your tardiness a pass on this account."

Peythone smiled smugly. "Indeed, Peyton is contributing to the defense of the species in a very meaningful way. But one does not wish to brag."

Oh, yeah. Riiiiiiiiiiight.

Idina placed her hands on either side of her décolletage and leaned forward as if they were going to share a secret—or perhaps she was going to flash him. "You must tell me, what are the Brotherhood like? They are *so* mysterious, so impressive, so frightening. I have only ever seen them from afar at meetings of the Council. Tell me, you *must*."

Okay, he hated everything about the female. From her rapacious eyes, to those big diamonds, and that accent. God, what was up with that accent? It was like ninety percent right, but there was something wrong with her *r*'s. She couldn't seem to roll them properly. And then there was the sire. Upon closer reflection, his features were coarser than one might expect, and that tuxedo—it had a shine on it like it had been rubbed hard with some KFC.

What was his father up to, Peyton thought. Of all the families they might want to associate with, why these people?

Then again, the Founding Families in Caldwell were aware of Peyton's reputation. Maybe this wasn't so much the best his father could do . . . as the best the son could do.

"Well?" Idina of the Libido prompted. "Tell me *everything* about them."

Fuck this shit.

Peyton turned around and looked at the young female.

This shut everyone in the room up, a hushed disapproval slamming the door shut on all that social drooling.

The daughter recoiled, but then she collected herself quickly, shifting her stare downward as was appropriate considering his social *faux pas:* They had not yet been properly introduced.

She was lovely in a low key kind of way, her beauty not the sort that grabbed the eye immediately, but rather something that was revealed the more you stared at her. Her features were even and small, her limbs long and graceful, her body in that soft blue dress possessing all the curves a male could want.

A slight flutter off to the side drew his attention. It was her hands . . . her hands were shaking—and as if she didn't want him to notice that, she clasped them together in her lap.

What have you done to deserve me, you poor thing, he thought.

"I'm Peyton," he said, much to his father's horror.

As he spoke up, the female's eyes lifted to his, and there was surprise in them. But she immediately glanced to her parents.

Her sire cleared his throat with a disapproving grunt—like he wished this were going better, but knew he had no right to expect shit in that department.

And then he muttered, "This is my daughter, Romina."

English, not the Old Language. An insult to which one of us? Peyton wondered.

In any event, he bowed low. *"My pleasure to make your acquaintance."*

Before he straightened, he tried to communicate with her telepathically: *It's going to be okay. We're going to get out of this.*

As if they were both prisoners.

Take out the "as if."

And clearly, they were on death row, at least in the female's opinion. The girl was flat-out terrified.

FIFTEEN

s Saxton stood beside the open sliding door of his penthouse, he didn't feel the freezing cold or the punches of the wind gusts or the hunger that had been agitating his belly. The male before him took all of that away, Ruhn's big body tensed as if he were ready to bolt off the top of the Commodore, his hair blowing asunder, his eyes too bright and very wary. But that scent . . . that *scent*.

Dark spices. Arousal.

Sexual need.

What fantasy is this, Saxton wondered. Was he asleep and dreaming?

"Don't go," he said in a rough voice. Except then he caught himself and tried to pull back from a tone that was too close to begging. "I mean, come in and tell me what happened. At Minnie's. Please."

Ruhn's stare shifted so that he seemed to focus on the interior.

"There's no one here but me." Saxton stepped back even farther. "We're alone."

Dear God, why did that sound like an invitation?

Because it was.

"Stop it—" As he realized he'd spoken aloud, he closed his eyes and tried to pull himself together. "Sorry. Please, it's cold."

Or maybe it was sweltering hot. Who the hell knew.

"All right," Ruhn said in a low voice.

As the big male turned sideways and came in, Saxton couldn't keep from closing his eyes and inhaling. He had never smelled anything so sensual in his life. *Ever.*

With shaky hands, he closed them both in together by pulling the glass back into place. "I was . . . well, I was just going to make—would you like some coffee?"

Ruhn looked around and crossed his arms over his chest. "I'm fine. Thank you."

"Won't you sit down?"

"This shouldn't take long."

And yet the male did not start to speak. He stayed there right by the exit, his boots planted on the pale gray rug, his black leather jacket and blue jeans making a mockery of all the carefully constructed minimalism around him, a giant in a dollhouse.

"Tell me what happened?" Saxton went across and sat down on his sofa. "Is anything wrong?"

Ruhn seemed to take a deep breath, his chest expanding so much that that jacket creaked. "I went out there, to the farmhouse, to make sure Mistress Miniahna was all right. There was a truck parked in the driveway, just before the circle in front of the house. Black, with darkened windows. I waited, and after a moment, two human males got out and looked at the trees. One had a sensor in his hand."

"They know we removed the cameras."

"Yes." Ruhn put his hands into the pockets of his leather jacket. "They do."

"And?"

"Well, I couldn't just leave with them there."

Here we go, Saxton thought.

"What did you do?"

"I dematerialized around to the back and approached them as if I were coming around the house. The men were surprised. I told them I was staying with my aunt and was out chopping wood when I heard them come up the lane. I asked them what they were doing on the property. One said he and his buddy were concerned for her, what with her being all alone. When I pointed out that she wasn't alone, that I was there, they said they knew she lived by herself. Then they went on about how the neighborhood was really changing and that she should consider selling. I told them that there was no more reason to worry about her as I was going to take care of things at the house and that I would deal with any trespassers. Then I asked them what their names were and why they were on the property at all, and that was when things got interesting."

"Did they threaten you, too?"

"They gave me these." He pulled out some papers that had been folded in quarters. "And told me that they were for Mistress Miniahna. They had tried the front door during the day a number of times, they said."

Saxton sat forward and held out his hand. "Did you show these to her?"

"I can't read." Ruhn came forward only far enough to give whatever it was over and then he immediately dropped back. "As I didn't know what they were, I didn't want to show her something that would upset her for no good reason. I wasn't sure what to do for the best. That's why I called you."

Saxton unfolded things, and a quick scan got him right up off the cushions onto his feet. Then he paced around as he did a more careful read.

"What is it?" Ruhn asked.

Saxton stopped and looked over at the male. "They're accusing her of being a squatter."

"How? It's her property."

"It is, but she and her *hellren* made a mistake with the property records. I discovered it late last night. They didn't file redundant real property contracts over time."

"What is that?"

"It's a strategy for vampires who hold real estate in the human world. Every twenty years or so, generally, you want to pretend that you've sold your house or your land to what appears to be a fellow family member. Otherwise, you have what Miniahna is going to have to deal with here—which is that the records show a single owner since 1821. Needless to say, that is impossible for a human to pull off, and clearly, the developer has discovered the issue, even as he cannot guess the truth about our species. Anyway, tell me—did you wait for them to leave? The humans?"

"Yes. They took off right after they gave me those." Ruhn frowned. "Can you do anything to help her?"

Saxton walked into the kitchen area and went straight for the coffee machine. As he poured himself some Starbucks Breakfast Blend, his mind was racing.

Backdating documents. Yes, he had to create an artificial paper trail—

When he turned around, he caught Ruhn wincing as the male gripped under his arm and seemed to stretch his torso.

"Are you all right?" Saxton asked.

"Just fine."

"Then why are you looking as if you're in pain."

"It doesn't matter."

"It does to me."

Ruhn opened his mouth. Closed it. Opened it again.

Saxton shook his head sadly. Abruptly, he was tired, horny, and totally confused by the male—oh, and he was truly pissed off at the human race and its meddling ways. So, indeed, he was done with being socially appropriate and polite.

"Look," he muttered, "whatever it is, just say it. We're working together, right? And I don't want you involved in all this if you're compromised."

There was a long silence. And then Ruhn re-crossed his arms over his chest with mostly no grimace. "I've always known you didn't approve of me."

Saxton recoiled. "I beg your pardon?"

"I don't see what the problem is."

As Novo spoke, she tried to look as strong and powerful as she could. Okay, fine, so she was still in her hospital bed with wires and tubing in places she would really prefer to be wire-less and tube-lacking, and she was, in fact, wearing a johnny that had little pink bouquets of flowers all over it, but damn it, she was perfectly fine.

And she had every right to—

"You're not leaving this facility." Dr. Manello stood over her and smiled like he held all the cards. "I'm sorry."

To keep from throat-punching the human, she looked down at herself . . . and blamed those frickin' rosebuds that were all over her johnny. Why couldn't the hospital gowns have prints of, like, Deadpool's mask. Knives. Bombs with the wicks lit. Vials of poison.

"No, you're not sorry," she bitched.

"You're right, I don't give a shit that you're pissed off at me. What I care about is your heart. Now, I'll spare you the be-a-good-little-girl speech, because I don't want to get castrated—but do me a favor and don't screw up all my nice knit-one-purl-two and stay where you are, 'kay."

"I feel fine."

"You passed out going to the bathroom."

"I got dizzy, that was all."

"I found you on the floor, in a heap."

"I had my IV still in."

"But not your catheter, which you had taken out yourself." He put his palm up to stop her from arguing. "Tell you what, I'll award you the Patient of the Night trophy for all your efforts. Congratulations, your prize is a jelly donut and a whole lot of going-absolutely-nowhere."

Novo grunted and tried to link her arms over her chest—when that caused an arrhythmia that made some alarm go off, she had to let them sulk back down to either side of her body.

"I'm fine."

"No, you will *be* fine." Dr. Manello went around and reset whatever monitor had started talking. "In another night or two. Provided you stay put."

"FYI, I'm giving this establishment a really crappy Yelp review."

"I would be honored." The doctor put his hand on his heart and bowed. "Thank you—oh, and your mother called."

Novo went to sit up and hissed before collapsing back. "My mother?"

"Yeah, she'd been trying to reach you? She was afraid you were dead. Needless to say, I told her you were breathing. Didn't mention that I knew that because of an oxygen sensor clipped to your finger, but at least I was confident that I was giving her accurate information."

Novo tried to look like she didn't care. But that fucking alarm, the one connected to her fucking heart, started going off again.

"What did she say? I mean, what did you tell her?" She shut her lids. "Not that I got hurt, right?"

"I'm not authorized to report on the condition of my patients." He leaned over to whatever was beep-beep-beep'ing and silenced things again. "I informed her you were in class for the rest of the night. But you may want to call her when you feel up to it."

How's never, on that one? "Can you give me a doctor's note that says I don't have to."

"Will you promise to stay in bed?"

"Sure, but I'm pretty certain that's something I'll break."

"Fair enough. Quick question. If you don't want to hop on the horn with your family's version of Carol Brady, I'm not sure her getting a note from your surgeon is going to de-escalate whatever is going on, am I right?"

"Look, Doc, if you're going to continue to be logical and reasonable, I'm going to have to ask you to reassign my case to a crazy person."

"Right, 'cuz why be difficult when you can be perfectly unreasonable."

"Exactly."

Dr. Manello smiled and then headed for the door. Before he opened the way out, he hesitated. "Is everything okay in your family?" He held up his palm again. "You don't have to go into specifics if you don't want to. It's just . . . she was worked up, and it's very clear you're avoiding her."

"My mother is always worked up about something—and usually it's my sister. Who's getting mated. As her bridesmaid—oh, sorry, I guess I'm the honor maid, or something?—I'm supposed to be planning things, not doing my job to protect the species. Yeah, 'cuz really, picking out dresses and organizing a goddamn bachelorette night out is more important than fighting *lessers.*"

"I didn't know vampires did that kind of shit. Bridal showers and stuff."

"We don't. My sister needs all the attention in the world, however, so one species' traditions are not enough for her. She needs two."

"What a charmer." Her surgeon smiled even more, his handsome face crinkling at the eyes and around his mouth. "And may I just say, in a totally non-creepy way, that you are going to look fantastic in bows and ribbons. Especially if they are the color of bubble gum."

Novo closed her eyes with a groan. "Can you just knock me out?"

"Nah, I'm afraid if I hit you in the face, the rest of your classmates will beat my ass."

"I was talking drugs."

"Ah, where's the fun in that." The man got serious. "You rest up. If you're stable by the time the night's over, I'll consider letting you go home, 'kay?" As Novo flipped her lids back open, he glared at her. "But you have to feed. I don't care who from, and that is mandatory."

After the doctor left, Novo thought about the bride-ette night, or whatever you call it, and decided she should take all those females to The Keys.

Yup, surprise! It's a sex club! Now get your nipple clips on there, young ladies, and go find yourself a glory hole.

As she pictured her sister trying to make it through just the wait line, she had to laugh—and the sharp-shooter that came in response made her worry that she had sprung herself a leak.

No alarms, though. Just the regular beeping that seemed to suggest some kind of circulation was happening on a regular basis—

All at once, she was back in that empty cold house, on the bathroom floor, bleeding from between her legs. Pain, different than now, was deep in her belly, twisting her like a rag until she thought she would snap in two.

No medical help then. No nice doctor with a sharp wit and kind eyes, no medical equipment, no drugs. No clear understanding of what was happening to her until something had come out of her.

Her young. Not alive, although perfectly formed.

There had been so much blood. She had been sure she was going to die.

Fate had had other plans for her. In fact, she had lived. It turned

out that just because you wanted to gain entrance unto the Fade didn't
mean you were granted what you prayed for. No, she had survived, but
she had never been whole again.

Wait . . . that was wrong. She hadn't been whole even before the
miscarriage had happened, and afterward? How could she not blame
herself for the loss. Her body had failed her young, had let that innocent being down—

No, not her body. Her mind, her character. She had been so dis-
traught over Oskar leaving her for Sophy that her emotional meltdown
had caused the miscarriage: She had not been strong enough for her
young, hard enough, tough enough. *She* had failed.

"Stop it," she snapped. "Just . . . fucking *stop*."

To get her mind off the past, she focused on getting herself the hell
out of the clinic. Feeding, she thought. She needed to get the feeding
thing arranged.

With a grunt—that suggested the doc had a point about the whole
not-yet thing—she reached out to the rolling table closest to her. Batting away the can of ginger ale, the rose-colored plastic bedpan, the
Kleenex box, and the remote to the TV she had yet to turn on, she finally grabbed her phone.

Her ringer had been off when she'd been in the field, and what a
good choice someone had made in not turning that back on. As she
triggered the screen, there was a raft of texts. A lot were from her fellow
trainees . . . there was one from John Matthew . . . and a couple from
the Brothers. Also one from Rhage looking to see when she would be
well enough to give a statement about what had happened in the alley.

And then about . . . oh, seven hundred and fifty from her sister.

As well as some voicemails from the female. And their *mahmen*.

Novo closed her eyes as she felt like screaming. Then she refocused.
Feeding. She needed to feed.

And on that subject, now would be a great time to make good

choices, she told herself. She needed to hit up Craeg, Axe, or Boone and ask one of them if they could help her out.

Yup. She was just going to text one of those guys, and she knew they would come as soon as they could arrange transportation. And then she would be one more step closer to having this all behind her—and a step further away from complications she could do without.

Read: Peyton and his blue-blooded vintage.

Yup, she was going to hit up Craeg . . .

Or Axe . . .

Or . . . Boone.

They were going to do just fine, she told herself as she signed into her phone. Just fine and dandy.

SIXTEEN

fter Ruhn spoke up, he fell silent and really wished that he hadn't said anything. Actually, wait, what he would have preferred was not to have come here at all. Because if the latter had been true, then the former never would have been a problem.

I've always known you didn't approve of me.

Had he really said that? "Never mind, it is hardly relevant—"

"What gave you the idea I disapproved of you?"

"I should not have brought this up."

"No, I'm glad you did." Saxton shook his head. "We need to talk this out. I'm trying to see how I could ever have given you that impression."

For a moment, Ruhn got too busy falling into those gray eyes, those big, beautiful pearl-gray eyes. He loved the way they looked up at him, the thick lashes framing that stare, the brows arching perfectly, the head tilted in polite inquiry . . .

The mouth ever so slightly parted as if the male were still surprised.

"Whyever would you think that?" Saxton prompted.

"I cannot read."

"And that matters how? Reading is a measure of something that can be taught, not intelligence, and certainly not worthiness. Ruhn, you gave up Bitty to parents who loved her for her own good. You let your bloodline go for her benefit and others. How could I not appreciate a male who could make such a selfless, loving act?"

"I couldn't sign the documents."

"You gave your mark . . . beautifully." Saxton's voice grew forceful. "Worry not ever, Ruhn, over my opinion. I could not respect you more. In fact, I have always been"—those eyes shifted away—"struck by you."

An unfamiliar blooming sensation warmed Ruhn's chest, relieving the pain there—and at the same time, the walls of the elegant penthouse seemed to shrink into them both, drawing them closer together even though neither of them moved.

Ruhn's heart began to beat harder, and he coughed a little.

"Have I made you feel uncomfortable?" Saxton linked his arms. "I apologize. I assure you, I offer this only in the spirit of friendship."

"Of course."

"Regardless of my orientation."

"Orientation?"

"I am gay." As Ruhn recoiled, Saxton's face tightened and his voice lowered. "Is that going to be a problem for you?"

More like a solution, Ruhn thought—before he caught himself.

Coughing again, he said, "No. No, it will not."

"Are you certain about that?"

When Ruhn didn't reply, Saxton looked away. "Well. In any event, thank you for updating me about Miniahna and I'll take it from here. Your services are no longer required—"

"I'm sorry?"

"You heard me—"

"Wait, are you firing me?"

"Just so you and I are clear, I have been beaten for being what I am." Saxton went over and opened the sliding door. "I have been dis-

owned by my bloodline because my sire regards me as an embarrassment and a disgrace now that my *mahmen* is gone. So I can assure you,
I've survived far worse alienation than your disapproval, and I will not
apologize for something about myself that I am not ashamed of—
simply because it makes you or anyone else uncomfortable."

Ruhn took a deep breath.

After what felt like an hour, he walked over to the open door and
the male standing stiffly and with dignity by the way out. As freezing
air swirled into the penthouse, it ruffled through Ruhn's hair and he
wondered what it would be like to have Saxton's fingers do that.

"Forgive me," Ruhn said quietly. "I mean no offense. I honestly do
not. I have . . . trouble expressing myself, especially around people like
you."

"Gays. You can say the word, you know. And it's not like you can
catch homosexuality like a cold."

"I know."

"Do you." Saxton tugged at his cuffs, and as he did, there was a flash
of red rubies. "I'm not sure that is true, and incidentally, a sexual preference should not be threatening. I'm not going to jump you or anything. People are as principled or unprincipled as they are. Whom I
choose to sleep with does not affect my ability to recognize boundaries
any more than a heterosexual male would not aggress on every female
he comes across."

"It's not that."

"So you believe I am morally wrong. Ah, right. It's that, then."

"No—"

Saxton put his hand out. "Actually, I'm disinclined to argue with
you. Your reasons are your own. It's cold and I would like to shut this
door. Thank you."

Later, Ruhn would wonder where the courage came from. Where
the honesty did. The answer to that, when it occurred to him, was both
simple and profound: Love had wings that demanded flight.

"I am attracted to you and I don't know what to do about it."

Saxton's eyes grew wide, his shock altering everything about him.

"I mean no offense." Ruhn bowed low. "I do not expect you to be complimented by that, nor do you have to worry I will embarrass you. I just did not expect to find a male attractive, and . . ." He looked away. "The only reason I tell you this is because I cannot abide you thinking that I would shame you or anybody else in that manner. So I'm sorry."

There was a tense moment of silence.

And then Saxton reached out . . . and slowly slid the door back into place.

The downstairs male guest bathroom in Peyton's family's mansion was a small but dramatic space tucked in under the grand formal stairs. The floors, walls, and ceiling of the asymmetrical, slant-roof'd room were tiled with slabs of golden agate, and the fixtures and sink were gold. Brass sconces on either side of a gold-leafed mirror threw orangey illumination that had always reminded him of the end of a lit cigar, and the needlepoint rug underfoot had the family's crest woven into it.

There was no bladder imperative to have come here. He'd just needed a break from all the shoot-me-now polite conversation in the dining room, and to waste some time, he took out his phone to see if someone, anyone, had texted or emailed him.

It was the first time he had ever prayed for spam. He didn't give a shit whether it was Viagra from overseas, or a webcam scam telling him to text SUCKME to some number . . . or the president of Nigeria needing to hide money: He was in. Anything but going back out to that table, where his father and Salone were trying to one-up each other on who they knew, the *mahmen* was getting drunk and leering across the table at him, and that Emily Dickinson waif was pushing her food around without eating anything.

"I've quit better jobs than this," he muttered as he checked the phone's screen.

On that Annie Potts note, maybe he should just put the OG *Ghost-busters* on and watch from under his napkin—

Four texts. Three of which were from the club set. And one that made his heart pound like he'd been hooked up to a car battery.

As he went to type in a response to that last one, he stopped halfway through—and called instead.

One ring. Two rings . . .

Three.

Shit, it was going to go to voicemail. Did he hang up or—

"So is this a yes?" Novo said in a husky voice.

Instant erection. The kind of thing that tested the tensile strength of his tux's zipper and suggested there was no way he was leaving the loo without giving himself a hand job.

"Yes," he answered. "It is."

"When can you come here?"

Now! Fucking right now! his cock said. *You get that on that bus and you go to her right now!*

Listen, little Pey-pey, you need to chill—

"Excuse me?"

Peyton shut his eyes and leaned into the agate countertop. "Ah, yeah, sorry—"

"Little Pey-pey? I didn't know you had a younger brother."

It was more like living with a frat boy who never lifted a finger until he had a bright idea that could burn the house down.

"It's . . . nothing." Actually it was more like eight inches. Hard. "And I've got a . . . I'm stuck in a family thing, but it's just a meal. As soon as it's done, I'm coming in."

"How long? They said I had to feed before I can leave."

"Not long. An hour. The cheese and fruit course is about to be served, and after that, there will be sorbet." Thank God it wasn't Last

Meal or there'd be another two hours ahead of them. "I'll arrange for transport and tell my father I have to go."

"So dependable you are."

"When properly motivated."

"And altruistic, too. Or do you still feel like you owe me?"

Peyton looked at himself in that mirror over the gold sink. His eyes were rapt and hungry, a high color of arousal on his cheeks. In the golden glow, he was all tiger in a gilded cage.

"You don't want me to answer that," he heard himself say in a guttural voice.

"Don't do me any favors."

"Fine. I want you to take from me. I want your mouth on me anywhere I can get it. And I know better than to think you'll let me fuck you, but just so we're clear, the entire time, I'll be back between your legs in my mind. That honest enough for you? Still want me to come . . . to you?"

He deliberately double-entendre'd that last one because he was a prick. And he wanted her so badly he was losing his frickin' mind.

When Novo didn't say anything, he let his head drop and decided to kick his own ass. Way to be supportive—

"Yes," she said roughly. "I still want you to come."

Holy thundering blood pressure, Batman.

"This time . . ." He bared his descending fangs, his upper lip twitching. "I want your fangs in me, I want the pain and the rush. And I want you at my throat."

"Anything else?"

Okay, those two words, in that erotic drawl, were sexier than all the actual sex he'd had for the last year.

"Let me inside of you, Novo. You don't have to explain anything or repeat it, but I just need to know what it's like to finish in you."

"You're admitting weakness."

"I'm telling the truth."

"Why start now."

He shook his head. "When have I lied to you?"

There was a pause. "When it comes to Paradise, you've been lying to yourself."

Oh, no, he thought. That's a wrong turn off a road he wanted to stay on, heading into a set of brambles he could totally do without.

"I'm not in love with her."

"You're just proving my point about the lying. Remember last night in that alley? Don't pretend you weren't being a bonded male with her, putting yourself and everyone else's best interests aside to protect what you think of as your female."

"Why are we talking about this?"

"I really don't know."

There was a beat of silence, and before she could change her mind, he jumped into the quiet. "I'll be there as soon as I can. I just need to get through this dinner with my father. If I could leave, I would, but with him, everything is a goddamn problem."

A soft laugh came over the connection. "That exasperated tone in your voice is probably the only thing we will ever have in common."

"Family problems, too?"

"You have no idea."

"Tell me."

There was a long pause. "I thought you were having dinner with your sire. Why are you on this phone with me?"

"I'm hiding in the bathroom. You're giving me an excuse to stay a little longer."

This time, when Novo laughed, it was shockingly natural—and he realized he'd never heard her like that before.

Lifting his hand, he found himself rubbing away an unexpected ache in his chest.

"Come on," he said. "Spill. It'll be your humanitarian gesture for the night. Keep me in here some more."

The exhale was long and slow. "Come when you can. No hurries. Bye."

As the connection was cut, Peyton refocused on his face in the mirror. Even though he knew the address of the house he was in, the zip code and the street and the number . . . in spite of the fact that he had been in most every room in the mansion, for all of his life . . . he was utterly lost.

And he had been for years.

Closing his eyes, he pictured Paradise, with her blond hair and her lovely face and her quick smile. He remembered her laugh coming over the phone, her sorrow and her pain, too. He heard her voice and her accent, her consonants and her vowels.

All those phone calls, all that time, day in and day out, while the raids forced them to stay indoors in their safe houses away from Caldwell.

What he had fallen in love with was her constancy. Her reliability. Her always-there, and her kindness . . . and even more than all that, the fact that she had never, ever judged him. He had told her things that had made him feel pathetic and things that had frightened him. He had talked about nightmares and the demons in his own mind. He had related his father's hatred of him, and his *mahmen's* absentee dismissal, his drugs and his drinking, his females and his women.

And still, she had stood by him. As if none of that ugliness made her think less of him.

Talk about family issues. He'd never had that support from his bloodline or the *glymera*. He had kept his secrets to himself, not because they were particularly unusual or shocking or perverse, but because there had been no one to trust his underbelly with. No one to care. No one to accept him as he was and forgive him for not being perfect.

That was why he had loved her.

But that was less about her, wasn't it.

And more about what he'd needed.

Paradise had been, for a time, the paint on his canvas, the compass in his pocket, the light switch he could flip on when he needed illumination in the scary dark. Her good nature had offered him those salvations, although similarly that was not about him; she would have done that for anybody, because that was the way she was.

He had never been sexually obsessed with her.

She had never been like Novo to him. Novo was a bonfire he wanted to jump into. Wearing a suit of firecrackers and carrying a gas tank on his back.

No, he had stared at Paradise because he had mourned the loss of that tight connection, its absence thrusting him back into this world of gilded frames and plastic smiles and no grounding whatsoever.

Sometimes gratitude could be mistaken for love. Both were warm feelings that endured. But the former was about friendship . . . the latter was something else entirely.

And for some reason, he felt a driving need to explain this all to Novo.

Turning away, he reached for the door. He was going to leave the second he could—

Peyton jumped back. "Whoa!"

"Forgive me," Romina said softly.

The young female was pale and shaky as she stood before him, and she checked over her shoulder with the paranoia of a field mouse in a cat's path.

"I must speak with you alone." Her eyes clung to his. "There is little time."

SEVENTEEN

As Saxton slid the door back into place, the resistance of the panel meeting its jamb was the kind of thing that dimly resonated through his hand and up his arm.

Oh, you beautiful male, he thought as he noted Ruhn's blush and lowered eyes. For all the power in that body, there was a vulnerability that made one want to offer the male a safe haven. Then again, Saxton had always had a soft spot for strays.

"Forgive me," Ruhn mumbled.

"For what?" Saxton inhaled and held more of that delicious scent in his lungs. "Why do you apologize?"

"I do not know."

"It is no imposition that you are attracted to me. At all. Look at me. Come now . . . raise your eyes."

It was forever before that glowing stare lifted to meet his own.

"I don't know what to do," Ruhn whispered. Except then the male focused on Saxton's mouth.

Oh, yes, you do, he thought. *You know perfectly well what to do.*

But it wasn't in the male's nature to take charge. Fortunately, Saxton had a remedy for that one.

"Do you want me to kiss you," he prompted softly. "Just so you know what's it's like. Just so that you don't have to wonder."

None of it was in question. The answers were in the sexual charge that leapt to life between them, a wall of fire that promised to melt their bodies . . . and maybe their souls.

Except then Ruhn glanced outside.

Saxton sighed. "No one will know. I promise."

It was sad to have to reassure the male of that, as if this were dirty business, the kind of thing that made others change their opinions about you and made you feel lesser about yourself—but there was no reason to be naive. Most civilians, like Ruhn, had a much more conservative view of these things than aristocrats did. In the *glymera,* there was a look-the-other-way sort of tolerance, provided you were willing to get properly mated to a female, produce an heir and a spare over time, and never, ever come out of the closet.

None of which Saxton had been prepared to do in service to his sire and his bloodline. Which was one of the reasons why he and his father were estranged.

Along that whole privacy note, he leaned to the side and triggered the interior drapes, the great swaths of blackout fabric swinging into place, shutting out the world, creating a vault of privacy.

"No one will know," he said in spite of the disappointment in his chest.

In response, Ruhn reached out a trembling, workman's hand . . . only to stop just short of touching Saxton's mouth.

"Is that what you want," Saxton breathed.

Ruhn lowered his arm. "Yes."

Saxton stepped in close, but not too close, keeping a distance between their pecs. Then he took Ruhn's face in his palms.

The male's entire body shook, all those muscles and heavy bones poised to jump—but whether it was to him or away from him, he did not know.

"I won't hurt you," Saxton vowed. "I promise."

And then he drew the taller male down slowly, the subtle pressure something that Ruhn gave readily into.

Tilting his head to the side, Saxton pressed his lips to Ruhn's—and the gasp that came out of the other male was that of a lover surprised. Saxton felt the shock, too, and he would have said something.

But he didn't want to stop to speak.

Gently, softly . . . he brushed over that mouth again and again. At first, there was no response, the lips against his own frozen. But then they parted, and stroked back, with a sweet hesitation.

Saxton's body roared, his erection straining to get out and be stroked, and sucked. And in return, he wanted to learn every square inch of the male *rightfuckingnow.* Patience was a virtue more likely to be rewarded than fumbling greed, however.

Saxton inched back and searched Ruhn's face. "How was that?"

"More," came the moaned response.

A purring sound left Saxton as he brought himself against Ruhn's body. Wrapping an arm way up over those big shoulders, he urged that sweet mouth back to his own as he slid his other arm around a waist that was tight and smooth as polished stone.

The shaking in Ruhn's torso was erotic as fuck. What was even better? At those hips, an erection in total proportion to that tremendous body was a hard ridge, ready to be set free. Saxton knew not to rush things, though—because he didn't want to seduce the male against Ruhn's hesitations. Rather, he wanted the male to come along willingly on what was surely going to be an incredible sexual ride—

As Saxton's phone started to ring in the kitchen, they both jumped.

"Shouldn't you get that?" Ruhn asked in a husky voice.

Perhaps, yes, Saxton thought. But only to flush the goddamn thing down the toilet—or maybe hit it with a hammer. Except . . .

"It may be the King." Saxton eased back. "Wait for a moment."

With quick feet, he rushed to the black granite counter where he'd left his cell by the coffeepot. "Hello—oh, yes, but of course, my Lord. Tell me? Uh-huh. Yes. Right . . ."

Saxton closed his eyes. He could not be rude or shirk his duties, but he needed to get Wrath off the phone so he could pick up where he'd left things—and hopefully take the kissing further.

"Yes, my Lord. I will prepare the appropriate documentation and will serve it to the other party tomorrow evening—when? Now?" Saxton mouthed a word silently that was not appropriate. "Yes, I will come to the Audience House now and bring—what? Yes, that, too. Thank you, my Lord. My pleasure."

As he hung up, he thought, actually, his pleasure was standing right over—

"Goddamn it," he muttered as he turned back around.

Ruhn had disappeared through the sliding glass door, leaving nothing but the subtle undulations of those drapes in his wake, the cold evening air ruffling the fabric as it blew away the lingering scent of sexual awakening.

There was an instinct to follow, but he let it go. Ruhn had made his choice, at least for now.

No telling if he would come back.

Saxton touched his mouth. "But I hope you do," he whispered into the vacant penthouse.

The bus trundled into the training center at a pace that seemed only slightly slower than that of water evaporating from a glass. In a refrigerator. Over the span of a hundred and fifty motherfucking years.

As Peyton sat on the left-hand side of the aisle, right up against the window, he focused on the black glass while trying to ignore his own reflection. There was no one else riding with him, and he couldn't decide whether that was good or bad. A distraction might have been nice . . . but then again, chatter in his ear would have irritated the hell out of him—and no, thanks, on having to respond to anything or anyone.

Relief came when the vehicle slowed to a stop. And resumed. And then a little farther on . . . decelerated again.

Finally, they were getting to the sequence of gates. Like all the other trainees, he'd never seen what they looked like, and he couldn't have told even the Scribe Virgin herself how to get onto the road that led into the training center. But he was well-familiar with this stop-and-go as they entered the Brotherhood's property and descended underground to the facility.

I must speak with you alone. There is little time.

The image of Romina standing outside of that bathroom, her blue dress gathered in her hands, her eyes wide, her pale face drawn in haunted, hunted lines, made him shake his head and rub the bridge of his nose.

Romina needed a friend, badly. She also needed Peyton.

I'm afraid you're being sold a bad bill of goods. Declare tonight that I am not to your approval, and then you will be spared.

When he had demanded to know what the hell she was talking about, she had told him a terrible story, one so horrible, he couldn't bear thinking about it.

And in the end, she had not lied. She was indeed spoiled in the eyes of the *glymera*—and not as in privileged and pampered. According to all standards, Romina was ineligible for mating, although not by her own fault—assuming she was telling the truth, and really, considering what had happened to her? Why would you admit that to a stranger otherwise?

He admired her honesty. And he felt broken, too, unmateable for a lot of reasons, so they shared that.

I know that you will do the right thing for yourself. I just didn't want anyone else hurt.

With that, she had returned to the table. And he had tried to follow in her footsteps—only to fail at the finish line. Instead of going back into the dining room, he'd kept right on going out the front door. His father had yelled after him, but nope, Peyton was done. He'd dematerialized to the pickup location, texted his arrival, and waited twenty-five minutes in the cold without a winter jacket for the bus to arrive.

By the time he'd gotten on the transport, his fingers had frozen into claws in his pockets and his jaw had locked down on his clapping molars. The warm-up of all his corporeal merchandise had been an exercise in burning pain, but he'd barely noticed.

It was a sad commentary on where he and Romina came from that both of them were nothing but pawns in a social chess game to their families.

God, that poor female.

And he had no idea what he was going to do about it.

What was clear? His absence during that cheese and fruit course had been duly noted. His phone had rung three times, and his father had left him voice messages. Peyton didn't listen to them. Why bother? He knew what they said; he could dub the words and the tone in just fine—

"We have arrived, sire."

Peyton jumped in his seat. Fritz, the loyal *doggen* butler who served as the bus driver most nights, was both concerned and smiling, his wrinkled face peeled back like a set of curtains in a friendly house.

"Sire? Are you all right? May I get you anything?"

"Sorry." Peyton rose to his feet. "Sorry—I'm fine. Thank you."

Bullshit, he was fine. Matter of fact, he was so far from fine, he couldn't see goddamn Fine-landia from where he was.

As he got off the bus, the butler escorted him over to the reinforced steel door, their footfalls echoing throughout the multi-layered concrete parking area. And then they were inside, proceeding down the long, wide corridor. When Peyton stopped in front of the closed door to Novo's hospital room, Fritz bowed low and kept on going to his next duty.

Before Peyton knocked, he brushed his hair back with his fingers. Made sure his cuffs were down. Checked his—

"You can come in."

At the dry sound of Novo's voice, Peyton straightened his spine and pushed into the hospital room.

Okay . . . wow.

She looked so much better. She was sitting up, a couple of the monitors were gone, and there was a tray with the remnants of food on it: fresh Danish, a half-eaten bowl of fruit, toast points, and a little pot of strawberry jam. She'd obviously eaten the scrambled eggs.

Hospital food here was not "hospital" at all.

"So formal," she murmured. "You didn't have to dress for the occasion."

He glanced down at himself. "I'm wearing my tux."

"You sound surprised. What did you think you had on?"

When he looked back at her, Novo sat up a little higher on the stack of pillows that was holding her to the vertical—and the grunt and grimace she tried to hide told him that much as she might appear stronger, she wasn't going home at the end of the night.

Feeding or no feeding.

"You okay?" she asked.

He considered tossing a jocular fish back, but then thought about Romina. "No, I'm really not."

"Unrequited love got you down? You want me to get you a card or something. Teddy bear to cuddle. No, wait . . . chocolate and a glass of wine?"

Peyton ignored all that and went over to the far corner, his legs going loose right on schedule so that he fell into the chair there. Putting his head in his hands, he just stared at the floor. He wanted Novo like all get-out. But he couldn't get his head away from what he'd been told by that other female. Where he was with his own family. How bad things could get when you had money, but nothing else, to back you up in the world.

"Jesus," Novo murmured, "you look like you're having a nervous breakdown."

"Tell me about your family," he heard himself say. "What are they like? What do they do that hurts you?"

Novo looked away. "We don't need to go into that."

As disappointment surged, he told himself he shouldn't try to re-create that friendship he'd had with Paradise with anybody else. That had been a time-limited period in his life, something that had passed now that she had moved on and he was still where he had always been.

God, he wanted a smoke.

Patting the inside pocket of his jacket, he felt around—oh, thank you, motherfucker, he thought as he discovered a couple of old joints in there.

He took one out and snagged the gold lighter he kept in his slacks.

"You can't smoke in here."

Peyton glanced across to the hospital bed. "Do you not like the smell?"

"I don't care. But there's an oxygen tank over there, and I'm pretty sure the docs won't appreciate it even if you don't blow us sky high."

With a groan, he got up and went to the metal cylinder. There was a valve on the top and he thought, Rightie-tightie. The Brothers had taught him that. And yup, the thing was closed.

He flicked the lighter open on the way back to the chair and had his first draw as he sat down. Holding the hissing inhale deep, he waited impatiently for the buzz to come and froth up his frontal lobe until the piece of shit took a chill.

"Please," he said on the exhale. "Just . . . tell me something, anything. I need to talk."

EIGHTEEN

aybe it was the drugs, Novo thought. Maybe it was the reminder the night before that she was mortal. Maybe it was all the text messages and voicemails that had come in about her sister from her mother, her sister, her sister's friends. Maybe it was the fact that Peyton wasn't looking like his regular, James Spader circa *Pretty in Pink* self.

But something made her open her mouth.

"My sister is not like me," she blurted into the silence. "At all."

"So she's dumb?" Peyton exhaled more smoke and loosened his black bow tie. "Ugly? Uncoordinated? Wait, she throws a baseball like a—"

"Stop." She shook her head at him. "I can't be real with you if you're going to do the Peyton dog-and-pony show."

He put the joint between his teeth and shrugged out of his tuxedo jacket. Then he unbuttoned the top quarter of his dress shirt. As he resettled, he exhaled again and spoke through the smoke.

"I'm serious about all of that. I think you're smart, beautiful, and a great fighter."

There was no twinkle in his eye. No lift to his lips. No *har-har-har* in his tone. And then he just stared at her as if he were daring her to refute his opinion.

Well, crap, she thought. He was dangerous like this . . . all sexy as he sprawled in that chair, his arms draped over the sides, his legs now crossed at the knee. In that pose, with that loose bow tie and the V of golden skin at his throat, he looked like he could please a female any way he liked—and the impression was probably correct.

He sure had the anatomy for it. She knew that firsthand.

But more than all that physical stuff? He was focused on her as if what she might tell him, whatever it was, was the only thing that he cared to hear in all the world. He seemed to really see her, no distractions, no side glances somewhere else, no tapping feet or drumming fingers.

To a female who had always been second fiddle to a loud, pink, gardenia-smelling lace-and-bows nightmare? It was just as addicting as the taste of his blood.

How far did she go, though.

She had told no one, not even the Brotherhood during her psych eval, what had happened to her. The first was true because she hated pity. The second? Well, duh, she didn't want to get kicked out of the program for being mentally unstable.

Which she was not.

But they might think she had reason to be.

"So tell me about your family problems," he prompted.

"It's nothing, really," she muttered. "Sibling stuff, you know."

As her hand moved over to rest on her stomach, she caught herself even though he couldn't possibly guess at why she would feel protective.

"Come on." He took another inhale. "You have to do better than that."

As if on cue, her phone rang on the table that she'd pulled over her knees. Tilting the cell up, she cursed when she saw who it was.

"And here it is." She rolled her eyes. "My sister, again. She's getting mated, and she picked me to be her little bitch through the whole thing. I am soooo touched, you can't imagine."

"When is the ceremony?"

"Wedding," she corrected. "And very soon."

"What about you being injured."

She shook her head as the phone went silent. But it didn't stay quiet for long. The text that binged was from Sophy as well.

Novo read it out loud because why the hell not. *"Fine. I guess I will have to take care of my bachelorette party. Miss Emily's doesn't have a reservation for us on Friday. Clearly, you never called them. Thanks so much for all your help."*

Letting the cell fall back down onto the tray, she took a deep breath—and could swear she was catching a contact high from the weed.

"You're in a hospital bed," Peyton said.

"Really?" She looked down at herself. "And here I thought this was a hot tub."

"Be serious."

"This coming from you?"

He slashed his hand through the air. "You're recovering. Why are they bothering you with anything?"

She made a show of folding the top of the blanket down and smoothing it across her chest. "Well, to be fair, they didn't know I got hurt."

When there was just silence, she glanced over at him. And as if he had been waiting for the eye contact, he shook his head.

"That's just like I am with my father. I don't tell the male anything, either." He frowned. "What would they have done if you'd . . ."

"Died out there? Or on the table?" She shrugged. "Probably just put our first cousin in as the head bridesmaid and moved right along."

"Wait, bridesmaid? What the hell?"

"Oh, yeah. She's adopting the full human routine and expecting my parents to pay for it, me to go along with it, and all her friends to put it out on Insta. I think she believes she will set a trend, and who knows. Maybe she will."

"Who's she mating?"

Novo cleared her throat. "No one special. Just another civilian—well, he comes from a little more money than we have, so it's a step up for her. And listen, my issues aside, Sophy is beautiful, so it's a good exchange on the mating market. I'm sure they'll be very happy together, him buying her the things she wants, her giving him the young he . . ."

Novo couldn't go on.

It was as if she had been heading down a road, toolin' along, moving at a reasonable pace while not paying much attention to the landscape or the weather conditions. And then BAM! Black ice, skidding, gripping the wheel . . . and slamming headfirst into a rock face.

"So yeah." She took a couple of deep breaths. "You know, that weed is strong."

"It is."

"Only the best for you, huh."

"Something like that." He looked at the joint's glowing tip. "Is she going to put you in a bad dress?"

"I'm sorry? Oh, Sophy—you mean at the ceremony? If she doesn't kick me out first."

"When is the mating—or is she calling it a wedding?"

"Let's just call it circus, between you and me." As he smiled a little, she said, "Why the grin."

His eyes bored into hers. "I like the idea of you and me having a secret."

And then he got serious. Fast.

Rising to his feet, Peyton headed for the bathroom to put the joint out—and along the way, he did absolutely nothing to camouflage the erection he was sporting.

It was so thick, so hard, she could see the outline of the head under the tuxedo's slacks.

As a rush of lust hit Novo, she had to close her eyes. Also had to lick her lips—which made her glad he was in the little bathroom.

From behind the partially closed door, there was a trickle of water, and she imagined him bent over the sink, extinguishing the joint. Then he was standing in between the jambs, his handsome face grave.

With his eyes locked on hers, he tucked one of his hands down into the front of his pants and he not-discreetly-at-all rearranged himself so that the tent effect was gone.

After which he just continued to look at her.

She knew exactly what he was waiting for. And the interesting thing was . . . she got the sense he was content to stay like that for the next hour. Or twelve.

It was another thing that was totally unlike him.

"Come here," she said in a low voice.

Peyton did exactly as he was told, approaching the bedside so that he stood over her. His scent was incredible, and for once, the smell of weed, which usually she wasn't that into, didn't bother her in the slightest.

With an elegant hand, he rolled up one of his sleeves. And then the other. His forearms were heavily muscled and veined from the workouts, his body adapting to the rigorous exercise by growing stronger.

She focused on his throat.

As if he knew what she was looking at, he let out a pumping growl. "Let me lie down beside you."

If he did that, they were probably going to have sex, she thought.

Take out the "probably"—

The door was thrown open, and, man, Dr. Manello was not a happy camper, the surgeon's face in full glower mode.

He jabbed a finger at Peyton. "That shit in the alley might not get you tossed from the program, but I will guarantee you that smoking weed in one of my patient rooms will." He looked around as if searching for a bong, a bowl, or a pipe. "And clearly, the two of you must have realized that and stopped, am I correct. You flushed the joint down the toilet because you thought, wow, in a room with an oxygen tank, around a patient on a complex regimen of drugs, using marijuana would be a *really fucking stupid idea*. Am I right?"

They both nodded.

"And am I also correct in assuming that this is a mistake that will never happen again, because you two fucking assholes recognize that at that point I would have no choice but to turn you in to the Brothers for a beating?" They nodded again. "Good. And your punishment"— he pointed that finger at Novo—"is you get to stay here all through tomorrow during the day."

The instant she opened her mouth, he talked right over her. "And thank God you're too smart to fucking argue with me right now, because my bad mood just went nuclear because of the smell in that corridor."

With that, the surgeon marched out and yanked the door shut behind himself.

Except then he put his head back in. "Do you have any left?"

Peyton's brows shot up. "I'm sorry, what?"

"Weed, you dumb-ass."

"Ah . . . yeah. It's old, though. I don't wear this tux more than four or five times a year and I found 'em in my pocket."

The surgeon put out his hand. "Gimme. And in lieu of payment, I'll put a sign on the door that says PATIENT SLEEPING, DO NOT DISTURB."

Novo spoke up. "We're not doing anything in here."

"Oh. Right. You're just going to hold hands while he feeds you. Which is why I'll put the sign up and you'll lock the door on the inside." He jogged his palm. "Why I am not holding any weed right now?"

Peyton took out the two remaining joints and handed them over. "You need a lighter?"

"Yes, I fucking do. And I'll give it back to you. Because I don't ever smoke. And especially not weed."

"Okaaaaaay, I'm going to go out on a limb here and suggest there's some empirical data happening at the moment to suggest the contrary, but that's your issue, not mine. I gotta ask, though, what's wrong? Can we help?"

"You don't have enough time to listen to it all. But at the top of the list is a drug company, halfway down is UPS, and the bottom is I ate a burrito at Taco Hell at about five in the afternoon when I was trying to get more Cipro on the black market—and I've been shitting liquid ever since."

Peyton's gold lighter changed hands. "You deserve this."

"No shit." Dr. Manello rolled his eyes. "And FYI, I hate that word right now, I really do."

The surgeon left on that note, and Peyton looked down at her.

It was hard to say who cracked up first. Maybe it was him, she wasn't sure. But a split second later, the two of them were wiping their eyes and trying to breathe and laughing so hard, they were limp.

And then they heard a rustle at the door.

Peyton went over and cracked the panel. "Nice work, Doc," he murmured as he shut them in again.

And then his hand hovered right above the lock's mechanism.

He could have turned the thing mentally. But he was obviously giving her a choice—and the control.

For some reason, she thought back to the very moment when that slayer had plunged her own dagger into her chest. "Surreal" did not begin to define what it had been like to know that she was going to die.

Funny . . . she hadn't thought of it until now.

She focused on Peyton. "I'm sorry."

As his eyes closed, he seemed resigned. "That's okay. I'll just let myself out—"

"For the way I acted in the PT suite. I was in . . . a really bad headspace and honestly, I was trying to get into the sex with you. My brain was all fucked up, though, and then I took that out on you. It was not fair. I apologize."

He blinked. "You are . . . always a surprise."

"Am I?"

"Yes."

She fiddled with her blanket again, re-smoothing it. "Things have not improved much. In my head. I mean, with everything that . . . you know, landed me here."

"I don't want to force myself on you."

"I wouldn't let you do that."

"I know. But I wanted to say that." There was a pause. "Novo?"

"Hm?"

"Look at me." He waited until she did. "I'll be slow, okay? I'll be . . . gentle. And if it's not right, I'll stop, no matter how far things have gone."

She shook her head. "Come on, Peyton. I'm as far away from being a virgin as you are. I don't need to be handled like some fainting flower—"

"You can trust me, Novo. I'm not going to hurt you. I promise."

For no good goddamn reason, her eyes teared up. No—that was wrong. She knew the why of it. She had been strong for herself for so long . . . that she had forgotten what it was like to have someone else shoulder any of her burden.

She never would have called herself lonely or identified herself as alone.

But Peyton's unbidden, unexpected, and totally unwarranted support of her—particularly around sex—made her feel the distance between her and everyone around her with an acute sensitivity.

"I'm not big into trust, Peyton," she said roughly. "It has never proven to be a value add in my life."

"That doesn't change what I said. Not one word."

"Why?" she whispered. "Why are you being like this?"

"The truth?"

"It fucking better be."

"I don't really know. That's the truth. All I am certain about . . . is that I don't want to ever see you hurt by anyone or anything ever again."

Don't believe him, she told herself. *Don't fall for one second of this bullshit. He wants to fuck you, and that's why he's saying it. You have been through the sweet-talking thing before, and remember where that got you?*

Pregnant and alone.

Miscarrying alone.

Alone for evermore.

And yet even as she forced herself to remember what had happened in that cold house a lifetime ago? Even as she told herself it was safer to think she was getting played?

She looked into Peyton's steady, grave eyes and found it hard not to take him at face value.

"I'll stop at any time. You say the word," he repeated softly.

A nervous panic vibrated through her, making her very bones feel unreliable. She had had a lot of sex since Oskar, since losing the young. Lots of her body parts meeting the body parts of others. But she had never really shared herself with anyone.

That was a bonus of not telling her story to a single soul. As long as the other person didn't know, she could pretend it hadn't happened for however long the hookup lasted.

Tonight, though—probably because it was a mere twenty-four hours after she had died a couple of times—the veil of time between the tragedy and who and where she was now seemed to have dwindled from over two years . . . down to a matter of minutes.

Everything that she kept separate was in danger of merging.

Peyton, however, seemed similarly vulnerable. And though she didn't know his details, that made it fair, did it not.

"Lock the door," she said.

NINETEEN

eyton kept his eyes on Novo's as he followed her instructions and flipped the lock into place. He was quite confident that the medical staff had a key to things. But with that sign on the door, and the fact that the training center was empty because Wrath had ordered everyone off rotation, privacy was a good bet.

Before he went over to her, he cut the lights so there was nothing but a glow coming from the little bathroom. In a way, he hated the dimness because the lower the illumination, the brighter the readouts on the monitors around the head of the hospital bed.

She still had two IVs in.

But she had been well enough for a shower, her damp hair once again braided, the end curling up tight. And she had eaten a little of that meal.

As he approached, she lowered the top half of the bed until it was all flat, and his heart beat faster as he realized he was actually going to lie down beside her.

"Let me just move . . ." She tried to rearrange the tubing that fed into her arm. "Damn it, this is ridiculous. Let's just take it out—"

"Yeah, not going to happen. Here, let me help you."

He ran the clear plastic lines up by the pillow so that they didn't get pinched. And then he put down the rail, and sat on the very edge of the mattress.

As he took her hand, her skin was softer than he'd imagined. A warrior like her? Her palm should have been spiked. Still, he could recognize the tensile strength in her and feel the calluses from weight bars and rowing and fighting.

When she pulled him down, he went more than willingly, stretching out on top of the blankets that covered her.

"So are you going to kiss me or what?" she demanded.

"Yes, I am."

He found her mouth and oh, fucking hell—his brain shorted out, all higher reasoning and rational thinking just packing their bags and leaving for someone else's skull. Her lips were delicious and her tongue was a thrust of aggression in his mouth and her scent made him feel higher than the weed. And holy shit did things move fast, especially south of his waistband. He wanted in her so badly, he was panting and out of control already.

The one thing he was careful of? He made sure not to put too much of his weight on her healing chest. Other than that, it was sensation only, his hips rolling into her thigh, her torso arching under him, her hands clawing into his back—

"Take off your shirt," she moaned.

"Yes, ma'am."

He eased off of her slowly and sat back on his heels. The buttons were stubborn, his fingers were sloppy, his breathing was too hard—but she didn't seem to care. Novo just stared up at him with ravenous eyes, her tongue tracing her upper lip, the tips of her descending fangs flashing white.

"I'm hungry," she growled.

"Take it all."

"Be careful. I might kill you."

"So let me die in your arms."

Peyton tossed his white shirt down on the floor, the loose bow tie going with it, and then he lay back down. As they tilted their bodies together, though, he got on some of her wires, and an awkward re-alignment had to happen—which was something he tried not to focus on. Should they even be hooking up like this?

Fuck yes, his cock announced. *Shut the hell up with that.*

Stop it—

"What?" she said.

"Nothing. Let me keep kissing you before I come in my pants."

"That's not a very threatening threat." Her lids lowered over her burning eyes. "Because that's what I want you to do."

As he hissed, she stroked over his pecs and went down onto his hard stomach. When she stopped at his waistband, he gritted his teeth. "Fuck—"

"That's the plan. Help me get these off."

At first, he wasn't sure he'd heard that right. But then she was tugging at his belt with her free hand—and hello, he was more than willing to be a Good Samaritan for this cause. With a rough series of tugs, he got the strip of smooth black leather through the white-gold buckle and then he was fumbling with the button and the zipper.

Her hand slipped inside as soon as she had access and the instant she touched him, he jacked forward with such force, he nearly snapped his spine.

"Watch me," she commanded.

He groaned and looked down, seeing her palm circle his thick shaft—and then she stroked him, up and down, the sensations creating a mad rush of hot and heavy all over his body. Then she was kissing him, her mouth taking over, her braid slipping free of her shoulder and landing with a heavy thump on his arm.

"Fuck, slow down, I'm going to come—"

"What I say."

Just as the pleasure was cresting, she went for his throat, those razor-sharp fangs scraping down his skin, finding the right place at his jugular. She struck at the very onset of his orgasm and he barked out her name, the pain and the pleasure mixing, the alchemy ramping everything up until he thought he would blow apart.

Cupping the back of her head, he urged her on as she started to pull from his vein, her head close to his own, her scent the only thing in his nose, his cock hard and kicking and hungry for more as she pumped him off.

She owned him.

Through and through.

Whatever vulnerability he had sensed—and not understood, but certainly accepted—was gone now as she ruled everything about him.

He'd never been one for getting Dom'd. That had never interested him much. After this? He wondered how much further she could go . . . how much he could take from her.

And he wanted to find out.

As Novo sucked at Peyton's throat and gave his arousal a workout, she wanted him in her sex. But the feeding had to come first—and okay, maybe she was chickening out a little, shying away temporarily until she could trust herself to stay separate.

But it was good, all of it. That taste of him down the back of her throat, the feel of his erection, both velvet and hard, the sense of control, of mastery—not just over him, but her own emotions. And on his side? Peyton was defo all about the orgasms, his beautiful male body riding the waves she called from him, his hips moving with her, the rhythm getting faster and harder the more releases she gave him. He was spectacular in her grip, those heavy muscles flexing and easing, his cock the kind of thing that fantasies were justified by.

And then there was the powerful rush of his blood. He was so pure that he made her head buzz and her heart pound, the strength he gave her so willingly making her feel like she was on a very long, rejuvenating vacation while at the same time being in Vegas and winning a million dollars at the slots.

She could have done this forever.

Yet the tipping point came when an alarm bell started to ring. At first, she shifted her eyes over to the monitors. Nope, it wasn't a machine informing her she'd pushed her repaired cardiac muscle too far.

No . . . it was an instinct in her own head that was telling her she was on the verge of taking too much.

Prying herself off his neck took some inner arguing, but then she forced her lips to break the seal and made her tongue lick the puncture wounds closed—

Okay, wow. She'd chewed him raw, multiple bite marks marring his flesh, the raw red slashes of her fangs making him look like Wolverine had hit him with a hand job. God, she hadn't even been aware of striking more than once. Clearly, though, she'd bitten him many, many times.

How long had they been at this?

Not a clue.

And she really had to stop. Extending her tongue, she licked up the side of his throat again and again, sealing everything up. With that job done, she pushed herself back and kept stroking him—before deliberately running her thumb over the slick head of his erection. His response was violent, his body jerking like a puppet at the end of strings, his torso arching and then his hips punching up. His eyes, glassy, unfocused, crazed, met her own as he bit into his lower lip and sucked a breath in through his teeth.

Blond hair was all messy on the pillow. Color on that handsome face was high. A delicious sweat made his bare skin glow.

He was . . . mind-numbingly beautiful.

Unfair. Totally unfair.

And she was still hungry.

Fortunately for them both, he had another kind of sustenance to give her.

Novo moved down him to his hips, opened her mouth, and took his sex in deep. In response, Peyton pulled another all-body spasm, his expression shocked as if he'd expected things to be over.

When she was sure he was looking at her, she sucked him in and out of her lips, his girth so wide, she felt the stretch in the corners of her mouth. And then she paused at the top and went into a swirl.

Sure enough, he started to orgasm again.

She caught all of it her mouth and swallowed what he gave to her.

Then she kept right on going.

TWENTY

or Saxton, the end of the working night arrived with a whimper, not a bang, a series of uncomplicated mating blessings and a property-line dispute that was easily adjudicated by the King capping off eight hours of same. As he entered his office in the staff hall and put his folders and his mostly used-up yellow pad on the partner's desk, he stared at his laptop, his orderly-everything, his pens in their little holder.

Rubbing his eyes, he tried to mentally compile a list of what he had to get in order before he could go home.

And pretty much failed at the task.

His head had functioned fairly well when he'd been engaging with the King and the citizens. Now that there was no overriding imperative to focus on, he couldn't seem to gather the cognitive reins, his thoughts bouncing from one thing to another.

Actually, that wasn't entirely true.

Ruhn was the prevailing topic. And the particulars were whether Saxton was remembering their kiss . . . or the flecks of chocolate in those pale brown eyes . . . or the feel of those strong shoulders. Or the fact that he just wanted to do it again.

Unfortunately, what he really needed was to train his brain on the fact that the male had left without saying a thing. Which was hardly a volunteer for a repeat.

On that note, he slipped his hand into the inside breast pocket of his suit jacket and took out his phone. Nope. No texts, no calls.

Okay, that would be no calls, given that Ruhn wouldn't be able to text.

And honestly, the fact that Saxton was as let down as he was seemed ridiculous. He didn't know that male but as a mere acquaintance, and he had certainly had full-on sex with people he had gone on to either not see again or not hook up with again and all that was fine. He was also self-aware enough to realize that with Ruhn's retreat, he had been reminded of another departure, one far more serious and consequential.

Naturally, all roads led back to Blay.

"Forgive me for intruding, sire?"

At the soft inquiry, he turned to the open doorway. One of the *doggen* who serviced the house was standing with her wool coat on and her hat and scarf in her hands.

"Oh, no worries, Meliz." He made sure he smiled at her so she didn't mistake his mood for a dissatisfied commentary on her efforts. "Are you off, then?"

She bowed low. "Yes, sire. I will restock the pantry after I aid the others at Last Meal back at the big house. Everyone else has departed for the day and I have made sure the fires are out, the flues are shut, and the doors are locked."

"Well done, then. Thank you. I shall see you on the morrow."

The *doggen* bowed even lower. "It is my pleasure to be of service."

She took her leave, and a moment later, he heard the alarm system chime that there was a door that opened and shut.

Right. He had to get things organized here. And then . . .

Well, home, he supposed. It was around four a.m., and even though there were still two hours of darkness left, he did not fancy a trip out into the city's nightlife. And no, he wasn't interested in filling the day with another sex-as-gym-equipment workout, either.

Somehow, though, the idea that he was going to be stuck in that glass box in the sky, all the drapes drawn against even the winter's anemic sun, made him want to scream—

Someone was outside.

Standing in the snow. Watching him.

Saxton turned to the glass panes and instantly recognized the huge body, the tense stance, the dark hair that was teased by the cold wind.

Not knowing what else to do, he pointed to the right, in the direction of the kitchen and its back door.

In response, Ruhn nodded and started for the rear of the house through the snow.

With quick feet and a faster heart, Saxton made his way down the staff hall, past the pantries, and into the vast kitchen. He opened the back door immediately, that signal going off once again, and he listened as the heavy footfalls squeaked and crunched through the snow-pack.

And there he was, bigger than ever, more reserved than usual.

Ah, yes. The re-framing conversation. "Do come in," Saxton said remotely.

As the male entered, Saxton closed things back up and wished that Ruhn was literate—because then this could have been done over text: *That was a mistake. It's not you, it's me. I don't know what I was thinking. Please do not tell anyone.*

"Worry not, no one else is here," Saxton muttered as he noticed that the sugar tin was ever so slightly out of place by the stove. "So whatever you'd like to say can be done without risk of eavesdropping."

He went across and righted the corners of the metal box. Then he fussed with the flour container, which was even bigger. Also scooted over the smallest of the three, the one that had salt in it.

When he turned back around, he was sick and tired of waiting for the other male to speak.

Trying to keep his frustration out of nuclear territory, he clapped his hands together and got with the program. "Look, I'll just dub in the words, okay? I've had a long night, I'm tired, and as much as I respect your journey or your exploration or whatever it is called, I think we can save us both time and aggravation by stipulating that you tried it, you were not into it, and you need some reassurance that I meant what I said about keeping things private."

"That is not why I came."

Work, then. Of course. "What of Minnie now?"

In lieu of a reply, Ruhn walked forward . . . and it was about when he was halfway across the distance that separated them that Saxton realized . . .

The male was aroused.

Very aroused.

Ruhn had not come here for a never-again, but rather for some-more.

Saxton's body responded instantly, his blood rushing, his cock hardening, his annoyance, frustration, and exhaustion instantly evaporating.

As the other male came to a halt with mere inches between their faces, Saxton had to smile a little. "I guess I read this wrong, huh."

"Yes," came the growl. "You did."

Holy from-out-of-nowhere.

Ruhn took hold of Saxton by either side of the throat and yanked him forward, the male's kiss nothing tentative or shy, nothing experimental. It was full on, tongue pushing inside, that big body thrusting hips and an erection the size of a baseball bat into Saxton and forcing him back against the countertop.

Oh . . . my God. It was a case of hang on for dear life as he was devoured, the power and hunger in Ruhn the kind of thing that was as shocking as it was unexpected and undeniable—

And then Saxton was spun around and bent over, a rough hand forcing him down by the shoulder blades onto the counter.

As Ruhn ground his cock into Saxton's ass, the male said in a guttural voice, "Say no now. If you're going to, say it now."

Saxton turned his head to the side, his cheek squeaking over the granite. Opening his mouth, he began to pant.

"Don't stop. Oh, God . . . *do it.*"

All at once, the lights in the kitchen went out, the space plunged into darkness as Ruhn clearly willed it so. The hands that went for Saxton's fly were rough with impatience—and then his fine loose slacks were hitting the floor. A blunt head probed and then Ruhn spit into his own palm—

The possession was hard and very deep.

The ride was a pounding to the point of violence.

The orgasm that poured into him was soul shattering for them both.

And Ruhn did not stop. He shoved a hand under Saxton's chest and locked a hold on the front of his opposite shoulder. Then the male steadied his stance and pistoned, their lower bodies slapping together, Saxton's head banging into those metal canisters, something getting torn—his suit jacket. Throwing out a hand, he put his palm against the wall under the cabinets just so he didn't end up with a concussion—and then he searched for purchase with his other hand.

He didn't find it, his arm flapping around.

Thank God he had something underneath his torso or his legs, which were now loose as satin ribbons, would have gone out from him.

Except then he located something to hold on to. Reaching between his thighs, he gripped his erection and instantly came, his sure strokes throwing him over the brink. He didn't care where he was ejaculating or how much cleanup was going to be required.

When you were having the sex of your life, the aftermath was not what you concerned yourself with.

• • •

Ruhn finally collapsed on Saxton's back—after God only knew how many orgasms. And yet even though he stilled, there was no silence. He was panting so hard that his front teeth were whistling, and beneath him, Saxton was nothing but harsh inhales as well. The scent of sex was thick in the air, and his cock, which was still hard as a rock as it twitched inside of the male, seemed to be suggesting this was a pause, not an all-finished.

With a groan, he opened his eyes. Across the way, the oak table with its orderly lineup of chairs pressed into its flanks was a surprise.

Where were they—oh, right. The kitchen. In the Audience House.

He had come in the back. So he could come . . . in the back.

Okay, that was the worst joke he'd ever thought up. And by the way . . . dearest Virgin Scribe. What had he done here?

Putting his palms on the granite countertop on either side of Saxton's shoulders, he intended to push himself up and off, but that went nowhere fast. He was too exhausted, and it felt too good to leave.

The male felt too good to leave.

As he tried to find the energy—and the will—to disengage, he thought of the other times he'd had sex. They had been exclusively with females, and only during his previous life. The encounters had been because he had been sought out by those wanting to be with an animal, and he had been provided to them for that specific service. His body had performed because of the timing of it all and because they had been naked and on him and his cock had risen to the occasion.

But he had never chosen them.

Saxton . . . he had chosen.

"I'm sorry," he said roughly as he summoned movement unto his arms. "I . . . am very sorry."

With a lithe twist, Saxton looked up at him. "Why in the world would you apologize for *that*?"

Ruhn felt a blush burn his face, and then he was ducking that direct stare and retracting. The air was cold on his arousal, and as he looked down, he was struck by an overwhelming need to do this all again. He had left a slick mess behind, but it was . . . the most erotic thing he'd ever seen.

Yet what did they do now? he wondered as he did up his jeans. That initial drive sated, he now couldn't believe he'd had the nerve to be so aggressive, so wanton, so—

Saxton straightened and pivoted around.

Fates, that face, those eyes, that hair . . . that erection, which seemed both a foreign and a familiar anatomy. Ruhn had never seen an aroused male up close before—and he was struck by an insatiable need to explore with touch and taste.

Indeed, this male was the answer to the "why."

"I ripped your suit," Ruhn said as he focused on the torn shoulder socket. "I am so sorry. I will pay to—"

Saxton reached over, grabbed the lower part of the sleeve—and yanked it clean off. As he dropped the cloth to the floor, he smiled. "Would you like to work on the other side?"

Ruhn laughed. He couldn't help it—and then he covered up his front teeth with his hand out of shyness. As Saxton grinned back at him, he had to look away. It was just too much beauty, too much excitement . . . too much everything.

"Have you eaten?" the solicitor asked as he reached down and pulled his slacks back into place.

"No, I have not."

"Let me make us Last Meal." Saxton passed a hand around the kitchen. "We are well stocked here. I will just excuse myself for a moment upstairs."

As Ruhn hesitated, Saxton took his face in his hands, and urged him down to the male's mouth. The kiss was as sweet as the sex had been possessive.

"I have to go to Mistress Miniahna's," Ruhn heard himself say. "To check on her before the dawn comes."

"All right, I understand." Saxton took a step back, a reserve tightening his features. "I shall see you at nightfall, then. We need to pay a visit to those real estate developers."

"Good."

There was an awkward silence. And then Ruhn blurted, "When?"

Saxton exhaled as if he were changing tracks in his head with effort. "Ah, let's say five forty-five. End of business for them, dark enough for us. We'll need to take your truck—"

"I mean us. When can we . . . do this again?"

Saxton's smile was quick and sustaining. "Anytime you like."

Ruhn reached up and brushed the male's face with his knuckles . . . before running his forefinger across that lower lip. Flashes of what they had just done replayed with a soundtrack of their moans and gasps.

"Thank you," he said.

Saxton shook his head. "I rather think I'm the one who should be saying that."

No, Ruhn thought. Not at all.

He leaned in and kissed the male. As his blood began to stir, he knew he had to go—or he was liable to never, ever leave.

"It is I who am grateful to you," he whispered against those lips.

TWENTY-ONE

"Who is Oskar?"

As the question was whispered in her ear, Novo came fully awake. At first, she had no idea whose chest she was lying all sprawled and warm on—but a quick inhale solved that problem. Peyton. She and Peyton were—

Yes, the hospital room. She was in the clinic, still recovering from surgery.

Lifting her head, she looked at the male she'd turned into a throw pillow. Peyton seemed perfectly content to be used in such a fashion, his naked body relaxed, his eyes heavily lidded, the mess at his throat already beginning to heal itself. Over on the floor, his tuxedo was all fallen-soldier-on-the-battlefield, scattered in pieces from having been cast aside.

His cock was much the same, resting flaccid and exhausted on one of his thighs.

She had the sense it would be back in working order at the drop of a hat.

"A lover?" he prompted.

"Who?"

"Oskar. You said his name in your sleep just now."

"Oh, that's no one."

"Really? You seemed upset—or your voice did."

"Must have been a nightmare for no good reason."

"Yeah." He brushed a wisp of hair back from her cheek. "Can I ask you something?"

"Sure."

"You want to go on a date with me sometime?"

Novo cocked a brow at him. "A date."

"Yup. Dinner. Dancing. This kind of thing."

"Are you thinking there will be sex involved?"

"Hoping, sure."

"Maybe."

His smile went straight into the center of her chest, sure as that dagger had: slow, confident, sexy. "I love a challenge."

"I'm not a challenge, though."

"You are as far from easy as anyone I've ever met."

"You can never win me. That's why I'm not."

"Isn't that the very definition of a challenge?"

"No, it's called a brick wall. You're welcome to try me, though."

"Somehow, someday," he held his forefinger aloft, "I'm going to get through to you."

"Ask yourself why you're bothering to try. You'll get far more out of that endeavor, I assure you—"

"She's soooooooooooooo hiiiiiiiiiiiiiiiiiiiiiiiigh, hiiigh above me—"

Novo recoiled and had to talk over all the off-key. "Why are you singing?"

"—she's soooo looooovely—"

Novo had to laugh. "You are a total freak, you know that—"

"—liiiiiike Cleeeopatraaaa, Jooooooooannn of Arrrrccc—"

"Oh, my God, you are tone deaf."

As she covered her ears, he really turned up the volume. "—or Apppphrooooodiiiiteeee—"

His arms wrapped around her and he kissed her and kissed her again. But it wasn't about sex. He seemed to like the fact that she was laughing, and the mouth-to-mouth was his way of telling her that.

"Why are you such a whack job?" she said against his lips.

"'Cuz I will do just about anything to see that smile of yours."

"Why do you care?"

"How can I not?"

Novo rolled her eyes. "Listen, you need to stop."

"I did. I'm no longer singing. But if you want me to go through my repertoire of Wham!, I have that shit on deck right now for you. I also do a mean Flock of Seagulls, wassup."

"I'm talking about being charming. I hate it. Just be yourself."

"What if I am being myself."

"Frustrated lounge singer?"

"Someone who wants to make you smile."

She shoved herself off of him and sat up—at least until her IV lines stopped her. "I think you need to go."

Peyton just put his hands behind his head and continued to lie there like a lion sunning himself. Except he was not king of the jungle and, hello, the light source was fluorescent and coming from the bathroom.

Damn it, that roughed-up blond hair and those sleepy blue eyes were too fucking attractive. Especially considering they were the cherry on top of one hell of a naked-ass sundae.

"I can't," he drawled.

Wait, what had they been talking about? Oh, right. The Peyton charm. "You sure as hell can cut the shit."

"By the way, it's two in the afternoon." He nodded at the clock over on the wall. "Daylight is a real buzzkill, so you can't tell me to go. As annoying as you find me, I'm very sure you don't want my death on your conscience."

"Do not underestimate how irritating you can be." Novo pointed to the door. "And no matter what time of day or night, you can always leave this room."

"Make me."

She blinked. "What . . . ?"

"You heard me, hard-ass. Unplug yourself, pick me up, and toss me out there like litter. Otherwise, I'm just sooooo comfortable right here. I mean, this two-inch pillow—that's basically like putting my head on a Frosted Mini-Wheat—is diiiiivine. And don't get me started on these sheets. I mean, hello, I'm throwing my Porthault out as soon as I get home and replacing it with this sandpaper. My ass is getting buffed to a high shine with me just breathing."

Novo mostly kept the laugh to herself. Mostly. "Stop. You're not funny."

"No? Not even a little?" He winked at her. "How about I do my best joke ever."

She crossed her arms over her chest—and then abruptly froze. As she looked down at herself, she took a ragged breath.

Instantly, Peyton was all serious and sitting up. "What's wrong. I'll get the doctor—"

"No, I'm okay."

With hands that shook, she reached up to the hospital johnny's ties. Loosening the top one, she gently parted the two halves . . . and stared down.

In a barely audible voice, she whispered, "It's gone. The scar . . . is gone. It's healed. My heart . . . has healed. There's no pain."

Peyton leaned in. And then he reached out and brushed his finger down the perfectly regenerated skin. There wasn't even a mark.

"I didn't want to die." She cleared her throat, but she was still hoarse. "Out there. When it happened . . . I didn't want to die."

"You sound surprised."

Novo closed her eyes. "I am."

"I'm sorry."

Trying to snap out of it, she shut his sympathy down. "You already apologized for the mistake."

"No." He shook his head. "I'm sorry there was a time when you wanted to die."

"I never said that."

"You don't have to."

Before she could try to slam that door closed, he did the strangest thing.

Peyton took her hands, drew them away from the ties, and then turned them over. Dipping his head, he kissed her on both wrists, his lips the softest of brushes. And afterward, he gathered the ties she had been holding . . . and executed a perfect bow, the two loops exactly the same, the pair of ends of equal length, the johnny now re-closed.

Placing his hand over her heart, he whispered, "I am so glad you're okay."

Without another word, he wrapped his arms around her and urged her back down onto his chest.

She resisted. For a little bit.

But then she stopped fighting.

As the hours of daylight passed, Peyton did not sleep. He just stroked Novo's back with a slow hand, the contours of her spine and muscles a landscape he learned better with each pass.

He had often recognized her strength. How could he not? There was a lot of pain underneath all of that, though—and he was struck by a need to find out her secrets, get in and help her conquer those demons. But come on, what could he really do for her? He was more boat-with-a-hole-in-it than competent-rescuer-on-the-high-seas.

At some point, he must have drifted off, because the wailing of that patient with the mental breakdown woke him up. Listening to the howling, he wondered how much longer anyone could last in that condition.

A quick check of the clock on the wall and he cursed. Five o'clock.

Damn it, he didn't want to leave her and he most certainly did not want to go where he was expected at five-thirty. But he was used to doing shit he had no interest in.

With slow, careful movements, he repositioned Novo—and prayed that she stayed asleep. She looked like she was really making the turn, what with that scar healing up already and her brows relaxed now, not furrowed in pain. When he was standing on his own two feet and she had curled onto her side, he eased the blankets into place and realized that they had never been skin to skin. She hadn't taken her johnny off, and he hadn't even gotten in under the covers.

Seemed like a metaphor for all the things she was keeping to herself.

As he pulled on his tuxedo slacks, he had some notion that he should leave well enough alone. Sexual attraction did not a relationship make, and neither did it justify demands for emotional connection. And hell, he knew firsthand from those hours on the phone with Paradise that people talked about themselves on their own timeline and no one else's.

Just leave her be, he told himself. Those defenses of hers were in place for a reason.

His tuxedo shirt was a wrinkled mess and he hated that as he pulled it on, but it wasn't like the thing was going to stay on him for longer than the walk down to the males' locker room. He'd take his shower there and throw on a set of scrubs.

Over at the door, he stared back at Novo sleeping on that hospital bed. She was in the position of a young, her knees tucked up tight, her arms, too, those hands of hers that were so good with weapons curled into innocent rolls under her chin. Black lashes rested on cheeks that were no longer so pale, and that heavy black braid was like a rope as it lay along the archer's bow of her back.

He had some thought that he was never going to see her like this again.

This moment, right here, was a one-off, an artificially constructed instant limited to the final phase of her recovery. The next time he saw her, she was going to be up and at him and everyone else, her body whole and fully functioning, her mind sharp, her faculties no longer dimmed, but firing on all cylinders.

He had been granted a gift the now. Not by her, though. She never would want anyone to see her like this.

Stepping out of the room, he took off the piece of paper that had been taped to the door and folded it a couple of times so that Dr. Manello's shitty handwriting was no longer visible. Then he put the thing in his pocket and hustled down to the locker room.

A quick shower, shave, and change of clothes, and he was ready for what was ahead, another hurdle to be jumped, a hoop to go through, a "t" to cross, an "i" to dot—and then things were done here. He left his tux in one of the lockers and was stuck wearing his formal patent leathers, the little grosgrain bows and glossy pointed toes looking absolutely ridiculous sticking out from underneath the hems of the scrub pants.

Back in the hall, he paused by Novo's room. Then kept on going. No one was out and about. Dr. Manello was probably sleeping off his toked-up version of a rager, and Doc Jane and Ehlena were no doubt getting ready for First Meal at what they called "the big house." There were no Brothers around, and certainly no trainees.

There were going to be soon enough, though.

They were supposed to be having a meeting at eight. That was why this particular appointment of his had to happen so early.

Peyton stopped at the glass door of the office. Peering in, he almost hoped there would be no one at that desk. But of course, that was a not-happening.

The Brother Rhage's *shellan,* Mary, was sitting at the computer, her head down, her eyes trained on the screen. As if sensing his presence, she looked up and waved for him to come in.

Run, Forrest . . . run! was all he could think of as he pushed his way inside.

"Hey." She got to her feet. "How are you?"

"I'm great. Thanks."

"Good. You ready to have a little chat?"

As far as he knew, Mary was a human—or had been one—until the Scribe Virgin had interceded and, for some reason, taken the female out of the continuum of time. He didn't know much more about it, but she certainly seemed as serene as an angel or a deity or whatever she was. And she was very different from Rhage. She was small, especially compared to her *hellren,* and she had an unassuming beauty, her brown hair cut practically, her face always free of makeup, her clothes simple, functional. The only jewelry he'd ever noticed on her—not that he paid much attention—was an enormous gold Rolex, which had to have belonged to her mate, and maybe a pair of pearl studs.

She was wearing both tonight.

Bottom line, she was just what you'd think a shrink would be like: calm, sharp as a tack, and bonus for him, she didn't seem judgmental in the slightest.

"Let's get this over with," he muttered as he went to take a seat in the chair across from her.

"Oh, not here."

He looked around at the office. "Why not?"

"It's not private."

"I don't have anything to hide," he said dryly. "If that were the case, I would have stopped streaking at human concerts years ago."

"No, let's go."

"Where?"

Mary came around the desk. "There's an old interrogation room down the hall—no, this is not being filmed, and before you ask, I will not divulge to anyone what you say. It's just that if we're in there, no one will interrupt us."

"Wait, if you won't tell anybody anything, why are we doing this?"

"I'll be making an assessment. But I will not be sharing specific details."

"About whether or not I'm sane?"

"Let's go this way."

As she smiled, it was calm, but he had the sense she wasn't going to go into any further detail.

Whatever, he thought. This was all just a formality before they kicked him out.

As Peyton followed her into the corridor, he shrugged. "FYI, you can tell the world as far as I'm concerned. I made the bad call out in the alley and I know I'm leaving the program. So we could save a lot of time and just have you check that box on the form."

She stopped and looked up at him. "No one's made that determination yet."

"You mean telling me to leave? Come on, we both know that's where we are. And it's fine."

"Do you not like what you're doing here?"

The question was not phrased in an offensive way, as if she were criticizing him for his lack of commitment or something. It was more an invitation to talk.

He should be ready for a lot of that tone from her, he thought.

"No, it's fine. Whatever happens, happens."

After she made some kind of an mmm-hmm sound, they started walking side by side. As they went along, only one set of footfalls, his, echoed around. Mary glanced down at his feet.

"Those shoes look awfully fancy," she said with a smile.

"I wanted to impress you."

"That's not your job or mine." More with that smile. "But they're a very nice pair of tuxedo shoes. I've learned all about men's fashion from Butch."

"He and I use the same tailor now."

"I believe that."

When they got to an unmarked steel door with no window in it, she knocked, waited a moment, and opened the way into an anonymous room with gray walls, a table in the center, and only two chairs.

"I'm sorry this is so dour," she murmured as they entered and she closed them in together.

As she sat down, he realized she'd brought a yellow pad and a pen with her. Huh. He hadn't even noticed she'd taken anything from the desk.

"Join me," she prompted as she motioned to a chair.

"This won't take long," he muttered as he sat down. "Not long at all."

TWENTY-TWO

As Ruhn pulled the truck over in front of the Commodore's impressive front entrance, he was thinking about cologne— something that was not on his normal list of musings. Which was the point.

Leaning forward so he could regard the skyscraper's towering steel-and-glass facade, he found himself finally understanding why people used the stuff. Previously, with no one to impress, the idea that you would deliberately scent yourself with something formulated by a bunch of humans and marketed to great expense seemed a ludicrous exercise in lost wages.

Now? With the prospect of Saxton joining him in this cab?

He wished he had the sophistication to know what was the right cologne and the money to buy it—

One side of the double doors opened and Saxton strode out into the cold, the male's breath leaving in a puff of white that drifted over his shoulder. He had on that pale brown coat of his and a red scarf knotted and tucked in at his throat. His slacks were navy blue or perhaps black. His hair was thick and shiny, brushed back from his beautiful face. He had a brown satchel in one of his gloved hands.

Before Ruhn could stop himself, he put the truck in park and got out, going around to open the passenger door.

"You are so kind," Saxton said with a smile as he approached.

Ruhn had to stop himself from leaning in for a kiss. And as if Saxton recognized this, he brushed Ruhn's forearm as he got inside.

Shutting the door, Ruhn proceeded to resume his position behind the wheel. "Is it warm enough in here for you?"

"It's perfect." The male looked over. "How are you?"

An easy-enough question, but those gray eyes were pointed without being demanding. More was being asked, wasn't it.

Ruhn cleared his throat and then focused on the male's mouth. All at once, the air became thick and charged.

In a very low, very deep voice, Ruhn answered with the truth: "I am hungry."

During the daylight hours, he had thought of nothing but their time together, replaying that erotic scene in that kitchen over and over again—until he had had to relieve himself. About a hundred times.

Being attracted to someone of the same sex still seemed strange.

That sex they'd shared had been the most natural thing he had ever done.

"Well," Saxton murmured. "After our work is done, we'll have to see if we can take care of that for you. A male must eat, doesn't he."

"Yes."

As the promise of orgasms and pleasure and exploration swirled between them, Ruhn put the engine in drive—and prayed this meeting with the human developers did not take long.

"I know where we're going," he said.

"As do I," Saxton chuckled.

Ruhn blushed as he glanced over. "I mean across town."

"Me, too." Saxton reached over and squeezed his hand. "I shouldn't tease you. It's just that blush. You know."

"It's not manly."

Saxton frowned. "What an odd way to put it."

"I don't know what I'm saying. I'm not good with words."

"You do just fine." Saxton squeezed again and released his hold. "You need to stop apologizing for yourself. You are not less than. People are only ever different."

Given that Ruhn wasn't sure what to say—as usual—he made a noise that he hoped seemed supportive. Agreeable. Something like that.

Fates, he was in over his head here.

"So," the solicitor said briskly, "I have everything all arranged. Backdated contracts, which are already in the process of being filed with the humans, a cease-and-desist letter to threaten the developer with, and a partridge in a pear tree."

"We're bringing them a bird?"

Saxton laughed. "It's a saying."

"Oh."

Ruhn put the directional signal on and headed down toward the river. At the bottom of the decline, he nodded toward the ramp that would take them up onto the highway.

"Is this way okay?"

"However you wish to go. I trust you."

With a nod, and a feeling of pride for that vote of confidence, Ruhn took them up onto a congested stretch of the Northway.

"Lot of traffic."

"Mmm-hmm," Saxton said. "Tell me, was Minnie okay? When you went to see her right before dawn?"

"Ah, yes, yes, she was. Nothing was out of order. When I knocked on the front door, I told her I was just checking on her. She said all was well—oh, and I fixed her downstairs toilet for her. It was running."

"That was kind of you."

"The bathroom sink was also leaking. And the furnace was making a clunking noise when it kicked on. I may investigate all that further."

"I can understand why she doesn't want to leave that house."

"But it is too much for her to take care of. It really is."

"Agreed."

Somehow, the accord between them seemed so much more profound than just a meeting of the minds on the subject of Mistress Miniahna.

But perhaps he was merely romanticizing.

Back at the training center's interrogation room, Peyton was having a hard time following Mary's line of questioning.

Eventually, he had to *no mas* it.

"I'm sorry," he said as he interrupted her. "I don't mean to cut you off, but I thought this was supposed to be about work? I don't understand why you're asking about my family."

"Just getting additional background."

"I was already screened right after orientation by the Brother Butch. I mean, it's all in my file."

"I like to collect my own background." The female smiled. "Is there some reason you're uncomfortable speaking about your family?"

"Not at all." He shrugged and eased back in the hard chair. "It doesn't bother me. It's just a waste of time."

"And why is that?"

"Look, I told you. We both know what's going to happen with all of this."

"All of what."

He motioned between them. "This conversation. The statement I gave your mate about what I did. It would be more efficient to kick me out of the program now as opposed to waste all this paperwork. It's not like I'm going to sue you guys for wrongful termination or some shit— sorry, stuff."

"You make it seem like you're very dispensable."

"What do you mean?"

"Well, you're taking for granted you're going to be dismissed."

"But I am. Why wouldn't I be?"

Mary intertwined her fingers and sat forward, resting an elbow on her pad. "You're part of the team."

"Isn't that the Minions' song?"

"I'm sorry?"

He shook his head. "I'm just being a smart-ass."

"I know. It's one of your coping mechanisms—but your deflection through humor is a topic for another time." Again with the smile. "So why do you think that you don't matter to everyone else in the program?"

He focused on the little pearl stud in her left ear. "Whether I matter or not isn't the issue."

"So it's one-mistake-and-you're-out in your opinion?"

"Excuse me, and I am not being a smart-ass this time—it's not like I got a math problem wrong."

"You're still deflecting. If Paradise had acted as you did in that alley, would you ask her to leave the program?"

"No, but she's not me."

"Why are you different?"

From out of nowhere, his head began to pound and he closed his eyes. "I don't know. And I'm not the person in charge—for good reason. Can we be done?"

"Why couldn't you be in charge?"

"Why did I know you were going to say that," he muttered as he sat forward and put his hands on the metal-topped table. "I don't know. I don't have answers to these questions. So how about you throw me out because of that?"

"Would you like to know why they asked me to talk to you?"

"I put Novo in a hospital bed."

Mary shook her head. "No, you didn't. You made an unfortunate decision that, frankly, was more an indication that the training failed than you did. The Brothers asked me to talk to you because they want my sense about whether or not you're taking this seriously. The responsibility, that is. Everyone who's worked with you recognizes your skills. You're a really good fighter, you're smart, you're quick. But you're a quitter. When things get tough, you walk. They saw it during orientation when Paradise essentially carried you through the gym and into the pool challenge. They've noted it during exercises. And, to be honest, this whole just-kick-me-out is part of that characteristic of yours."

"I'm not a quitter."

"So prove it."

"What?"

"Stay."

Peyton shook his head. "It's not up to me."

"That's where you're wrong." Mary's voice was grave. "It is entirely up to you."

As Peyton got quiet, he noticed that the top of the table was reflective . . . and if he stared down into the surface of it, he could see himself.

He'd never really thought about it like that, but all those females and women he fucked and left? The schools he'd been suspended from halfway through? The things he'd dropped out of, the commitments he'd made and failed to follow through on . . . ?

Hell, the closest relationship he'd ever had had been over the phone.

And Mary was right. This whole getting-kicked-out thing? He'd been practically begging for that outcome.

Was this what his father had always found so frustrating about him? This floating-above, never-committing thing? His sire was still an unsupportive shit all the way around, but Peyton had to wonder if he himself hadn't deliberately given the male fodder for the cannons, so to speak. And what about the club douches that were Peyton's closest set of "friends?" They were just like him, living off family money, asshat'ing around, developing drug habits instead of inner character.

He was from the land of labels. Which was not the same as quality, was it.

Who do you want to be? he asked himself. *Who are you really?*

The memory of Novo lying asleep on his chest, of her warm weight and her even breathing, of her subtle twitches as she dreamed, came back to him sure as if she were with him now.

Sometimes life brought you to corners that you saw coming, big changes altering your direction and focus thanks to a given event, like a mating or the birth of a young. Other times, though, the glacial shifts came without warning, popping out of nowhere.

He had never expected to run into this brick wall of self-reflection tonight. While in hospital scrubs. And tuxedo shoes.

At least the shoes might have been predicable. Maybe the scrubs. The rest of it? Hell, it was the shit he deliberately didn't want to think about.

"What are you going to do, Peyton?"

"I want to stay," he said roughly. "I want to keep going in the program. If they'll have me."

"Good." As he looked back up her, Mary nodded. "That's all we wanted to hear."

TWENTY-THREE

"Forgive me for being blunt," Saxton remarked dryly. "But this place is a dump."

More like a meth lab than anywhere you'd build houses out of, he added to himself.

As Ruhn parked them grille-in to a low concrete building that had been painted the color of bile, Saxton wasn't sure what he expected—but certainly not this window-less, single-doored tomb in a part of town usually reserved for businesses that had a shady side to them.

These were not just developers they were dealing with.

And of course, there was no signage identifying things as a going concern, nothing with a name on it or advertising—and the place had been hard to locate. There had only been a P.O. box listed on the letterhead that had been sent to Minnie, and Vishous had had to do some digging to find this address.

These humans wanted to be found only on their own terms.

"Is that the truck you saw at Minnie's?" he asked as he pointed across the shallow parking lot.

"Yes." Ruhn turned off the engine. "That's the one."

"Okay, shall we do this?"

"Yes."

It was not hard to note the change in the other male. Ruhn was scanning the empty environs as if he were searching for aggressors, his hands tightened into fists—and they hadn't even gotten out of the Ford yet.

Grabbing his satchel, Saxton opened his door, and before he even got a foot on the ground, that single entrance swung open, a big human filling the jambs—with one hand tucked into his jacket.

"Can I help you," the man demanded.

Saxton smiled and walked around behind the truck bed. As he caught up with Ruhn, a second human came to stand behind the one who in the doorway. Both had dark hair, squat builds, noses that were off-center—and eyes that were as warm and welcoming as pistols.

A set of guard dogs, trained to bite trespassers.

Number two also had a hand inside his coat.

"How nice to see you again," Saxton said as he stopped in front of Big and Bigger. "I believe you recall my associate from the other evening."

"What are you doing here."

"Well, you were kind enough to offer some insight into Minnie Rowe's ownership of her parcel, and thanks to you, we were able to get everything sorted. I have in here," he lifted his satchel, "copies of the documents that should have been filed with the appropriate agencies, but which had, for reasons beyond her control, not in fact been submitted properly. I'm happy to provide you with copies of—"

As he went to open the flap, both of the men outed their guns.

"That's enough," the first one said.

"Now, gentlemen,"—Saxton feigned shock—"whyever would you need to defend yourselves as such? My colleague and I have come here on a routine property matter, which actually does not pertain to you or the man you work for—as neither you nor he is in an ownership position relative to the—"

"Shut up." The man nodded to the truck. "Get back in that thing and leave."

Saxton tilted his head. "Why? Don't you like people showing up on your property unannounced after nightfall?"

That front human outed his gun and leveled the muzzle at Saxton's head. "You don't know who you're dealing with."

Saxton laughed, his breath condensing into a white puff. "Oh, my God. I feel like I'm in a Steven Seagal movie from 1989. Do you use these lines and they actually work? Incredible."

"They won't find the body—"

The subtle growl that percolated up into the cold air was bad news. It was all well and good for Ruhn and him to play push and shove with the humans like this—although all the posturing was such a bore, really—but what absolutely could not happen was anything vampire-ish entering this scenario.

Saxton looked over his shoulder and shot Ruhn a glare. But the male did not show any signs of noticing or stepping off—and his upper lip was starting to twitch.

Damn it.

Refocusing on the pair of humans and their metal show, he elbowed Ruhn and was relieved when the noise stopped.

"Leave Mrs. Rowe alone," Saxton said. "Because you also have no idea who you're dealing with."

"Is that a threat?"

Saxton looked to the heavens. "You gentlemen must get a better script to work off of. I suggest *Taken* with Liam Neeson. At least that's in this century. You are stale. Realllllly stale."

"Fuck you."

"You're not my type. I'm so sorry."

As he turned away, he grabbed ahold of Ruhn and pulled him along.

Once they were back in the truck, Saxton stared over at the pair of guards, memorizing their features. He was very sure he and Ruhn had been photographed as if they were on the red carpet. There had to be cameras all over the place.

"We need to get Minnie out of that house until this is finished," he muttered as Ruhn reversed them and headed onto the road beyond. "Things are going to escalate even further, I fear."

"If she leaves, I could stay in the house. So it's not unattended."

"That is not a bad idea." Saxton glanced across the seat. "That is not a bad idea at all. Let me call her granddaughter first and see if we can get buy-in on that—and then we'll talk to Minnie. Maybe if it's just a short-term thing, she'll be more open to it. You're smart."

Ruhn's little smile was the kind of thing he wanted to remember forever. And then the male came up with another piece of brilliance.

"Would you care to have something to eat?" Ruhn asked. "Whilst we're out?"

As Ruhn drove them off, he waited for Saxton's answer. It had felt a bit forward to ask for a date, but he was in fact hungry—and the idea of sharing a meal, and prolonging their time together?

"I would love that," the solicitor said. "Is there somewhere in particular you want to go?"

"I do not know."

"What kind of food do you enjoy?"

"I do not have a preference."

"There's a wonderful French bistro that I just adore. It's a little bit of a drive, but then again, from this neighborhood? We'd have to travel to get to a 7-Eleven."

In the back of his head, Ruhn counted how much money he had in his wallet. It was about sixty-seven dollars. But he did have his debit card and his bank account had just under a thousand dollars in it— which was his entire net worth.

His lack of financial status made him hope that his old landowner would do as he promised and help him find a job in Caldwell. The conversation over the phone the previous evening had certainly seemed promising, although there was no telling what was available for work up here. Still, aristocrats of the stature of the one he had long worked for tended to be very well connected.

He had to believe something would turn up—and provide him with both purpose and a living wage.

"Would that be okay with you?" Saxton prompted.

"I'm sorry, yes. Please. Where are we going?"

"Take a right up here and I'll direct you."

About fifteen minutes later, they were in a far better part of town, the little shops and quaint eating establishments lined up flank to flank as picture perfect as any city street could be. The snow had been plowed well and he imagined human pedestrians traveling down the sidewalks in the daylight, cheerful even though it was cold. And in the warmer months? It was no doubt very busy on weekends and populated by people like Saxton: urban sophisticates with nice manners and elevated tastes.

"Here it is," the male said as he pointed ahead. "*Premier.* There's a parking lot behind. Just head down the alley right here."

Ruhn took them back into a cramped foursquare stretch of asphalt, made even smaller by the plowed piecrust edges of snow. Fortunately, there was only one other car so he was able to squeeze the truck into the far corner, and then he and Saxton were walking on the packed ice to the rear door.

He went forward and held things open, and as Saxton passed by, Ruhn traced with his eyes the male's hair and shoulders, his tight waist, his fine slacks and pointed shoes.

Inside, the smell from the kitchen was amazing. He didn't have any idea what the aromas were made of, but his spine loosened with every breath he took. Onions . . . mushrooms . . . soft spices.

J. R. WARD

"Ah! You are back."

A human man in a black suit and a blue tie came down a thin hall-way with both arms out. He and Saxton kissed each other's cheeks, once on each side, and they slipped into a language Ruhn did not recognize.

Abruptly, the human switched back to English. "But of course, we have always the table for you and your guest. This way, come. Come."

It was not very far at all before things opened up to the restaurant proper. As with the parking lot, there were few places to sit, and a couple was just standing up to leave. Probably the owners of that other vehicle in back.

"Right in front of the house," the human said proudly.

"Merci mille fois."

The human bowed. "The usual?"

Saxton looked at Ruhn. "Would it be okay if the chef used her discretion?"

Ruhn nodded. "Whatever is easiest."

The human man recoiled. "It is not easy. It is our honor."

Saxton put his hand out. "We are so looking forward to whatever Lisette prepares. It will be a masterpiece."

"You may be so assured."

As the man left in a bit of a huff, Ruhn squeezed himself into a chair that would have done well by Bitty's toy tiger, Mastimon. In fact, the entire place made him feel big as an elephant and as coordinated as a falling boulder.

"I think I offended him." He sat back—and then got with the pro-gram as Saxton put a napkin in his lap. Following suit, he murmured, "That was not my intention."

"You will love Lisette's food. That is all they will care about in the end."

Wine appeared. White. Ruhn took a sip and was astounded. "What is this?"

"Chateau Haut Brion Blanc. It is from Pessac-Leognan."

"I love this."

"I am glad."

As Saxton smiled, Ruhn forgot all about the wine. And he was still distracted as the male started to talk about what he had done during the day for Minnie and some of the other cases he was working on for the King. It was all so interesting, but more than that, the rise and fall of the solicitor's voice was hypnotic.

Food was served, small, colorful portions arriving on tiny, square white plates. More wine. More of Saxton's conversation.

It was all just so . . . peaceful. Even with the undercurrent of sexual need, and in spite of the restaurant's mini-sized everything, Ruhn felt an unfamiliar ease. And the food was, in fact, absolutely amazing, each course building on the previous, the totality satiating his hunger in a way that was subtle, but powerful.

When they were finally finished, some two hours later, it was well after midnight—and he felt as though they had been at it for about five minutes. Sitting back, he put his hand on his belly.

"That was the most incredible meal I have ever had."

"I am so happy." Saxton motioned to the human man who had sat them down. "Marc, if you please?"

The man came right over. *"Monsieur?"*

"Tell him, Ruhn."

Emboldened by the wine and a full belly, Ruhn met the human's eyes without giving it another thought. "That was incredible. Amazing. I've never had a meal like that in my life and I never shall again."

Okay, apparently, he'd said all the right things. The man went into a positive swoon of happiness—and promptly rewarded them with a plate of pear slices and chocolate something-or-other.

"I will get the bill tonight," Saxton said as he took out his wallet and slid free a black card. "This is my treat as it was my choice. Next time, you pick and you pay."

Ruhn flushed. Yes, he had tried to guess in his head what this might have cost—although that had all been only in theory as they had not had menus and no dollar amounts had been discussed—and he could only imagine it was incredibly expensive. And he did appreciate Saxton's nod to the fact that he wanted to contribute.

After the check came and the card was exchanged, Saxton then signed things just out of sight, and the two of them got up and gave further compliments to the human—at which point, a woman in a white chef's outfit came forth and there were exclamations to her as the person who had provided them with such a glorious meal.

When they were finally back outside, Ruhn found that he could remember little in terms of detail: If asked what precisely he had eaten or drunk, what had been said, where they had sat, he could not have pointed to many particulars.

And yet the whole was unforgettable.

"Aren't they wonderful?" Saxton was saying as they walked over to the trunk. "Such a great couple. They live above the restaurant. It is truly their life."

As if on cue, a light flared in a window on the upper level, a shadow passing by drapes that were pulled.

"Thank you," Ruhn murmured as he looked at Saxton. "This was amazing."

"I am glad. I wanted to show you something special."

Shifting his eyes lower, Ruhn recalled the taste and feel of the male's kiss—and oh, how he wished that they were on the human schedule. It would have been wonderful to find this the end of the day instead of the start of the night, the two of them winding down together back at Saxton's sleek penthouse, entwining themselves, legs about legs, arms about arms, in a bed, with nothing but hours of pleasure ahead.

There was much to explore.

So many things he wanted to taste and touch.

"If you keep staring at me like that," Saxton groaned, "I am going to lose my job for failure to show up."

"I'm sorry." He was not. "I'll stop." He did not.

It was cold and the wind was blowing, but it might as well have been an August night for all he was in a rush to get under cover in the truck. He could have stayed just where they were forever, suspended between a good meal and the good-bye that was going to have to come because of Saxton's responsibilities.

"Can I visit you at the end of the night?" Ruhn asked.

"If you spend the day with me, yes." Saxton's smile was slow and full of promise. "I'm going to need more than a half hour before the dawn's ugly light."

"That is—"

Later, he would wonder exactly what it was that broke the moment and brought his head around, but he would be forever grateful for whatever instinct had his back——because they were no longer alone.

Two figures were in the shadows about fifteen yards away, standing just out of sight behind a shop's back porch.

He knew who they were without confirmation from their scents.

"Get in the truck," he ordered Saxton.

"What?"

Ruhn grabbed the male's arm in a hard grip and started marching for the cab. "The truck. Get in there and lock the doors."

"Ruhn, why are you—"

The men who had been at that two-bit office stepped forward, silencing that line of questioning. And a quick triangulation to the passenger-side door of the truck made Ruhn nervous. It all depended on how fast those humans moved.

"Let me call the Brothers," Saxton said as he put his hand inside his coat, clearly going for his phone.

Keeping his voice down and his eyes on the approach, Ruhn shook his head. "I've got this."

"They could be armed. They probably are. Let me—"

"This is why I'm here. Get in the vehicle."

He unlocked things remotely and then jumped ahead, opened the door, and pressed the keys into Saxton's palm. "Lock yourself in. Leave if things go badly."

"I will never leave you."

With a rough shove, Ruhn all but airlifted the other male in, and then he shut the door and glowered at the solicitor.

Thunch went the locks.

Ruhn walked around and stood at the back of the bed. The humans were not in a hurry on the approach, but that didn't mean anything. Aggression was best played as a second card, and maybe they knew that—

As if on cue, the two men rushed forward on the attack. One had a knife. The other was empty-handed—if there were guns, they were holstered for now, probably because even though it was late, there were still humans around in short-stack apartment buildings or over their businesses, like the restaurant owners.

Settling into his fighting stance, Ruhn returned to his previous life in between one heartbeat and the next, his brain flipping into a different gear that was rusty only for a split second. Then everything, for better or worse, came back to him.

And he started to fight.

TWENTY-FOUR

"A wheelchair. You want me to go down the corridor . . . in a wheelchair."

As Novo glared a hole in the back of her surgeon's head, Dr. Manello seemed woefully unaware that his skull had sprung a leak and she was the one responsible for his brains evac'ing all over the place. In fact, the man seemed nonchalant and utterly unconcerned by her Laser Eyes of Total Domination.

Which was pretty fucking frustrating. Especially when it was compounded by the fact that she was still relegated to her hospital bed. Still in a johnny with flowers on it. Still hooked up to things that beeped.

"Come on." He patted the chair's seat. "You don't want to be late for the big meeting."

"I am perfectly fine walking on my own, thank you very much. I'm not a goddamn cripple."

"Okay, that counts as a micro-aggression. Or something. Or, like, disrespectful to the physically handicapped."

"What are you, the thought police, too?"

"Non-negotiable." His smile was about as charming as a toe infection. "So let's do this."

"I'm not getting in that thing." She crossed her arms—at least until her IV line got squeezed and she had to put them back down. "And when can I get rid of this bag."

"I am so relieved."

"Excuse me?"

"The bitchier my patients get, the more they are improving." He pumped his fist like Rocky. "Woo-hoo!"

"I'm going to hit you with my bag."

"I didn't know females like you had purses. I thought you just fanny-packed your shit like a dude."

Novo burst out laughing and pointed a finger at him. "That is not funny."

"Then why are you—"

"Fine, bring that thing over—but I am driving."

"Oh, of course, Danica. Aaaaaabsolutely."

The fact that she grunted as she sat up and swung her legs around probably proved his point, but he had the good sense not to bring that up.

The wheelchair wasn't more than three feet from the mattress—and it was a shock to find that even within that short distance, she was ready to take a load off by the time she turned herself about and positioned her ass over the seat.

She thought of Peyton.

His blood was solely responsible for the recovery she'd had. After the two times she had fed from him, she'd taken huge leaps in her forward progress. Without him? She doubted she'd be upright at all, and yet she was still frustrated.

"Let's get you set up here." Dr. Manello transferred the IV bag to a pole on the back of the chair. "Okay, hit it."

He jumped ahead and held the door open.

It took her a minute to get a hang of the ambulation thing. Her hands were sloppy and her arms were weak. But then she was rolling along.

"If you salute me, I'm going to—"

Dr. Manello snapped to attention, all Benny Hill with his palm flashing out.

"Really?" She started to laugh again and had to hold under her rib cage. "Ow."

"Come on, badass," he said. "Let me help you."

Before she could tell him to fuck off, he took control of the driving, and it was a little hard to argue that she didn't need the help as she breathed through the sharp-shooter.

Which seemed to be getting worse. To the point where she had to bring it up.

"Am I having a heart attack?" she asked as she massaged under her left arm. "I . . ."

Panic made her feel like she was suffocating, and the good doctor was right on it, pulling a stethoscope out from his white coat and coming in front of her. He listened to things for a little bit. Asked her to sit forward. Listened some more from the back.

Then he unplugged the thing from his ears and stood back, observing her. "I think you're fine," he said. "Heart is regular as a metronome. Your color is great. Your eyes are fine."

"I feel like I can't . . ."

A sudden muffled burst of talk made her frown. "Are they in the gym?" she asked.

"Yup."

"Why aren't we in a classroom?" Usually if there was a meeting, it was only the six trainees, and one or two Brothers, tops. "I mean, we don't need all that space—"

"You ever have panic attacks?"

"No, never," she lied.

"Okay. Well, you might have some anxiety spikes over the next little bit. It's not uncommon. You've been through a lot—and it wouldn't be unusual for you to be jumpy as hell."

"Is that a medical term of art?"

"Tonight it is, yup." He sank down on his haunches and got serious. "The tricky thing is to recognize that the shortness of breath is more likely anxiety, not your heart exploding in your chest, 'kay? If you can believe in that, you'll do better. You're medically sound. I promise you that or we wouldn't be out here in this hall."

"Right. Okay."

"You got this."

"I'm not normally . . . weird."

"When was the last time you got stabbed in the heart?"

She pshaw'd with her hand. "Whatever, man. I mean, it's been at least a week. Maybe two. Guess I'm just out of practice."

"That's my girl." He put a hand on her shoulder and squeezed. "Let's do this. And I'm going to hang right with you."

"I thought you said I'm medically sound?"

Dr. Manello started pushing her down the concrete corridor again. "Belt and suspenders, my friend. Belt and suspenders."

They went forth at a pace that was all about the slow and steady, and as they trundled by the weight room, she wondered whether she was ever going to work out again.

The closer they got to the gym, the louder the voices became and she gathered her long braid, holding it in the center of her chest as if it would offer her some kind of protection—even though she knew not against what.

One of the sets of doors opened before they were in range, and as Vishous stepped out, she wondered if they had been sensed by the Brother.

That diamond stare narrowed on her, the tattoos at his temple distorting. "How you."

"Ready to fight."

"That's right." He offered his knuckles out for a pound. "Gimme some."

Something about knocking her fist against his gave her some additional strength, and holy crap, it turned out she needed it. As Dr. Manello pushed her into the gym, she was stunned by the number of people who had lined up at the bleachers. It was the entire Black Dagger Brotherhood, all the fighters and her fellow trainees.

Everyone went silent.

At least until they started to clap. Those who had been seated rose to their feet, and people whistled and cheered as well—to the point where she was tempted to check and see if someone else, someone who was important or who had actually done something significant, was behind her.

"Oh, God, please stop," she muttered into the din.

What was she supposed to do? Pull a Queen Elizabeth and do a white-glove wave?

One by one, the Brothers and fighters came over to her, everybody from Rhage to Butch to Tohrment, John Matthew to Blay and Qhuinn, giving her shoulder or hand a squeeze—or in Zsadist's case, offering a brief nod. What truly saved her was that there wasn't any pity or gooey sympathy. No . . . it was like they were welcoming her into a club that they themselves had been a part of for quite some time.

It was a survivors' club.

Of course, she thought as she started to relax. The Brothers had all been critically injured in the field at one point or another in their long careers—likely, a number of times.

She had cut her teeth in that regard.

Phury was the last Brother to come up to her, his limp barely noticeable thanks to his state-of-the-art prosthetic lower leg.

"Don't let it get into your head," he said as he bent down. "Your body will heal more quickly than your mind. Your job is to place this in a perspective that allows you to still be effective out there. A loss of confidence is worse than going into the field unarmed. Talk to Mary if you need help, 'kay?"

His yellow eyes were warm and kind, his head of multi-colored hair reminding her of a lion's mane.

And as he went to step away, she almost called him back just so he could say that to her all over again.

But she would remember.

She had to, she thought as she put her hand to her sternum and rubbed. There was no sense getting herself killed . . . just because she had managed to live.

The trainees came next, Axe giving her a high five that was more like a medium to maybe a low four and a quarter. And then Boone was hugging her and Craeg and Paradise were offering words of encouragement.

Peyton was the only one who didn't make an approach. He stayed standing on the bleachers, a couple of rows up from the bottom, dressed in scrubs and tuxedo shoes. His hair was streaked back as if he had been pulling his hands through it.

She was glad he stayed put. The last thing she wanted was any of the assembled to know that they had spent all day together. That was not happening again, for one thing. And even if it was—and it most certainly was not—that was their business and no one else's.

He wasn't even looking at her, his eyes trained down on the wooden bench in front of him . . . as if *War and Peace* had been inscribed there and he was reading it word for word.

She had no idea when he'd left her room. She had woken up reaching for him, though—and she told herself she was relieved when she found that he wasn't there.

Tell me about your family. What are they like? What do they do that hurts you?

Someone was talking to the whole group now, but Novo couldn't follow the voice or the words. She hated that she was glad her surgeon was right with her, the equivalent of a comfort blanket who happened to have a medical degree and hands that were magic with a scalpel.

Her eyes wanted to dwell on Peyton—for reasons she knew were bad impulses to give in to. She needed to not look to him for security, safety, strength. Oskar had taught her all the reasons why that was not a good idea.

In truth, the biggest problem Peyton represented wasn't a sexual one, but something far more dangerous to her well-being.

He got into her heart? He was going to do more damage than that *lesser* with the dagger had, for sure.

Novo would not have wanted him to go down to her. Nope. No way.

As Peyton stayed on the bleachers and tried to feel comfortable with some other male rolling her around in that wheelchair—even if the guy had, okay, fine, been the one to put her heart back together—his only solace was that the distance was what she needed.

He'd never met someone more determined to be on their own.

Where did she live? Was she safe there during the day?

These things interested him way more than whatever the Brothers were talking about, but as he thought about what Mary had said to him, he forced himself to tune in.

"—more training is needed," the Brother Phury was saying, "just so that you're more clear what the proper procedures and operating principles are. So after we've talked it over"—he indicated his fellow Brothers—"we've decided to fall back into even more classroom training and take you out into the field in pairs, instead of in one whole group. This new paradigm is going to remain in place for quite some time. We were so impressed by your skills development that we jumped the gun taking you out. We're all learning here, and we're going to constantly assess and reassess how things are functioning—but we want you to know that we remain totally committed to this program—and to each and every one of you trainees."

At that, the Brother looked directly at Peyton.

"Any questions?"

Paradise put her hand up. "What will the schedule be like? For the times we're in the field. I mean, how often will we be able to get out there?"

As that question got answered, Peyton thought back to his talk with Mary . . . and then he looked at Novo.

The training program wasn't the only thing he didn't want to give up on. It was a good guess that Novo was going to try to pull back from him. He had seen her in her healing state and she was going to want to separate herself from that by keeping her distance from him. But he wanted to be with her again—to lie with her on some bed, somewhere, her head on his chest, his arm around her as she slept.

"Okay, so let's break for tonight," Phury announced. "This class has been working pretty much straight through since you started, and now's a good opportunity for everyone to regroup in their heads and hit it fresh on Saturday."

It wasn't until after people started to disperse that Peyton realized he'd been in an enclosed space with Paradise and hadn't given her any thought at all.

In the back of his head, notions of being proud of himself warred with the idea that maybe he'd just traded one addiction in a female form for another. Now he was all about Novo.

And yet the shit with her felt very, very different.

As he wide-stepped it down to the floor, he was not surprised to find his head was fucking pounding, and he loitered on the periphery as the Brothers walked out and the trainees went with them—with Novo in that chair in the middle of the pack. Like she might be using the others as a shield.

"The bus is leaving in ten minutes," Rhage called out. "We're going to beat the shit out of you first thing midnight Saturday, so sleep well, children!"

Out in the corridor, Peyton glanced to the office and wondered if he could find her address in a file or something—but that was a no-go. For one, it was automatic dismissal under the whole privacy deal. For another, it put him squarely in stalker territory.

Which he was so not.

As he trailed behind her.

Wondering how to get her alone.

Yeah, he was sooo far away from emergency-order-of-protection territory.

Besides, she was not being discharged tonight. No way.

In the end, he let her be, hanging back as her surgeon returned her to her room. And God, as that door eased shut behind her, it seemed impossible that they had spent hours together, him naked, her as soft as he had ever seen her.

Peyton was all the way down at the end of the corridor, about to go through the steel door to the bus, when he realized he'd left his tuxedo shoved into one of the lockers. Whatever. He had two more at home.

As he pushed his way into the parking garage, he decided to—

Craeg was standing by the bus. Like he had been waiting.

On the approach, Peyton did a quick review of the male's stance. Weight was down in the legs. Hands were curled into fists by his sides. Jaw was locked and loaded.

Shit. Really? They were seriously going to do this?

Standing beside her male, Paradise was urgent. "Craeg. Come on. Get on the bus." And then she put herself in front of the guy. "Craeg. Don't be stupid."

Peyton was the one who addressed her. "Give us a minute, Paradise."

"Don't you fucking tell her what to do." Craeg's pecs swelled as he took in a deep inhale. "She is none of your fucking business."

The female reached out and touched her male's shoulder. "Come on. Let's get on the bus."

"No," Craeg said without looking at her. "Gimme a minute."

Paradise glanced back and forth between them, as if she were hoping one of them would come to his senses. But nope.

"Fine, get yourselves kicked out," she snapped. "You're a pair of hotheaded animals."

After she disappeared onto the transport, Peyton closed the distance and said in a low voice, "Do it."

"Do what," Craeg growled.

Peyton flashed his palms . . . then deliberately linked them behind his back and spoke in the Old Language. *"I hereby offer you a* rythe. *I do so in recognition of my disrespect and disregard of your status as a bonded male unto the female Paradise, with whom you have been mated. It is not my intention to justify this behavior in any fashion, and I wish to make up for my lapse in judgment according to the Old Ways."*

Craeg's face became remote, his anger banking.

Switching back to English, Peyton said, "Take the free shot and let's put this behind us. I'm not aggressing on your female. I recognize she is yours and you are hers. I had a knee-jerk reaction that came from a friendship situation, not a romantic one, and I'm willing to swear on that shit. But in the meantime, come on, man, just do it."

There was a period of silence, only the low hum of the bus's diesel engine filling the quiet. Dimly, Peyton was aware that Axe and Boone had crowded into the open door of the bus, the two trainees staring over.

Boone looked worried. Axe was smiling like he was filming this for Barstool Sports' Insta account.

"So be it," Craeg said.

Peyton didn't bother to brace himself. He just stood there and let that huge fist come flying at his face.

The impact was like a bomb going off on his cheek, and he spun like a top, doing a Three Stooges three-sixty on one foot as the crack echoed around all the layers of the parking area's concrete floors.

Bag. Of. Sand.

He went down—or maybe the ground came up to him—like a deadweight, his bones bouncing all tiddlywinks in the bag of his flesh. It took a minute or so before his breath came back to him, and even after it did, he just lay there, because the cold happened to be right under where he'd been hit.

A pair of combat boots came into his line of vision, and he had the random thought that they looked awfully stable, the kind of thing that built you a solid foundation on which to stand. And throw righties at assholes.

"Do you need a doctor?" Craeg asked.

"KBgfaod jkfdoo lkd."

"What?"

Peyton tried to swallow, and in doing so, he tasted the copper milk-shake of blood. But none of his teeth seemed loose.

#bonus

"ImokayrealIam."

"One more time?"

"Okay. I am. Help me up."

"That's better." A huge palm came from above as if the Creator Himself were resurrecting him. "I gotchu."

Peyton grabbed on to what was offered and found himself hoisted up off the asphalt like he was a sunken ship being brought back to the surface of the ocean. And you want to talk about waves? His head went on a wobble that translated all the way through him to his ankles.

Craeg's steadying grip on his biceps was the only thing that kept him on his feet.

"Did that feel good?" Peyton mumbled. Then he pointed to his own chest. "Not hating. Swear."

"Yeah, actually it did." Craeg put his arm around Peyton's shoulders. "It felt real good."

"Good."

They mounted the shallow steps that took them up onto the bus, and oh, man, Paradise was pissed—and clearly not prepared to be quiet about it.

"You two are such goddamn good friends," she said as she crossed her arms over her chest, "you can sit together." She put her palm up to Craeg. "Don't even speak to me."

"If you need somewhere to stay," Peyton said with his new lisp, "I have plenty of space."

"May take you up on it," Craeg muttered as they slid into a seat side by side like two twelve-year-olds who were in trouble at school.

As Peyton slumped and started to slide off into the aisle, Craeg propped him up.

"You know," the guy remarked, "I kinda feel like I'm your car seat, buddy."

"This whole soldier thing doesn't work? I think you'd make an excellent boxer. Serious."

"Thanks, man. That means a lot. You still up for helping with Paradise's birthday? And by that, I mean do everything that's supposed to be classy?"

"Hell yeah."

"Good deal."

Boy, whoever thought up the *rythe* thing got it right. With one non-sucker punch, the air was cleared and they were done with it.

Well, except for Paradise.

Craeg was going to be sleeping on the couch for a lot of days, that much was for sure.

With a shimmy and subtle surge, they were off for the outside world. And Peyton was not looking forward to whatever was cooking at his father's house. Given the way he had bailed on First Meal with Romina and her parents, he was going to be in trouble with his pops.

What was the saying, though?

Same shit. Different day.

Whatever.

TWENTY-FIVE

S axton twisted around so he could see out the back of the truck's cab. As the two human men approached Ruhn, they were on a saunter—until suddenly they weren't, their bodies rushing forward in a coordinated attack.

"The hell I'm not calling," Saxton muttered as he fumbled with his phone.

As soon as he sent the text, he flipped his eyes up just to make sure Ruhn was still alive—and caught the rather alarming sight of one of the men flying through the air, ass over teakettle. The guy landed in a heap on his head, flopping over like a loose bag of potatoes.

Ruhn grabbed the other one and slammed him face-first into the side of the truck. Then came the hits: to the gut, to the jaw in an uppercut, to the groin. Ruhn's fists were controlled, vicious weapons and he used them as if he had a repertoire of offensive and defensive moves so vast, this was just child's play.

The bag of potatoes rallied and got up on loose legs, his drunk-walk back to the fray suggesting he might better head in the opposite direction. What wasn't a joke? That knife in his hand.

Saxton pounded on the rear window and then lunged for the driver's door, throwing it open and jumping out.

Ruhn was already on it. He glanced behind him at the human and then refocused on the one he was working on, bending the man's arm at a weird angle—and driving the lower part of it down onto the high, hard edge of the bed. The bones broke instantly and Ruhn was smart enough to clap a palm onto the mouth that cranked open, to muffle the scream.

Throwing the man to the side like litter, Ruhn spun around.

He wasn't even breathing hard.

And he was not the male Saxton had just had dinner with, that was for sure. His eyes were cold and curiously flat, as if his warmth and shy kindness had given his wheelhouse over to a serial killer. In fact, his face showed no expression at all. It was a frozen mask of the features Saxton had loved staring at over the French cuisine and the candlelight.

The human with the blade staggered over, a trail of bright red blood drops behind him in the snowpack. Clearly more aggressive and angry than competent, one got the sense this was not going to end well for him.

And it didn't.

Ruhn overpowered him instantly, grabbing on to the wrist that controlled the knife, and spinning the human around, so that he also banged headfirst into the side of the truck—and instantly, the knife was down in the snow.

The human was not far behind. Ruhn forced the man to the ground, mounted his back, and grabbed on to the sides of the man's head.

He was going to twist until the neck broke. Saxton saw it clear as day.

"No!" He jumped forward. "Ruhn, stop!"

At the sound of Saxton's voice, Ruhn went statue, nothing on him moving even as he was poised to snap that cranium right around.

"Let him go. We don't need the police involved—and there could be a lot of eyes on this." Saxton glanced up at the apartment over the restaurant. "Come on, we need to go."

The shades were all still down on those second-story windows, and the upper floors on either side of *Premier* were dark. But all it would take was a single set of curious eyes, drawn by an unusual sound, and there were going to be complications all over the place.

Saxton reached down and touched Ruhn's shoulder. "Come with me."

God, the male wasn't even breathing hard. Even as those humans were panting from exertion and pain, great puffs coming out of their mouths like steam from old trains, Ruhn was a robot, something mechanical that did not have to concern itself with oxygen.

"Ruhn, look at me."

Beneath the male, the human was straining, grunting, begging, his coarse face red as a neon beer sign.

"Ruhn."

Ruhn's head cranked around and those matte eyes focused for a moment—and chilled Saxton to the bone. Who could ever have guessed a demon was behind that placid, timid exterior? This was another personality entirely.

From out of thin air, Rhage and V arrived on scene, the Brothers dressed for fighting in black leathers and jackets that held arsenals of weapons. The surprise on their faces? He totally understood.

Rhage stepped forward and addressed Ruhn. "Hey, son, what are we doing here?"

The human in that hold was struggling to breathe, spit and blood running out from between his crooked teeth, but it wasn't as if Ruhn seemed to notice or care.

Rhage got down on his haunches and started to talk quietly to the male. Meanwhile, V closed in from behind.

"You need to step off, Hollywood," the Brother said. "We're done with the chatting."

After a moment, Rhage nodded, and V went into action, going behind Ruhn, snagging a hold under each of his arms, and yanking outward so that the grip was broken. As the human's face landed in the snow with a bounce that reminded Saxton of a plate hitting the kitchen floor, Ruhn was dragged off onto his ass.

Now came the breathing.

Like a spell had been broken, Ruhn started to inhale and exhale in great pumps, his hands coming up to hold his head, a strangled sound like a moan leaving his mouth.

Saxton stepped back as the humans were packed off by the Brothers, the two men scrambling for that truck that they had parked around the corner. There was a good chance short-term memories were being erased, and Saxton didn't want that. He wanted them to be scared into leaving Minnie alone.

But he had other things to worry about.

With eyes that were now dazed, Ruhn looked up at him. "I didn't want you to see this part of me," he whispered.

Staring down at the male . . . Saxton had no idea what to say.

Saxton left the scene about twenty minutes later, dematerializing to . . . wait, where was he going?

As he re-formed in a stand of pine trees, he looked around, and was nominally amazed he'd been able to pull off the disappearing trick at all. Ah, yes. Minnie's farmhouse. That was right.

Walking through the snow to the front door, he recognized he was ruining his loafers, but he didn't care. And it was a relief that things were opened up for him before he even mounted the steps.

The female who stood in the doorway was the one from the portrait in the parlor, the younger version of Minnie, only taller and without the laugh lines. With dark hair that was long and straight, and a lithe body in jeans and a Syracuse sweatshirt, she was casual—until you met her pale eyes.

This was a very sharp, very protective female. And he liked her instantly.

"Hi," she said. "Welcome. I'm Minnie's granddaughter, also called Miniahna—but I go by Ahna."

As he approached her, he tried to reconnect with his purpose here, his job, his reality. It was so hard. He kept seeing Ruhn's mask-like face, and with that image in his mind, it was hard to focus on anything else—impossible not to obsessively try to reconcile the violence he'd witnessed firsthand with the rest of what he knew, and liked, about the male.

"I am Saxton," he said as he stepped onto the stoop and bowed low. "It is my pleasure to be of service to you and your *granhmen*."

"Thank you so much for all your help." The female dropped her voice. "This has been a nightmare like you can't believe."

"We're going to take care of this," he affirmed in equal quiet. "Oh, there you are, Minnie."

He smiled at the older female as he entered the parlor. "How are you?"

"I am well, thank you." Minnie glanced at Ahna from her seat. "But I don't see why I have to leave. What happened? What's changed?"

Saxton went over and sat down beside her on the sofa. "As we discussed, I went and spoke with the humans. I don't want to alarm you, but there was, shall we say, a bit of an altercation."

Read: Ruhn almost decapitated one of them. With his bare hands.

"And in light of that, we feel as though you should stay with your granddaughter for a couple of nights."

"I can't leave the house unattended." The female shook her head, her eyes worried and sad. "This is all I have in the world. What if they—"

"I could stay here," he offered. "If you're worried about the property, it would be my pleasure to stay in a guest room, or even sleep here on this sofa, so that you are assured all is well in your absence."

Minnie looked at Ahna, and the granddaughter was right on it. "*Granhmen,* be sensible. Come downtown. It is a most generous offer by Saxton. Most generous."

Miniahna refocused on Saxton. "I cannot ask you to do that."

"Madam, you did not. And if it will give you peace of mind, that is all the repayment I shall ever need."

Besides, it wasn't like he was leaving his own home behind. More like a hotel suite with an elevation.

Ahna went over and dropped down to her knees by her *granhmen.* "Please. This has gone on long enough. I'm so exhausted losing sleep, and with everything that is coming up in the next few weeks, please. I'm begging you."

Minnie's fallen shoulders were answer enough. "All right. If I must."

"Well done." Saxton got to his feet. "Now, perhaps there are some things you'd like to gather? If there is much to be transported, I shall summon a car."

Fritz might have his hands full running the Brotherhood's lives, but there was nothing that *doggen* liked better than a problem to solve.

"Come, *Granhmen,* let's get you packed."

"But I could come back. Shower and change here each night and—"

"*Granhmen.*"

Minnie rose from the sofa and looked around. With her white hair and another version of the same loose dress she'd had on the other night, she seemed every one of her years, not just old, but worn out and discouraged.

"I'm worried that if I leave . . . I won't ever come back."

"That is not true," Ahna said. "This will always be your home."

"You want me to move in with you."

"Of course I do. But I'm not going to make you leave here for good. This is about safety, not because you're frail and can't live independently. You will absolutely come back if that's what you want."

It took some more cajoling, but then the females were heading for the second floor. In their absence, he took out his phone to call for the butler to send a car. And then he cursed. He had to work all night, yet he'd promised to babysit the house.

As if on cue, his phone rang and he answered it without checking to see who it was. "Hello?"

There was a pause. And then Ruhn said, "I'm so sorry."

Saxton closed his eyes. "Are you all right?"

"Yes. I am uninjured."

Are you who I thought you were, Saxton amended in his own head.

"Where are you?" he asked.

"I'm in the truck, going back to the Brotherhood's compound."

"I'm sorry I left without saying anything, but I was concerned about a retaliation against Minnie—I'm at her house now. She's leaving with her granddaughter as soon as she has some things gathered."

"Good. That's good."

There was a pause. And just as Saxton was trying to re-form the "are you okay?" thing, Ruhn spoke up. "Listen . . . I want to explain things to you. I know that you are shocked, and I just . . . I'm not that person. I mean, a part of me is. But . . ." The male took a deep breath. "I am very good at something I hate, and I used that skill for a number of years for my family. That is not me anymore, however—and I don't want it to be. That is my past. It stays . . . in the past."

Saxton thought about the male who had sat across from him at that little table. The one who had been so careful as he had eaten things he could not pronounce, but had loved. The one who had sheepishly tried to tackle *escargots à la Bourguignonne* and ended up with one shooting off onto the floor. The one who had sipped white wine and held the delicate glass as if he were afraid he would break the stem.

Then he thought of the lover who had bent him over in the kitchen. Passion. But not rage.

That could be a thin line to walk, however.

In the end, he had to go with his gut. "Could you do me a favor?"

"Anything."

"Can you come to Minnie's? We need to transport her stuff downtown. She and her granddaughter can dematerialize to the address, but if you could bring her things to them, that would be great."

"I'm on my way."

"See you in a bit."

"Thank you. Yes."

As the call was ended, Saxton took the phone from his ear and stared at it.

"Everything okay?" Ahna asked as she came down the stairs.

"Yes, indeed. Is that suitcase all?"

"She has a carry bag, toiletries, and some pictures of my grandfather she would like to bring."

"Perfect."

He got up and walked around the little parlor, coming to stand in front of the fireplace with its blue and white tiles. As he thought of the love that had brought the pieces of art across a vast, dangerous ocean, he wanted that force of grace and warmth and stability in his own life.

But it was hard to find the courage to open oneself again. There was such risk involved, and though the reward was great, the chances were slim.

Funny . . . that this was occurring to him as he considered Ruhn.

Clearing his throat, he said, "Can you please tell me how to operate the security alarm? I work nights, but if it goes off, I can be here, with reinforcements, in an instant."

"But of course. There's a pad over here in the kitchen."

As they went in, and she wrote various codes and cell phone numbers and her address down, he looked around and noticed that there was a light out in the recessed fixtures in the ceiling. And the faucet was dripping over at the sink. A whistling by the back door onto what he assumed was a porch suggested some weather stripping had to be replaced.

It had been two years since Minnie's *hellren* went unto the Fade, if he remembered correctly.

If he were handy with these things, he would help her.

"Let me go check everything is in order downstairs in the guest quarters." Ahna headed for what had to be the cellar door. "She's going to need to make sure everything is in order as she wants you to feel like the honored guest you are. But I don't want to waste time or back-slide."

"I will be fine."

"I'll be right back."

After a minute, Minnie came around the corner, pulling on a coat the color of mulberry wine. When she saw the basement door open, she became flustered. "Oh, I must go down and—"

Ahna appeared at the head of the stairs. "Everything is in order, *Granhmen.* Come now, let's go."

Minnie looked around as if she were saying a good-bye that tore at her heart. "I, ah . . ." She glanced at Saxton. "Your friend is more than welcome to stay here as well?"

Saxton covered his own awkwardness as he bowed. "You are most kind."

It took another ten minutes to get the older female out of the house, but then she and her granddaughter left her things by the front door and dematerialized from the closed garage. Left by himself, Saxton returned to the kitchen, took off his coat, and started up the Mr. Coffee machine. As the unit burped and hissed, he got out one mug. Added a second. And then sat down at the circular table in the alcove.

Funny how each and every home had its own smell, its own accent of creaks and groans, its singular impression. And as he looked around, he saw the Old Ways preserved . . . and old love enshrined. It was a sad commentary on the relentless progress of life that there was visible decay and aging happening, one half of the happy couple trying desperately to sustain that which had been a two-handed carry.

He thought of Blay and his time with the male.

And was still locked in his memories when he heard a truck pull up to the front of the house.

Ruhn, he thought, as he got up and headed for the front door.

Or perhaps the shady developer had sent reinforcements.

His heart pounded equally over either.

TWENTY-SIX

uhn stepped up to the front door of the farmhouse and found himself straightening his wool jacket. There was blood on it. His knuckles were busted. And he had been hit a couple of times in the face, although the pain was muted from the cold.

He was a fucking mess.

After Saxton had dematerialized out of the scene behind the French restaurant, Ruhn had spoken with the Brothers for a time. They didn't seem particularly bothered by any of the violence or the fact that he'd nearly killed the human. But their opinion was not what mattered to him.

He knocked on the door and stepped back, stomping his boots in preparation for going in. And then things were open. Saxton was on the other side, his coat having been removed, his blond hair flopped off his cowlick as if he had been dragging restless hands through it.

His stare locked on Ruhn's left eye, the one that had its own heartbeat from the swelling.

Ruhn lifted a hand and covered whatever was going on up there. But that was stupid. "May I come in?"

Saxton seemed to shake himself. "Yes, please. It's cold. I'm making coffee?"

As the male indicated the way in, Ruhn followed the direction and then just stood there in the little entry area at the base of the stairs. Saxton's eyes traveled around, but always returned to Ruhn's face.

Maybe his injuries were worse than he thought? They didn't feel like much. But then, with his high pain tolerance, they never did.

"It's fine," he said as he touched his face. "Whatever this is."

Saxton cleared his throat. "Yes. Of course. Ah, coffee?"

Ruhn shook his head and proceeded in the solicitor's wake to the back of the house. Sure enough, there were a pair of mugs on the counter and the scent of fresh brew in the air.

"Do you like anything in yours?" Saxton went for the pot and pulled it out from its base. "I just like a little sugar in mine—"

"I was conscripted into a fighting ring. For a decade."

Saxton slowly pivoted, coffeepot in his hand. "I'm sorry?"

Ruhn paced around and tried not to get lost in how much he hated talking about the past. "It was an indentured fighting ring, run in South Carolina. Humans do them for dogs and birds. Vampires do it for our own species. I spent ten years getting in the ring with other males so that people could bet on the outcome. I was very good at it and I hated it. Every second."

When Saxton didn't say anything, he stopped and looked across the homey kitchen at the other male. Such surprise. Such stunned shock.

Fates, he wanted to throw up.

"I'm sorry," he blurted. Even though he wasn't sure exactly what he was apologizing for.

No, wait, he knew. It was the fact he had anything like this to confess to such a fine, upstanding male—and also now that he'd spoken of the past, Ruhn was drowning in it once again.

He remembered the stench of the stables where the fighting males were kept. The spoiled food. The kill-or-be-killed reality that had meant he had been in the ring even with those just out of their transitions. He had had to beat others who were weaker than him and be beaten by those closer to his level. And all the while, the masters of the fighting ring had profited from the bodies that had been maimed, crippled . . . destroyed.

The young ones were what haunted him the most: all those begging, bloodshot eyes, and pleading mouths, and heaving chests from pain and exertion. He had cried every time at the end. When the moment had inevitably come, his tears had run through the dirt, sweat, and blood down his face.

But if he did not do the job, his family was going to pay the price.

And so he had learned that in fact you could die even as you lived.

"I'm sorry," he croaked again.

Saxton blinked. And then put the coffeepot back in the machine without pouring anything. "I'm not . . . ah, I don't believe I knew of such a thing in the New World. I have heard stories about betting on males in brokered combat in the Old Country, however. How did you . . . if you don't mind me asking, how did you come to be a part of the practice? 'Conscripted' means in servitude. Were you . . . how did this happen?"

Ruhn crossed his arms over his chest and let his head hang. "I loved my father. He was a male who provided well for my *mahmen* and his family. We never were rich, but we never were left wanting." Images of the male chopping wood, and building things, and fixing cars, replaced the ugliness of the fighting ring. "He had a weakness, though. All of us do, and those of us who think they do not are not being honest. He had a gambling problem. He bet on the fights for some time, and eventually racked up so many debts that not only was he going to lose our house—but my sister and my *mahmen* . . . well, they were in danger. They were going to be conscripted for . . . activities of another sort.

Do you understand what I'm saying?" As Saxton paled and nodded, Ruhn continued, "I had to do something to cover what he owed. I mean, I wasn't going to stand by and have those two innocent females pay . . . Fates, I can still hear the sound of my father begging the boss, weeping for some more time to try to pay up."

When his voice cracked, he coughed a little. "You know, I think I will have some coffee, if you do not mind."

"Let me get it for you—"

Ruhn put his hand out. "No. I will do it."

He needed something to occupy him for a moment; otherwise, he was liable to break down. The memories were too clear, like lasers burning through him. He could still remember the banging on the door when the boss had shown up and threatened to take his sister and use her to work off the debts.

The male had said if their *mahmen* came, too, it would go quicker. Five years instead of ten. They had until dawn came to make good.

Instead, Ruhn had departed before the sun had risen and he had traveled farther south, to the deep woods that had hidden within them an extensive operation of fighting, illegal gambling, and prostitution. They had tested him out in the offices, sending in a male who had been half his height and twice his weight. Ruhn had taken a brutal beating, but he had just kept getting up, over and over again, even as he had bled from his mouth and from cuts and bruises all over his body.

After they had accepted him, he had made his mark on some kind of document he hadn't been able to read, and that was that.

Coming back to the present, Ruhn looked down and found a full mug in his hand. Guess he had poured himself the coffee.

Taking a test sip, he found that the taste was perfect—but a sting suggested his lower lip was split. "As I said, I needed to be the one who fixed it. My father was too old to fight, and I was out of my transition by about twenty years at that time. I've always been big and very strong.

Sometimes what we do to survive . . . is harder than what we do when we die." He shrugged. "But my parents were able to rebuild their lives. My sister . . . well, that was another story." He looked at the solicitor. "Please know, it was not something I would have chosen freely. It is not in my nature to be violent, but I learned that I will do anything to take care of those I love. I also learned that if someone is trying to hurt me . . . I will defend myself, to the death."

He shook his head. "My father . . . he never got over what happened. He never bet a single penny after I went away, and by the time I came out, they were both working and in good health. I couldn't see them, of course, while I was fighting. You were not allowed out of your stall."

"Stall?" Saxton said with horror.

"They kept us underground in stalls, as you would horses. The spaces were six feet by six feet. We were allowed out only to fight, and we had no visitors except for the females they gave us to feed from. That's what they wanted to use my sister and my *mahmen* for." Through a tight throat, he added, "And sometimes we had to service . . . well. Anyway."

Saxton seemed to wipe his eyes. "I cannot imagine what that was like."

"It was . . ." Ruhn touched the side of his head. "It did something in here. It rewired me, and I wasn't sure whether it was permanent. . . . Until tonight, I hadn't been in a position where I was fighting again. It came back, though. All of it."

He took another draw from the mug, not because he was particularly thirsty, but because he was done with the conversation. The facts had been shared, and he had tried to be honest without talking too much about how ugly it had all been.

How ugly he had been when he'd been there.

As the silence stretched out, he risked a glance at Saxton—

His breath caught. The male's eyes were full of compassion, not disgust or fear.

"Come sit down," Saxton said softly. "You're bleeding and I want to clean you up. Sit."

When Ruhn continued to just stand there, Saxton went over, took the male's hand, and nudged him toward the table. As Ruhn sat down, the coffee in his mug was wobbling because his hands were shaking.

That made two of them on the trembling front, Saxton thought as he walked to the sink and started the water to warm up. Peeling free a couple of paper towels from a roll mounted on a dowel, he tried to comprehend what Ruhn had been through.

No wonder the male's affect had changed as it had during the fight behind the restaurant—that blank stare had been more upsetting than the violence itself. Indeed, after living with the Brotherhood for this long and hearing their stories of being in the field? Saxton was more than well-versed in violence. No, the disturbing thing had been the fact that Ruhn had disappeared into some other part of himself and had had to be all but pried off his prey.

A wild animal unleashed.

Saxton tested the rush of water with his forefinger. It was warm enough. Pumping a little soap onto the Quicker Picker Upper, he got the towel wet and then turned back around. Ruhn was staring into the mug, his brows down, his shoulders tight.

One did not have to guess where the male had gone in his mind.

To have to save his sister and *mahmen* from being used as veins and no doubt sexual outlets for the fighters? Kept in a stall? All for the mistakes of his sire?

For ten years, penned up like a tiger, not knowing at any given hour whether he was going to be sent back into the ring to be beaten or killed. And along the way, he had to have been injured and learned to live with loneliness and pain.

It was too sad to even contemplate.

Walking over, he expected Ruhn to look up. When he did not, Saxton put his hand lightly on the male's shoulder.

Ruhn jumped and knocked his mug over. "Oh! I'm sorry—"

"I've got it." Saxton went back and snagged the paper towel roll. "Here. I've got it."

Unraveling a bunch of the Bounty or whatever it was, he threw the stuff down and let its absorbency work its magic.

"Turn toward me." He hooked his forefinger under Ruhn's chin and brought the male's face around. "That's it."

Ruhn flinched when he made contact, but Saxton was pretty sure that was more because, for him, reality was a jumbled-up mess at the moment.

"This is quite a cut," Saxton murmured as he went to work on a laceration over Ruhn's brow. "And it's getting more swollen by the moment. Maybe we should take you in to have Doc Jane or Dr. Manello look at this."

"I've had worse."

Saxton paused. "Yes. I'm sure you have."

As he resumed cleaning off the dried blood, he wished he could say the right thing, the proper thing . . . anything that could possibly relieve some of that decade. There were no words, however.

But there was a remedy.

"Is the fighting operation still ongoing?" he asked tightly.

Ruhn shook his head. "There was a revolt by the fighters about a year after I left. They got themselves loose, killed the guards and the enforcers, and slaughtered the boss. The compound is all overgrown now." He cleared his throat. "I went back, you see. Not once, but a couple of times. I was trying to . . . make sense of it all. Ultimately, I failed."

"I don't know how you could."

"As I said, I did it for my family. That is the only peace I have ever found." Ruhn exhaled long and slow. "But you know, I also regret that I let my sister down. Maybe if I had been home, she wouldn't have fallen in with that violent male. Perhaps I could have done something before he moved her so far away, up here to Caldwell. After I got out, I tried to find her, but she'd left no trail. My parents knew that he was dangerous—I think he must have relocated her as a form of control. I hate that she died without me there to save her."

"You did what you could," Saxton said sadly. "At the end of the night, that's all any of us can do."

He went back to the sink with what was left of the roll and got some wet with nothing but water. Over at Ruhn once again, he made sure he wiped all the soap away. The rest of what was on the male's face was bruising, and you couldn't clean that up.

"You say that I did an unselfish thing with Bitty," Ruhn said roughly. "I didn't. I saved her from me. What I did to those men out in that parking lot? I've got a bad side, and in the end, I knew she was safer with Rhage and Mary. Plus . . . what if she ever found out? She couldn't have a father like me."

"What do you think Rhage does for the race?"

"That's different. I wasn't saving anyone."

"Other than your sister and *mahmen*."

"I don't know."

Saxton dried off the area. "This looks bad."

"It'll be all right." Ruhn glanced up. "You are very kind to me."

Saxton brushed a fingertip over the male's jaw. And then he stroked the thick hair back, and touched Ruhn's lower lip.

"You're cut here, too," he whispered.

Leaning down, he gently kissed the place that had been torn by a human's fist. And as he straightened, a warning started to go off at the base of his brain.

As much as he was attracted to Ruhn, and wanted to be with the male, hurt people . . . hurt people.

Yes, yes, it was the kind of thing you could see with a sappy image as a meme on Facebook, a trite little four-word construction that seemed custom-fit for the snowflake generation's perpetual, depressive sensitivity. But as a rescuer, it was entirely like him to take in a stray who had been abused. How did he know that Ruhn's past was truly over, though?

He thought of that look in the male's eyes—or rather the absence of expression—during that fight, especially when Ruhn had been about to snap the human's neck.

"It's okay," Ruhn said roughly as he pushed his chair back and got to his feet.

"What is?"

The other male took a step back. And then another. "I understand."

"Understand what?" Saxton asked.

"I don't trust me, either."

"What are you talking about?"

"I can see it in your eyes." Ruhn nodded. "And I get it. You're trying to reconcile what you saw with what you wish me to be. I live with that all the time. Every day when I close my eyes, I am reminded of the things I did. And if I forget, I just have to look in the mirror."

"Ruhn, don't make up my mind for me."

With rough hands, the male took off his jacket. Then he turned around and yanked his shirt all the way up to his shoulders.

Saxton gasped. That broad back was covered with a pattern of welts—except no, that wasn't it. They weren't marks made by a whip. The four-inch-long cuts were far too regular, too surgical—and there were at least thirty of them, fanning out from the spine. They had to have been brined into place, salt being poured over the open wounds when they had been made to ensure that the things didn't close and disappear as the skin regenerated.

"Thirty-seven," Ruhn said baldly. "I killed thirty-seven males with my bare hands. And every time I did, they took a knife to me and added to my tally. It was done for the crowd, so they would bet more money. It was for the show."

Saxton covered his mouth with his palm, tears spearing into his eyes.

As Ruhn pivoted back around, all Saxton wanted to do was throw his arms around the male and hold him until the memories didn't hurt quite as badly.

But it was obvious that was a no-go.

Ruhn pulled the shirt back into place and put his jacket on once more. "I'm going to go now. But you need to tell me where to drop Mistress Miniahna's things off." In a dead voice, the male tacked on, "And not to worry. I will not interact with the females. I'll leave the things in a safe place and stay away from them."

"Ruhn, please don't—"

"So where am I going?"

"You are not lesser than, Ruhn."

"Oh, I'm worse. I'm a straight-up killer. None of those males wanted to be there any more than I did. They were all conscripted, too, working off debts. They were not killers, not any more than I was—at least not when I first arrived there. But I am a walking trophy to what I turned into. I have blood on my hands, Saxton. I am a murderer."

The male walked over to the archway. "So tell me, where am I dropping off the—"

"You're not a murderer."

Ruhn's head lowered in defeat. "That's an emotional declaration, not a legal one, and you know it."

"Ruhn, you—"

"Look, I don't like to talk about all of this." Ruhn's eyes skipped around the kitchen. "I sweep it under the rug during the waking hours and I pray during my sleep that I won't remember my dreams. The only time I ever discussed it before now was when the Brothers looked into my background because of Bitty—and even then, I didn't . . . well, it doesn't matter. I guess I'm telling you all this because I feel like you deserve the honesty. There was something happening between us, and it was on both sides. But see, I know who you are, and you don't . . . well, unless you know the truth, you don't really know me. And that look in your eyes? The wariness, the suspicion, it tells me I did the right thing."

"I can trust you."

"You don't have to." Ruhn touched over his heart. "One thing that I have learned after all these years working for the *glymera* is that the poor have only their dignity and pride to offer the world. My father taught me that. And I cannot have my dignity if I lie to someone I'm falling in love with."

Saxton's breath caught in his chest.

But before he could respond, Ruhn shook his head and turned away. "You know, I actually think it's best that someone else make that trip into town. I've got to go."

"Ruhn—"

The male stopped, and did not look back. "Please, just let me go. Just . . . let me leave."

Every instinct in Saxton's body told him to stop Ruhn from going.

But it wasn't up to him.

A moment later, the front door of the farmhouse shut quietly, and Saxton fell into the chair Ruhn had been sitting in. The coffee was still warm in his mug.

That did not last, however.

TWENTY-SEVEN

"**J** know you want to fuck me."

Peyton looked up as the human woman addressed him, and it took him a couple of seconds to focus on her—then again, Ice Blue, the club he usually hit, was hoppin', the music was loud, and he'd done half a dozen bong hits before he started drinking.

Oh, and then you had the blue lasers spearing through the smoky air and the fact that he hadn't slept properly for a day or two.

"Did you hear what I said?" she purred.

She was dressed in a skintight white latex dress that was cut low to show off her spectacular breasts and hemmed high to give plenty of leg. The shoes were strappy and tilted her delicate feet so far forward, it was like she was *en pointe,* and her hair was dark and flowing in curls around her shoulders and her lower back.

In the VIP section, she was hands down, going away, the trophy of the night, the most erotic, beautiful thing there was, and she wanted him. Why? It was not his scintillating conversation—they hadn't said anything more than a quick hi-how're-ya. Hell, he didn't know his name—

Her name. He didn't know *her* name.

No, it was his suit-and-tie. His ostrich shoes. The fact that he and his crew had come in the back where they didn't have to worry about getting said shoes ruined by the snow or being inconvenienced by the wait line. It was also the bottle service here in this private banquet, and the way security deferred to him, and the hundys he flashed around as drinks were brought over. He was an apex spender and she was prepared to use her physical assets to get on the money train.

And hey, he was wearing white, too, so it was, like, totally, predestined.

"Let's take a selfie," she said as she straddled his legs and took her phone out of a bag that was only big enough for an iPhone. The small-sized one, not the big-as-a-Pop-Tart variety.

"No." He put his palm out. "No pictures."

She giggled and put the phone away. "You telling me you're famous? I don't recognize you."

With practiced ease, she took his hand and guided it to her hip. "I'm up from Manhattan. I'm doing a photo shoot down by the river tomorrow. I hate the cold. I wish I were in Miami."

At that, she pushed her hair out of the way in a very calculated, *Oh, I'm soooo dissatisfied by my glamorous lot in life—and b.t.dub, my hair is just such a buuuuurden.*

It was the mating call of the female club rat.

And usually, he'd start strategizing about dark corners and blow jobs at this point. For some reason, though, all he could think of was . . . *If you'd rather be in Miami, hop a plane, and you paid for those damn extensions. If you don't want the shit covering your tits, pull it back in a rubber band, for godsakes.*

As she started talking at him again, he was very aware that this whole out-to-the-club thing was not following his playbook. Glancing over to his boys, he saw three other vampires dressed out of the same men's section of Neiman Marcus, the trio like variations on a set of cocktail coasters: The suits might have been different shades of blue or gray, but the cut was the same with skinny legs and thin lapels, and the shirts under those fitted jackets were subtly patterned in similar fashions. The watches were not Rolex, nope, too cheap. They were Audemars Piguet or Hublot. And in their breast pockets, they were packing coke and X. Oh, and there was a driver waiting in the back alley when they were through looking good while they polluted themselves. No Uber. Ever.

And this little *hors d'oeuvre* in the white shrink-wrap would know all that.

She also came with her own crew, her three friends the saltshakers to his buddies' pepper mills.

So yes, everyone had gotten the memo.

With no real interest, he squeezed her waist to test whether it was Spanx or dieting that had created that tight curve—and it was both, going by the whalebones of the corset she had on. She was too thin, he decided.

He liked Novo's build better. It was power. Strength. Solidity.

Man, this was so not happening for him. He was the plug out of the socket, his lounging sprawl for the first time because of boredom rather than entitled languor.

With a lithe shift, the girl stood up off him, extended her arms over her head, and did a slow turn that presented him with her ass. Looking over her shoulder, her plump lips kept moving like she was saying something, but she might as well have been lecturing him on astrophysics.

One of his buddies leaned into him. "You always get the good ones. But I'm coming up high and tight behind you."

As if to prove the point, the male spun the girl who was coming on to him around as if he were parking an R8 next to a 911 and comparing the rear spoilers of the two sports cars.

Peyton looked away—only to get one of those blue lasers right in his eyeball.

For some reason, probably because the flash of light gave him a headache, he thought of his father. His sire had thrown a spectacular fit the minute Peyton had walked into the mansion, complete with all kinds of you-are-a-disgrace fireworks. And as with this club scene, he had just sat back, removed from the show even as his body was right in it.

He'd thrown the guy a couple of bones to appease him, and then it had been upstairs to shower and dress. Three phone calls later had brought him right here.

He had done this how many nights?

Too many to count—

His lady friend lowered that ass right onto his Gucci belt—wasn't there a rap about this?—and started working it.

She was very aroused. He could tell by her scent.

Placing his hands on her hips, he closed his eyes and tried to get into it.

Saxton sat in Minnie's kitchen with that coffee for a while, listening to the porch door's whistle from its loose weather stripping. What he really wanted to do was talk to someone, but the only person that came to mind was Blay, and that would seem too much like he was trying to prove a point about moving on or something.

The weird thing about sexual attraction was its strength and power could create an illusion of closeness between two people: When the body was drawn to another person's, and desperate and hungry for a physical expression, it was like the brain felt it had to catch up by manufacturing an intellectual or emotional connection.

Surface compatibility thus being assigned deeper connective meaning.

But in fact, you didn't know someone until you knew them. What was that saying? Unless you traveled with somebody, you had no idea who they truly were . . .

Knowing them for a decade was even better.

The truth was, Ruhn didn't know him any better, either. The male had no knowledge of his relationship with Blay, his troubles with his sire, his background and struggle. And this stuff about Ruhn's past? It was absolutely horrific, and he hated that the male had gone through it. But he had to acknowledge that he'd rather liked the idea of protecting a shy, quiet, sensitive soul in the world, being the guardrail and interpreter of new and different experiences.

Over dinner, for example, he'd planned in his head all kinds of other places he could take Ruhn to eat, Vietnamese, Thai, Italian. And in spite of what he'd promised, all of the restaurants would have been way outside of Ruhn's price range to afford.

In his mind, he'd looked forward to providing all those exclusive new tastes and tempting treats.

There was control in bringing another out of their shell, wasn't there. Safety, because they relied on you in their unfamiliarity and inevitable discomfort.

Now, after what he'd witnessed in that fight, all that fantastical *noblesse oblige* on his part had to be recast. The gentle giant had been through torture, and anyone who could survive the likes of that did not need protection by anyone.

Lowering his head into his hands, he thought, wow, it was a good thing people didn't share their inner musings with anybody else.

Because this kind of truth-telling was best kept under lock and key: He was an utter asshole to be worried about his little psychological dramas in comparison with what that male had lived through. Ten years, in a cage? Killing males or being killed? Getting marked?

Saxton had never been through anything like that, and the idea that Ruhn's past was suddenly making this romance thing between them much too real was too ugly to contemplate.

I cannot have my dignity if I lie to someone I'm falling in love with.

Talk about courage. To say that and mean it?

With a curse, Saxton got to his feet. He had no memory of when he'd taken off his coat, but he found it in a chair next to where he'd been staring off into space.

As he pulled the thing on, he went into the parlor and looked over to the fireplace, to those tiles that lined the hearth. He tried to imagine Minnie and her *hellren* traveling all the way across the ocean to an unknown land with the specter of the sun looming every day, little money to their name, and nothing but love to shield them.

That was courage.

Shaking his head, he went back to the kitchen, and set the alarm on the panel by the door into the garage; then he closed his eyes and tried to concentrate. Eventually, he managed to dematerialize and leave in a scatter of molecules through the tiny seam in that weather stripping.

He resumed form all the way across town, miles away, on the rear stoop of the Audience House. As he entered through the kitchen door, his brain totally flatlined. There were some *doggen* around, doing . . . God only knew what . . . and he had some kind of interaction with them. Questions asked and answered, this type of thing.

And then he was in his office. The King was taking the night off, but there were still things to be filed and paperwork to be done . . . also the stuff that Wrath had called about . . .

Or had that been a different night? Another time?

Some other . . .

Sitting down, he put his head in his hands and tried to remember what had been said about which things when. But there was no piecing together the thoughts, no cognitive map materializing out of the soup of confusion to help him march his way back to an even nominal functioning.

A knock on the doorjamb brought his head up. "Oh. Hello."

As the Brother Rhage entered, he filled the entirety of the office with his preternatural beauty and incredible size and bracing charisma.

It was like Ryan Reynolds, the Jolly Green Giant from those frozen-vegetable ads, and twelve world leaders had rolled into one being and come in for a little chat.

"You look like shit," the Brother said as he sat down on the other side of the partner's desk. "What's going on?"

"Oh, nothing. Did you need something?"

"Not really. I came to drop off more of George's teeth-cleaning thingies. Don't tell Fritz. He'll freak—but I was going by Petco—what the hell is wrong with you? I'm serious. You've got a death mask going on."

As Saxton tried to find a place to start, a thread in the tangle to begin the unraveling, Rhage took a cherry Tootsie Pop out of his leather jacket and peeled the wrapper.

"Hello? Have you stroked out on me over there?" Rhage's teeth were brilliant white as he opened his mouth to fit the lollipop in between his sharp fangs. "You want I get you a doctor?"

"Actually, what I need is . . ." Saxton cleared his throat. "I'm not sure I should be talking to you about this."

He didn't want to do anything to jeopardize Bitty and her adoptive parents' relationship with Ruhn. But who else could he go to?

"And I don't want this to change anything," he tacked on.

Rhage shrugged. "Well, considering I don't know what you're about to say, I'm not sure I can promise anything. But I'm good at the open-minded stuff. I mean, shit, I put up with Lassiter almost better than anyone else. Okay. Fine, better than Vishous. Wait, that probably isn't saying much. What was the question?"

"It's about Ruhn."

Rhage ditched the levity. "What about him?"

"His past. Specifically."

Instantly, the Brother changed, his big body sitting up, his eyes narrowing, the Tootsie Pop getting a hard crunch of some tense molars.

"What about it?"

Saxton picked a pen out of his holder and fiddled with the thing, twisting its cap in circles. Popping the cap off. Putting it back on.

"I know that Phury and Vishous went down there." Saxton looked up. "To his old master's estate. They found out about his background."

"They did."

"And so you know what happened to him."

There was a pause. "Yeah. The fight ring. But how did you hear about it? We were keeping a lid on it out of respect for him."

"He told me." Saxton shook his head. "I don't know how anyone lives through something like that."

Rhage sat back and stared across the desk, those Bahamian blue eyes so bright, they nearly cast shadows. "Can I ask you something personal?"

"Of course."

"Are you thinking of dating him or something?" As Saxton stiffened, the Brother shrugged. "It's cool if you are. I mean, I know he didn't have a female or anything down at his place, and he's never been mated."

"I don't know how to answer that."

"So it's a yes. And hey, I only ask because I'm curious. I can't think of any other reason why you'd bring this up. If he were just a guard for you, I figure you'd be glad he had the experience, even if the way he got it was extreme."

"I don't want to put you in an awkward position."

"But you want to know if he's going to kill you in your sleep, right?" As Saxton stammered, Rhage put up a hand. "Mary psych-tested him. I mean, Bitty invited him to live with us, and we were more than willing—because hello, he's our daughter's nearest blood relative. But with Wrath, Beth, and little Wrath in the house, we couldn't take chances. Mary gave him the tests orally as naturally he couldn't read them. He passed all the screenings. He's bog standard, non-psychotic.

She said he has a boatload of PTSD, of course. I mean, after what he'd been through, how could you not have it. And I don't know . . . after tonight? With him attacking those humans? Maybe this guarding you stuff is not a good place for him to be."

"Indeed."

"He's a good male, though. I trust him. And I know you're not usually around when he's with Bitty, but you should see them together. Every day before she goes to bed, the two of them come upstairs. There's this puzzle table that we set up in her room, you know? The pair of them sit there and work on puzzles—frankly, that shit makes me crazy. I mean, you want to talk about psychotic. Hello. Sitting with eight million tiny pieces that you can't pick up with your fingers, trying to match the colors—but I digress." He crunched the Tootsie Pop and started chewing. "They love it. And all the time? In this quiet voice, he tells her stories of her *mahmen* and her grandparents. What it was like growing up—it sounded like a great life. In the country, playing outside, horses and sheep, a *mahmen* and father who loved Ruhn and his sister so much. And Bitty, she eats it up. He's given her the side of the family that helps her feel like her *mahmen* is still with her. It's priceless. It really is." Rhage laughed a little. "And come to think of it, it's pretty much the only time I hear him talk."

Saxton nodded. "I'm so glad they have that connection. And yes, from what I have seen, they are very close."

"Ruhn's like a son to me. For real."

"I just never expected . . . well, I didn't expect everything that happened to him."

"Who would?" Rhage tossed the white stick with its pink stain on one end in the trash. "And listen, I've already talked to Mary about what went down tonight. She's going to pay Ruhn a little visit. See if he needs a tune-up, so to speak. She helped Z a lot with his shit, so tragically, she has some experience dealing with trauma."

"I don't judge him." As Saxton spoke, he realized he was trying the words out, seeing if they were true—and that made him feel like a bad person.

"Good. Because you shouldn't. And you shouldn't be afraid of him, either. Everyone deserves second chances. I am living proof of it."

"You're right. And what happened to him was nothing he volunteered for."

"Too right."

"I feel like I'm in mourning on his behalf."

"Anyone who's heard the story feels the same way."

Will my heart be safe with him, Saxton wondered to himself.

And to be fair, that was a question he would be asking no matter who he was contemplating a relationship with.

"I wish I could see into the future," he murmured.

"There are certain corners in life where that would be a nice bonus. I wish I could help you more."

"Thank you." Saxton smiled. "You are a gentlemale under all your bravado."

"Now let's not get ahead of ourselves."

After a moment, the Brother got up and sauntered out, leaving Saxton with his own thoughts.

After a while, he went to his file drawers. Getting down on his haunches in the far corner, he pressed his thumb to a sensor and sprang the lock. Documents pertaining to the Black Dagger Brotherhood and their families were kept there and he easily located Bitty's adoption papers.

Taking the file out, he opened the cover and flipped through to the last page, where Ruhn had "signed" his name.

The male had drawn a self-portrait of himself on the line where the signature was supposed to go.

It was a stunning rendering, and so realistic that Saxton ran his finger down the contours of the cheek and could swear he felt the warmth of the male himself.

For some reason, he thought of Blay and Qhuinn. From what he understood, Blay had always taken care of his partner, looked after him, made sure he was as stable as he could be. It had been an expression of love before that word had been shared between them.

The longer Saxton stared at that drawing, the more he realized why all of this with Ruhn was affecting him so.

He had the capacity to fall in love with the male.

And that meant the stakes were very high. He knew all too well what unrequited love felt like. This stuff with Ruhn? It had an even greater potential for destruction.

TWENTY-EIGHT

ovo saw the cane as a huge improvement. Come on, over the wheelchair? It also meant she'd skipped the walker stage.

Beating expectations was good, especially when you were in the vampire equivalent of cardiac rehab.

As she shuffled down the training center's corridor, she was keeping her pace at a solid geriatric, her feet in their hospital-issue shower shoes scuffing along with a minimal lift from the concrete floor. Everything was quiet, the Brothers elsewhere, the trainees gone home, the clinic empty of patients except for—

The disembodied howl that traveled out from the crazy guy was like a draft in the air, invisible and chilling.

She kept on going. She had made this trip a good ten times or so, even though she was pretty sure that Dr. Manello had only said once an hour. But really, she kept this up and she would hit that rate on average—provided she went against a two-week timetable.

He just needed to be more specific.

Coming up to the double doors into the gym, she looked through the chicken-wired glass. She couldn't wait to start sparring again.

Continuing on, she relied on the cane for balance, the wonky feeling more like an inner-ear problem than anything to do with her heart malfunctioning. They'd even sprung her of her IV, although she was wearing a Holter monitor to make sure her cardiac function was hunky-dory.

Glancing back, her room seemed like miles away. But fuck that. She went farther on. Eventually, a hundred and fifty years later, she came up to the pool's doors.

There was someone in there.

Craving company was as unfamiliar as this physical weakness she was rocking, and certainly the latter seemed to make the former more of a thing: Before she knew better, she was pushing her way into the little ante-hall and doing her old-lady dance over the tiles.

The scent of chlorine tingled in her nose and the warmth and humidity made her think of summer nights—

Splashing. And voices.

When she realized there was more than one person in the water, she nearly turned around. Except then she saw that it was Ehlena at the edge, the nurse crouching down and encouraging somebody who was trying to swim.

"Oh, hey, Novo!" the female called out with a wave. "Come talk with us!"

Novo checked to make sure the double-johnny situation she'd jury-rigged was covering her naughty bits in the back and then she caned her way forward. The tiled ring around the Olympic-sized pool was dry, so she didn't worry about slipping, and that heat and moisture helped ease the aches she still had in her ribs.

"Hi, Luchas," she said to the male hanging on the edge of the pool.

"Greetings," came the grunting reply.

His thin, deformed hands, with their missing fingers, were like claws on that lip, his frail body floating out behind him, his remaining leg churning through the water slowly.

He was so pale, and she had to look away from the hard cut of his shoulder blades under his thin skin.

"I wish I could join you," she said as she leaned on the cane and lowered herself down into a sit.

"Not with that monitor on, I'm afraid." Ehlena smiled. "But you're almost home free. You should be ready to go tomorrow."

"I can't wait." Novo kicked off her slippers and put one foot . . . and then the other in. "Oh, this feels good."

Luchas's workout created waves in the water, and she closed her eyes so that she could concentrate on the buffering sensations against her calves and the soles of her feet.

She also didn't want the male to feel like she was staring at him.

From what she understood, Qhuinn's brother had been abducted during the raids, and it had been assumed that he had been killed along with the rest of the bloodline. The truth had been more grue-some. The male had been found stuffed in an oil drum, surrounded by the Omega's blood. He'd been barely alive, and he'd had so many broken bones and missing parts, he'd been all but poured onto a gurney.

Although he'd been rescued some time ago, he had been living in the clinic ever since, not dead, but not particularly alive, either. Qhuinn always visited him, but there was no joy, no laughter, no prospects, it seemed. And for a young male that had once had a life of privilege, it was sad reality.

"Good job," Ehlena said to him. "Now that you're warmed up, let's work on arms."

"All right."

There was some splashing, and then the nurse coached the male through various stretches and then some breaststrokes that crisscrossed the shallow end of the pool.

Luchas's concentration was complete, as if his life depended on his ability to follow directions and perform the movements—and certainly, if he stopped swimming, he would, in fact, sink. There was no fat on him.

Although she had seen him around the training center, she had never expected to have anything in common with him. But here they both were—except she was going to get better, and there was a chance he would be forever in this neither healthy nor dying netherworld: By tomorrow night, she was going to be walking normally, and in another twenty-four hours after that, she was going to be in the weight room, goddamn it. Luchas, on the other hand? It was hard to imagine him any different than he was now.

"I think I better head back," Novo said as she plugged her cane in and got to her feet.

"I'm glad you stopped by to see us." Ehlena lifted a hand. "Let me know if you need anything."

"Thank you—and I'll talk to you later, Luchas." Novo offered a little wave. "Take care."

"You as well," came the gruff reply.

The male didn't look up, and she was glad to leave. It was hard to be around somebody as infirmed as that when you yourself were rocky. It made you wonder why you were the one who got picked to get well whereas they were on the Leave Behind list.

Considering how much it mattered, the randomness of such good fortune was the kind of thing that bent your brain.

As she reemerged into the corridor, she shivered in the relative cold, and by the time she came up to her hospital room, she was done. Like, just having run a marathon done.

Back at her bed, she hung the cane off the foot and dragged herself onto the mattress. As loneliness settled over her like a toxic cloud, she was too tired to fight it—

Her cell phone rang on the rolling table she took her meals on and she turned her head to the sound. The thing was facedown, and she had absolutely no interest in checking to see who it was. She already knew. Her *mahmen* and her sister were livid that the bachelorette party, or whatever the hell it was called, was happening the following evening and Novo hadn't done shit with the preparations.

But come on. Thanks to Sophy, they had a reservation down at that place. What else did they need—oh, riiiiiiiiiiight, the goddamn sash, a crown and a scepter, feather boas.

The usual Instagrammable shit.

Yeah, 'cuz you aren't really living life unless you can create "moments" to prove how sparkly fresh your existence is.

Throwing out a hand, she grabbed the phone and flipped it over—

Novo sat up as she accepted the call. "You again."

Yet her tone was far from hostile. In fact, there was a plaintive quality in there that she really needed to kick in the ass.

Peyton's voice was muffled. "Hi."

In the background, there was all kinds of noise. He was at a club. Of course.

Except he was calling her. "What are you doing, big spender?" she drawled.

Better, she thought. Yes, that was how she wanted to sound. More like her old self—her regular self, she amended.

"Oh, you know, same night, same drill."

"So why aren't you fucking some random in the back room?"

"I had the option."

"And you passed? Not feeling well, are we?"

"What are you doing?"

"Laps up and down the corridor. Then I'm going to play around with some particle physics, bench-press a Prius or two, and read the collective works of Shakespeare. So yeah, busy night for me."

His laughter sounded good, so good. "You up for a visitor?"

"Depends."

"On what?"

She looked around the mostly barren room. "I don't know," she said softly.

"I'm lonely."

"You're out with those guys, right? The matched set of douche canoes."

He chuckled. "Yeah."

She moved her phone to her other ear. "And you're surrounded by human women, right? The hot ones who have throat muscles that go lax on command and enough silicon implanted in them that they could qualify as an inert molecule?"

"Pretty much."

"So why are you on my phone?"

"Because I'd rather be with you."

Novo closed her eyes. "That fight with your father really must run deep, huh."

"This is not about him."

"You sure about that? 'Cuz I'm not."

"So what do you say. And this is not about sex."

"Good. Because I'm walking with a cane and I feel about as sexy as a toaster oven."

"Okay, quick side note on that. Toaster ovens are hot. I mean, that's their purpose. That's how you warm up pizza and how Hot Pockets get their name. Without toaster ovens, they'd be Room Temperature Pockets, and who needs that."

Novo started laughing. "You're a freak."

"My point is, if you're trying to say you're not feeling sexy, go with a different metaphor. Like . . . I feel about as sexy as a bottle of Tums. Now, they put *out* heartburn so—"

"Shut the fuck up and call for the bus."

As she hung up, she was smiling. And then, for absolutely, positively, no reason whatsoever . . . she went into the bathroom, brushed her teeth, washed her face, and re-braided her hair.

It took a good hour for Peyton to get to the training center, and when he finally got off the transport, he found himself nearly running down to Novo's room. As he came up to her door, he smoothed his hair and made sure that his suit was properly buttoned.

Opening the way in, he stopped.

She was sound asleep, her head cocked to one side as if she had been trying to stay awake for him. The IV was out of her arm, he noted, and short of some wires on her chest that were hooked up to a tiny receiver thingy, all of the monitoring equipment was gone.

He let the door close silently on its own and kicked his loafers free so he made no sound at all in his socks. Halfway to the bed, he peeled off his jacket. Right next to her, he removed his belt, untucked the tails of his button-down, and popped out both cuff links.

"It's me," he said as he carefully lay down with her.

Novo muttered something in her sleep. Then she turned to him and nestled in close, her body fitting perfectly with his, her scent flooding his nose, a grand sense of peace settling in.

He willed the lights to dim and shut his eyes.

The quiet hum of the heating system overhead was the most perfect white noise on the planet. And the deep sigh of relaxation Novo let out made him feel a hundred feet tall and strong as an ox.

"You came," she said into his chest.

"You're awake."

Novo lifted her head. Her eyes were so languid and sleepy, her thick lashes nearly on her cheekbones. And the flush on her cheeks was because she was warm from sleep.

"Yes, I came." He brushed a strand of hair back. "You look amazing."

"Are you kidding me."

"No. Never."

Later, he would have to wonder who kissed who first. Was it him, pressing his mouth to hers? Was it her, dropping her lips to his? Maybe they met in the middle.

That was probably it.

Slow, so very slow. Soft. Gentle.

"Come under the covers with me," she whispered.

"With or without my clothes," he asked.

There was a pause. "Without."

His heart began to pound as he sat up, and before things went further, he willed the door lock into place. Then he pulled his shirt over his head and let it fall where it did. Peeled his socks. Hopped off the bed, released the waistband of his slacks, and unzipped them. His cock was fully erect, and he tucked it up onto his lower abdomen and held it in place as he turned back around.

Novo was letting her hospital johnny drop to the floor.

For a moment, all he could do was stare at her. She was amazing, her golden skin glowing against the white sheets and blankets, her taut, tight-nippled breasts, the curve of her waist and her stomach.

"Will you help me get this off?"

Get what off? he wondered. "Oh, the wires. Sorry."

"Just unclip these things from the pads."

He eyed the sensors that provided the data feed to the heart monitor. "Are you sure we should?"

"I'm allowed to take them off when I shower. It's fine. And Dr. Manello said this is out of an abundance of caution anyway. Come into the bed first."

With a shaking he couldn't hide, Peyton slid into the warm spot her body had created. And he did what he could to keep his hips back, even though there wasn't a lot of room—it seemed rude to be rubbing all up on her while she was unclipping the—

Her nipples were small and pink and very perfect.

And though he meant to help her with the wires, instead, his fingertips sought out one of her breasts, drifting across her smooth skin. She gasped as he touched the tip.

"I have to taste you," he said hoarsely.

In response, Novo arched, offering him exactly what he wanted and oh, God . . . he covered that tip with his mouth, sucking, licking. Her fingers dug into his hair and urged him on—and that scent. Her arousal made his head short out.

Yet he held back.

Impatient and starved, he kept himself in check nonetheless.

And when his stroking hand got tangled in a wire, she pushed his shoulders back. "Let me—hold on, there's one left."

Novo did away with the final lead, and then she smiled in a lopsided way. "Try and ignore the pads."

He stared into her eyes. "I only see you. Trust me."

Dropping his head down again, he nuzzled his way across her sternum and paused to kiss where her heart was. After a silent prayer of thanks, he continued on to her other nipple, running his tongue around it before taking it into his mouth.

Beneath the covers, his hand caressed her hip and stroked her thigh. She was muscle and sinew, so strong, so powerful, and holy shit, that was fucking hot. And even though he wanted his cock in her, he took his time, petting her, getting her more and more hot, until she was sawing her legs across the mattress, her breath was coming in an urgent beat, and her spine was undulating as her pelvis rolled in frustration.

It was only then that he licked and nibbled his way up to her collarbone, her throat . . . her lips. Delving into her mouth, he swept his palm down the inside of her leg, heading for her heat.

"Yes," she said into his kiss. "Oh, God . . . yes."

Her slick sex, so open and ready, nearly made him orgasm. But this was about her. Holding himself back once again, he penetrated her and found a rhythm, helping her along with his thumb. When she found her release, he swallowed her moans.

"I want you in me," she demanded.

As her hand found his erection, she did not have to ask twice. He rolled on top of her, finding a home as she split her thighs to make room for him. And then he retracted his hips, angled his arousal . . .

"Oh, *fuck*," he groaned as his head entered her.

He slid deep, so fucking deep. And she was tight, like a fist. And she was hot, like raw fire. It was as he had known it to be from before, except so much better. Because she was with him now, hungry as he was.

He pulled back, all the way back, and slid in again. And back. And in.

His lower body wanted to pump like a piston, but he kept the penetrations slow and steady. Beneath him, she was a live wire of impatience, and she even sunk her nails into his ass to get him to go faster.

He refused.

And he was glad he did.

Because when she came again, he was able to be aware of every pulse, the contractions working his cock—

The orgasm tackled him from behind, hitting him and his will like a ton of bricks, taking him down a rabbit hole of pleasure from which he could not escape.

He'd wanted to last longer. But as he filled her up, and dropped his head into the fragrant nest of her throat, he couldn't say he regretted a thing.

How could he.

He'd never had anything or anyone so good before.

TWENTY-NINE

When Ruhn got back to his guest room at the Brotherhood's mansion, he closed himself in and looked around at the fine decor. Everything was so beautiful, from the wallpaper, which certainly looked like silk, to the antique dressers and desk, to the canopied bed that was draped in the same kind of heavy fabric that the walls seemed to be covered in.

He'd always thought it looked fit for the King.

He'd never felt comfortable under that canopy with all those fancy pillows and the monogrammed bedspread—and he had even contemplated sleeping on the rug with a blanket over him. He had been worried, though, that word would get back through the maids that tidied up every night and his hosts would take offense.

Crossing over to the walk-in closet, he had another jolt of I-don't-belong as he opened the double doors and confronted the rows upon rows of barren hangers and shoe shelves. His two or three T-shirts, two pairs of jeans, and work boots took up no space at all on the right. The sweaters and slacks that Bitty, Rhage, and Mary had gotten him as the household had celebrated the human holiday, Christmas, had seemed like way too much when he'd been unwrapping them. In this vast wardrobe containment space, they made no dent at all.

He removed his clothes and put everything into the hamper.

He'd had to get used to his laundry being done for him. In the beginning, he had fought tooth and nail to have Fritz and the staff leave his things alone so he could take care of them, but in the end, he had caved.

That hangdog face the butler assumed when he was denied work was more than what Ruhn could withstand.

Walking naked into the bathroom, he was tempted to leave the lights off, but he needed to see the truth of how badly he'd been hurt—

"Oh."

Going over to the stretch of mirror above the two marble sinks, he shook his head. "Oh . . . dear."

His face looked bad. Really bad. One whole side was puffy and distorted, and he leaned in closer to the glass and prodded the bruising gently with his finger. The answering pain suggested that Saxton might be right; that cheekbone might well be broken and maybe he did need a healer.

And then there was his split lip.

"Maybe a shower will help."

He had no idea who he was speaking to.

Moving across to the glass enclosure, he opened the see-through door and turned on the water. The fact that there were six different showerheads had always seemed like a ridiculous luxury to him—but he never complained once he was in the spray.

He certainly did not tonight.

His body was aching in places, and he hissed as the open cuts on the backs of his knuckles came in contact with water. His left arm was sore, but he didn't dwell on the why of it. That would have required him replaying the fight in his mind and he wanted to pretend nothing had happened.

After he had soaped and shampooed—he didn't condition; he didn't understand why people got their hair clean just to put crap right back in it—he stepped out, toweled off, and tried to win an argument with himself for not going to the clinic.

Bitty made up his mind for him, however.

If she saw him like this, all banged up? Or if things healed wrong and that side of his face ended up contorted permanently? She might think he was the monster he had been.

He couldn't bear that.

Back in the closet, he pulled on fresh jeans, a clean Hanes undershirt, and that blue sweater Bitty had gotten for him.

He wore the sweater for good luck. For strength. For—

The knock on his door was soft and that was not good news. Maybe it was his niece, having seen his truck parked out in the courtyard with the other vehicles.

"Who is it?" he said.

There was a pause. "Me."

As Saxton's voice registered, Ruhn was so shocked he couldn't move. But then he snapped into action and went for the door.

Opening it, he found himself gripping the knob so hard, his forearm hurt. "Hello."

"May I please have a moment of your time? In private?"

As Novo felt Peyton go still on top of her, she froze herself. This wasn't supposed to happen—not so much the sex, although she had surprised herself with wanting him even though she was train-wreck tired still. No, what she didn't want was the *kind* of sex they'd had.

Fucking. She only ever wanted raging sex, the kind that rattled your teeth and broke beds, that you were sore for the night after from, that made you feel like you'd been in a car accident.

Not this soft, gentle stuff.

The former was athletic and aggressive, and so it was easier to keep a guard up. What she and Peyton had just done? It was too close. To . . . intimate.

"What's wrong?" he asked her.

As he pulled back, she couldn't meet his eyes. "Nothing. It's fine."

After a moment, he withdrew—and she hated that her body missed him immediately. That was also something she did not need.

"You know," he said in a level voice, "sooner or later, you're going to have to decide whether you like me or not."

A pang of conscience made her more honest than she would ordinarily have been. "It's not you. Honest."

"Oh, my God, what a line." His smile was dry as he swung his legs around and sat on the edge of the bed. "And you know, I've used it, too. It's always a lie."

"Not always."

"Well. Most of the time."

There was a long period of silence, and she tried not to trace his shoulders and upper body with her eyes. The extra muscle suited him. And it wasn't the only place where he was big.

She shut her lids as a blast of pure erotic heat whipped through her like a solar flare.

"I do like you," she heard herself say. "I'm just not . . . good at the whole relationship thing."

He looked across his shoulder at her. "Annnnnnd I have also used *that* line! Hey, give me back my playbook."

"It's true."

Peyton seemed to focus on the floor as he shook his head. "No, frankly, it's bullshit. 'Cuz who is good at relationships? And is that where you saw us going? Wait, don't answer that—because it's in the past tense now, clearly."

Novo sat up. "Peyton. I'm serious."

"My given name. I guess you are." He slid off the high bed and pulled on his slacks. "And it's cool. It's whatever, you know. I am not going to push you."

"I'm just not interested in anything."

"Evidently. Although I guess I should be complimented by the fact that you're threatened by me. It's a backhander, to be sure. But you probably only give this strong-arm speech to people you think maybe, possibly, just might get past your badass shell. So hey, sign me up for that merit badge, 'kay? It'll probably be a middle finger against a background of female empowerment, but I'm sure I can find a jacket to put it on."

As she stared at him, the words came to her, but only in her mind: *I lost a young. After the male left me for my sister—and Sophy only came on to him to prove she could win, okay? I miscarried alone, in a cold house, and promised myself I would never, ever get involved emotionally with anyone ever again.*

And then you come along, and for a while, I got to write you off as a rich asshole . . . until you promised me you would never hurt me and then made love to me instead of fucked me.

Now I want to run from you because I don't want to learn that lesson twice.

Okay, fine, that would all be so much better spoken instead of merely thought and kept to herself. But she couldn't seem to make that leap. She couldn't seem to open her mouth and tell him about all the reasons why no one, not just him, was allowed to get through to her.

"I'm going to go," he said, "before you have to throw another line of mine back at me. Which, I'm willing to bet, is going to be the whole *I'm so sorry, but I have to crash now because I have to work*—which, at least for me, was actually a bold-faced lie up until I came into the program. But there you go."

Bending down, he picked up his socks and shoved them in his pants pockets. Grabbed his shirt and put it on. The jacket as well. His loafers—were those made of ostrich skin?—went on first the left and then the right. He finger-combed his hair. Snagged his cuff links.

As he added more and more clothing to his formerly naked frame, he moved faster and faster, as if his departure were a train gathering momentum.

"So I'll see you when I see you." Peyton paused by the door. "And the message has been received, okay? I'll leave you alone, especially now that you're back on your feet."

He gave her a smile that was right out of a fashion magazine, all cocky and full of perfect white teeth. "Take care."

He knocked on the jamb like a judge putting the gavel down on a case, and then he was gone as if he had never been.

In the silence, she told herself it was for the best. He felt too good. He got past her defenses too often. He was the kind of surprise she did not need in her life.

And his departure couldn't be better. By the time she saw him next—and that would be Saturday night—he would be re-categorized appropriately and all would be well.

She wasn't going to have it any other way.

THIRTY

As Saxton stood at Ruhn's open bedroom door and waited for his answer, he took deep breaths and smelled that wonderful combination of soap and shampoo that the male used.

"Please," Ruhn said as he stepped back. "Come in."

Saxton entered and thought immediately that the decor did not suit the male. It was not that the room was ugly or even badly done. In fact, it was a very elegant example of what he liked to think of as neo-monarchy, everything damask and silk and gilded up the yin-yang. The dark blue was okay, and worked well with the Old Masters paintings and all the gold leaf, but for what Ruhn would be comfortable in? It was too fussy and fancy.

That farmhouse of Minnie's was better, everything handmade and practical, with clean lines and wood that was polished from years of hand waxing versus all kinds of layers of varnish.

"Would you prefer me to leave the door open?" Ruhn asked.

Saxton looked over his shoulder. "No. Please close it, thank you."

There was a soft click, and then Ruhn stood to one side, his hands clasped loosely in front of him, his shoulders down and brought into his chest.

It reminded Saxton of the first time they had sat together on Minnie's sofa, when the male had tried to make himself smaller than he really was.

"I just want to tell you that . . ." Saxton laughed roughly as he paused. "You know, for a lawyer who deals with words all day long, I find myself curiously tongue-tied."

"I will wait," Ruhn said. "For however long you require."

As Saxton found himself over by the bed, he stopped and was surprised to discover that he'd been pacing. Turning around, he spoke clearly. "I am sorry that I seemed so shocked by everything. And I apologize for giving you any impression, if that's what you came away with, that my opinion of you has been altered in any fashion. I also want to tell you that I am a coward."

The male's brows shot up. "I . . . don't understand."

Saxton moved down to the foot of the bed. "May I sit here?"

"Yes. Of course. This is more your house than mine."

"That is actually not true, but we hardly need to debate the point."

Saxton glanced overhead at the canopy and then regarded the drapes that came down the four posts. God, it was as if Tallulah Bankhead had left her gowns from the forties behind.

He swung his eyes back to the male. "I am a coward in comparison to you."

"Because you stayed in the truck when those humans came up to us?"

"No, because . . ." He took a deep breath. "I was in love with someone. I say 'was' because the depth of my feelings were not reciprocated and I have had to live with that reality for a while now. It has been a very awkward situation for me."

Ruhn blinked. "I am . . . I am so sorry. That must be so hard."

"Yes," Saxton said softly. "It has been difficult to be regularly reminded of what I had wished for, and it is hard not to feel lesser than even when one is well aware that it is not an issue of fault—the heart wants what it wants." He shrugged. "And you know, I am also not the first, nor the last, to grapple with such a thing."

Ruhn crossed his arms over his chest and stared at the floor. "Was it someone in this household?"

"Yes."

"Who?"

Saxton hesitated. "Blaylock, son of Rocke." When there was no response, he sighed. "Blay is the one. Was the one."

Ruhn was quiet for a time. "I find myself rather jealous of the male at the moment."

"You are so honest." Saxton shook his head with admiration. "I am amazed at how transparent you can be."

"Is that a good thing or a bad thing?"

"I love it. It's almost as attractive as your smile."

The male glanced up. Blushed. Looked away. "Blaylock is a very handsome male. He is kind, too."

"He is also a fighter. Just as you were tonight."

Ruhn frowned. "Are you trying to make me feel less guilty for my past?"

"Yes, I can't help it. I have thought of little else since we parted. I hate that you feel badly for the torture you were subjected to. You were a victim."

The male crossed his arms as if he were holding himself. "I don't want to talk about it anymore."

"We don't have to. But I guess . . . you were honest with me and I want to be honest with you. I got my heart broken very badly, and I never thought that anyone other than Blay would reach into that part of me. I think I've believed that he broke something fundamental in my makeup. That I was forever changed. And then I met you."

Ruhn's head whipped up, his eyes widening.

"I remember the moment I first saw you." Saxton smiled. "It was at the meeting with you, Rhage, and Mary pertaining to Bitty's adoption. I couldn't stop looking at you."

"But I thought it was because you didn't trust me or disapproved. I've always—anytime you looked at me, I figured it was . . ."

"You are a very captivating male. But I assumed you were straight."

"Well, I never thought in terms of straight or gay before. I always thought females were the only . . . you know, option. Until I met you."

Saxton smiled again. "Just so you know . . . I think I could fall in love with you, too. And I didn't imagine I would say that about anyone, or to anybody, ever again. The truth is, though, I want to see where this connection is going. If it's something you're interested in. You were brave by saying what you did . . . and I want to be brave, too."

The blush that hit Ruhn's face was one for the ages—and his shy happiness made Saxton feel like he was doing the right thing.

You couldn't soar if you didn't leap.

No one knew what the outcome of this was going to be. But he'd wanted to go traveling. He'd wanted to leave Caldwell and get out of this rut he'd fallen into.

There was a journey to be had with Ruhn.

"Yes," the male said. "I would like to know, too."

"Can I kiss you now?" Saxton asked.

Ruhn moved across the room and felt transformed. It seemed impossible to travel such a vast emotional distance when going only a matter of feet, but as he came to stand in front of Saxton, he felt renewed.

It was extraordinary. The world had previously seemed gray and closed off, but now it had a horizon with a glorious night sky full of stars. And all of that universe was contained in the handsome face that looked up at him from the foot of the bed he slept in.

"Yes," he said as he touched Saxton's blond hair. "You may always kiss me."

Except he was the one who bent down and it was his mouth that found the other male's. So sweet, so soft . . . and he instantly hardened in the place that counted most.

"Lock the door?" Saxton said against his mouth.

"Yes."

One of them took care of it. He didn't really track which. And then he sank to his knees in between the thighs of the male. As he was tall, he was able to keep the contact going at their mouths as his hands found all kinds of things that had to go: jacket, shirt . . .

He paused when he got to the male's button and fly.

Saxton was also hard, his arousal a thick shaft under the fine fabric.

Looking up, Ruhn drank in the sight of the bare chest, the shoulders, the collarbones. "I don't know how to do this?"

"Oh, God . . . you do, you do."

"Would you like me to . . ."

"I'm about to come just looking at you between my legs. Do anything you want to me."

Ruhn smiled and then fumbled with the pants. He didn't want to rip them—well, actually, he wanted to tear them off the male, but he didn't want to damage things. The slacks were polite, though. They all but melted open, revealing a pair of black boxer briefs . . . and that erection.

Saxton rose to his feet. "Allow me."

And then the male was naked.

Magnificent was the only thing Ruhn could think of as he stroked up smooth thighs to a flat stomach and graceful hip bones.

The erection was even better. Stiff, proud, begging for attention.

Ruhn gripped it. Warm and hard. And Saxton moaned, the male's head falling back so only the point of his chin was visible.

Leaning in, Ruhn opened his mouth. He'd thought it might be

awkward. Instead, it was as the sex in that kitchen had been . . . the most natural thing to suck the cock in, and stroke it, and tease the head with his tongue.

When Saxton collapsed backward onto the bed, Ruhn went with him. And he watched the King's venerable, proper solicitor arch with abandon—especially as the release arrived.

Which Ruhn was more than happy to attend to.

More than once.

And then Saxton began to return the favor: Ruhn rolled over and watched with awe as he himself was stripped bare. That blond head dipped down and the sensation of wet suction had him cursing and fisting the duvet. Focusing on the canopy above him, he strained until sweat broke out all over him.

He couldn't look. Not because he was ashamed or it was ugly.

The glances he spared himself were too hot, too erotic, Saxton's beautiful face and stretched lips too much to handle.

He came into the male's mouth.

And called Saxton's name until he was hoarse.

THIRTY-ONE

O n Friday night, Novo pulled her black leathers into place, buttoned the fly, and pivoted around to the mirror over her bathroom sink. Her black muscle top was more than willing to get tucked in and stay put. Hair was back and braided. And in another minute and a half, she was going to have her combat boots on.

It felt so fucking good to be in her own skin again. To have her energy back. To stop wondering, every second, whether her heart was going to go into a fatal arrhythmia.

Too bad this wasn't her first shot back in the field.

No, no. It was bachelorette party time. Yay.

No, really. YAY.

But hey, at least she wasn't fresh out of surgery, peeing into a bag. The comparison was . . . well, at least a moderate improvement in terms of torture.

Okay, fine, the two were neck and neck.

In this scenario, though, she only had to endure an hour or two before she returned to her real life. With the stabbing and operation, she had had to die a couple of times and dig herself out of the owie-hole over the course of days and nights.

Walking out into the main room, she went over to where she kept her weapons in a locked fire safe the size of a small refrigerator. The safe was the most expensive thing she owned in the shithole she lived in, but as soon as she had gotten into the training program and received her first stipend, she had invested in the beast. The last thing she needed was a human breaking in and getting a bunch of guns with no serial numbers, knives made by a master smith who was a vampire, and explosives.

And let's face it. This wasn't the best of neighborhoods.

The hundred-foot-by-hundred-foot shoebox she rented was part of the basement of a walk-up and it had no windows, which was secure, but it meant things smelled a little moldy even in the winter. The building was owned by a vampire, however, which made everything easier, and the best thing? It was hers.

Her family didn't even have the address.

Pulling the blanket up off the safe—yeah, 'cuz, oh, that was savvy camouflage—she put in the code, cranked the door open, and took out her nines and one short-bladed dagger. On second thought . . . no, just one nine. Any more firepower and she might be tempted to turn her sister into Swiss cheese.

Oh, wait. That was going to happen anyway.

She holstered both the knife and the gun on her hip in such a way that they looked like nothing more than a cell phone on one side and a walkie-talkie on the other. Then she grabbed her wallet and her phone, threw on her jacket, and she was out into a cramped, cold hallway. At the end, there was a door and a short flight of concrete steps up to street level.

Outside, the wind was in the same mood she was, aggressive and nasty, and as it whipped around her body, it was like being on the subway and having people bang into you as you held on overhead.

Her last thought, before she dematerialized into hell, was that Peyton hadn't been in touch.

It had been the plan, and what she'd asked him to do. But he'd still surprised her. And it was embarrassing, really, how often she had checked her phone for texts or calls. Thank God she lived alone.

What was really pissing her off? How frustrated she got every time it wasn't him—which was each time she picked up her phone, as it turned out. She'd gotten a number of texts: Paradise asking her to come to some birthday party, Boone wanting to know if she'd like to read any of his books, Axe to see if she was interested in working out. No Peyton.

And her sister and her mother had Bridal-mageddon'd her, of course.

OMG, guys, I'm feeling so much better. Yeah, that was a close call, that whole almost-dying thing. But I'm good and you were soooo helpful during my recovery. Thanks! *heart made from two fingers/two thumbs over chest* Love you!

Jesus Christ, this night was going to make her stabbing seem like a cakewalk.

Going around the corner of the building, she found some dense shadows and dematerialized across town to—

Holy. Mary. Mother of all that was estrogen.

Like an ocean swimmer surrounded by chum, she looked left and right, not because she couldn't recognize that there was a great white with bad dental work heading right for her churning legs, but rather because she was searching, praying, for a lifeboat of any kind on the horizon.

Nope. No one was coming, and more sharks were on the way.

The venue was pink on the outside and uplit by purple lights. Inside, through the glass bay windows, she saw lace curtains and framed posters of Paris. Lots of round tables and mismatched, cheerfully painted chairs. Flowers. Teacups. Towers of tea sandwiches even though it was eight o'clock at night.

Imagine My Little Pony meets *KUWTK* and serves gluten-free food.

The only thing that was a surprise was how big it was inside. As she entered, the air was thick with powdered sugar and melted butter, but it turned out the front tea room was just the start of things. Behind that section, there was a proper French-ish restaurant that had a very un-frat-boy, Cosmo's-only bar, and a dancing area that had certainly never had a mosh pit anywhere near it.

Things grew dimmer the further in you went, but the decor never lost its seven-year-old, pink-and-purple girl palette. And the waitstaff did get a little more intense, although it was more like you just added extra red dye food coloring to the frosting: In the front part, you had human women in pink forties' dresses with white aprons; in the restaurant, you had men and women in soda-fountain hop clothes; and finally, around the dance floor, security was one-hundred-and-twenty-pound swizzle-stick men with climate-change-awareness T-shirts and facial hair that was right out of Paul Bunyan's playbook.

Then again, those boys were unlikely to have to ask anyone to leave, much less throw somebody out. The clientele were so Sophy's peeps, eighty percent of them women with pressure of speech and the kind of hand gestures that professional boxers couldn't keep up with for long.

Novo felt like a fly in a bowl of vichyssoise—and as she went down into the restaurant proper, she certainly got that kind of attention. All the pretty girls in their pretty clothes looked over at her, their expressions ranging from who-let-*that*-in to bless-her-heart, depending on where they were on the Mean Girls spectrum.

She found her sister presiding over her court of like-minded intellectuals at a special lineup of tables by the dance floor. There were a good number of them, well over a dozen, and that was not a surprise. A queen needed her ladies in waiting.

The second Sophy saw her, the female looked down at her place setting. Then she glanced over at her right-hand girl as if drawing strength. When the other female, who looked a lot like old-school Lynda Carter, nodded and squeezed her shoulder, Sophy put her napkin on the table and got up.

That smile was as bright and false as a pair of dentures.

"Novo, I'm sooooo glad you're here."

It was like getting embraced by a powder puff, and as Novo stepped back, the female's spring-bouquet perfume lingered on her leather jacket like somebody had smacked her with an Easter lily.

"I've saved a seat for you. Down there."

Novo looked at the other end of the table. There were a couple of empty chairs there, and she was willing to bet that was on purpose.

"Thanks."

Joke's on you, Sophy, she thought as she sauntered her way to her dunce-cap seat.

This was the best thing that had happened to her all night: If you took the infectious-disease model, there was no inoculation that could work against the Pollyanna pathogen, so isolation was best.

"So what do you think?"

As Saxton posed the question, he looked across the restaurant table. Ruhn was chewing slowly and looking as if he were trying to understand the dialect of a language he was only nominally familiar with.

"It's delicious," he announced after he swallowed. "What is it called again?"

"Chicken tikka masala."

"And this?"

"Garlic naan."

The waiter came up to the table and spoke with a beautiful, fluid accent. "Is everything to your liking?"

"Oh, yes," Ruhn said. "May I please have another plate of this? And more of the rice?"

The human man bowed. "Right away, sir."

Saxton smiled to himself. And was still smiling when the second wave arrived twenty-five minutes later. Ruhn ended up having thirds, too.

He was a precise eater, nothing sloppy or loose about his forkfuls or his hands, and he wiped his mouth constantly. He also asked very good questions.

"And then what did the sire do?" he was saying.

He was also so very handsome in the light of the little candle that sat between them, his eyes luminous, his face accented by the shifting shadows from the flame on its wick. As Saxton stared at those lips, he remembered how they had spent the day downstairs at Miniahna's farmhouse, intertwined in that old rickety bed, the heat of their bodies providing all the warmth they needed, their passion banked, not extinguished.

Ruhn was proving to be the kind of lover Saxton had been looking for all his life. There was great hunger and rough dominance, but all of that was mediated by a wellspring of consideration and caring. It was the yin and the yang of sex, the grabbing and the caressing, the biting and the kissing, the pushing down and the cradling.

"Saxton?"

"Sorry, just admiring the view—and the memories of the day." On cue, that blush was enchanting—and there was the temptation to stay on the subject of making love. But he let it go for the time being. "Anyway, the sire relented. She will be allowed to mate the male she wants. In the end, love wins."

"I like that outcome."

"Me, too." Saxton sat forward as the male seemed to retreat into his head. "What are you thinking of?"

"I would like to believe I'd let Bitty choose. I mean, not that I'm her father or anything. But I would hope I would do that for her as long as the male was not a bad or dangerous guy."

"You will. You're a good father."

"Rhage is her father." Ruhn shook his head. "And I'm okay with that. It's hard to be a father—I'm intimidated by the role. My father . . . he was my everything, my hero. He was strong and he honored my *mahmen*. He worked hard and provided well. All I ever wanted to do was be like him and live up to his standard. I never felt like I quite got things right."

"Relationships with family are complicated."

And it must have been so hard to learn the male wasn't perfect, Saxton thought. That he had endangered the family through his gambling. That Ruhn had had to make good on the debts of his hero.

Those words stayed put, however. It seemed cruel to remind the male of what he had lived through. Ruhn knew too well the price that had had to be paid.

"My father was the opposite." Saxton sat back as their plates were cleared. "I never wanted to be like him. I still do not."

"He could not . . . accept you?"

"Merely not accepting me would have been a blessing. He hates me for who and what I am. He would rather I were dead. It didn't used to be that way. But once my *mahmen* passed? Everything changed. I feel as though he went bad."

"I am so sorry. But . . . forgive me, I thought the aristocracy was more . . . I don't know what the word is . . ."

As Ruhn trailed off, Saxton nodded. "Oh, it's permissible provided it is neither seen nor heard. When I refused to mate a female from an appropriate bloodline, Father kicked me out of the family, out of the house, out of the will. I was supposed to walk in his shoes, after all. Be a solicitor, take over the estate and finances. Procreate to produce the next generation of the *glymera* who deny what they really were—see, my father is gay. But in his opinion, which is the only one that matters in his world, he chose the proper way to mediate the proclivity—namely, cheating on my *mahmen* for their entire mating. Of course, she was tolerant of the arrangement. None of that messy sex stuff. In that regard, they were perfectly matched."

"I am glad you did not mate a female you did not care for."

"Me, too. What it cost me in terms of my family has been more than made up for by my being who I am without apology."

"Do you think you would ever want young?"

Saxton took a sip of water to try to hide a sudden rush of emotion. "I just might. You know . . . I just might."

"I never thought about it until I started to spend my time with Bitty. I like telling her the stories of her *mahmen* and me, and the family traditions we had, and the foods her *granhmen* made. The toys her grandfather made. They are all I have to give her, really, but she seems to truly want the stories. It makes me feel like I'm keeping my parents alive, her *mahmen* alive. I loved my family so much. Even more so now that I am in Bitty's life."

"You are a very good person, Ruhn. And I wish I'd grown up the way you did. We had all kinds of material things, but no emotional ties among the people living under that expansive roof."

"When you are poor, all you have are the people in your life. Who they are and who they are to you? That is the wealth you have in the world. That is the wealth you pass down to the next generation. That is what I am giving to Bitty, and I am so grateful her new parents understand and accept me in her life."

When the check came, Ruhn reached for it. "I have some money. As of three nights ago, Wrath has put me on the payroll and I feel as though I have earned it."

"Well, I'll have to thank you for the meal later tonight."

Cue that blush. Oh, yes . . . that lovely blush.

After Ruhn took out some bills and placed them on the little plastic tray with the check, they both got up and walked through the maze of tables and other diners.

It felt good to be a part of the world, to be out with a lover he cared deeply for, to be eating and drinking, talking and walking, going to work and looking forward to coming home. Things seemed more vivid, the smells of the food, the sounds of the human talk . . . the sensation as Ruhn reached behind himself and Saxton took the palm that was offered, flesh on flesh, warmth magnified.

Outside, the cold was a welcome brisk kiss on the cheek instead of something to brace oneself against, and the slippery, partially salted walkway was a fun excuse to cling to Ruhn's arm as around the corner they went together, to the alley that led to the back of the restaurant.

There, in the shadows, they kissed for the longest time, bodies straining for contact through winter clothes and scarves and gloves, the hours they were to be apart like an obstacle course to be surmounted.

"I'm going to go to Mistress Miniahna's to check the house," Ruhn said as they finally eased back.

"I shall go back there as soon as Wrath and I are finished."

"Okay, then. See you soon."

"I cannot wait."

As Saxton closed his eyes to dematerialize, a barreling gust shot down between the restaurant and the card shop next door. But it might as well have been a light, tropical breeze.

Indeed, the rejuvenating warmth of new love brought spring to the whole world, no matter the calendar's season.

THIRTY-TWO

*T*wo hours of eating and drinking later, and Novo was ready to chew her own leg off to get out of Café Estrogen. Not that she ate. Or drank.

No, it was kind of like being at a zoo for Victoria's Secret shoppers: As she stayed down at the loser end of the table, she watched the females play with their hair and get into debates over whether to have the ceviche something or another over the kale-rolled organic what-the-fuck.

She had to give her sister credit, though. Sophy was in her element, so solicitous of the others, leaning forward with a manicured hand to touch a thin forearm in inquiry: "Is that chicken all right? Do you need it done differently?"

Or something to that effect. And the females were just as treacle-icious back, all, "Oh, noooo, it's fabulous. Really . . . even if it is underdone."

To which Sophy would say, "I will get the waiter. I want this night to be perfect for you."

"But you're the bride!"

"You're my best friend! I'm just soooo glad you're here . . ."

Blah, blah, blah.

It was performance art at its best, and Novo knew the flip side to this bright and shiny silver dollar: At home, Sophy would deconstruct everything the other females were wearing, what they'd eaten, how their weight was, whether their hair was on fleek.

On fleek? What the hell did that mean?

A working definition seemed to involve hair extensions, four different shades of "natural" blond, and enough hair spray to turn them into a potential Roman candle. Other than that? She was working in the dark on that one.

At least this had to be almost over—

The four vampire males who approached from behind her wouldn't have registered ordinarily. One of them, however, carried a scent she remembered all too well.

Her first instinct was to turn around and see if she was right, but Sophy's eyes lit up and then she got to her stilettos and clasped her hands together as if she'd won the Sephora version of Powerball.

Of course Oskar had showed up.

Novo should have seen this coming.

Keeping her eyes down on her empty plate, she relied on her peripheral vision. He was still the same height, still wore that same cologne—but the clothes were different, skinny jeans and a black three-quarter hipster coat instead of the preppie khakis and North Face jacket he would have worn back in Novo's era. Hair was longer and pulled back into a man-bun.

And he'd grown a beard.

And taken to wearing heavy black-rimmed glasses.

Dollars to donuts, she could guess who was responsible for this new "look."

The three with him were variations on the evolved male, the one on the left going so far as to be wearing a We're All Feminists T-shirt over his turtleneck.

Not that being a feminist was a bad idea. Not at all. It was just Novo assumed sporting a pair of ovaries probably meant you had a little more skin in that game. But whatever.

On cue, the table went into girl-gasms at the new arrivals, everybody tittering, the smiles popping like glitter bombs, the laughter an overflow of mirth, as the males went and greeted their girlfriends or mates.

From her distance away from the hub, Novo decided screw it and focus on her old love. His face was stiff, she thought—but maybe she was reading into that. And he looked bored, although again, her own predilections could be assigning that to him—

Oskar took a step back and that was when his gaze swung around—and he did a double take.

Sophy noticed immediately and she covered up the calculation in her eye just as quick. With the broadest smile yet, she motioned down the way, clearly telling him to go greet her dearly beloved sister.

Oskar shoved his hands in his coat and walked forth with his head down, a dog who'd gotten its ass paddled with a newspaper for tearing something to pieces. When he came up to Novo, he cleared his throat.

"Hey, there." His voice was still the same. Soft, a little husky. "It's good to see you, Novo."

She'd wondered for a long time how this would play out. What it would be like to see him, scent him, hear him speak. She had always assumed she would be crippled with pain and that tears, those hated external signs of weakness, would blur her sight and leak out onto her cheeks. Her heart would thunder, her palms would sweat, her . . .

I'm looking at a boy, she thought.

This was not a full-grown male standing before her, and chances were good, no matter his age, he would always be as such. This was someone who needed a Sophy, somebody who would provide him with the contours of his life, tell him what his wardrobe should be, order him into some situations and out of others.

Novo had ascribed much to him, in her naiveté.

Maturity through hard experience wiped that away.

"Good to see you, too," she murmured.

His eyes roamed around the human crowd. "I heard you're in the Brotherhood's training program."

"I am."

"Pretty impressive. I was surprised when Sophy told me. How's it going?"

"It's a lot of work. But it's good. I'm happy with it."

She stopped there for two reasons: One, she didn't think it was any of his business, and two, she didn't want to seem defensive.

"I always knew you'd do something big." Now his eyes shifted to hers and stayed put. "I mean, ever since I first met you . . . you were different."

"Sophy has her own unique characteristics." She shrugged. "To each their own."

"Yes. To each . . ."

As he let the sentence drift, she expected him to say a quick, awkward buh-bye and head back to Mama, as it were. But he didn't. He just stared at her.

Novo was the one who broke the eye contact. And yup, guess who'd had enough of the reunion BS?

Sophy came up to her male and linked her arm in his. "Dance with me, Oskar. Come on."

Novo got to her feet. "I'm going to head out, Soph."

"Oh, you mustn't! It's time to dance—stay a little longer." Those eyes narrowed. "It's the least you can do considering that Sheri has had to do all the work for tonight and for the wedding ceremony."

On that, the female pirouetted away and took her deadweight with her—after she made him take his coat off and leave it at the table.

Novo dropped back in her chair. The way she looked at it, she could either blow another thirty minutes here, or end up with double that on her phone later tonight and tomorrow. At least sitting at the table, she didn't have to talk to anyone.

Sophy's blond hair gleamed under the lights above the dance floor, and her thin body in its floaty dress made Oskar seem even bigger and stronger. The pair of them were quite a picture, young romance caught right on the precipice of the rest of their lives.

Provided you didn't look too closely.

As Oskar held his female in his arms, he was looking over her head, his expression bland. On her side, Sophy was talking to him with an urgency she was masking with that Proactiv commercial smile of hers, the one where she was just so Happy and Centered in Her Life. Clearly, there was trouble in paradise. Then again, it wasn't uncommon for couples to have issues as they came up to a mating ceremony. Lot of stress, especially if you insisted on straddling traditions and being Queen for the night—

"Fancy meeting you here."

Novo jumped out of her chair and spun around. *"Peyton?"*

It sure the hell was. The fighter was standing right behind her, and he was dressed as if he were on the way to one of his clubs, his slick suit and open-collar shirt the kind of thing you could get away with in Caldwell this time of year only if you had a chauffeur.

"What are you doing here?" she asked.

He looked around. "Just thought I'd drop by for some overpriced, badly prepared, pseudo-French food in the company of human posers and vampire suck-ups—and oh, hey, 'urprise, I find you here. Not your usual gig, is it."

"Not even close. And you really were just dropping in?"

"Yeah. Totally. Absolutely dumb luck."

"And, like, not at all because I mentioned to you when and where this fiasco was going to take place?"

Peyton made elaborate work of grimacing and then did a spot-on imitation of the groom's cake lady from *Steel Magnolias:* "Guuuuuuillllllty."

Novo tried to swallow her laughter, she really did. But goddamn it, she was glad to see him even though she shouldn't be.

Except then he got serious. "Actually, I had something I had to ask you. It's the kind of thing . . . well, I didn't want to do it over the phone, and besides, I wasn't sure if I called whether you would answer."

She stayed away from that last one—because she didn't even want to think about all that phone-checking no one needed to know about.

"What did you want to ask me?"

Those amazing eyes of his dropped to the ground and he cleared his throat. After a moment, he seemed to collect himself and he looked back at her.

"What the fuck is a douche canoe?"

Novo barked out a laugh that was so loud, she turned the heads of the humans seated across the room even though the music was playing. There was none of that from the females at the table, though. 'Cuz they were already staring at her.

And geez, she couldn't decide whether all their shock was because a male was addressing her. Or because Peyton looked like exactly what he was: a privileged son of the *glymera*.

"Well?" he prompted. "I was hoping to get a working definition."

"It is not a compliment," she said. "And it is worse than a douchebag."

"Bigger payload, huh," he murmured with a slow smile.

"Yeah. Pretty much. You can fit a hell of a lot more douche in a canoe than a bag."

"Hey, is this chair next to you taken? I had to walk all the way back here and I got a blister."

"Really," she drawled. "You're going with that?"

Peyton leaned in. "Is it going to work?"

She looked away. Looked back. God, she really wished she would stop smiling. "I don't know."

"I'll take that as a yes," he said as he parked it beside her chair. "And may I just say . . . hallelujah."

Peyton knew he was taking a huge gamble crashing this bridal's maiding or whatever the hell the humans called it. He'd made that vow not to bother Novo quite sincerely—and he'd had every intention of keeping it . . . at least for the first twenty-four hours or so. Unfortunately, not seeing or talking to her had proven more difficult than he'd anticipated—and in the end, he thought, what the hell. Plausible deniability. He was a free agent and out in Caldwell, and hey, if he happened to show up at the same place she might possibly have mentioned as where she might theoretically be on a Friday night?

Well, that was just the breaks.

Sorry.

Not sorry, actually.

And here she was, looking better than any female or woman in the place with her skintight black leathers and her muscle shirt, her strong shoulders and arms shown off, her body once again as it had always been.

Powerful. Sexy.

Oh, God, he just wanted in her again. He didn't care the terms or the whys or the wheres. Just once more.

"You want something to eat?" she asked him. "Or are your boys waiting for you in the car?"

"The douche-mobile is empty at the moment." He smiled. "And I—"

"Aren't you going to introduce us?"

At the sound of the higher-pitched female voice, he looked at what had come up to them: a lollipop blond with big white teeth, a knock-off Valentino-ish lace dress, and eyes that were too close together. Oh, and look, she had an accessory. The male in her wake might as well have had a leash hooked to a proverbial collar, his hangdog expression and cultivated hipster vibe the kind of thing that made you question whether he had balls or not.

Probably did, Peyton decided. But they were in the female's purse.

"Novo?" the female prompted. "Let's not be rude to your guest."

Okay, that smile was to fine china what Dixie was to plates.

"This is Peyton, son of Peythone," Novo muttered. "He's in the training program with me."

There was a pause. And then the Pomeranian shot a look at Novo and put her hand out. "Well. How lovely. And allow me to introduce myself as my sister, Novalina, seems disinclined to do so. I'm Sophya."

Those eyes bounced up and down him, from his shoes to his suit to his cuff links, and he could have sworn he heard the chatter of an adding machine in the background as she assigned a monetary value to everything.

Talk about instant dislike. He was really not impressed.

So, yeah, he deliberately stayed seated and crossed his arms over his chest. "Hey."

"Are you, ah, are you joining us for dancing?" She smiled stiffly as she lowered her hand. "Because everyone has to dance with the bride-to-be, you know."

He ignored that and focused on the male standing behind her. Funny, for someone who was apparently getting mated sometime very soon, he didn't seem terribly interested in the female he was going through the ceremony with.

Nope. He was staring at Novo.

On the one hand, Peyton could understand it. Novo was hot as fuck, a Bugatti in a parking lot full of minivans. On the other hand . . . he really just wanted to castrate the motherfucker and feed his own cock to him.

Then field-dress him in the middle of the dance floor.

Maybe cut him in quarters with a saw while the humans screamed and ran for the exit.

Then light the corpse on fire.

Yeah, 'cuz you really should clean up your messes.

"—of course, I've always had a flair for style." Novo's sister paused to take a breath. "I mean, the wedding is going to have to be just right for—"

"This is your *hellren*-to-be," he said, cutting her off.

"Oh, yes! Yes, I'm sorry." She stepped aside and made like Vanna White. "Peyton, this is Oskar."

Oskar.

The name Novo had called out in her sleep.

As a cold bucket of water splashed down over his head, Peyton got to his feet. "Named after a hot dog." He got to his feet and extended his hand. "Quite a bastion of honor there, bro. Or do you prefer wiener?"

Everyone froze.

And then Novo started laughing so hard, she nearly fell over.

THIRTY-THREE

It was rude to laugh. Novo knew this. She honestly did. But the evening, which had started on a low note and then sunk to sub-basement levels, had suddenly turned on a dime—and was looking more like an adventure than an endurance contest.

"I'm sorry, buddy." Peyton clapped Oskar on the shoulder. "Just joking."

Sophy recovered quick and stepped in between the two males. "Yes. Indeed. Well, ah, Peyton . . . you must tell me all about yourself. Come, let's sit down together. Waiter!" Sophy called out. "Waiter, a menu for my guest!" She actually snapped her fingers. And then pulled out a chair for herself and one for Peyton. "I want to hear all about what the Brotherhood is like. You must have some amazing stories."

And there it was. The charm. The batting eyes. The touch on a male's forearm.

In response, Peyton looked back and forth between Sophy and Oskar—but Novo couldn't tell whether he was taken by her sister or not. And God, that would be . . . really sucky. Even though she had no claim to him at all.

A pit formed in her stomach—except almost instantly, she thought, nope. If her sister wanted to pull another Oskar here, the joke was on Sophy. There was no way in hell Peyton was going to mate a civilian: in spite of the fact that Sophy was beautiful, and certainly had the so-cial aggression to try and take a further step up, there was nowhere to go on that staircase for her.

Paradise was much more his style as the daughter of the King's First Adviser.

"Peyton?" Sophy prompted. "So? Will you sit down with me?"

Okaaaaaaay, wiener references aside, the night was once again tak-ing a torpedo into its hull, and Novo glanced over her shoulder at the way out. Time to go. Hey, if Peyton wanted to get to know her sister better—hell, if he wanted to fuck her just because he could? More power to him—

"No, we're not staying."

Popping her brows, she turned her head back around—to see Pey-ton picking up her leather jacket from the back of her chair.

"Come on, Novo," he said. "I'm taking you out on the town."

"You can't leave," Sophy protested. "Wait, you can't."

Peyton leaned in and looked the female right in the eye. "I can do anything the fuck I want, sweetheart. And what I am *not* going to do is play windup toy for you as you ignore the poor SOB you're mating and disrespect your sister. I'd say it was a pleasure to meet you, but I gave up lying a couple of nights ago, so that's a no-go. And I'd wish you a happy life, but that is not what you're heading for." He pegged Oskar with a hard stare. "And neither are you, my friend. If you have any brains left, you'll either leave her or blow them out. Good luck."

Novo was so stunned, she let herself get escorted out. But come on. Come *on*.

The two of them strode past the other humans eating full meals and entered into the tea room section of the place. And then they were out into the cold.

She started giggling as soon as she hit the night air.

Putting her fist up to her mouth, she stuttered, "That was awesome. That was fucking awesome."

Peyton indicated the way forward. "My car is over here."

Taking her elbow, he led her over to a—oh, wow, nice—blacked-out Range Rover and opened things up so she could slide into the back.

"Oh, my God, you did that." She was still laughing and talking to him even as he closed the door and went around. "You fucking did that."

There was a *doggen* behind the wheel, a young one, and he twisted around in his seat. "I'm sorry, madam? Whatever did I do?"

She batted her hand through the warm, new-car-smell air. "Nothing. I was just—I was talking to him."

Peyton got in and ordered, "Drive."

"Where may I take you, sire?"

"Anywhere, I don't care."

As they pulled away from the curb, it was clear that Peyton was not laughing.

"What's wrong?" she asked.

"Who is Oskar to you?"

Well, that double-tapped her happy-happy, joy-joy. And now she became just like him, serious as hell.

When she glanced at the driver, Peyton said, "He is discreet."

"Just because your servant won't talk to anyone else doesn't mean I'm all about discussing my personal business around him—or with you."

"So you admit that you and Oskar were together."

"Jealous?"

"Yeah. Especially because he was staring at you the whole time. He's getting mated to that nightmare female in how many nights? And he only has eyes for you. What did you do, dump him when you got bored and he dated her because that was as close as he could come to having you?"

"Try the other way around," she said in a low voice.

"What?"

She turned to the window and looked out. They were passing by other restaurants that were locally owned and operated; in this neighborhood, there were none of the commercial chains that were closer to the exits of the Northway or the skyscrapers of downtown. And through the fogged-glass fronts of the eateries, she saw humans on dates, families gathering, waiters and waitresses hustling food and drinks on trays.

"He left me for her," she heard herself say.

Okay, she needed to stop—

"What the *fuck* was he thinking?"

Novo told herself not to be complimented. Hell, Peyton had to be saying that just because he was hoping to get some later.

"I mean, your sister is fake," he continued. "I'm sorry, I know she's your blood, but that is one of the most transparent females I've ever met in my life—and I'm in the *glymera,* for godsakes. We invented that kind of horror."

Novo pivoted back to him. She couldn't help it.

Peyton was sitting deep in his seat, but he wasn't looking at her. He was staring straight ahead, his eyes unfocused as if he were reliving the whole scene.

"She didn't pay any respect to him," he said. "That's her future *hellren.* She should be concerned about him over anyone, especially some asshole like me she doesn't know. But she sized up my clothes and decided . . . well, anyway. And Oskar deserves what he gets if he picked something like that over a female like you. I mean . . . you're so strong and beautiful and smart. You're a real person."

Novo blinked once. Twice.

And decided she really wanted to fuck Peyton. Like, right now.

She leaned in to the driver. "Take us to The Keys. Do you know what that is?"

The *doggen* shook his head. "No, madam. I'm sorry, I don't."

"Take a left up here. I'll tell you where to go."

Peyton's blood thickened and his cock got hard the instant Novo said the word "Keys" and he almost didn't think he'd heard right. But then her efficient directions took them to the unassuming entrance of Caldwell's most notorious sex club.

Hell, from what he understood, the place was well known even down in New York City.

"Am I dressed appropriately," he asked as the Range Rover came to a stop.

"We'll get a mask from Staff."

Novo got out her door and he did the duty on his side. Leaning back in, he told the driver to park and wait.

He had no idea how long they were going to be in there. Or what was going to happen next.

Before he straightened, he tucked his erection up so it lay flat on his lower abdomen and closed his suit jacket. Meanwhile, Novo left her jacket behind so she was just in that muscle shirt and those leather pants, which—oh, God, he wanted her so damned bad.

Especially as she walked ahead, her strides taking her to the head of a wait line that was at least fifty people long.

There were two guys standing at an unmarked door, and as she flashed a key, they let her in immediately—and he was waved through clearly because he was with her. Inside, he could catch the scent of sex, and hear music, but he couldn't see past heavy curtains that delineated a kind of anteroom.

Hello, naked lady.

From out of the shadows, a woman with both her breasts painted red and nothing on her lower half emerged to offer them masks that were black and reminded him of *The Phantom of the Opera*. Once they were in place, Novo pulled the curtain back and walked forward.

And once again, Peyton followed . . . only to stop just inside the barrier.

Hieronymus Bosch, he thought as he resumed making his way into the vast, dimly lit space. That was the only thing that came to his mind.

As music pumped through speakers he could not see, his eyes were overloaded with images of naked, contorted bodies. Some were strewn over benches and sofas. Others were in Lucite boxes. There were sunken pits where writhing forms twisted and turned into human fists and lineups of women and men face down or up on tables with all kinds of people covering them.

This would have been quite the scene for him a couple of years back.

Hell, he had been living it on a smaller scale as recently as a week or two ago.

And it wasn't that it didn't interest him. He was curious how it all worked, although that was more like a *huh* than any sort of erotic impulse.

There was only one person he wanted to fuck, and she was taking him deeper and deeper into the club.

"Does this turn you on?" Novo asked as she looked back at him.

Enough, he thought.

Snagging her arm, he whipped her around and slammed her body right into his own.

"You turn me on," he growled.

With a roll of his hips, he ground himself against her and it was then that her eyes got hot behind that mask. And he couldn't not respond to that. He grabbed her by the ass—hard—and pushed her up against a wall. Clamping a hand on the front of her throat, he squeezed just enough to make her have to work for air.

"Is this what you want?" he said harshly. "Do you want it hard and where people can see?"

"Fuck you." She bared her fangs and hissed at him. "And yeah, I do."

Her hand shoved itself between them to find his cock, and she didn't so much stroke him as rough him up—and he *loved* it.

Sweeping his hand to the front of her muscle shirt, he peeled it down so that it trapped her arms. No bra. Fuck, yeah . . . no bra. He held her in place by the throat and went for her nipple, nicking her with his fang so he could suck her blood while he suckled on her. In response, her fingers raked into his hair and one of her legs lifted and wrapped around his ass.

Why the *hell* wasn't she wearing a skirt?

Screw the preamble, they were both panting for it. So he turned her to face the wall, jerked her hips out, and took out the switchblade he always carried with him in his breast pocket.

"Don't move."

When she looked back at him, he released the blade and waited until she nodded. Then he ran his free hand up and down her crack, rubbing the leather, stroking her sex through the pants. That didn't last long. Taking the razor-sharp blade, he cut into the seam that went right up the center of her, put the knife away, and slid four fingers, two from each side, into the hole he'd made.

It was a clean jerk.

And underneath, her bare, hairless sex was open, ready, wet for him.

He sprung his cock so fast, he ripped his own fly. And then he entered her on a single, powerful thrust that drove her face-first into the wall. She called out something, maybe it was his name—over the din of the music, he had no clue—and braced her arms as she spread her legs farther apart.

Peyton rode her like an animal.

Fuck his fancy clothes. And fuck the people who were watching them, too. He didn't care about anything but coming inside of her. Filling her up. Doing it over and over again until he leaked out of her in rivers of come.

Halfway through, he realized he was marking her.

Somehow, along the way, he had bonded with her.

THIRTY-FOUR

Saxton couldn't wait to leave the Audience House. His sense of responsibility and duty to Wrath ensured that he got all his work done, but the instant he could, he was out the back door and dematerializing to Minnie's.

He entered through the seam in the weather stripping, but as he did, he was aware of a great deal of resistance. And as soon as he was fully re-formed, he understood why.

The explanation was lying on the floor, head under Minnie's sink, long legs stretched out, arms cocked and working at something in there.

"Okay, this is a fantasy of mine," Saxton drawled. "Who knew I wanted you to cosplay being a plumber?"

There was a clank and then a curse. And then his hot pipe-worker was sitting up and wiping his forehead on his arm. Wow. Hanes T-shirt and blue jeans. Muscles underneath. Male everything, everywhere.

Be still my heart, Saxton thought.

"You're back," Ruhn said with a smile.

Saxton put his satchel down on the counter and took off his cashmere coat. "I am indeed. And you are dirty and sweaty."

"I'll take a shower—"

"Don't you dare."

Saxton walked over and got down on his knees in between Ruhn's legs. Running his hands up those corded thighs, he made quick work of the button fly—and then he brought his mouth to what he'd been thinking about all night long.

Ruhn's explosion of breath was followed by a loud series of flopping bangs.

Then the male dropped his monkey wrench.

Whatastinkingpity.

"Saxton . . ." There was another gasp. "Oh, God, yes—"

Saxton looked up. Ruhn was rubbing his head as if he'd knocked it against the lip of the counter—but the male didn't seem worried at all about the bump at his temple. No, his eyes were full of wonder and heat. Indeed, there was always a degree of surprise behind Ruhn's erotic passion, as if he couldn't believe his body was capable of feeling like it was. And Saxton loved that. The surprise and joy, the powerful instinct and urgency—all anchored by a sense that it was a first time, every time.

Saxton got back to work, sucking and licking, and he could tell by the way Ruhn's hips started to jerk up and down that he was getting close—

"Hello!" came a cheery voice.

Whipping his head up, Saxton looked in panic to the front of the house. Then he popped off that floor as Ruhn scrambled to get the button fly back into place.

With a quick lunge, Saxton leaned over Ruhn and hit the hand soap at the sink, knowing that the flowery fragrance would cover up the scent of male arousal. Turning the water on, he started to wash his—

"Not the water!"

A deluge came out under the sink, soaking Ruhn's back and the floor just as Minnie walked into the kitchen. The female stopped dead.

"Hi!" Saxton said as he turned off the faucet with his elbow. "How are you?"

And then he stood there with his soapy hands dripping suds into the sink—as Ruhn looked around him, drenched from head to shoulders.

Minnie started laughing. "You two remind me of Rhysland and me. I can't tell you how many times he stuffed himself under that sink and tried to fix that pipe. And he always asked me to run the water."

Ruhn stood up with a blush so vibrant it was as if he were wearing rouge. Reaching for the paper towels, he passed one to Saxton and used several to dry his hands and the back of his neck. "This has gotten loose before?"

"Oh, yes." The older female came forward with a canvas bag. "I made you some bread. And there are preserves here. Strawberry. I had to buy them. The strawberries even at Whole Foods looked too tough for me— oh, the lights! You replaced the lights that were out in the ceiling!"

"Yes, madam." Ruhn bowed. "Even the one that got stuck in the socket."

"That one over there?" As she pointed across the kitchen, and he nodded, she smiled again. "It always does that, too. Did you use a potato to get it out?"

Now Ruhn smiled. "I did, yes. My father taught me that. Just as he was the one who showed me how to work pipes. Also, were you aware that there is a leaky toilet upstairs?"

"No, I didn't realize."

"I need to go to Home Depot and buy another set of guts for it. But I can do that first thing tomorrow night."

"I shall give you some money—"

"No," Saxton cut in. "You shall not."

As she looked back and forth between the two of them, her cheerfulness dissolved into a misty emotion, the kind of thing that tugged at the heart. And while her eyes watered, she fumbled in her coat for a tissue to dab away her tears.

"This is such a big house," she said. "And it needs so much . . . of everything. I try to keep up with it, I truly do. But it is only me and I'm not as strong as I used to be."

Ruhn moved as if he wanted to hug the woman. But he didn't quite make it, his shyness seeming to freeze him in place. "We will take care of it all for you. And when you come back, anytime something goes wrong and you need a handymale, you can call me. I will come and fix it."

With a determined sniffle, Minnie marched across to the male and threw her arms around him. For a moment, Ruhn just stood there, looking like he was going to panic. But then he eased his enormous arms around the frail older female and gave her the gentlest of hugs. And then Minnie came over to Saxton.

He was right with the embrace thing, and when they stepped apart, he took his handkerchief out of his hip pocket. "Here, madam."

Minnie snuffled and patted at her face some more. "I didn't know how much the decline here was bothering me, until a solution presented itself. I didn't know . . . what a burden I've been carrying. I've felt as though . . . I've felt as though I've been letting Rhysland down."

"Well, we have a solution," Saxton said as he glanced at Ruhn. "And we're going to make sure you never worry about your house again, aren't we."

As Ruhn looked over and nodded, Saxton felt a warm glow in the center of his chest.

"You two are in love, aren't you," Minnie said abruptly.

Immediately, Saxton cleared his throat, unsure of whether this was going to be a problem. "Madam, we are . . ."

Just friends? That was a lie he would not speak. But Ruhn had crossed his arms over his chest and seemed as if he wanted the floor to open up and swallow him whole.

"In love," Minnie echoed as she took one of each of their hands. "You know, love is the greatest gift the Scribe Virgin bestowed on her species. I'm happy to see it in this house again. Rhysland and I had so many years of it together here."

Ruhn's exhale was accompanied by a release of his arms. And then he started to smile.

I will remember this for the rest of my life, Saxton thought. *This kitchen with the cupboard under the sink wide open, his hair and shirt wet, Minnie beaming like it was a festival night.*

It was the moment when he truly let himself go.

The little rich boy turned out to be a fearless, horny exhibitionist.

As Novo danced against a tall female in latex, she only had eyes for Peyton: He was standing off to the side, watching her hands as they skimmed the woman's body, and her hips as she moved, and her ass as she turned around.

He was starved for her. Even after all the sex they'd had, he was ready to go again . . . but only with her.

Other women—and men—had approached him, performed in front of him, offered him all kinds of things, but he waved them away with impatience. And some of them had been stunningly beautiful.

Peyton didn't give a rat's ass. He only seemed to see her.

For a female who had been left for another, it was a revelation. In fact, she didn't know that she had needed to feel wanted this badly—but she was well aware that shit was a slippery slope to go down. You never wanted to be centered by another: Because when they left, and they would eventually, they took that part of you they'd filled with them and you were hollow once again.

But for tonight? For this one night?

She was whole, in a way that she thought she would never be again.

And evidently, Peyton had had it with her being in someone else's arms. He strode over and all but shoved the woman out of the way. Then he was kissing Novo, his mouth full of demand, his body hard again, his hands rough and greedy.

Next thing she knew, she was bent over something—she didn't

know what and didn't care. And he was inside of her once more, pumping, pulling her braid like it was the reins of a bridle, her spine torquing under the pressure. Her orgasm was so intense, she clamped her molars together and felt the sting at the top of her head.

Closing her eyes, she opened herself up to all of the sensation: the weakness in her thigh muscles, the rough material under her cheek, the compression of her breasts, and the slapping pounding that her sex was taking.

Tears came to her eyes underneath her mask.

With desperation, she tried to catch the tail of the emotion and drag it back into its cage, but she couldn't get the upper hand.

It was as if the release opened the casket of everything she had held inside, the old pain rolling out like a corpse, the smell of it, the sight of it, too overpowering to be ignored.

She sobbed in the darkness, into the mask, into the sex of strangers and the loud music.

Opening her mouth, she screamed the pain out of herself, cast the past into the club's uncaring anonymity, used Peyton's fucking as the exit ramp.

And no one knew.

It was completely private.

Eventually, Peyton fell upon her back, his heavy weight a beautiful grounding that brought her back to earth, his harsh panting in her ear a confirmation that he had been there while she had come through the ghost land, that she had not been alone, even if he had had no idea he was helping her.

Moving her arm around, she searched for his hand. When she found it, she brought his palm forward . . . and kissed his lifeline.

It was the closest she could come to thanking him for a gift he would never know he gave her.

The healing had finally started.

THIRTY-FIVE

"Come back to my place."

As Peyton opened the way out of the club for Novo, he prayed she said yes. He didn't want the night to end. He didn't want to spend the day anywhere else but next to her. He didn't want to wake up alone, without her.

"What is your driver going to think of us?" she drawled.

"I sent him away two hours ago. Come back with me."

As she stopped and looked up at the sky, he followed suit. A thick cloud cover had rolled in, and there was a winter humidity in the air. More snow was coming.

Who gave a shit about the weather.

"My father is away on business," he said. "We'll have the place to ourselves. He took his butler with him, and the other servants are glad to have a night off. And okay, fine, so I told the driver to clear the house out or he was fired."

Novo pivoted around. "Where do you live."

"Is that a yes?"

"No, it's a question about where you live."

He smiled. "You never give an inch, do you? And my blood is in you. Follow the way. After we fuck in the tub, I'll make you Last Meal down in the kitchen."

There was a long silence. Off in the distance a siren wailed. A horn honked. Three people spilled out of the club, the clutch of humans wrapped in each other's arms, laughing.

"All right," she said.

Peyton took her hand and gave it a squeeze. "Thank you."

When she pulled away, he let her go. And then he closed his eyes and dematerialized. When he re-formed on the front lawn of his father's mansion, he had no idea whether she would actually show or not. She was like that. Hot and cold.

His heart pounded as he stood in the snow, the wind rushing around and whistling through the evergreens at the edge of the property.

Lights were on inside, and for a moment, he regarded the mansion as if through Novo's eyes. Would she like the old place?

Somehow, that didn't matter, and not because he didn't care about her opinion. It was just that, for the first time in his life, the fact that none of this was really his hit him. His father's life, his bloodline's expectations, his social sphere's demands . . . he was not required to buy in to any of it, and maybe his addictions had represented his struggle to come to this realization.

At that very instant, Novo appeared beside him.

"Welcome to my humble abode," he murmured as he swept a hand toward the house's grand expanse.

"You know, I thought it would be bigger." As he recoiled, she nailed him a good one in the arm. "Gotcha. This place is like a goddamn castle, are you kidding me."

Drawing her in close, he kissed her on the top of the head—and was surprised when she let him. And then he took her to the front entrance. As he hipped open the heavy door, he was surprised at how tense he was.

She walked in with those split leathers and her athletic body moving with power and her head up as she looked around.

Her eyes seemed to miss nothing of the antiques and the grandeur, the crystal chandeliers, the grandfather clock and the tapestries.

Pivoting to him, she said dryly, "You never mentioned you lived in the Smithsonian museum."

"I hate to show off, you know." He kicked the door shut, the sound of the thing hitting home echoing up to the high ceiling. "It's fucking tacky. Come. I want to introduce you to my tub."

As they went upstairs, she asked him how many rooms there were; he hesitated.

"Come on," she chided. "Can't count that high?"

"I'm not good with math, it's true." He took her to the left at the head of the stairs, down the corridor that had so many doors. "I'm going to guess fifty or sixty. Maybe more. There are parts of this place I've never bothered to go in."

"I live in a single room. No, I have two rooms, a bathroom and an everything."

"You'll have to show me sometime."

"It wouldn't hold your interest any longer than a Kleenex box."

He stopped in front of his bedroom suite. "It's yours. So I am very interested."

Novo did the job with the knob, probably as a way to duck the intensity that he was throwing out. That was another thing he was learning about her—she was big into diversions, and this was not a surprise. The female avoided closeness at every turn, making him think of a bird landing and taking off at the slightest provocation.

She did seem to keep coming back to his palm, though.

God, she was so different. Unexpected. Fascinating.

With a whistle under her breath, Novo walked into the enormous spread, checking out his bed, his movie screen–sized TV, his sofas, and the bathroom beyond.

"It's so cozy, right?"

She laughed. "If you're comparing this place to a hotel lobby, sure."

He walked over to his dressing room, the doors opening on their own thanks to motion sensors. Inside, he stripped by the dry-cleaning hamper.

When he came back out, he was naked. "You have way too many clothes on."

"And you no longer have that problem."

Her eyes gleamed as she kicked off her combat boots, disarmed, and peeled that muscle shirt and those ruined leathers. Then she stood before him in the flesh. Her body was . . . so amazing. Lean, muscled . . . incredibly sexy.

"Fuck," he heard himself say. "You are the most beautiful female I have ever seen."

"FYI, I'm a sure thing tonight. You don't have to compliment me—"

"Shut up." He came forward and took her hand. "Until you leave this house at nightfall, just let me say what I want and be who I am with you, okay? I'm not asking you to pretend that you're one of those doormat females in a dress with their pinkies in the air over a teacup. But for the next bunch of hours, leave me alone with the corrections, okay?"

She looked away. Looked back. "Fair enough."

With that settled, he pulled her into the bath and started the water flowing into the tub. And in the mirrors, he watched as she wandered around and investigated sinks and towels, bathrobes and windows. She was so stunningly sexy, he nearly let things overflow onto the floor.

"That is a pool," she announced. "Not a tub."

"Wait," he said as she lifted a leg to get in. "Your hair."

With a graceful twist, she turned to him. "What about it?"

Peyton came forward slowly and took the end of the long rope where the band was. "Take it out."

Before she could shake her head, he whispered, "Please. I just want to see you with it loose. Once."

As a haunted look came into her eye, he braced himself for a no.

Instead, she took the thing out of his fingers. "Let me do it."

With her back to him, she brought the length around and there was some snapping as she undid the banding . . . then she was working the braid apart, unleashing acres of gorgeous black hair.

When she was finished, she pivoted to him and pushed it all over her shoulders so that he could only catch sight of the part of it where the indent of her waist was. With her downcast eyes, and tense body, it was as if she were braced to be slapped.

Reaching out, Peyton fanned her hair back into place.

"You take my breath away," he said softly as he regarded the waves cascading down below her breasts, nearly to the cleft of her sex. "Now . . . and forever more."

It was just fucking hair, for godsakes, Novo thought.

But the truth was, no one had seen her with the stuff loose since Oskar. And in the end, the only way she could stay with it down was by reminding herself, over and over again, that this was just for the day ahead. As soon as the sun lowered itself on the far edge of the horizon, she was going to tie everything back up again and set herself to rights once more, everything buttoned, braided, and bound, her emotions impenetrable once more.

As Peyton started speaking to her, she heard more the tone than the syllables, and yes, he was telling her things that in her lonely, battered heart she was hungry to hear and believe—but which her self-preservation told her to shut out.

She could not ignore the way he looked at her, though.

Or the fact that he got down on his knees.

His hands were like a summer breeze traveling over her thighs, her hips . . . her breasts. And his lips were velvet soft as he brushed them across her lower belly. When he hooked an arm under her leg and moved it over his shoulder, she went with him, allowing him the access he wanted. His mouth on her sex was so good, too good, slick against slick, heat against heat.

Staring down past the hard tips of her breasts, she watched him work her out, his tongue licking free as he looked at her looking at him. His eyes were on fire, the sexual worship in his blood transmitting into his expression.

She came once. Twice.

Then she was on the soft rug on the floor and he was mounting her, his hard cock sticking straight out of his hips as he lowered himself onto her.

She closed her eyes so she couldn't see him, so she could pretend it was some other male, any other male. The distance and insulation that lie offered seemed crucial.

Except her body knew it was him.

And oh, God . . .

. . . so did her soul.

THIRTY-SIX

As Saxton sat beside Ruhn in the truck several nights later, he was unsure whether in fact hours had passed since Minnie had interrupted their liaison under the sink . . . or whether years, decades, or centuries had transpired. Indeed, time had become a rubber band stretching and releasing between extremes, moments and eons seeming to be one and the same.

"It's up here," he said. "On the right. Number two-one-oh-five."

"This one?"

"Yes . . . this one. The Victorian."

Saxton was very aware of a churn in his stomach as he braced himself to turn his head and look up at his former home. And in truth, he became absolutely nauseous as his eyes shifted over to measure the dark green, gray, and black paint job, and the cupolas, porches, and shuttered, long-paned windows. In the snow-covered landscape of winter, it was like something off a New England Christmas postcard, picturesque, perfect, and pretty as any painting.

"It's beautiful," Ruhn said as he put the engine in park and shut things off. "Who lives here?"

"Myself. I mean, I used to." He opened his door. "Come with me."

Together, they got out and walked up the unshoveled path to the front porch. Taking out a copper key, Saxton unlocked the deadbolt and then he was pushing the big door wide, a subtle creaking releasing from the hinges.

Ruhn was careful to stomp the snow off the cleats of his boots and Saxton followed the example, clapping his Merrells before stepping over the threshold. Inside, it was warmer than the great outdoors, but not balmy by any means. He had left the thermostats on at sixty-two back on Columbus Day weekend in October when he'd come to make sure the furnace was working. But other than that, no one had been in.

It still smelled the same. Sweet old house. But it was no longer home.

He shut them in and looked around.

Like something out of a Vincent Price movie, all of the furniture, which was period, was covered with sheets and he went randomly into the front parlor and lifted up the corner of a king-sized draping. Underneath, the fainting sofa was classic Victorian, all heavy carved and veneered mahogany, the fabric a deep wine color.

Ruhn came in behind him. "How long did you live here?"

"Quite a while actually. I loved this house."

"What changed your mind?"

Saxton let the sheet fall back into place. "This is where . . . well, Blay and I would come here sometimes."

"Oh."

"After we broke up, I couldn't bear to be in these rooms." He walked farther on, proceeding into the library. "Too many memories."

Behind him, Ruhn followed, and when he turned about, the male's expression was remote.

"Which is why I wanted to bring you here tonight—" At the sound of the door knocker, Saxton focused over the male's shoulder. "Wait here, I'll be right back."

Saxton strode out to the front foyer, and it took him a moment of collection before he could open the door. But then he inhaled slow and deep and did the duty.

On the other side, a tidy female vampire with a briefcase and hair that had been bowl-cut into an unfurled umbrella on top of her head was standing at attention.

"Saxton, I'm so glad you called me, darling."

Kiss, kiss on both cheeks. Pat, pat on his forearm.

"I was surprised, but so very pleased to hear from you," she said as she came in. "I am glad that—oh, who's this?"

Saxton closed them all in. "This is my . . . this is Ruhn."

"Well." She marched right up and put her hand out. "It's a pleasure, Ruhn. Saxton has impeccable taste, and I can tell he's exercised it to his benefit once again. I'm Carmichael."

Ruhn blinked and looked over in a panic, rather as if an exotic bird who was not house-trained had landed on his shoulder.

"You mentioned you have a buyer for this place?" Saxton smoothed over.

The distraction worked perfectly. Carmichael was instantly refocused.

"I told you months ago that I did. When you bought that penthouse without me. Tsk, tsk. That was rather rude of you, but you are forgiven if you give me this listing."

"You're selling?" Ruhn asked softly.

"Yes." Saxton locked eyes with the male. "I find that I'm ready to let it go."

"Well." Carmichael all but tap-danced it out. "This is splendid news. I have a listing form for you to sign right here."

With admirable efficiency, she somehow managed to whip out a sheet and a pen from the briefcase without having to put the thing down: balance on a knee, pop the locks, out with the paper and a Bic.

"Here. Let's get this done and I'll bring them through in an hour."

With a pounding heart, Saxton took the listing form and the cheap pen.

"While you sign that, I just need to confirm some dimensions." For that, she put the briefcase down, got out a tape measure and her iPhone, and headed off. "You're a lawyer. You know where to put your John Hancock."

As her caffeinated footfalls clipped down in the direction of the kitchen, Saxton glanced at Ruhn.

The male was standing close by, his hands loosely linked, his eyes calm, but worried. "You don't look like you're comfortable doing this."

And that was when it happened. A feeling of total peace came over him, as unexpected as a blessing that had been prayed for by an agnostic. And it was grounded in the pale brown of Ruhn's eyes.

"I love you," Saxton said abruptly.

That beautiful stare flared so wide, the whites around those pupils flashed like moonlight.

Saxton waved the paper around. "This house, this . . . shrine? I was keeping it as a testament to something I thought I'd never find again. And I realize, I don't need to keep this anymore. I'm letting it go just as I've let Blay go, and that's all because of you." He held up his free hand. "Which is not to say you have to reciprocate. I brought you here because I just—"

Ruhn silenced the rush of words: "I love you, too."

Saxton started to smile.

And he didn't stop. Even as he used Ruhn's broad back to put his signature on the line.

In order to move forward, you had to let the past go—and sometimes that meant mental shifts that happened on the inside . . . whereas with others, it was about things in the physical world.

Often, the two were interrelated.

With Ruhn in his life, he was now infinitely more interested in the future than he was the past.

Which was as it should be, he thought as he put the cap back on the Bic. Life, after all, was so much more than nostalgia and regrets.

Thank God.

Standing in the training center's gym, Novo pointed at Peyton. "Him. I want him."

The Brother Rhage clapped his hands together. "Fair enough. So it'll be the two of you—then Craeg and Boone together—and Paradise will fight Payne. I'll take Axe. Let's square off, people."

Novo mostly kept her grin to herself as she assumed her attack stance, her legs bent, her hands up, her shoulders tensing as she got ready to punch. Peyton, on the other hand, didn't bother being discreet. He was smiling like a motherfucker as he fell into the same pose.

"On my count of three," Rhage barked out. "One . . . two . . . *three*."

As the whistle blew, Novo went down to the mats, swung both of her legs in a fat circle, and caught Peyton right at the ankles. The male went over like a tree in the forest, all that weight going into a free fall that left him bouncing on his face. No time, no time—after that hard landing, she gave him not even a second to gather his wits.

She jumped on his back, caught him by the throat in the crook of her arm, and then rolled him, split her legs around his ass, and clamped down with all her strength. Peyton grunted and strained, thrashing around as he tried to pivot over on top of her or get free of her hold on his airway. Squeezing, squeezing . . . she started to sweat, the burn in her arms, shoulders, and thighs making it feel as if her bones were on fire.

Every time he shifted one way, she threw a leg out. And then when he went the other way, she switched to her opposite side. Then she grabbed on to her own wrist and pulled, pulled . . .

Peyton started to slow.

Slower.

Sloppier.

And then he put out his arm and slapped his palm once . . . twice . . .

On the third clap, she released everything and flopped onto her own back. She was breathing so hard she saw stars, her lungs like a pair of twin volcanoes in her chest—

She started to giggle. And she let the girly sound go because, fuck it, she had just made a male nearly twice her size tap the fuck out.

Peyton rolled over and retched a couple of times, his head hanging loose, his arms bowed out.

And then he, too, was on his back and laughing.

As they looked at each other across the blue mats, they laughed even harder.

It wasn't until Novo sat up that she realized—oh . . . right. Everyone in the class had stopped what they were doing and was staring over at them.

They had been spending the days together at his house ever since the night of the bridal shower—and the subversive part of her loved sneaking up the staff stairs and avoiding his father and the servants: She liked the idea of fucking Peyton under the roof of a male who would never, ever approve of a scrub like her.

And there had been another bene, one that was perhaps expected. Courtesy of the bridal shower/bachelorette fiasco, she'd been kicked out of the wedding/mating party, her job title and duties revoked by her sister. Which was just fine. She was, however, still on the guest list.

Guess she'd have to see how long that lasted. And also whether she decided to go at all.

Lying next to Peyton during the days, she had begun to wonder why she had to attend an event like Sophy and Oskar's mating at all. Sure, it was family, blah, blah, blah. But she wasn't treated like family. She was an embarrassment to her parents for not being feminine enough and a cudgel for her sister to use to feel better about herself.

Who needed that?

In fact, the more she thought about it, the more she wondered why blood relatives were given such importance in people's lives. The genetic lottery, which no one volunteered to play, spit you out wherever it did, without regard to compatibility, and yet somehow you were supposed to imbue that accident of procreation with all kinds of emotional weight and significance—simply because your parents managed to help you stay alive until you could get the fuck out of their house.

So actually, no, she didn't think she was going.

And suddenly, she didn't really care that the entire trainee class and two professors were now on to the fact that she and Peyton were studying anatomy together.

"High five," she said to him as she put out her palm. "You'll get me next time."

As he slapped her hand with his own, he shrugged. "And even if I don't, I'll always enjoy the ride."

The saucy wink was totally him. And so was the way he jumped to his feet and helped her up.

He was always a gentlemale. Even at his raunchy finest, he never quite shed that aristocratic upbringing—and somehow, it didn't really bug her anymore.

It was just another side to him.

"Let's call it a night," Rhage announced. "Hit the showers. Bus is leaving in twenty. Tomorrow, we're in the weight room for the first half. Then target shooting and a refresher on poisons for the second."

There was all kinds of chatter on the way to the locker rooms, the males paring off first before she and Paradise went into their facilities and headed for their individual shower cubicles. Peeling off sweaty clothes felt liberating, and then there was the release of her braid. Pure heaven.

Hot water. YAY. Except . . .

"Hey," she said over the din of rushing water, "can I borrow some of your shampoo? I'm out and forgot to bring more."

As she leaned through her curtain, Paradise looked around her own. "I thought you always hated the smell of mine."

Novo shrugged. "It's not so bad."

"Well, of course. Anything I have is yours."

"Thanks."

With efficiency, that shampoo bottle was passed between them, and Novo was back under the spray and lathering up.

"Do you need this back?" she asked.

"Nope. I'm conditioning? I'll pass that underneath the curtain."

"You're the best."

"So . . ." There was a pause next door. "Looks like you and Peyton are getting along."

As Novo arched into the spray and started the ten-minute-long process of getting her hair clean of suds, her gut tightened.

"I saw him smiling at you back there," Paradise prompted over the rushes of water.

Was she jealous? Novo wondered. *God, let's not get weird here.*

"He's a pretty chill guy," she murmured.

In the changing part of the stall, the conditioner slid into view, and Novo picked it up even though she wasn't quite ready. She was still rinsing when the other female turned her water off, and by the time Novo emerged in her towel, Paradise was dressed and at the mirrors by the sink, a pink hair dryer going.

Heading around the stand of lockers, Novo dried off and threw on a fresh set of leathers and a muscle shirt. She was just starting to comb out her hair in preparation for braiding when Paradise put her head around the corner.

"Okay, I'm dying over here."

Novo popped her brows. "Really? 'Cuz your coloring looks fine and you don't seem to be in respiratory distress."

"What's going on with you two?"

"Why don't you ask him?"

"I could do that. I could."

As the other female just stood there, looking like a page out of *Vogue* with her patrician blond beauty and her elegant, expensive, I'm-rich-just-like-him clothes, Novo started to braid things up. And as she went down the lengths, she studied the other female. There wasn't any anger or possessiveness going on. Just a wide-open, slightly surprised curiosity.

Novo didn't say anything until it was rubber-band time at the ends. "You really are just friends with him, aren't you."

Paradise nodded. "Only ever just friends." The female smiled. "He's a good male, though. And I love the way he looks at you. It's what I've always hoped he'd find."

"We're not together or anything. I mean. You know. Not like in a relationship or anything."

Shit, she sounded defensive. Then again, she could never have imagined having this kind of conversation—for a whole crap load of reasons.

Paradise smiled. "Sometimes relationships sneak up on you. Feelings and emotions can be like ninjas, all stealth and—"

"Deadly. They're deadly."

Paradise frowned. "No, I was going to say they come out of nowhere."

"Well . . . look, I don't have much to say on this."

"I'm sorry." Paradise's perfectly arched eyebrows tilted in at the corners in worry. "I shouldn't have brought it up. It's none of my business."

"Nah, it's cool. We're cool."

As the female seemed to be honestly relieved, Novo had a wholly unexpected urge to hug her—but she stomped that down real quick.

Was she melting or something? What the hell?

"I'll see you on the bus," Paradise said as she shouldered her duffel. "And I won't say anything to anyone, not even Craeg."

"It's okay." And interestingly, that was the truth. "I don't have anything to hide—because there's nothing emotional going on."

After Paradise left the locker room, she took a moment to be astounded. Ordinarily, a conversation like that would have rattled her. Not anymore. Or . . . at least not tonight.

Odd.

Gathering her things and putting them in her own duffel, she checked her phone just out of habit—

All that chill, no worries, Bobby McFerrin shit went right out the window as she saw who had texted her.

Opening up the message, she had to read it twice. Then she put her phone away and scrambled-egg'd her way out into the corridor.

She was halfway to the parking area when a voice in her ear drawled, "Can we have a rematch, only naked?"

Novo jumped and spun around to Peyton. "Oh! Yeah, sorry, absolutely—where are you headed?"

"Home. And I was hoping to see you."

"Yeah. I have to go start some laundry and stuff. I'll meet you in like an hour?"

"Hey." He put his hand on her arm. "You okay?"

"Totally." She shrugged out from under his touch. "My shoulder's aching and my place is out of control. I just need to get things sorted on the home front and then I'll be over."

"Roger that." His eyes became remote. "And listen, if you need some time off, I totally understand."

"Nah. I'm good." As she shook her head, she was struck by a surprising impulse to give him a quick kiss.

As if he sensed this, he smiled slow and on one side. "Take your time. I'll always wait for you."

Together, they walked down the corridor and got on the bus, sitting across the aisle and facing one another, their legs stretched out so that their running shoes knocked. As the bus began to move, Boone started to listen to old-school U2 and she was able to track the *Joshua Tree* album by the rhythm of the hisses of his earbuds. Craeg and Paradise were in the back, in each other's arms, not hooking up, but just relaxing. And Axe started to snore.

When they got to the designated drop-off spot, everyone disembarked and Peyton lifted a hand to her before ghosting away.

Novo loitered as everybody dematerialized. Then she scattered herself into the night air . . . in a direction away from where she lived.

When she re-formed, it was in front of an Irish bar called Paddy's in a section of town she had avoided for over two years.

She took a deep breath as she pushed her way into the pub. It was mostly empty, but there was a male vampire sitting all the way in the back, in a booth.

He stood up as soon as she came in. And after a moment, she walked down toward him.

"Hello, Oskar," she said as she stopped in front of him. "This is a surprise."

THIRTY-SEVEN

*A*fter Novo spoke, there was an awkward moment, and she made good use of it by sitting down and arranging her duffel bag—so that there was no chance of a hug or anything.

Oskar cleared his throat and then re-lowered himself into the booth. "Would you like something to drink?"

Maybe a beer, she thought. Ordinarily, she liked a good Scotch, but this was not an ordinary situation.

"Yeah, Coors." Then she tacked on. "Light."

He raised a hand and when the bartender came over, he said, "Two Coors Light."

"We close in a half hour."

"Okay. Thanks."

The human man grumbled away and came back immediately with a pair of longnecks. "You want to pay for 'em?"

Oskar nodded and shifted over so he could get his wallet out of his pocket. "Keep the change."

"Okay. Thanks—but we still close in thirty."

The guy was still muttering under his breath as he returned to washing glasses on the far side of the counter.

"I'm glad you came," Oskar said softly.

As she picked at the label on her bottle, she could feel his eyes searching her face, her hair, her body.

"You look different," he murmured. "Harder. Stronger."

"It's the training."

"It's not all physical—"

"Look, Oskar, I don't know what you're hoping to get out of this, but I'm not interested in rehashing the past, okay? I lived through it, and it's done. You've moved on with Sophy and so have I."

"I just . . . wanted to see you."

"Right before you mate—sorry, marry—my sister. Really? Come on. What kind of game are you playing here—"

"I knew you were pregnant."

The words were quiet, but they hit her like a bomb, stopping her heart and her breath. "You did?"

"Yes." He nodded and looked down at his own bottle. "I mean . . . I wondered. You were getting sick first thing at night all the time. Or at least that's what Sophy said. She thought it was the flu. She didn't want to catch it."

Of course she didn't.

And now Novo was studying him. He was thinner. There were bags under his eyes. That beard was like a trimmed garden hedge on his face, and the glasses? The lenses in them were without prescription. They were just one more prop in the outfit.

When you only looked at the superficial, she thought, standards were too easily met—and altered.

"What happened to the young?" he asked roughly. "I mean, where did you go for the abortion?"

As her stomach rolled, Novo pushed the beer aside. "What makes you think I had an abortion."

"I saw you, like, ten months later. You weren't pregnant anymore."

Oh, riiiiight. She remembered that happy little reunion. She had come to her parents' for dinner, having been invited by her *mahmen*. It had been after she had moved out and she had been feeling guilty that she hadn't been back. So, yeah, sure, Mom, I'll grin and bear it for a meal.

And naturally, it had been all about Sophy bringing her new boyfriend home to "meet" the family. Evidently, her sister had chosen that meal to tell the 'rents that there had been a little switcheroo on the dating landscape—and she had even maintained that it was important for Novo to be there so that everyone could feel good about the way things had ended up.

Novo had gone home and not been able to eat for three nights.

Sophy, on the other hand, had basked in a glow of I-win-the-game for weeks afterward.

"I mean, it was your decision," he said. "I wouldn't have stopped you. We weren't ready to have a young at that point."

"Yeah, 'cuz you were fucking my sister. Details, details."

He winced at that. "I'm sorry." He scrubbed his face. "I just . . . I didn't know what to do."

It was on the tip of her tongue to suggest that, once again, probably not fucking her sister was a good place to start. But then she stared at his face again. First loves were by definition passion with training wheels on. Sometimes you lucked out and the future was long and full of self-discovery on both sides that only brought you closer together. But more often than not, you had too much to learn about yourself.

He had been her first. On all the levels that counted.

But compared to a certain blond aristocrat? Who was a wiseass and gave zero fucks about almost everything?

There was no comparison, actually.

And come to think about it, the fact that Sophy had stepped in and interrupted the natural devolution of things really was a neither-here-nor-there. The true tragedy hadn't been about losing Oskar. It had been more about the young and the betrayal by her own bloodline.

"I'm okay," she blurted. "It's all okay."

Which was a shocking truth.

"I'm glad," he replied.

"I didn't say those words for you." She touched over her own heart. "I said them for me. I am . . . okay."

At least about losing him. The young? Well, that was a different story—and none of his goddamn business. If the male had known she was pregnant and left anyway? He didn't deserve her secrets.

Truth, like trust, had to be earned.

Oskar cleared his throat and ran his fingernails over his beard like the stuff itched. Then he took off his heavy black-rimmed glasses. Placing them on the table, he rubbed his eyes like they hurt.

As the silence stretched out, Novo shook her head. "You've decided you're making a huge mistake mating Sophy and you don't know what to do."

He let his hands flop down to the table. "She's driving me insane."

"I can't help you with that. Sorry."

"She's . . . totally demanding. I mean, I never actually asked her to mate me. She took me to this jewelry store, and the next thing I know, she's trying on rings—and I'm buying the one she wanted. It's this diamond. With a halo, or something around it. Whatever that is." Oskar resumed the rubbing of the stubble, like he was trying to erase his life by scrubbing off what Sophy had no doubt made him grow. "She got us this apartment. I can't afford it. She says she can't work because of the ceremony—wedding, I mean. There's crap everywhere—party favors, napkin rolls, centerpieces. She starts one thing, stops, yells at me, tries to get her girlfriends to step in. It's a nightmare, but what's worse—"

Novo put her hand up. "Stop. Just . . . stop."

As he looked at her, she slid out of the booth with her duffel. "This is none of my concern. And really, it's not cool for you to ask me to come here just so you can bitch about my sister. Mate her or don't. Work on the relationship or not. This is your shit to deal with, not mine."

"I know. I'm sorry. I just don't know what else to do."

In that moment, the essential weakness of him was so obvious, she wondered how in the hell she had ever found him attractive. And she knew exactly what was going to happen. He was going to walk down that aisle, or whatever the humans called it, and he was going to mate Sophy, and they were going to squeeze out a kid, maybe two. And after that, he would spend his entire life wondering how it had come to pass that he had ended up with a *shellan* he couldn't stand, kids he didn't like, and a house he couldn't afford. It would be a mystery that would never be solved, even as he walked into his grave on a path he had set himself upon.

"You know, Oskar, no one's got a gun to your head."

"What?"

"You're choosing this. You're picking all of this—and that means if it doesn't feel right, you don't have to do it." She shook her head at him. "But that's on you. All of this . . . it's on you."

"Don't hate me. Please."

"You know . . . I don't. I don't hate you at all . . . I feel sorry for you." She gave him a nod. "Good-bye, Oskar. And good luck. I really do mean that."

As she was walking out of the pub, the bartender called out, "Come back and see us sometime."

Over her shoulder, she said, "Thanks. He'll definitely be back, I'll tell you that much."

Peyton was out of the shower and getting into a monogrammed robe when his phone rang. As he answered, he didn't bother to see who it was because he was paranoid that Novo might be canceling.

"Yeah?"

"Peyton?"

As he recognized the female voice, he closed his eyes for a moment. Then he went over and sat on the edge of the tub. "Romina. Wassup?"

There was a pause. "Listen, I don't know if you're aware of this, but our fathers are making an appointment at the Audience House. To see the King."

He popped right back onto his feet. "What? Why?"

"I think a payment has been set and things are . . . progressing."

"No. Absolutely not." As it dawned on him that that was a colossal insult, he quickly said, "Listen, it's not about you—"

"Of course it is. And I don't blame you."

"No, I'm . . ." In love with somebody else. "I'm seeing someone."

It felt strange and wonderful to say that. And also like he was tempting fate. He'd had the sense that things were really thawing with Novo over the last couple of nights, but he wasn't a fool. She was still on a hair trigger for trust, and come on. They hadn't been together that long.

They weren't even technically *together*.

"I'm happy for you," Romina said. "And in which case, we really have to do something to stop this."

"They can't force us to consent."

"If your father accepts the payment, mine will expect you to follow through."

He frowned. "I'm sorry—what?"

"Your father established a price, and if what I understand is true, my father has agreed to pay it. So if the money changes hands, the deed is done. It is the Old Way."

So he was being sold? Like a head of cattle?

Dragging a hand through his wet hair, he was so stunned, he couldn't think. "Fucking hell, now I know how females feel," he muttered.

"I'm so sorry. And I had a feeling you didn't know. I think they might be trying to get the King to sign off without even a ceremony. In which case, I don't believe we can override anything. The word of Wrath, son of Wrath, is law. We would be mated then and there."

"Motherfucker—"

There was a rustle over the connection and then Romina's voice dropped. "I have to go. You have to stop this. You work for the Brotherhood. Somehow, you must be able to get to the King. I don't want this for you."

"Or yourself."

"I'm not worried about me."

As the call went dead, he ran the conversation through in his head—and wondered if there was anything going on he didn't know about. Financially for his family, that was. Except no. There was plenty of staff around and his father didn't look worried. The price set was no doubt just a way to recoup a failed investment in a first blooded son.

"Peyton?"

At the sound of Novo's voice out in his bedroom, he spun around. Shit, he needed to take care of this. Right away. And also had to tell his female what was going on.

"In here," he said. "Listen, I have to go out for a—"

As she came into the doorway of the bathroom, he knew instantly something was really wrong. And then he saw the tears in her eyes.

"Novo? What's going on?"

He rushed over and put his arms around her. The sobs that came out of her were so violent, her body shook against his own and he drew her deeper into the bathroom and shut the door so that no one would hear her for her privacy's sake.

"Novo . . ." He cupped her head and stroked her back. "Novo, love . . . what happened . . . ?"

Eventually, she took a shuddering breath and broke away from him.

As she paced around, her arms were locked on her midsection and she was hunched over as if in agony.

When she stopped, she looked at him with eyes that were so full of pain, he could barely stare into them.

"I lost my young . . ." As she spoke, the emotion came out anew, sobs shaking her. "It was a little girl. I held her in the palm of my hand . . . after I lost her . . ."

THIRTY-EIGHT

ovo had thought she was tight. That she was just walking away from that pub and Oskar and all that past shit perfectly right in the head. And to that point, she had dematerialized without a problem, re-forming back behind the garage of Peyton's family's mansion, slipping in through the door in the library using the code Peyton had given her.

She had even laughed a little as she had dodged that butler, the one Peyton hated so much.

But sometime down the long hall to his room, an unraveling had started, some thread of her inner fabric catching on the heel of her stride, until she was naked by the time she reached the open doors of his bath.

And then he had looked at her and she had breathed in the scent of him . . . and the dam had broken completely—such that she had named her truth to him, shared her secret, told him that which she had told no other.

His shock and horror as he stared at her made her want to run.

"I'm sorry," she stammered. "I shouldn't have come—"

In a panic, she went to race out, but he jumped ahead and blocked her with his body.

"Tell me," he said. "Tell me what happened, oh, God . . . Novo . . . I never knew."

She shook her head back and forth for the longest time, her tears falling past her body, landing in a semicircle at her feet.

"No one knows. No one knew . . ." She sniffled and shivered as the images returned—and dear Lord, the memories of that old, damp, cold house. "I told no one."

"Oskar," Peyton said in a dead voice. "It was Oskar."

She nodded. "He left me just after I went through my needing. I thought we'd been careful, but obviously . . . it was about three weeks afterward when I didn't bleed and then I knew. I kept it a secret. I moved out of my family's house, telling my parents it was because I needed space—they didn't know until later what Sophy had done. That Oskar had gone with her."

"Here. Take this."

She stared at what he was holding out to her, not understanding what it was—oh, a Kleenex box. She snapped free some tissues and tucked the rest under her arm.

Her nose sounded like a foghorn as she blew it.

"I was eight months along when the pains started. About two weeks later, I was in this house I'd rented . . . I started bleeding and . . ." She blew her nose again and pressed the tissue wad to her eyes as the pain came back. "I lost the young. She came out of me . . . and she was so tiny, so perfect. My daughter . . ."

The image of the young was carved into her brain, deep as a ravine, never to lose its contours no matter how many times she recalled it or how many years passed.

All of a sudden, she felt a warmth around her, a body against hers. Peyton.

The sobbing came back and she gave herself to it, fisting the thick robe he had on, hanging on as her legs went out from under her.

"I got you . . ." he said. "I have you."

"I never told him. He'd guessed I was pregnant . . . but I never told him what happened . . ." Abruptly, she looked up. "He called me tonight and asked me to come see him. He wanted to . . . vent about Sophy. He thought I had an abortion."

Peyton's brows tightened. "Wait a minute . . . he knew? That you were pregnant with his young? And he went with your sister?"

"When he was talking tonight . . ." She pulled back and then had to pace around. "He asked me where I went to have the abortion. I didn't tell him I miscarried." She looked down at her flat belly. "I buried the young by myself. Out in the field behind the house. While I was still bleeding. I . . . covered the grave with stones, and planted a stupid little bush because I didn't want her not to have a headstone or any marking." She shook her head. "He doesn't deserve to know what happened. That is my life, my private pain. He didn't want her and he didn't want me. And I don't think he deserves . . . he doesn't deserve either of us."

Novo closed her eyes. "She's still with me, you see. She died before she knew anything of the world—but I keep her here." She touched over her heart. "She is here with me. Always."

Abruptly, she looked at him. "And you are the only one who knows."

There were so many different ways to say "I love you."

As Peyton went back over to Novo and pulled her against him once more, he reflected that those three words were certainly the most common transmission of the sacred emotion between two souls. But there were other ways. Gestures, gifts, the rebuilding of a barn after a fire, the shoveling of a walkway, even something as simple as carrying groceries in from the car.

Novo was telling him she loved him by sharing this terrible truth, a loss so great that he couldn't fathom how she had made it through the tragedy or why she had kept going afterward: By inviting him to play witness to her history, her pain, by opening herself up to him in this way, as she had done with no other, she was proclaiming she had love for him.

"I have hurt for so long," she said when she had calmed a little. "Held this in for so long."

He imagined her somewhere by herself, in a medical emergency, with no one to hold her hand or ease her in any way. And then she had buried the young—

He squeezed his eyes shut as he imagined what that had taken out of her.

"Come with me," he said as he took her hand and brought her into the bedroom. "Lie down. Let me hold you."

She crawled onto his monogrammed duvet as if she hurt all over. And when he joined her, he put his arm around her and ran into the corners of the Kleenex box, which she clutched like a child did a toy for comfort. As she shivered, he brought himself closer to her.

"What was her name?" he heard himself say.

Novo jerked against him as she looked up. "I . . . I did not name her."

He stroked wisps of her hair back from her hot, red face. "You should name her. And you should go back and bring her a proper marker. She lived inside of you. She existed."

"I thought maybe . . ."

"What did you think?" he whispered as he brushed her hair away. "Tell me."

"I wondered if I should give her a name. But I wasn't sure . . . I feel like I didn't deserve to. *Mahmens* give names to their young. I couldn't keep mine . . . I let her down, I killed her—so I am no one's mother to give any name."

"Stop," he croaked out. "You did nothing wrong." With a surge of hostility, he tacked on, "Which is more than I can say for others. And you should name her. You keep her in your heart, you are a *mahmen*—and that innocent little soul is up in the Fade, watching over you. Your daughter is an angel, and you should name her if only so you can address her when you're talking to her in your head."

"How did you know?" Novo asked roughly. "That I talk to her?"

He traced her face with his eyes and wished he could hold all of her pain for her, take it as burden out of her tired arms and carry it for the rest of their lives.

"How can you not? She is your daughter."

Fresh tears welled and he took a Kleenex from the box and dried them one by one. When they stopped, she whispered, "I am so tired all of a sudden."

He ran his fingertips down her cheek. "Sleep. I will watch over you. You will not have any nightmares tonight."

"Promise?" she said.

"I promise." He closed her lids. "I won't leave you. And no nightmares. Just rest."

Novo's strong body released its tension with a shudder. And then she cuddled into him.

"If I could sing, I would give you a lullaby," he said softly. "About a place where there is no pain and loss. No worry. But I can't carry a tune."

"Thought that counts," she mumbled.

Not long thereafter, her breathing became slow and steady, little twitches of a hand or a foot signaling she was deep, deep, deep at rest.

Staring at her in his arms, he knew that he would lay his life down for hers without regret. He would slay dragons and move mountains for her. He would conquer whole worlds at her command and starve to skin and bones just to ensure she had food. She was not his sun or moon, but his galaxy.

"I love you, too," he said by her ear. "Forever and always."

THIRTY-NINE

ovo woke up ten hours later. She knew this by the clock on the bed stand, which, naturally, wasn't some digital POS you could get from Amazon, but an antique Cartier thing that seemed to be made of marble and had hands with diamonds on them.

She had turned away from Peyton in her sleep, but they were far from separated. He was tucked in tight to her back, that robe of his still on, the pair of them on top of the duvet instead of in between those incredibly soft sheets of his.

Man, she had to pee.

Okay, that was hardly the most important thing on her mind, comparatively speaking, but in terms of urgency? And the fact that it was a simple walk to the bathroom to take care of it?

#goals

As she moved carefully out of Peyton's arms, he surfaced briefly from his rest to mumble something that sounded like "Where going?"

"Bathroom," she said quietly. "You go back to sleep."

He nodded against the pillow and let out a mutter of affirmation.

Standing over him, she wanted to smooth his tousled blond hair and erase the black circles under his closed eyes. She was willing to bet that he had stayed up most of the day to watch over her, and she hated the position she had put him in.

But she was glad, too. She was . . . relieved, kind of the way you would be after you excised an infection. It hurt like hell to get the boil cleaned out, but afterward? Clean was like bright sunshine in what had been a dark, damp place.

"You are so much more than I thought you were."

And that was true not just because she had underestimated him from the start. It was because he had this way of hanging in with her, of seeing her, of supporting her without smothering her.

It was an incredible commentary on who he was to her . . . when the male who she had conceived her young with was not the one she had gone to with the pain of that death. No, it had been Peyton.

Peyton was the only one she had wanted. Had trusted. Had needed.

She had fallen in love with him.

And admitting that didn't feel scary, actually. Which was a shock.

"I will name her and I will go back there," she said softly. "And maybe you will come with me someday so I can introduce you two."

In accepting him into her life, she wanted him to go with her back there sometime. It was not only a part of her, but had been the defining term for what had felt like the longest while.

Tiptoeing into the loo, she shut herself in the toilet room, took care of business, and then washed her hands and dried them. As she looked at her reflection in the mirror, she was surprised that she appeared exactly the same. You'd think some of the inner transformation might have translated into different-colored eyes or hair that was of another style.

But no, it was still her.

And that was rather the point, wasn't it. Since the miscarriage, there had been two sides to her: What had happened and the pain, loss, and grief that went along with it—and then everything else. The latter had been responsible for existing and navigating the world at large. The former had been this shadowed entity that had haunted her. And she had protected both with a hard shell.

Because either she kept all the contradictions held in tightly or she wouldn't have been able to function from the splitting apart, the falling apart.

After telling Peyton her story and crying it out, the two halves seemed to be integrating a little. She wasn't sure how to explain it.

Who the hell knew.

"I'll see you in class," she said to Peyton as she came back out and put her boots on.

He mumbled again in his sleep and then roused well enough to properly focus on her. "Class? See you in class?"

"Yes. In class."

As she leaned in and kissed him, she had the urge to say, "I love you"—and the impulse was so strong, she nearly spoke the three words aloud.

In the end, she settled for "I can't wait."

"Me, too."

"Go back to sleep. You have at least an hour, maybe a little longer, before you have to get up."

"Wish you didn't have to go."

"Me, too," she parroted.

Over at the door, she took one last look at him. His lids were back down and he let out this long, slow exhale as if all were right in his world.

She felt the same way.

Out in the hall, she headed down for the stairs, striding along, her head both muddled and strangely clear. There was so much she hadn't expected, from him and from herself . . .

It was as she came to the stairway that she realized she had made a mistake. In her distraction, she had gone right instead of left and ended up not at the head of the staff stairs, but rather the main, grand staircase.

"And who, may I ask, are you."

She turned around. The male who had spoken was dressed in a three-piece suit that was dark as a shadow. He had thinning hair that was the same color as Peyton's and autocratic features that would have been considered handsome but for his expression of total disdain.

"Well?" he demanded as he came toward her. "An answer, if you will."

Up closer, she thought . . . no, Peyton's father wasn't as handsome as he appeared to be at a distance.

"I'm a friend of your son's."

"A friend. Of my son's. Well. Has he paid you for your services, or are you looking to steal the silverware on the way out."

"Excuse me?"

"You heard me."

"I am not a whore," she snapped.

"Oh. Forgive me," he drawled. "So you just spent the day with him for free? That must mean you are hoping to become his *shellan*—but allow me to cut your aspirations short. He is to be mated unto a female of appropriate bloodline this week, so I'm terribly sorry, my dear, but there is no future for you with him."

"Mated?" she whispered. "What are you—"

"He has consented and he has met her. And lest you think there will be a role for you on the side, I must disabuse you of that notion. Go ply your wares elsewhere. Off you go. Good night."

She stumbled back, the words not translating into any comprehensible meaning.

"Not that way," the male barked. "You are not front-door material. You must use the rear stairs—"

Novo turned and ran down the grand red and gold carpeted expanse, her feet flying over the steps as Peyton's father continued to yell after her. At the front door, she fumbled with the locking mechanism, freeing herself just as a male servant came running in from some other place in the house.

Bursting out into the cold, she slipped and fell in the snow. Got back up and continued to run across the lawn, leaving a messy trail in the pristine snow.

Her heart was pounding and her head was swimming. Mostly, she was aware of being in pain once again; the reprieve she'd had, her head popping up out of a proverbial churning ocean for a breath of sustaining air, had lasted no time at all.

She did not cry, however.

It was the cold in her face that coaxed tears from her eyes. Only the cold.

FORTY

axton was late for work. As he rushed up the farmhouse's basement stairs, he was pulling his suit jacket on at the same time he tried to fasten the buttons on his shirt. Things did not go well, any efficiencies lost in the face of attempting to do two jobs at once.

"I have your toast!" Ruhn called out by the sink. "And I put your coffee in your mug!"

Saxton skidded to a halt. The male was spectacularly naked, and all Saxton could think about was how he had ridden that . . . posterior region . . . to very great delight twice during the day. No, three times, including what they had just done in the shower together. Which was the reason for the lateness.

"How am I supposed to leave the house with you like that?"

Ruhn, always a rule abider, for once had no time for flirting. "Come, you will be late! I do not want it to be my fault."

Saxton would have joked about that, but his love was so earnest that such levity was liable to be in poor taste, no matter the intention.

"Promise me, when I return, that you will be dressed exactly like this?"

"Saxton, eat."

As a plate was shoved at him and his travel mug waved in his face, he just stood there, shirt half buttoned, jacket askew.

And p.s., what a great word . . . "askew." It sounded just like the disorder it described.

"Saxton—"

"Promise."

"Fine! I'll be naked as you please!"

"A thank-you." He bowed a little and quickly righted all that was wrong with himself. "And I am awaiting our reunion with bated breath."

"I shall be here." Ruhn smiled. "I'm working on the cellar today."

"You are going to have this place like new by the time we leave."

"That is the plan."

Saxton paused. "I love you."

The kiss Ruhn gave to him was like his breath, easy and necessary. "I love you, too," the male said. "Now go—wait, your proper coat is over there on the table!"

"I don't need it. I have you to keep me warm."

Minutes later, Saxton dematerialized . . . and re-formed at the rear entrance of the Audience House. Immediately, as soon as he walked in the kitchen, he knew he was out of sync. The *doggen* had already taken out the trays of Danish and turned on the restaurant-sized coffeepot, and there were voices down in front, civilians having already arrived for their appointments.

"Shit," he said as he skidded through the staff hallway's flap door and jumped into his office like it was a pool.

The coffee mug went down on the partner's desk and it was only then that he realized he'd taken his piece of toast and his plate with him. He put the plate down as well, and threw the toast in his mouth, grabbed the folders, which—thank God—he'd set out before he'd left to go home to—

"Wrath is going to be late."

Saxton swung around. Blay was standing in the doorway and dressed for guard duty, his clothes casual, his loose, zip-up fleece hiding all kinds of weapons. His red hair was still damp, as if he, too, had just arrived from his home, and the cherry Danish in his hand took Saxton back to Sunday evenings when they'd just woken up.

But it was extraordinary.

The appearance of the male, the recollection of their past, carried no pain. Not even nostalgia, really. It was more like part of the grocery list of prosaic events Saxton had lived, like when he'd bought a new suit from his tailor, or the last time he himself had had a Danish here at the Audience House . . . or even the fact that, yes, indeed, his own hair was also a little wet.

The absence of complication was a peacefulness that he drank in.

Saxton took the piece of toast out of his mouth. "I am so glad. I'm late as well. I just couldn't get out of—" He stopped there. "Anyway. We've got a full docket. What's his arrival time?"

Blay shrugged and finished his last bite. "I'm not really sure. Everybody who's here to see him is being understanding. I guess George threw up his breakfast, so Wrath is calling in a vet to make sure that the poor guy didn't get into anything."

"Oh, no." Saxton patted around for his phone. "I should call the house—no, wait. I don't want to interrupt. Nothing can happen to that dog—"

"Nothing can happen to that dog."

They both laughed. And then Blay got serious.

"Listen, my parents are so grateful for what you and . . . Ruhn . . . have done for Minnie. I guess you've taken care of those developers? Minnie is such a wonderful female, and the situation has been really bothering *Mahmen* and Dad. You know how my *mahmen* is. She's a worrier."

Saxton went around and sat down. "You have the two best parents I have ever met."

"They love you."

"And I love them."

There was a quiet moment.

"I'm really happy for you and Ruhn, by the way," Blay said softly. "And I hope that doesn't sound weird. It's not meant to be, I swear."

"I, ah, I didn't know anyone else was aware of us. Not that I was deliberately keeping it a secret or anything."

"Minnie told my parents."

Saxton took a deep breath. And then he reached for his travel mug, slid the top over, and took a sip. The coffee was just the way he liked it, sweet and not too harsh.

Somehow, the fact that Ruhn had made it seemed to put the male here in this room.

"May I be honest?" Saxton said.

"Always. Please."

He looked up at his old lover. "I'm happy for me, too. It's been hard."

Blay came a little farther into the room. "I know it has been. I didn't know how to help, what to do. I hated seeing you hurting like that. It just killed me."

"I tried not to show it too much. I thought I did a pretty good job at that."

"But I know you."

"Yes, you do." Saxton ran his finger up and down the metal flank of the mug. "I was not expecting him. Ruhn, that is. At all. I didn't think I would ever . . . feel like this again, and it changes everything. He is—okay, fine, it sounds corny, but he's my other half. It's happened so fast that my head is spinning and it's terrifying sometimes, too—but more than anything, it's brought me such joy and happiness."

"It only takes an instant," Blay murmured. "When it's real, it's like turning on a light switch. Click, and then there is illumination everywhere."

"Yes. That's it." Saxton found himself smiling up at the male. "I'm at peace. I was thinking about leaving, you know."

"Caldwell? You were?"

"I didn't have a lot to look forward to. I mean, setting up all this"—he motioned around the office—"was a great distraction. But when it started running right and was less demanding, I began to drift. The harbor appears to have presented itself once more, however."

"He's a good male. I didn't know he was gay?"

"He didn't, either."

Blay chuckled a little. "You can be irresistible. I know this firsthand."

"I am complimented by that, kind sire." Saxton put his hand over his heart. "Quite."

They both laughed—but then a pair of *doggen* hustled by in the hall, jointly carrying a Shop-Vac, the hose of which bounced along the floor.

"Oh, God, no," Saxton muttered as he got back up and went across to the office. "That bathroom better not have let go again." He stuck his head out into the corridor. "What has gone wrong?"

The two servants stopped and bowed, and the one on the left said, "The toilet upstairs."

"We fixed it," the other confirmed. "But there is water on the floor."

"I'm going to have that replaced. Thank you. Continue on."

The pair of flushed and happy *doggen* trundled off as Saxton turned back again. Looking into the eyes of Blay, he smiled.

"All is well."

"All is well, indeed," the male said as he reached out and squeezed Saxton's shoulder. "Very well—"

"Oh, excuse me. I didn't mean to interrupt."

Saxton looked over. One of the trainees, Peyton, son of Peythone, was standing in the open jambs with an expression of urgency, his weight shifting back and forth on his combat boots as if only the upper half of him knew he'd come to a stop.

"It's no problem." Saxton stepped back. "Come on in. Do you need something?"

"I've got an issue."

Blay clapped palms with the trainee and then glanced across. "I'll let you know as soon as Wrath gets here."

"And also about George."

"Absolutely."

Saxton waved and so did Blay, and then he took a moment to measure his new place in life, his proverbial new address, which was such an improvement over his previous abode.

All truly was well that ended well.

Then he refocused and went back around to his seat. "Tell me what's going on and how I can help?"

Peyton had woken up alone, but he remembered Novo saying goodbye to him—and then he'd had to snap into action because he'd slept through the alarm on his phone. He hadn't even bothered shaving. He just showered, threw his clothes on, and cracked a window, dematerializing to the Audience House.

Even though he was going to be late to the pickup, and would probably miss the bus to the training center, he had to take care of this first.

"May I shut this door?" he said.

Saxton, the King's solicitor, nodded. "Of course."

After they were closed in together, Peyton paced back and forth in the narrow area between the file cabinets and the built-in shelves.

"My father wants to mate me to a female and neither she nor I consent. We've talked things over. I'm in love with someone else, and she is . . ." He didn't think it was appropriate to share Romina's story. "She wishes to remain single. The problem is . . . our sires have come to some kind of financial agreement and we're worried they will execute it and we'll be stuck."

"So your father is paying a dowry, then."

"No, he's getting paid."

Saxton showed surprise. "Really. Okay."

"My sire has been trying to get rid of me for years," Peyton said dryly. "It's like a garage sale. Except I gather my price tag is considerably higher than five dollars."

"And just to be clear, both you and the female do not consent. She is firm on that as well."

"Yes. But from what she told me last night, our sires have made an appointment with the King. They're coming here. I don't know when, except it must be soon. My father's been down to South Carolina, where the other family lives, a number of times already."

"Peythone is your sire's name?"

"Yes."

Saxton signed into a laptop, and after some typing, he sat back.

"They do have an appointment."

"When?"

"I can't tell you." As Peyton started to protest, Saxton held up a hand. "Ethically, I have to be careful not to violate any confidentiality. But that doesn't mean I can't help you."

"Can we stop it?"

"I'm assuming the female has gone through her transition." When Peyton nodded, Saxton said, "Good. So you both are legally of age. My initial thought is that you are not even third parties to such a contract. Two adults who have a meeting of the minds can bind each other to an agreement, but such an agreement cannot encumber anyone else who does not have an interest or consideration in its terms."

Peyton rubbed his eyes. "I'm not following?"

"Your sires can agree to whatever they want between the two of them. But that agreement can't be used to compel you or the female into actions you would not voluntarily assume on your own. Unless you or the female are accepting part of this payment?"

"No. I mean, not that we're aware of. I haven't seen the contract and neither has she—but our sires do not commonly look out for our interests, if you know what I mean."

"The only thorny part of this is the Old Laws and how they relate to the financial consideration sometimes paid with regard to matings. I'll need to go through that. But don't worry. I'll take care of this."

Peyton sagged. "Thank you, oh, God, *thank you*. And listen, on my side, it's not that the other female is a bad person or anything. It's just . . ."

"You love someone else." The solicitor's smile seemed old and very, very wise. "I understand completely. The heart wants what it wants."

"Exactly. And again, thank you, you're a real lifesaver."

"I haven't saved you, yet. But I will. You can trust me."

"I already feel better about this. I've got to go to class now."

"Be safe," Saxton offered.

"Promise."

Out by the reception area, Peyton called for the bus, and cursed when he was told it was going to be another hour. But what could he do—

"Hey," Blay said, "you looking to go to class? We have a van here and one of our *doggen* can take you?"

Twice in one night, he thought. Man, things were just going his way. Finally.

"That would be awesome," he told the fighter. "Just really incredible."

Because the truth was, as much as he wanted to fulfill his classroom obligations, what he really wanted was to see Novo again. As soon as possible.

And never, ever leave her side.

FORTY-ONE

As Novo sat on her futon and stared straight ahead, there was nothing particularly on her mind, and that was a blessing, she supposed. What she was aware of, however, was that the great weight was back and heavier than ever, that familiar sinking in the center of her chest making it hard to breathe and difficult to move.

Overhead, she could hear people walking around, the humans settling in for the night. A glance at the clock told her it was just after ten p.m., and it was impossible not to think of the time in relationship to classes and what, under normal circumstances, she would be doing— if she hadn't called in sick.

They were meant to be in the weight room at the beginning of the evening. And then they were going to be in class, and they were supposed to receive their new field assignments.

She was going to have to put in a request that she not be paired with . . .

She was going to need to go out with only Paradise, Craeg, Axe, or Boone.

Drawing her legs up, she linked her arms around her knees and rested her chin on her wrist. God, how could she have been so stupid—

Nope, she decided. She was done with the self-blame. She was absolutely not going to beat herself up over the fact that some male had turned out to be a shit. And besides, she'd already been through one kind of cardiac rehab. She just needed to look at this as another variation on the theme. Heart was broken. Stitch it up. Get strong again.

It was just that simple.

As she mulled on that imperative for a while, she was aware she was trying to convince herself of a truth she wasn't sure she believed in, but whatever. It was her only way to realign all of it: Tomorrow evening, at nightfall, she was heading back into the program, and she was going to have her game face on.

There was no way she was quitting just because a romance she should never have started had blown up in her face.

That was a girl move. And she was a female, not a girl.

She was a fighter—

The knock on her door brought her head up. It wasn't the first of the month, so it couldn't be the landlord. And it wasn't Peyton, she could sense that much.

"Yeah?" she called out.

"It's Dr. Manello."

With a frown, she got up and went across her everything room. Opening things up, she said, "Hey, what are you doing here?"

"House call." The human barged in past her. "How we doing?"

For no good reason, she looked out in the hall to see if he'd brought reinforcements. Nope.

Closing them in, she put her braid over her shoulder. "I don't understand?"

As her surgeon put his little black physician's bag on the table for two she'd only ever sat one at, she noted that the bottom half of him was in scrubs. The top half was in a down jacket. He had a

Mets baseball cap on, and yeah, wow, neon yellow and blue running shoes.

"You call in sick," he said, "with a complaint that you're nauseous. So I came to check on you."

Swallowing her frustration, she shook her head. "Listen, as much as I appreciate the concern, it's no big deal. I'm just not feeling—"

"You had a significant cardiac injury—"

"That was forever ago."

"Try days."

Jesus. It had seemed like another lifetime. "But I'm fine."

"Well, then, let's get this over with quickly, shall we?" He pulled out one of her mismatched chairs and spun it around. As he patted the hard seat, he said, "If you're A-Okay, this won't take but a moment."

She crossed her arms over her chest. "I'm fine."

"When did you go to medical school last?" He rolled his eyes. "And by the way, do you have any idea how often I find myself saying that to people around here."

As the human just stared at her, like he was prepared to stay put until either one of them dropped dead from natural causes, she cursed and marched over.

"This is totally unnecessary," she muttered as she sat down.

"I hope so. Any vomiting?"

"No."

"Fever, chills?"

"No."

"Abdominal pain or pain that radiates down either of your arms?"

"No."

"Feeling faint or passing out?"

"No."

Well, at least not since Peyton's father had dropped the hammer on her in that hallway. Ever since then? Piece of cake.

Coming around to stand in front of her, the doctor took a stethoscope out of his bag and plugged it into his ears. "You're going to have to lower those arms if I'm going to listen to your heart."

Gracelessly, she uncrossed things and let her arms flop down—and then he was doing the little disk walk-around over her chest area. As he made a number of mmm-hmm noises, she took that to mean he was finding exactly what she thought.

Which was that absolutely nothing was wrong. Physically, at least.

"Blood pressure time," he said cheerfully. "Your heart sounds perfect."

"I know."

His head popped up in front of her. "You have a terrible bedside manner, you know that?"

"Isn't that your problem?"

"Touché."

As the doctor put her through an examination, she resumed staring straight ahead, her mind retreating once again to that place where there was, at least ostensibly, nothing on it. In reality, she suspected her subconscious was plotting against her, planning all kinds of wake-up-screaming shit, scheduling nightmares like they were patients into a dental chair.

"—Novo? Hello?"

She snapped to. "I'm sorry, what?"

Dr. Manello stared down at her for a moment. Then he sank onto his haunches. "You want to tell me what's really going on here?"

"Like I said, nothing. I just ate something funny."

"What was it?"

"I don't remember." As his expression shifted into seeing-too-clearly territory, she got up and walked around. "Honestly, I'll be good by tomorrow night."

"You know, if you need to talk to someone—"

"I absolutely, positively, do *not* need to talk to anybody."

"Okay." He put his hands out. "I'll back off."

Dr. Manello reloaded his little black bag, and then he was back at her door. "Call me, though, if you start to run a fever or actually vomit?"

"That is not going to be necessary." She went over to let him out. "Thank you for coming—"

"I'm worried about you. And not from a medical standpoint."

For some reason, she thought of that patient down in the clinic, the one who screamed all the time. At least if she lost her mind, she thought, they had some experience dealing with the insane.

But that was not going to be her. She just wasn't going to have it.

"I'm not," she told him. "I'm not worried about me at all."

If she could live through what had come before? Then getting over the reality that Peyton was exactly who she'd thought he was wasn't going to be a problem. She'd already trained for it.

Where the hell was she?

As Peyton walked into the training center's weight room forty minutes later, he sifted through the various bodies on the machines and the mats . . . and came up with a resounding no-Novo.

With a frown, he went over to the Brother Qhuinn. "Hey, have you seen Novo?"

"She called in sick. Said she wasn't feeling well."

Peyton's first instinct was to get on a rocket ship and race across town. The problem with that? He had no rocket, and he didn't know her address—but, wait, he had fed her, hadn't he.

"Did she say what was wrong?"

"Nope. Just that she was sick to her stomach and staying in. She sounded nauseous, but not at death's door."

"Could it be something with her heart? A problem from—"

"I told Manny, so he went out there and checked her. He said it was garden-variety food poisoning or something. It's not a problem." The Brother's blue and green eyes leveled on him. "Can you think of any other issue that might be bothering her?"

"When she left me at nightfall, I—" He clamped his mouth shut. "No, I can't."

"Maybe she would appreciate a text or a call from a classmate?" the Brother drawled. "Or a visit after class?"

"Yeah. That's a real—may I be excused?"

"Yup. Then you gotta work."

"No problem."

Peyton hightailed it into the locker room and went to where he'd tossed his duffel on the floor, having not even bothered to put it in a locker. Rifling through his change of clothes and his weapons, he snagged his phone. Nothing from her.

His first call went into voicemail. His second . . . yup, went as well.

He kept the text short and sweet: *Are u ok? Can I bring u anything?*

Peyton waited five minutes. And then he had to go back to class.

An hour and a half later, on the break between the weight room and the target range, he checked his phone again. Nothing. So he called. Texted once more.

And then he did the same another ninety minutes later as they transitioned into classroom work. Nothing. Not even after he called again. Texted some more.

What if she had passed out—

He was on the verge of fucking off class and calling for the bus when his phone went off. The text was from her: *Fine. See everyone tomoz.*

That was it.

His fingers went flying across his phone's surface, typing out all kinds of *I'll stop by, bring soup, heating pads,* etc. etc. etc.

Nothing came back at him.

"You all right?" Craeg asked over at the door out into the corridor. "Everything okay with Novo?"

Peyton cleared his throat. "Ah, yeah, it's fine. She's great. She'll be in tomorrow night."

Even though phones weren't allowed outside of the locker room, he put his into his fleece pocket.

What the *hell* was going on?

Sitting through class was an exercise in torture, but he was relieved that at least he and Novo were paired with Blay and Qhuinn the following evening. They would be the first squad to go back out into the field—like the Brotherhood wanted to do a CTRL/ALT/DEL on the incident in that alley and start the new world order on a good note.

At the rate things were going, it would be the first chance he got to see her.

When the end of the night finally came, Peyton all but trampled people to get on the bus—which was stupid. It wasn't like that was going to get him off the property any faster. And Christ, could the butler drive any slower down the mountain?

He didn't track any of the conversation that happened around him, and people seemed to recognize he was *in extremis,* leaving him alone.

The second that bus stopped, he was at the door, but as he spilled out into the night, he realized he didn't know where he was going. Closing his eyes, he sent his instincts forth as his fellow trainees took off one by one.

He located the signal of his blood to the west. And not far away.

Traveling in a scatter of molecules, he re-formed in front of a four-story walk-up in a meh part of the city. It wasn't a dump, but it was certainly not a candidate for *Architectural Digest*. In the basement . . . he could sense her in the basement. But how to get in?

As if on cue, a human opened the outer door to its vestibule, and

Peyton took the seven steps three at a time. "Hey! Can you catch the inside—"

"No prob." The guy leaned back and kept the inner door open. "You forget your key?"

"My girlfriend's."

"Been there. Later."

"Thank you."

Peyton walked inside and looked around. There had to be a way to get to the lower level—there. In the far corner.

No one else was around, and so he could just will it unlocked—shit, why hadn't he thought about that on the outside?

Well, because his brain was fucking jacked, thank you very much.

Going over, he tried that mental trick out—but it didn't work on what proved to be a copper deadbolt. So clearly, there were vampires living among these humans.

He thought about calling her, but things were so weird, he had a feeling Novo wasn't going to let him in. Maybe that was paranoia, though. Who the fuck knew—

The door swung wide and he jumped back. As he saw who it was, he nearly hugged her. "Novo! It's you!"

"What are you doing here."

The tone of her voice was as lifeless as a computer's approximation of same, and she was pale as a ghost, her eyes dead.

"Are you okay?" he asked, reaching out.

She took a sharp step back. "I'm fine. What are you doing here."

"What's wrong? What . . . I don't understand what's going on?"

"I wasn't feeling well. I am better now. I'll be back in class tomorrow. I told you."

Her hair was plaited and over her shoulder, her jeans and sweatshirt nothing unusual, her feet in Adidas shower shoes with thick socks on—as if she were just in for a cozy night at home. Her eyes, though. They were as matte as old river stones.

"Where are you?" he blurted. "What—"

Her hands came up. "Okay, I'm done. I want you to leave. I didn't invite you here, and I resent the fact that you used my feeding from you as a way to hunt me down."

"Hunt you down? Excuse me?"

"You heard it right. I don't want you to come here ever again."

Peyton ground his molars a couple of times. "Okay, let's back up here. As far as I knew, when you left my bed at nightfall, everything was cool between us. And now you're acting like I'm some kind of stalker. I think you owe me an explanation—"

Her laughter was harsh. "Oh, I owe you, huh. Riiiiiight. Because everything has to be about you."

"What are you talking about?" He could feel his voice getting loud, but he couldn't stop it. "What is wrong with you?"

"Me? Nothing is wrong with me. And nothing is wrong with you, either. You're getting mated soon to a nice female from a good family, so all's right in your world. Congratulations—hey, maybe you two and my sister and Oskar can double-date as newlyweds." She clapped her hands together. "Yay! Selfie time!"

Before he could open his mouth, she leaned forward. "And don't pretend that you're surprised. You knew exactly what you were doing the whole time you and I were fucking. You knew you were getting mated to someone else, but you played it like—" She cut herself off. "Anyway, do me a favor and don't invite me to the ceremony, 'kay? I'm pretty sure it would be awkward for the *shellan*-to-be, and whereas your kind is perfectly happy to be cruel, we wouldn't want to be tacky, would we. Yeah, 'cuz that's wrong."

A pair of humans, a man and a woman, came down the stairs over on the left, and the fact that they were laughing and holding hands was a real kick in the balls.

Peyton stepped to the side to let them pass, and he waited until they were all the way through the vestibule to speak.

"It's not what you think."

Novo laughed again. "Really? Just how many ways do you believe this scenario is open to interpretation—or do you assume that because I'm just a piece-of-shit civilian that I would be nothing but grateful to be your hot, kinky side-piece for the rest of my life."

Peyton took another step back. And then a third. "So you've made your mind up. You've decided everything, huh."

"The math is not that hard. And I'm a very smart female."

"FYI, you haven't let me say one word about any of this."

"Why would I. Your version isn't going to matter to me at all. It's only air, not substance. Just like you."

Peyton felt that one go right through the center of his chest. And in the aftermath, he looked down at the floor. Dimly, he noticed the carpet was damp, the result of people coming in from the cold with snow on their boots and shoes.

He thought of how she had let him hold her through the night.

He had been so convinced he was finally in her heart.

But he should have known better.

Maybe at a different time in her life they could have had a better chance. A relationship with her, though, was going to be like running a marathon on a broken foot. There were accommodations that could be made, conversations to re-engender trust, reassurances and reexaminations to make sure she was comfortable, but over time, the fundamental weakness that she would never really trust him was going to break down the overall effort.

"I can't fix you," he murmured.

"What was that?" she snapped. "What the *hell* did you say to me?"

He swung his eyes back to hers. "I'm sorry that you were hurt. I really am—"

"This is not about Oskar! Don't you dare try to deflect—"

"Actually, it absolutely is. Maybe you'll figure that out sometime, maybe you won't. But either way, that's none of my business because I refuse to keep paying for the sins of another. Good luck to you. Hope you find peace somehow, some way."

He turned away and went for the double doors—and as he came up to them, he caught a flash of her reflection in the glass. She was staring after him, her chin up, her eyes flashing, her arms crossed over her chest.

Over her heart.

If that was not a perfect metaphor for who she was as a person, he didn't know what was.

Letting himself out, he went down the seven snow-packed steps one by one and looked left. Then right.

He chose a direction randomly and walked along, putting his hands in the pockets of his fleece. He hadn't bothered to put on a parka, and he'd left his duffel bag back in the locker room at the training center by mistake. The cold didn't bother him.

For some reason, as he went along, he thought of a wounded animal that nonetheless bit the hand that was trying to save its life.

All just part of the tragedy, though. Wasn't it.

FORTY-TWO

"No, fuck that shit. That pair of assholes can fuck right off."

As Wrath made his proclamation, he was sitting in the Audience Room, in the armchair on the left, in front of a blazing hearth. George was curled on his lap, the King's hand stroking that boxy, blond head, the dog feeling considerably better after he'd apparently tried to ingest the yellow fuzz of a tennis ball.

Things were working their way through. Not that Saxton had asked for a detailed accounting of what "things" or "working" or "through" meant.

One could guess, however.

"You have such a way of putting things, my Lord," he said with a grin as he looked back down at the ancient tome that he had opened with care and consulted with much deliberation. "And in this instance, I wholly agree. Peyton and Romina have every right to determine the course of their lives, and by revising the language in this antiquated passage, we can assure that non-consented dowries are not a problem going forward for either sex."

"Do you want to cancel that appointment?" Wrath lifted his head, those black wraparounds making him look like he was prepared to shoot the pair of sires. "Because if they come in here, they may not appreciate my delicate delivery. Selling your fucking kid. Are you kidding me."

"Yes, my Lord." Saxton made a notation on his schedule. "I think it would be best if I explained to them over the phone that there will be no avenue legally for them to accomplish their objectives. Otherwise, we will have call Stainmaster, won't we."

Wrath laughed softly. "We are a good pair, you and I."

"I am complimented greatly by your praise and could not agree more wholeheartedly." Saxton bowed. "I shall draft the revision to the Old Laws and enter it into my online database so that it is effective as of this evening. All will be well."

"That's the last thing on our agenda, right?"

"Yes, my Lord." He glanced at the dog. "Although, George, no more with the tennis balls, okay?"

"Yeah, we're not doing that anymore, right, big man?"

As the golden let out a groan, Saxton gathered his papers, got up from his desk, and bid his adieu. On the way out, he nodded at Blay, who had been on guard by the door.

"I think the pair of them are beyond ready to go home," he whispered. "Wrath is exhausted from worrying about his second child."

"And I think we're all scared to death anything will happen to—"

"—that dog."

"—that dog."

They nodded and then Blay went into the Audience Room to arrange for transport and Saxton went back to his office. The temptation to go home right away was nearly overwhelming, but in the end, he had to follow his procedure. It was a good hour before he could leave, and when he was finally done, he nearly trampled two *doggen* on the way to the back door.

Dematerializing to the farmhouse's front stoop, he paused to loosen the laces on his Merrells, and he was whistling as he entered the—

The scent of blood was thick in the air.

"Ruhn?" He dropped his satchel and his travel mug on the floor. "Ruhn!"

As sheer panic flooded every nerve ending he had, he raced into the parlor. Furniture had been knocked over, a lamp was broken . . . rugs were out of place, scrunched up in corners.

"Ruhn!" he screamed.

Not a sound. Not a moan. Not a groan.

But the blood was not human.

Wheeling around, he ran down to the kitchen and—

The pool of blood was over by the table and Saxton all but tripped in his rush to get over there—

"Oh, God, no . . . !"

Ruhn was sprawled on the floor facedown, blood . . . everywhere.

"Ruhn! My love!"

Saxton fell to his knees by the body, his stomach rolling to the point of vomiting, but he refused to give in to the impulse as he reached out to touch shoulder and back.

"Ruhn . . . ? Dear God, please don't be dead . . ."

With hands that shook and arms that were weak, he carefully rolled the male over onto his back. What he saw was the stuff of nightmare: Ruhn's throat was slashed, his eyes fixed and unblinking. He did not appear to be breathing.

Saxton screamed into the empty house. And then he cried out in further pain as he realized what Ruhn had been lying on.

The dying male had pulled Saxton's cashmere coat off the back of the chair it had been on . . . and had held it to him as he had bled as if taking comfort in the love they had shared.

"Please don't be dead . . . wake up . . . *wake up* . . ."

FORTY-THREE

Somehow, Saxton managed to get his phone out and call . . . someone. He didn't know who it was. But all of a sudden, he was not alone. He was surrounded by people . . . and somebody was easing him back so that someone else could look at Ruhn—

Blay. It was Blay's arms around his chest.

They were both kneeling in Ruhn's blood.

"I can't hear anything," Saxton blurted. "Is anybody saying anything?"

"Shh," came Blay's soothing voice. "It's okay. They're just looking at him . . ."

"I can't . . . what's wrong with my ears." He hit himself in the side of the head a couple of times. "I can't . . . they're not working—"

Blay captured his hand and stilled him. "We need to find out if there's . . ."

"Is he dead?"

At that point, the floodgates threatened to open, but he had no time for the blindness that came with tears or any further lack of hearing. He simply sobbed without crying and tried to focus through his wretched sorrow.

When he had to turn to the side to try to throw up, Blay held his head while he dry-heaved, and he could vaguely recognize the male's voice speaking to him again. But God, he couldn't think.

And then Qhuinn was crouching down to him. The Brother's lips were moving and his mismatched stare was earnest, concerned, compassionate.

"I can't . . ." Saxton tapped his ear again. "I can't hear what you're saying . . ."

Qhuinn nodded and squeezed Saxton's shoulder. Then the male looked at Manny and Doc Jane, who were bending over Ruhn.

Chosen—a Chosen was here, Saxton realized.

Wait, they wouldn't have brought her if he was dead? Right?

"Someone talk to me!" Saxton shouted.

Everybody froze and looked over at him. And then Rhage was blocking the way and pointing to another room.

"No." Saxton shook his head. "No, I'm not—don't take me away from him—I'm not—"

Rhage's face got right in front of his own. "He has a pulse. They're going to feed him and they're going to close the knife wound. I'm taking you to the parlor and we're going to let them do their job—"

"No! No, don't make me leave him—"

"Do you want them distracted by you or working on Ruhn."

Saxton blinked. Put like that, the logic was enough to quiet him for the time being.

When he tried to stand up, his legs gave out and he caught himself by throwing out a hand. Blay and Qhuinn ended up pulling him to his feet and leading him out to the parlor. And as he fell down onto the sofa, he looked at his palms. His knees. His shirt.

There was blood all over him.

He glanced toward the door. And heard himself say, "There's a camera. Mounted in the corner of the eaves."

The Brother Vishous stepped forward from God only knew where. "Do you know what it feeds into?"

Saxton cleared his throat and spoke in a hoarse voice. "There's . . . downstairs, there's a laptop. The password is *Minnie*. It's there."

"I'm on it."

As the Brother stomped out of the room, like he was on a personal mission, Saxton put his head down . . . and wept.

How could his love have been taken away from him so soon?

Across town, Novo was pacing in her apartment. Which wasn't saying much: It took her about four strides to cover the distance to the bathroom. Four strides back to the futon.

Rinse and repeat, so to speak.

There was an intense restlessness in her, as if the universe were shattering somewhere in Caldwell, some kind of cosmic realignment happening that resonated in her world. Then again, maybe she was simply hallucinating from not having eaten in almost twenty-four hours.

She had been doing much better before Peyton had showed up just now.

Not really a newsflash.

It had been a shock to sense the echo of his blood up above her basement shithole, but all things considered, she couldn't really be surprised he had come. And she had been tempted to ignore his presence, except sooner or later, he would have figured out a way down to her level—and really, who needed to wait around for the other shoe to drop.

Seizing the bull by the horns, she had marched up there and given him what for.

So it was done. And he was the asshole and she was the victim who refused to be a victim.

Yada, yada, yada.

The trouble was, something wasn't sitting right. *I refuse to keep paying for the sins of another.*

"Just words, just fucking words," she muttered as she made another trip.

A quick check of the digital clock by her pillows and she added up how many hours before dawn: two. She had about one hundred and twenty minutes before she was stuck here all day.

There was only one place she could think of to go. And unfortunately, it was the last place in the world she wanted to be.

Something wouldn't keep her inside, though.

Like a bird seeking flight, she made a sudden rush to leave, sure as if she were afraid destiny's hand would close the door of her freedom of choice and lock it for good.

Out on the street, she walked fast, following in the footsteps of countless humans, and a few vampires, who had trod over the snow-pack on the sidewalk. She went way farther than she had to to find a place to dematerialize, but she wanted to give herself as much of an opportunity to change her mind as she could.

The calling would not be denied, however.

Eventually, she ducked into a doorway that had no light above it . . . and after more than a few attempts, she traveled out and away from downtown, past the very outer ring of the suburbs, to a forest of trees and marshes.

When she re-materialized, she found herself in an unfamiliar familiar landscape.

The house she had once rented was abandoned now, its windows broken, a hole in its roof, the yard a tangle of vines, out-of-control bushes, and saplings that would soon be trees. In fact, the entire property seemed to have been returned to the wild, the six or seven acres overgrown such that the other houses in the area could not be seen at all.

The snow cover, undisturbed except for some deer prints, seemed to be the crowning glory on the home's death. Or more like the dirt on its coffin lid.

She must have been the last person to inhabit the place.

Maybe her tragedy had cursed the land and the little house.

Or . . . maybe its owner had simply forfeited the mortgage and the bank had repossessed the property and not been able to move it on to someone else . . . and then a season had passed and a winter had come and pipes had broken . . . and after more of the same, there you had it.

The real estate equivalent of cancer that metastasized.

Walking forward, she was in no rush to get around to the back . . . but as with all journeys, large and small, the end came when it did.

And then she was staring out at the marshes that seemed to go on forever. In reality, there was a good mile of them, and off in the distance, there were foothills that turned into the mountains that ultimately cupped Schroon Lake on the other side.

Even with everything so unkempt, she knew exactly the spot where she had buried the young. It was over there. Under that little bush she had planted that was now so much bigger and the pile of rocks she had made that had stayed the same height.

There was still a small mound, beneath the blanket of snow.

With each step she took, the heaviness in her heart grew . . . until she could not take a full breath anymore. And then she was crouching down and she was putting her bare hand out to the snow.

Turning her palm over, she remembered the blisters.

It had been as cold as it was now the night it had happened. But she had been determined to dig. She had used a kitchen knife to stab at the hard, frozen earth and then had clawed the loose dirt free with her bare hands. Three feet down, and then she could go no farther because her hands were too shot.

She had gone back into the house then.

The young she had wrapped in a dishtowel—a clean one that had no holes.

Back out by the grave, she had leaned down and placed the tiny bundle in the earth. Her tears had been the first thing that had filled what she had dug. And then that dirt, falling in chunks that she had had to press down, her blood mixing with the clay soil.

Concerned that predators would find the site, she had turned back to the house. Stones set aside for some kind of terrace project that had not come to fruition had been stacked by the back door. One by one, she had carried them over and made a cairn.

Then she had sat in the cold until she had shivered from hypothermia.

Much like she was doing now.

Only the blazing burn of the sun's earliest rays had motivated her to go back inside—and even then, she had retreated not because she wanted to live, but rather because she had been determined to clean up her blood on the kitchen floor.

And also because of that old wives' tale about not being welcomed in the Fade if you killed yourself.

At nightfall, she had dug up that bush and replanted it . . . and then she had left with no idea where she was going.

She had spent the first few days on the streets, keeping sheltered from the sun in alleys behind Dumpsters. She'd wanted to believe she could meet her young eventually.

She still wanted to believe that.

Oddly, she recalled how busy the city had been during the day. Having only known Caldwell at night, the amount of traffic on the city streets, and all the walking, talking humans, and the bustling activity had been a surprise.

Eventually, she had decided she had to do something with herself. She had found a job as a short-order cook at an all-night diner, taking the third shift that paid relatively well because most humans didn't want to do the late hours.

And then she'd seen that post on a closed Facebook group about the Brotherhood's training program.

Letting herself fall back onto her ass, she stared at the stones she had laid, one upon the other.

"Serenity," she said out loud. "I'm going to name you Serenity. Because I hope that is what you have found in the Fade . . ."

FORTY-FOUR

"You are my uncle's special friend."

At the sound of a small voice, Saxton turned away from the closed door of the operating room. Bitty was standing beside him in the training center's corridor, both of her parents behind her, a toy tiger dangling in her hand. The little girl was in a red dress, her dark hair curling at the ends, her eyes innocent, yet very old.

This one had known so much suffering. Thus, she was used to this sorrow, wasn't she, he thought sadly.

Clearing his throat, he eased down to her level so he could meet her eye to eye. "Yes, I am. How did you know?"

"My uncle told me all about you. When we were doing our puzzle the other night. He said you were his special friend and he loved you very much."

Saxton had thought that he was all cried out: After the trip in on the surgical van, with Ruhn coding twice, and then watching the door close as Doc Jane and Manny went in to put some kind of a tube or something in the male's throat, he'd assumed he was dry as a bone.

Nope.

His eyes started to water all over again. "I love your uncle very much, too. He is my special friend as well."

"Here." She held out her stuffed tiger. "This is Mastimon. He has always protected me. You can hold him now."

With hands that shook, he accepted the precious gift, and as he tucked it into his heart, he pulled the little girl close to his chest. Her arms did not fit very far around him, but he drew strength from her.

Rhage looked heartbroken as he spoke up. "Any news . . . ?"

Saxton stood and was surprised as Bitty kept her arm around him. It seemed so easy to rest his hand on her small shoulder, the pair of them hurting together.

"Not yet," he told the Brother. "They've been in there forever."

"Do they know who did this?"

"Vishous is looking into it. I can't really even focus on that right now. All I want is for Ruhn to . . ." He stopped himself. "We're just going to pray for the best, aren't we, Bitty?"

"Yes." The little girl nodded.

"Can we bring you anything?" Mary asked.

"No. Thank you, though."

Other Brothers stopped by, asked for updates, chatted. Someone brought him a coffee, but when he tasted it, all he could think about was what Ruhn had made for him just twelve hours ago.

That coffee had been perfect. Everything else was ruined.

He was never going to be able to drink the stuff again.

God, it seemed impossible that life had been going at such a happy pace . . . only to have this brick wall of horror slam into him—

Down at the far end of the corridor, the office's glass door opened and Wrath came charging through. The King's face was cast in a dark fury, and his Queen, Beth, seemed to be holding him back—and getting nowhere.

As Wrath came down and stopped in front of him, Saxton had trouble meeting his ruler's eyes even though they were blind.

"Who did this," the King snarled. *"Who fucking did this."*

"I think it was the humans who . . ." Saxton took a deep breath. "Ruhn and I were staying at the house to help that homeowner who was getting harassed."

"Why the *fuck* didn't you call for more help!"

As that autocratic demand was barked out, Beth yanked at her *hellren*'s arm. "Wrath! For crissakes, will you back off—"

"It's okay," Saxton said with exhaustion. "He is just upset this happened at all and it's coming out badly. We go through this on the job, he and I—"

The King's arm shot out and dragged him forward so hard and so fast, Saxton's head spun—at least until it banged into a chest of granite.

"I am so sorry," Wrath muttered. "I didn't know you two were together."

Abruptly, Saxton found himself clinging to the far-larger male, Wrath's undeniable physical and literal power exactly what he needed at that moment.

"I didn't know he was yours," Wrath said tightly. "I would never have sent him out with you if I had known."

"He wasn't mine then," Saxton choked out. "When we started . . . he wasn't yet mine."

At that moment, Manny and Doc Jane emerged from the operating room, sure as if they had been summoned by a royal decree. The two surgeons pulled their masks down in sync, and it was hard not to read into their tired expressions that things had not gone as they had hoped.

"So this is what we've got," Doc Jane said. "He's stable, but in critical condition. He's having a hard time finding a steady blood pressure and heart rate."

"He coded again," Manny added. "And since we can't give you all transfusions, it's just tough. His brain has gone without oxygen for a couple of minutes, a couple of times."

"I'm so sorry," Doc Jane concluded, "but we're not sure . . . whether he's going to wake up."

As Bitty ran to her parents, Saxton covered his mouth so he didn't start screaming again.

When he was able, he said, "Can I see him—can she and I see him?"

Doc Jane glanced at Rhage and Mary. When they nodded, the doctor did as well. "Okay, but only the two of you. Talk to him, tell him how much you want him to fight. We're not going to move him right now—and you can't stay in there long. He needs to rest."

"All right. Okay."

He took Bitty's hand and looked down at her. "You ready?"

When the little girl nodded, Manny opened the door for them.

It was cold inside the operating room, so much colder than he'd been prepared for. And there was a purpose to everything that was in the tiled space, from the medical equipment to the multi-light fixture overhead to the glass-front shelves with all their instruments and supplies.

His only thought as they approached the table was that he didn't want Ruhn to die in this horrible, clinical place. And not like this, with all these wires going in and out of him.

He was so pale, he was gray. And there were bandages all around his throat.

"What's the beeping?" Bitty asked as they stopped.

"His heartbeat."

Fates, maybe they shouldn't let the girl see this, he thought as the pair of them looked down at him. Ruhn's face was so hollow, and with that all-wrong color, his hair was so very dark in contrast. Further, his eyes were closed as if they were never opening again, and his breathing was unnaturally punchy—

Oh, right. He was on a ventilator thanks to a tube that went in through the base of his throat.

"Uncle, it's Bitty and Saxton. We love you."

The girl took her uncle's still hand in hers.

"My love," Saxton said as he bent over and kissed his male's forehead. "Come back to us. We need you."

There were so many things to be said, pleaded, begged—

Saxton recognized that his own mouth was moving and that he was continuing to speak. But that odd deafness had returned to him, his ability to hear evaporating.

When a hand landed on his shoulder, he jumped.

Doc Jane's forest-green eyes were grave. "I'm sorry," she said softly, "but we're going to ask you to leave for a little while."

It was like peeling his own flesh off in strips to turn away, but he allowed himself to be led out. And as he stepped from the operating room, he saw that Vishous, Blay, and Qhuinn had joined the crowd that had assembled.

The door closed on his lover.

In the silence, as everyone looked at him, something changed deep inside of Saxton. Gone was the nausea and the sorrow and the fear. All that was weak disappeared as if it had never been. In its place?

The rage of a bonded male.

In a voice that did not sound like his own, he heard himself say, "Will you all take Bitty for a moment?"

Rhage nodded immediately, the male recognizing exactly what was going on. "Hey, Bit, I'm hungry. Can you and Mary take me down to the break room for something to eat?"

The little girl stepped in front of Saxton. "Do you promise to come and get me if he wakes up?"

Saxton brushed her cheek. "I promise. With all that I am, dearest one."

She gave him a quick, fierce hug—that reminded him of her uncle—and then she was taking her father's hand and leading the Brother and Mary down the corridor.

Saxton waited until they were out of earshot to turn to Vishous. "Tell me you know who did this."

Vishous nodded. "I reviewed the security footage from the last couple of weeks. They were the same two human men who have showed up in a truck a number of times. One of them now has his arm in a sling. They came to the front door and they had weapons. Ruhn opened things up and they attacked him. The fight had to have been a brutal one because the total elapsed time was almost thirty minutes."

"They left in rough shape," Blay tacked on. "Ruhn hurt them."

"Bad," Qhuinn affirmed. "Like a true fighter."

In a voice that was all vengeance, Saxton said, "You find them. You bring them to me. I, and I alone, will take care of this."

All three of the males bowed low, paying deference to his position as bonded male.

And then Vishous unsheathed one of the black daggers that were strapped, handles down, to his chest. Opening his ungloved hand, he gripped the blade and yanked it free, his blood welling, dripping, landing on the concrete floor.

He extended his palm. "On my honor."

Saxton gripped the offering. "Alive. They come to me alive."

Blay and Qhuinn likewise cut themselves, and in turn, Saxton shook each of their bleeding palms.

And so it was done.

Whether Ruhn lived or died, he would be *ahvenged*.

FORTY-FIVE

*A*s the following night arrived, Novo recognized the sun's descent and disappearance by the dropping of the temperature and a dimming of ambient illumination. A quick check of her watch told her what she already knew to be true and she got to her feet on a slow, stiff creep.

She had spent the day in the cold house, sitting on the kitchen floor, the boarded-up windows coupled with daytime cloud cover providing her with the protection she needed.

She had not slept, her mind churning over things at a slow-and-steady that had consumed the hours.

You're choosing this. You're picking all of this—and that means if it doesn't feel right, you don't have to do it.

All of this . . . it's on you.

More than anything, she found that her own words haunted her, words that she had spoken to the male who had betrayed and hurt her.

But she didn't think about them in the context of Oskar. She thought about them as they related to Peyton.

He was right. She hadn't given him a chance to explain anything. She'd been so ready to replay the past, jump back into the I've-been-screwed pool, that she'd decided what had happened. Taken at face value what his father had said. Turned on a dime.

All of which made a lot of sense.

Except when she thought of Oskar's new glasses. The ones that were for show.

The ones that were just on the surface, not anything true or real.

Leaving the house by the door she came in, she returned to Serenity's grave and stood in the wind for a little bit.

"I'll be back to visit. You rest well."

With that, she was off, traveling to her apartment . . . where she showered, ate something that tasted like cardboard, and checked her phone. There were a bunch of messages on the trainee thread and she read through them quickly.

Classes were canceled for the night. Something had happened, the Brothers didn't go into what. Everyone checked in, though. Even Peyton.

He had not called or texted her directly, but she hadn't expected him to.

When she called his number up out of her contacts, she knew he wasn't going to answer, and started to compose a voicemail in her head—

"Hello?"

She coughed a little from shock. "Ah . . . hi. It's me."

"Yup, that's what my phone says."

"Listen, I . . . can I come see you?"

"I'm a little busy right now."

"Oh. Okay."

"If you don't mind carrying shit down stairs, though, come on over."

"I'm sorry—wait. Are you moving?"

"Yup. Anyway, you know where I live. Or used to live. Come if you want."

As he ended the call, she nearly lost her nerve. But she was picking this, wasn't she. She was going to choose the depth, not the surface. She was going to . . . trust in what her heart knew of the male, rather than what things appeared to be based on a two-minute interaction with a sire that Peyton didn't respect.

Her own past traumas aside, she owed the male a chance to explain. And from there . . . well, it was going to be what it was. But at least she wouldn't be punishing him for sins he hadn't committed, as he had said.

Outside on the street, she needed a couple of tries before she could dematerialize, and when she re-formed on the lawn of his family's mansion, she was surprised. There was a big white U-Haul truck with a sea lion and some facts about Maine on its side backed right up to the grand front entrance.

Like the stately home was a college dorm or something and it was the end of the year.

Walking up through the snow, she paused to look into the van's open bay. There was a sofa in there. Boxes. Wardrobe stands with clothes on hangers. Shoes in laundry bins.

"Hey, could you give me a hand with this?" came a distant voice.

She wheeled around. Peyton was at the bottom of the stairs inside, trying to corral a love seat and all of its pillows in his arms.

"Yeah, of course."

She stomped her combat boots on the mat, not because she cared about tracking dirt into his father's house, but because she didn't want to slip and fall on all the marble. As she jogged over, it was hard to have that scent of Peyton's in her nose.

Harder still to hear her own words in her head, the ones that she had thrown at him like daggers.

Grabbing the edge of the love seat, they both grunted as they got it stabilized between them, and then they were crab-walking the thing across the Smithsonian foyer and out onto the ramp that led into the truck's belly.

"Where do you want this?" she asked.

"Right here is fine. I'm not taking much else."

As they lowered the weight, she said, "So . . . you're leaving."

"Yeah." He slapped his palms on the seat of his jeans. "It's about time. My father and I were done a long while ago."

He refused to look at her. Not because he seemed mad, though. More like he was finished with drama.

Unease rippled through her like a toxin. "Where are you going?"

"A buddy of mine has a penthouse with an extra room. I'm going to stay with him for a while until I find a place of my own."

"So you're at least staying in Caldwell. What about the training program?"

"Oh, I'm not leaving that. Why would I. I am not a quitter anymore." He measured his things. Then focused on her. "So. What can I do you for."

His affect was calm and centered, not hostile or emotional. Just as he would be with a stranger on the street: polite but not wrapped up in anything.

Her heart pounded. And not from love seat–related exertion.

"I wanted to apologize."

"It's cool. You don't have to." He turned away. "I'm not going to be weird in class or anything."

She reached out and took his arm. "Please. Let me talk."

With a deliberate move, he took himself out of her reach—and she was reminded of all the times she had done that to him, literally and figuratively.

"Actually," he intoned, "maybe it's best that you don't."

"Peyton, I said things I didn't mean last night—"

"You sounded very lucid to me, FYI. And listen, you're not the first person to call me out for having no substance, for being a flaker." Suddenly, his face got serious. "You will be the last one, though. I promise you that."

"I didn't mean it. I was hurt and I jumped to conclusions after I—"

"Oh. By the way, I am sorry for what my father said to you. When I came back here after you and I had our little—discussion, shall we call it—he told me what he'd done and we had it out. I broke his favorite Tiffany lamp, but at least it wasn't over the motherfucker's head." He shrugged. "Incidentally, not that you care, that's the reason I'm leaving. He's not going to force me into mating anybody, and I am sure as shit done with living under the same roof with a male who could accuse you of being a goddamn prostitute to your face."

"So it was all a lie?"

"About the female? Why ask me that?"

"You rightfully accused me of not giving you a chance to explain—"

"No, why ask me a question when you won't believe the answer? I am very sure I could talk until I'm blue in the face, and you will do what you want with the words." He pivoted away and headed back into the house. "You know, recast them to suit yourself. Play a game of chess and move 'em around until you get the answer you've pre-decided is the truth—"

She caught up with him on the fancy stairs. "I went to see Serenity."

At that, he stopped.

"That's what I named her. I spent the day at the house. In the kitchen."

It seemed like a lifetime before Peyton slowly turned back around.

And oh, man, she was not going to waste this chance. She spoke fast and with the kind of urgency that came from desperation.

"You were right. I've been punishing you and everyone around me for what Sophy did to me and what Oskar wasn't strong enough to fight against. And then I've been punishing me for the miscarriage even though I didn't do anything wrong. I've had this . . . fury in my blood that I haven't been able to handle. And I'm so sorry. You told me last night you hoped I'd figure it out for myself and I'm trying, I really am. I just . . . I love you. Even though I'm broken, I love you. And not like I did Oskar. I was with him because he was the first male who paid any attention to me and I was too fucking stupid to know the difference between hope and reality. But you . . . you were the only person I wanted to see when it was time to tell my truth. You were the only place I wanted to go. And that's because this," she pointed to her heart, "knows more than this."

As she indicated her head, she prayed she was getting through to him. "I would do anything to take back those words I threw at you. You didn't deserve any of it. You have more than earned a chance to explain what actually was going on about that mating thing, but in my anger, I didn't have the ability to give you that. I know I don't deserve a second chance, but—"

"Shh. Just stop talking for a minute."

He put his head in his hands and took a deep breath. Then he focused beyond her, looking around her.

Novo's heart beat so hard, it rivaled an entire rhythm section.

"Let me ask you one thing," he said after a long time.

"Anything. I don't care what it is."

He shifted his eyes to hers. "Do you think we can fit my love seat and my couch at your place? Or just the love seat."

Novo shook her head to clear it. "I'm sorry, what—"

"I mean, how much square feet do you have?" As she stared at him in total confusion, he held out his arms and smiled. "Come on, the female of my dreams tells me she loves me and then she thinks that I, a homeless indigent, am not going to take advantage of that and move in with her? Really? Like, seriously? Even if I wasn't in love with you, too, you're bound to be a better roommate than Nickle."

Novo couldn't decide whether to laugh or cry.

So she did both as she leapt into Peyton's loving arms. "I don't deserve you," she choked. "I really don't."

• • •

As Peyton held Novo to his chest, he closed his eyes and breathed in. "Deserve me? Well, considering that many people think I'm a curse of Biblical proportions—"

She pushed back. "Says who. I'll cut a bitch."

"My father, for one. But he has poor taste."

Peyton kissed her quick. And then again for a little longer. When they eased back for air, he stroked the tears from her cheeks.

"You don't have to say it," he murmured. "I already know."

"Know what?"

"That you don't want anyone to know about this soft side to you. So I'm just going to tell them that you came over, kicked me in the balls, and took my liver when I coughed it onto the floor. I had to follow you home or I wouldn't be able to cleanse my own blood."

She laughed, and then searched his face as if she were re-memorizing it after a long trip. "It's okay. I'm not feeling like I have to protect myself all the time anymore."

"Good. 'Cuz I've got your back."

"And I have yours." She craned a glance toward the open door of the mansion. "And I think we need to leave your couch. Your wardrobe takes up more space than I've got already."

"Cool. I'll just take it out of the truck and leave it in the middle of the foyer. My father will probably want to haul the fucker back out and burn it on the front lawn because it's mine—but at least he won't have to have the *doggen* move it that far."

"You are a very considerate son."

"Aren't I?"

She kissed him again. "But listen . . . my place is a dump compared to what you're used to. It's small, it doesn't have any windows, and the neighbors can sometimes be pests."

Peyton looked around at the grandeur he had grown up in. His sire had vowed to take him out of the will and remove him from the family tree—so all this was going to be a thing of his past. And the amazing thing? He was so totally good with that.

Stuff was nice. Love was better.

Refocusing on Novo, he said, "I would rather be in a hovel with you than a castle with anybody else."

As she looked up at him, her smile was so resplendent, he basked in it for a moment. Then he held up a forefinger.

"And as for your pesky neighbors, I have the solution for that." Leaning to one side, he took a folded piece of paper out of his pocket. "I'll just put this on the door."

Flattening the sheet, he turned it around so she could see the note Dr. Manello had written and put on the door to her hospital room back when she'd been recovering.

"Oh . . ." she said as she touched it. "You were going to take this with you."

"I'm a sap. For you, that is." He smiled at her. "And sooner or later, I was going to cave and come try you again. You're irresistible to me."

"Even though I'm a bitch sometimes?"

Peyton gave her his sauciest wink. "I love a challenge, what can I say."

They made out for a little bit. And then he linked her arm through his own. "Let's unload the sofa and blow this Popsicle stand."

"Sounds like a perfect plan."

They were halfway across the foyer when Novo said, "Hey, will you go as my date to my sister's wedding . . . mating . . . whatever it is."

Peyton stopped and thought about it. "Yeah, but on one condition."

"What's that?"

"I get to hit him."

"Who? Oskar?"

"Yup. Right in the piehole." As Novo rolled her eyes and started shaking her head, he put his hands up. "One shot. I promise. And listen, because I'm a stand-up guy, I'll do it after the pictures are taken. Come on, you're my female. I gotta take care of you."

"I can take care of myself," she said sternly.

"True. But you have to admit, you'd like to see that. Admit it. Come onnnnnnnnnnn."

"Fine," she muttered. "I would. But you're not going to hit him . . ."

"Even a little?" he asked as they headed out into the cold. "How about I duct-tape his ass cheeks together? Short-sheet his bed? Ex-Lax his chocolate pudding . . . ? I have other ideas, you know . . ."

Novo put her hands on her hips and tried to keep a straight face. In the end, she cracked and started laughing. "You are out of control."

He came in for the clinch and she didn't fight him. "Not any longer. I know what I want and where I want to be. And it is to be with you. You're my home just like I'm yours."

She wrapped her arms around his neck. "Do we have to unpack the truck before we have sex?"

"Fuck that shit." He grinned. "Actually, I was planning on pulling over and doing you in the front seat on the way across town."

"I like the way you think," she said as she kissed him long and hard. "You are a male with great plans . . ."

FORTY-SIX

It was twelve minutes after midnight on the dot when Saxton dematerialized to the rear of the Audience House. He did not enter through the kitchen door. Instead, he turned around and faced the four-bay garage that was set back from the mansion. The Brotherhood's blacked-out van was parked there, and with a calm that would have shocked him under other circumstances, he started through the snow to the set of exterior stairs leading to the structure's second level. As he ascended, his breathing was as even as a metronome, his heart rate steady, his eyes unblinking in spite of the cold.

From what felt like a vast distance, he watched as his hand reached out and turned a knob. Pushing the way open, he stepped inside, into the dim light.

The moans of the human men were muffled by the gags that were in their mouths. There were three of them, weaving on their feet, all with their hands tied behind their backs and their terror making them sweat like meat left out too long in the heat. Two he recognized from the attack behind the restaurant. The other was not one he had seen before, but the fellow was of predictable ilk: big, beefy, short-haired, and ruddy-faced.

Vishous held one. Blay and Qhuinn the others.

There was plastic sheeting beneath their boots.

The humans struggled even more as his presence registered, and as they jerked against their tethers, he was reminded of hooves stamping in a stable, the rustle-thump of heavy-weighted bodies just the same.

No one said anything.

Vishous simply nodded over to a workbench. There was a single dagger on it. Black bladed. Was it V's or Qhuinn's, he wondered idly as he removed his leather gloves.

No matter, he thought as he went across and palmed it with his bare right hand.

For no particular reason, he looked around the raftered space. There were a number of inset windows that punched out into the roofline, but each was covered with black curtains. There was no glass in the door. None of the neighbors would be able to see this.

He didn't care if they did.

Approaching the first one, the human started to thrash against V's hold, his nose blowing out liquid, his cheeks puffing up around the gag.

As if the Brother wanted to make things easy, Vishous changed his grip so that his glove-covered hand, the dangerous one, slapped onto the man's forehead and he pulled back, exposing the throat.

A bead of sweat, like a tear, rolled down the human's cheek as he begged for mercy. Saxton heard none of it. No, all he had were visuals of Ruhn on the floor of that kitchen, his precious blood spilled, his body on a coat that had been his only comfort as he lay dying.

Saxton's arm acted before he was aware of making any kind of mental command. It lifted up the dagger . . .

And then it slashed the black blade across that exposed, fragile neck.

The blood flowed quick, spraying out so that it speckled Saxton's face. And V held the human up off the ground as the man began to spasm such that he tap-danced his way to death.

As Saxton moved on to the second, he found himself opening his mouth and hissing with fully descended fangs. Then he extended his tongue and licked the blade.

The human who was going to die next saw all this and screamed around his gag, fighting to get free of Qhuinn not just because he was going to be killed, but because he had discovered that something was very, very different about the male who was his executioner. In response, the Brother just tightened his hold around that barrel chest and yanked that head back by the hair.

Saxton threw the blade out in a fat arc, right across the throat, the cut as clean as the first.

And then there was the last one, the one who had attacked Ruhn behind the restaurant, whose arm had been broken.

Blay's eyes were stone cold as he jerked the man up a little higher.

Now Saxton took his time. Bending in to the man, he pressed the tip of the bloody blade to the flesh over the jugular.

The man was crazed with fear, his legs kicking like he was being electrocuted, his stench that of rank panic.

"This is for my love," Saxton growled. "This is for my mate. This . . ."

On each sentence, he pressed the tip in further and further and further still, until the geyser was struck.

"This is for that which was mine. This is for what you tried to take from me."

With that, he lowered the dagger, reared back, and bit the side of that throat so hard he hit bone. Ripping the flesh free, he spat it out and watched as the human gasped and heaved and bled his way to his demise.

When all three were still, their heads lolling to the sides, their bodies no longer animated with life, their debts collected, the fighters let them drop to the floor, one by one, faceup.

Saxton wiped his mouth with the back of his coat sleeve. Then he cut his palm, the one that had held the dagger. Going over to each of the bodies, he stood over their sightless, open eyes and put his hand print on their faces with his own blood, marking the kills as they did in the Old Country.

"What of them now?" he asked when he was done.

Vishous spoke up. "We're going to deliver them to their boss."

"And then we're going to talk to him," Qhuinn continued.

Blay finished with, "And he is never going to bother Mistress Miniahna again."

Saxton stared at the bodies for a moment. "So shall it be."

On his way to the door, he was careful to wipe off the dagger and put it precisely, exactly, absolutely where it had been placed for his use.

Outside, the cold cleaned his nose out of the copper scent of human blood. And he made it down the stairs and around the van okay.

But as he came to the spot where he had arrived at, he was overcome by nausea. Tripping and falling forward, he grabbed on to the picket fence that encircled the backyard and vomited all over his shoes.

When he next looked up, Blay was before him.

"I don't feel any better," Saxton moaned as he wiped his mouth with his handkerchief. "I feel . . . no better."

"You will. Later. This is the balance that is needed."

As Saxton lurched to the side, the male steadied him and then offered him a sip of water from a bottle that, absurdly, he noted was a Poland Spring. His favorite.

And then Blay was hugging him. "You did the right thing. You did as it was proper."

Saxton embraced the male. "I just want Ruhn to—"

"He's awake!" V called from the garage's upstairs. "Saxton! They've been trying to call you. He's awake and he's asking for you!"

As Saxton shifted his stunned eyes to Blay, the other male started to smile.

"I've never heard of an *ahvenging* bringing back a loved one," he said. "But there's a first time for everything. Go! Go now . . . hurry!"

As the one person in the world Ruhn wanted to see most barreled into his hospital room, his first thought was . . .

Why was human blood all over the love of his life?

But then all of that was forgotten as Saxton rushed over and threw himself across Ruhn's chest. "You're alive . . . oh, God . . ."

Ruhn tried to speak, except nothing but mumbles came out at first. Soon, though, soon, he was able to respond. "I . . . wasn't going to leave . . . you."

Saxton pulled back and seemed to be searching for signs he was serious about staying on this side of the Fade. "I thought I had lost you."

"I heard . . . you . . . Bitty and . . . you talking to me." Fates, his throat hurt. "When you were here—did I die? I think I did."

As Saxton stayed quiet, Ruhn got scared. "Did . . . I?"

"You're here now. That's all that matters."

"Throat . . . hurts . . ."

"I know, love." Saxton's eyes went all around as if he were looking for hidden injuries. "You don't have to talk—"

"The Fade. The door. To the Fade . . . I refused to open it . . ."

"What?" Saxton leaned down. "What did you say?"

"I saw a door . . . in the fog . . . I knew if I opened it . . . I would leave you. Many times it came to me. I refused . . . I wasn't . . . leaving you. I love . . . you."

"I love you, too."

Saxton's tears fell like rain, but it was the spring kind. The renewing kind. And as emotions of Ruhn's own welled, they got even more intense as Bitty came into the room with Rhage and Mary.

"Uncle!"

Ruhn smiled until his cheeks hurt, and he tried to talk, but it was no good. He'd worn out his energy and voice—not that Bitty seemed to mind. She was a jumping bean, full of joy, and wasn't that as good as the drugs he was on to lessen his pain.

As the little girl kept talking a mile a minute, he was very aware of Saxton backing toward the door. The male held a forefinger up— a signal he would return in a moment.

"—and I knew you were going to be okay! I knew it!"

"My man," Rhage said as he came over and touched Ruhn's hand. "I'm glad you're sticking with us. Can I buy you another truck or something?"

As Ruhn frowned and started shaking his head—because the Brother was just crazy enough to do something like that—Mary elbowed her mate in the side.

"Rhage. You don't need to buy people things just to show them how you feel."

"You know, you could have a great jewelry collection, I'm just sayin'." Rhage winked at Ruhn. "I swear, my female is Spartan."

Ruhn lay back and let them talk over each other. He understood the release of tension and worry even if he didn't have the gumption to participate in it—and then Saxton was back, smelling of fresh soap and shampoo, a set of scrubs on him.

In the end, Ruhn didn't have to ask what had been done. He knew his love had gone and found those men . . . and proceeded as Ruhn himself would have if Saxton had been the one attacked and left for dead in the very house they lived in. Still, it made him sad that his lovely lawyer had had to use the sword and not the pen in this case.

But he would not deny his love the expression of vengeance. It was what it was.

"Okay, how about we give Uncle and Saxton some privacy," Mary said. "Besides, your father hasn't eaten in at least twenty minutes."

Rhage looked at his daughter. "I am feeling a bit peckish, you know."

"Let's make tacos and bring one to Uncle!"

Considering the burn in his throat? Oh, no, Ruhn thought. Better that he start with vanilla pudding. In, like, a week.

After Bitty and her parents gave him more love and left, he looked at Saxton.

"Can't talk . . ." he said. "Hurts."

Saxton sat down on the bed. "You don't have to say a thing."

"Love you. Love you so much."

As he tugged on Saxton's hand, even though it was weakly, the lawyer knew what he wanted. With a smile, Saxton stretched out and put his head on Ruhn's arm.

"Never leave me again?" Saxton asked.

"Never. Promise."

As Ruhn closed his eyes, he thought . . . well, it looked as if he was going to have to call his old estate manager and tell the male not to bother trying to help him find a job with room and board in Caldwell. There was no way he was moving out of this household.

Not unless it was in with Saxton.

Little did he know, however, the surprise that was yet to come . . .

FORTY-SEVEN

Some two weeks later, night arrived and brought with it a stunning February moon. Indeed, the heavens were so clear and so cloudless that the face of the sky's largest sparkling diamond was like a mirror.

Saxton was straightening his bow tie in the visor mirror as his love parked their truck across from a . . . "Wait, this is a church? This mating is happening in a church?"

Ruhn nodded as he likewise looked through the windshield with surprise. "This is the correct address according to GPS."

"Huh. Well, to each their own. It's not that I have anything against human spirituality, it's just . . . this feels quite odd."

"Let me get your door."

As Ruhn beat feet out from behind the steering wheel, Saxton had to smile. The male was such a stickler for manners, and how could you not oblige? Especially as those eyes shone with such happiness every time he opened the way forth or pulled out a chair or offered a hand.

"You know," Saxton said as he slid off of the high seat. "Sometimes I think you like to take this truck just so you can help me out of it."

Ruhn leaned in and whispered in Saxton's ear. "It's rather like your pants in that regard."

Saxton chuckled and nipped at the throat so close to his mouth. "Naughty boy."

"You like me that way."

"Always."

They were kissing before they knew it, hands going under clothes, the heat instantaneous and intense—as if they hadn't made love three times in the shower, and then again as they got dressed in their suits.

"We'd better stop," Saxton said between gasps. "Or we'll be late."

Ruhn stepped back with reluctance boarding on a full sulk. "Then I expect to find a quiet place at the reception hall—whatever that is."

"And I can't wait."

They held hands as they walked across the street to the human church. And then they were inside and being shown to a bench. No, it was called a pew, Saxton thought. Yes, that was it, a pew.

As they settled in the very back and looked around at the assembled, it was clear that the other vampires—and there were a good hundred at least—were also feeling strange. But whatever. When you could spend a night out with the one you love, who cared where you were?

"You know, I hate to move out tomorrow." Ruhn looked up at the exposed rafters above. "I love that farmhouse."

"Me, too." Saxton thumbed the inside of his love's wrist. "It feels like home."

"It is home."

Fritz had cleaned up the horrible remnants of the attack, an unexpected kindness that had left Saxton in tears when he had braced himself to go back there and do the job himself. But no. All was in order, the furniture righted and fixed as need be, the scuffs out of the floor, the paint matched and retouched where it had to be.

The blood washed away.

And there had been another reason Saxton had been determined to take care of the gruesome deed: He had been concerned that Minnie would come back unexpectedly and see the violence that had happened in her and Rhysland's beloved home.

But as always, Saxton's family—his true family, not the one he had been born into—had taken care of everything.

"Did we ever meet Minnie's grandson?" Ruhn asked. "What was his name?"

"Oskar. That's what the invitation said—and he's marrying Novo's sister. Do you know Novo? The trainee?"

"Oh, yes. She works out. Proper. She is very strong, not just for a female, but for anybody—"

"You came!"

Saxton wrenched around and got to his feet. "Minnie!" He threw his arms around the older female. "But you're the grandmother of the groom, what are you doing in the congregation? Or . . . wait, is that the custom? I'm so confused."

Minnie was dressed in a beautiful pale pink lace gown, her white hair all done up, her makeup on. And she was smiling like she had a secret.

"I just wanted to say hello to you both before things get started."

"You look so well," Ruhn said as he in turn hugged the female. "So well indeed."

"How is my house?" she asked as she slid into the bench—pew, rather—with them. "Is it in tip-top shape?"

"It is." Ruhn bowed and lowered himself back down. "I did the final repair on the furnace last night."

"And we're very confident that you will be safe there." Saxton could not meet the female's eyes—and not because he was worried about her. It was more because he was very aware of what had transpired between V, Qhuinn and Blay, and Mr. Romanski. "We have had very productive . . . discussions . . . with the developer. He has decided he has no further interest in your property."

Actually, the bastard had decided to leave New York State entirely. Go figure.

"Well, that's good"—Minnie clapped her hands together—"because I've decided to sell the property to someone else."

A spike went through Saxton's chest. "Oh. Indeed. Isn't that marvelous news? And we were going to suggest that we move out tomorrow night anyway so that—"

"I want the two of you to buy it from me."

Saxton was aware of freezing solid. Then he glanced at Ruhn. "I'm sorry—what did you say?"

Minnie reached forward and took both their hands. As she squeezed them, her eyes became glossy.

"That house was built by love . . . and needs to be lived in by two people who are in love. I want you to have it. We can settle on a fair price, and I'll continue living with my granddaughter. I've thoroughly enjoyed it, and I have met some wonderful new people in her building—vampires and a couple of humans."

"But what about your grandson and his *shellan*. Wouldn't you rather they take it on, perhaps?"

"They're on their own," Minnie said dryly. "She hates the country, for one—and she made sure she told me this when I invited them to dinner so I could get to know her better. And for another, and this makes me sad to say, I'm not sure that love is what is tying them together. My grandson . . . he's a different sort, I'm afraid, and so is she. But it's not my life, and I will support them as best I can." She squeezed their hands again. "So please say you'll do it. It would bring me such joy to know that you two are taking care of my home."

Saxton looked at Ruhn again.

Okaaaaaaaaaaaay, so that beaming smile was the answer, wasn't it.

"One condition," Saxton said. "Sunday night Last Meal every week together—and you bring your granddaughter when and if she wants to come."

"Deal," Minnie said as she hugged them both at the same time. "I only wish Rhysland had met you both. He would have loved you."

After the female left, Saxton just sat there on the bench—pew, for godsakes, *pew*—and stared straight ahead at the altar thing with its cross and its depiction of a robed male with a beard and a beautiful face looking upon the assembly with compassion. There were males lined up to the right, and that suggested things were about to get started. He hoped.

"I think we just got our dream home," he heard himself say.

"We did! We did!"

As Ruhn laughed like a little kid, Saxton gave his love a kiss—and he was just pulling back when two people slid in beside them.

"Hey," the female said. "Can we sit with you? I'm Novo, from the training center—"

"Of course!" Saxton invited as he leaned around her and smiled at Peyton. "We would love the company—"

"Great, but we need to be on the other side, by the wall. Not on the aisle."

"Oh . . . uh, okay," Saxton said as he got up to let them pass. "But aren't you the sister of the whatever they call it? Bride? Aren't you in the wedding . . . mating, whatever this is?"

"I got kicked out, thank God." She greeted Ruhn and then made Peyton shuffle by her and settle in right by the stained glass window. "Long story. How are you?"

"We just bought a house!" Ruhn exclaimed.

"Congratulations," Peyton said with a high five. "That's awesome. Where's it located?"

"You'll never believe who it belongs to . . ."

The bunch of them chatted until an organ began to play and then they settled in with the rest of the assembly. Right before things really started, Saxton took Ruhn's hand and the male glanced over at him with love—and Saxton was aware of the other couple sharing a kiss and lingering stare.

And then Novo was leaning over. "Listen," she whispered. "Can you two help me with something?"

"Name it," Saxton said. "And it is done."

Peyton rolled his eyes. "I just want to hit the groom. Once. Is that too much to ask?"

Saxton popped his brows. "Is that a human tradition for this type of ceremony?"

"Why, yes," the male said. "As a matter of fact it is—"

Novo slapped her palm over his mouth. "No. It most certainly is not. And no matter how I might have felt about my sister in the past, I don't want her special night ruined, okay?"

Peyton mumbled a little longer. And when she dropped her hand, he muttered, "First of all, I volunteered to do it *after* the pictures—and if it's realllllly important to you, I could catch him in the gut and not the face. I'm willing to work with you."

Novo started to laugh. "I love you."

"I know you do." The male kissed her. "And I love you right back."

"Enough so you don't hit him. How sweet of you. I'm touched."

Peyton's exhale was one for the history books. "Fiiiiiiiiiiiiiiine."

Saxton looked back and forth between the two of them. "Why do I feel like there is more to this story?"

Ruhn cut in. "Shh! They're coming down the aisle."

Saxton let it drop and relaxed as best he could in the hard seat, leaning against his male's shoulder. As the music got louder, and a bunch of females in pink dresses with bows on their butts walked by, he just shrugged.

To each his own, he thought as he kissed the back of his lover's hand. To each his own.

And he certainly had his.

• • •

Novo craned around Saxton and his mate, Ruhn, to catch a glimpse of Sophy coming down the aisle. The female certainly looked happy, her face partially hidden by a white veil, a long, puffy white dress making her pretty as a doll.

"You okay?" Peyton asked softly.

She shifted her eyes to Oskar up at the altar. The male was decked out in a tuxedo, standing stiff and remote next to a lineup of male friends who likewise seemed like they wished they were somewhere else. On the opposite side of things, all the females from that bachelorette party were dressed in unflattering pink gowns, clearly chosen with an eye to make them look heavier and less resplendent than the bride.

Atta girl, Sophy, she thought.

"Yes, I am." She squeezed his hand and looked into his eyes. "I am very okay."

Living with her "poor little rich boy," as Peyton had taken to calling himself, had proven to be ridiculously easy. They seemed oddly compatible, and if there were arguments, they were over stupid stuff like what ringtone the alarm needed to be—dog barking for him, whereas she preferred the old-fashioned phone ringing—or how many darks could go into a white load of laundry—him, as many as were dirty at that particular moment in time, her, absolutely, fucking NONE.

In fact, everything seemed easier and more whole. And although she was sorry that he was now estranged from his bloodline, it certainly meant he understood why she was not interested in introducing him to her parents.

Maybe that would come later. Maybe it wouldn't.

But in the meantime, she had all the family she needed in him.

Down at the altar, Sophy arrived in front of her groom/mate/whatever, and a human in ceremonial garb began speaking from a human book.

Novo could only shake her head. Would they even do a vampire mating? Probably. More attention.

"I love you," Peyton said.

Novo glanced at him again. The emotions she was feeling were complicated, and . . . exhausting: She was clear that she wished her sister well with her choices—and that was a change which was welcome. As for Oskar? She'd said her piece to him back at that bar, and so she was as good as she was going to get with that.

The thing that really mattered? She had her own happy life. And nobody was going to take it away from her.

Not even herself.

"You want to skip the reception," she said softy, "and head back to our place to Netflix and chill?"

The pumping growl that came back at her was exactly what she wanted, but then her male was like that. Peyton always showed up when she needed him—and usually with an erection.

Okay, that was tacky. Even if it was true.

"I love you so much . . ." she declared, "that it doesn't hurt."

"That's my female. That's what I'm talking about."

There was a pause. And then he got that look in his eye. "How about I just tie his shoelaces together?"

"Peyton," she hissed.

"What? You know, accidents happen. And if he happened to fall through a plate-glass window when it does?"

"Shh. Before we get kicked out of here—"

"I knew I should have brought my air horn—"

As she started to laugh, she cozied up to her male. Whatever the future held, there were two things she was sure of: One, they were going to be side by side through thick and thin, and two? She was going to be laughing all along the way.

Life was good.

ACKNOWLEDGMENTS

With immense gratitude to the readers of the Black Dagger Brotherhood! I would also like to thank Kara Welsh and everyone at Ballantine. Thank you also to Team Waud—you know who you are—and to my beloved family, both those of blood and those of adoption.

And of course, thank you to Naamah, my wonderful WriterAssistant!

ABOUT THE TYPE

This book was set in Garamond, a typeface originally designed by the Parisian type cutter Claude Garamond (c. 1500–61). This version of Garamond was modeled on a 1592 specimen sheet from the Egenolff-Berner foundry, which was produced from types assumed to have been brought to Frankfurt by the punch cutter Jacques Sabon (c. 1520–80).

Claude Garamond's distinguished romans and italics first appeared in *Opera Ciceronis* in 1543–44. The Garamond types are clear, open, and elegant.

Do you love fiction with a supernatural twist?

Want the chance to hear news about your favourite
authors (and the chance to win free books)?

Keri Arthur
Kristen Callihan
P.C. Cast
Christine Feehan
Jacquelyn Frank
Larissa Ione
Darynda Jones
Sherrilyn Kenyon
Jayne Ann Krentz and Jayne Castle
Lucy March
Martin Millar
Tim O'Rourke
Lindsey Piper
Christopher Rice
J.R. Ward
Laura Wright

Then visit the Piatkus website
www.piatkus.co.uk

And follow us on Facebook and Twitter
www.facebook.com/piatkusfiction | @piatkusbooks

piatkus